D0477256

THE FRENCH LESSON

THE
FRENCH LESSON

HALLIE
RUBENHOLD

Doubleday

LONDON · TORONTO · SYDNEY · AUCKLAND · JOHANNESBURG

TRANSWORLD PUBLISHERS
61–63 Uxbridge Road, London W5 5SA
www.transworldbooks.co.uk

Transworld is part of the Penguin Random House group of companies
whose addresses can be found at global.penguinrandomhouse.com

First published in Great Britain in 2016 by Doubleday
an imprint of Transworld Publishers

A CIP catalogue record for this book
is available from the British Library.

ISBNs 9780385618892 (hb)
9780385618908 (tpb)

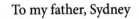

To my father, Sydney

Foreword and Dedication

To the Right Honourable Marguerite, Countess of Blessington

Little more than a year has passed since I sat in the drawing room of Gore House as the guest of the lady to whom this work is dedicated. The hour was late and we found ourselves quite alone when she pressed my hand and spoke in a low voice.

'I have often wished to enquire, my dear Mrs Lightfoot, how it was you came to make the acquaintance of Grace Dalrymple Elliot.'

At first her question startled me. I had not heard that name mentioned for some years and I wondered how it was she came to know of Mrs Elliot, or indeed my time in Paris during that period of revolution and bloodshed. Rarely did I mention either, and to no one but my most intimate of associates.

'Is it true what they say of her?' She raised an eyebrow into an inquisitive arch.

I folded my fan into my hands and smiled pleasantly in the manner I had learned to do when wishing to divulge nothing.

'I am afraid I have very few stories to tell of Mrs Elliot,' I said. 'Our acquaintance was but a brief one.'

My hostess did not for a moment appear satisfied with my response.

'Very well, my dear Mrs Lightfoot,' said she in a teasing tone. 'I know you well enough to understand your games. If you insist on refusing, I shall have to compel you to reveal your secrets.'

She then made me a very pretty little offer: in exchange for penning an account of my time in Paris during the French Revolution, she would settle upon me a tidy annuity of which, she claimed, she understood me to be in need. She then ventured to set forth her terms: I was to commit to paper a perfect record of all that befell me while I sojourned in that city. I was instructed to omit nothing, no matter how scandalous or indelicate. All my adventures, my opinions, all that I had witnessed or experienced, were to be laid plain so that at the conclusion of my memoir she would be in a fair position to judge for herself the truth of the rumours she had heard.

My conscience wrestled with her proposition for a good while before I saw fit to accept it.

And now, my dear Lady Blessington, I humbly submit to you in published form that story which you bid me to recount. I offer no apology for it, nor for the scenes in which I engaged, the philosophy I espoused, or the actions that my conscience urged me to take. As you and my devoted readers well know, I am blessed with numerous friends and champions, among which I have considered you for several years. Much to my detriment, I have also acquired an equal number of detractors, many of whom are my very own kinsmen. I bid you to peruse these pages carefully, for amongst the lines are the answers you seek. Only once you have discovered them will you be able to determine whether you wish to rank yourself amongst the former or the latter.

I am your eternally devoted servant,

H. Lightfoot
15th March 1837

Chapter 1

I should begin by stating this: until I found myself at Mrs Elliot's gate, I had no desire whatsoever to make her acquaintance. Only that afternoon I had endeavoured to prevent our introduction, and my scheme might very well have succeeded had I not suffered a terrible and sudden reverse. All at once, the lady I had sought most to avoid in Paris had become the nearest approximation of a friend that I possessed.

I cannot rightly say how it was I navigated a path to her home. I recall nothing beyond placing one foot before the other. At first I tripped and scurried, and then, once I had crossed the swirling Seine, my gait slowed into a heavy trudge. I believe it was Fortuna who, quite without warning, compelled me to draw to a halt. There, she caused me to lift my eyes to a sliver of light escaping from a shuttered window. It fell across a sign which read 'Rue de Miromesnil'.

Her *hôtel particulier* was simple enough to find amid the row of similar high gates. A lantern hung upon a hook above the entry, illuminating her entwined initials: G and E. I lingered for a while, my eyes set upon the dancing, silent candle flame.

I was in no fit state to pay a call upon anyone, least of all a woman who was no better than a stranger to me. I wore no cloak or shawl or gloves. My head was uncovered, and my coiffure was as slack and sodden with rain as a wet dog's pelt. My hem and stockings had been turned black from the streets. That city was slickened by a sludge worse than any you have ever had cause to see, and in wading through that gelatinous pudding of excrement and rotten matter I managed to tear right through my finest red satin slippers. However, my ruined attire was but the half of it. There was also the matter of the throbbing welt upon my cheek.

I breathed and exhaled in long vaporous clouds until at last I roused enough courage to pull upon the bell. I waited as the gate rattled and a porter lifted a light to my face.

I straightened my head and without so much as an ounce of hesitation announced myself as Lady Allenham, which of course was not my name at all.

He paused and examined me with a cautious squint. Once satisfied that my bearing spoke more of my breeding than did my wretched appearance, he showed me into the house and up the stairs. A pair of doors were opened on to a lime-green antechamber lined with gilt mirrors. Here he bid me wait and abandoned me with six reflections of myself. Briefly, I caught the eye of one of them before shame forced me to turn my gaze. I lowered my head and crept my hand along my injured cheek so as to hide it from the view of my hostess.

Within a moment there came the sound of frantic footfall from the adjoining room. The doors flew wide and with great alarm Mrs Elliot came towards me.

'Oh, dear, dear Lady Allenham!' she cried, aghast.

She stood before me, just as I had imagined her, just as she had been described to me by my friends in London, like some majestic rare bird of vast height. Her head of dark curls rose in a tower of blue and white ostrich feathers while a shimmering length of pale silk streamed from behind her. It spilled forth from her waist to the floor in a cascade of rippling fabric. She studied me down the bridge of her Roman nose, her rouged lips parted in horror.

'Heavens, my lady, have you suffered some accident?'

I could not think of an appropriate response, for the awkwardness of my humble circumstances had silenced me. I nodded and then slowly removed my hand from my cheek.

'Good Lord, madam!' Her eyes widened. 'Victoire!' She called for one of her servants. 'Victoire, you must make up a compress for this lady's injury, and bring some hartshorn . . . and some brandy . . . at once!' Her arms then flew about me, one around my waist and the other at my elbow. 'There now, there now,' she purred as she led me through to a sofa in her drawing room. Only two of the candles had been lit, which led me to conclude that she had been preparing to pass the evening elsewhere until I had intruded.

'My dear, I do believe you have had a most frightful shock. Have you been robbed? Are you in need of a physician?' She placed herself beside me and gathered my small hands into her elongated fingers. 'Dear Lady Allenham, I implore you, you must inform me what has occurred . . .'

Had you seen her expression, you would have perceived beneath her paint and powder that she possessed the purest, most saintly countenance. Her gentle eyes beguiled me with their warmth. Such a look of kindness had not been directed at me for many weeks. I exhaled in a slow sigh and carefully met her gaze.

Chapter 2

It was in April of 1792 when I found myself in Paris. Of course those were the days before the gas lights arrived, before the tyrant Napoleon rose and fell. It was after the Bastille was stormed, after the constitution was drawn up, after the court was forced from Versailles and locked into the Tuileries Palace.

I need not recount to you the events of the French Revolution. I would wager you have read enough of that in newspapers and chronicles to know something of its horrors. The devil himself could not have devised the scenes of bloodshed and murder enacted upon the streets. There was such suspicion, such fear; neighbours betraying neighbours, servants betraying masters, all in the name of the Republic. The worst of it was the dreaded pounding at the door. It might arrive by day or by night. The guards would not scruple to turn over an entire house, rummage through every drawer, poke at every mattress had they reason to suspect conspiracy. The denounced were routinely pulled from their beds, husbands torn from their weeping wives, and mothers from their babes. They were marched away through the streets, more often than not to a certain death at the guillotine.

But that was when the flames of revolution burned at their

highest; when I first passed through the barriers of that city they had only just begun to lap at the foundations. Nevertheless, to an Englishwoman, the alterations to life were most striking. I learned that the distinction of aristocracy had been abolished. No Frenchman or -woman of rank was permitted to be addressed as anything other than Madame or Monsieur. Coats of arms were removed from coach doors and from the architecture of great homes. Any display of wealth or hint of privilege was viewed as highly suspect. A life of moderation became de rigueur for all. Ladies fastened tricolour rosettes in place of jewelled buckles. Gentlemen abandoned their silk brocade coats for those of wool. It was considered prudent to speak in hushed tones when expressing a political opinion, and it now seemed every Frenchman and -woman was in possession of one of those. Few epithets were deemed more offensive than those of 'enemy of the constitution' or 'aristocrat', one who favoured the old regime. However, to be regarded as a 'counter-revolutionary' was worst of all. No one was to be trusted. Not a soul.

When I first landed upon that nation's shores nothing was further from my mind than its troubles. As I was neither a Frenchwoman nor one of our country folk foolish enough to cross the Channel and play at patriot, I concluded that I was unlikely to be inconvenienced by political matters. This was not the first occasion upon which my judgement had deserted me. Indeed one might even suggest that it was on account of a similar miscalculation committed two years earlier that I landed at Mrs Elliot's gate.

At the tender age of seventeen, I had fled the home of my father, the 4th Earl of Stavourley, and thrown myself under the protection of a gentleman. The fact that I had fallen in love with George William Allenham, the 4th Baron Allenham of Herberton, the man to whom my late half-sister had been betrothed, was not the error to which I refer. His affection for me was as true as mine was for him, and returned with as much devotion and ardour. In that regard we had sinned no more than had my father and my mother, Kitty Kennedy, a celebrated woman of the town. Our *affaire de coeur* was enacted with far more discretion than was theirs. For a time we lived privately in a cottage on Lord Allenham's estate, and passed our days as simply as might plain country folk. No, my misstep was not that I ruined my character so that I might live as my heart dictated, but rather that I had abandoned Orchard Cottage and set out in search of Allenham when he vanished from it. I ought not to have taken my leave of it for London with scarcely a ha'penny to my name. While this sort of adventure generally ends well for young men, it rarely does for young ladies. I shall spare you the sorry tale of my descent into the demi-monde, but merely say that as the winds of dissipation and debauchery whirled about me, my heart remained fixed on Allenham alone. My constant thought was of locating him and, in time, fortune favoured me and directed me to sail for Calais.

Allenham was delighted at our reunion, but in the days that followed took pains to explain the circumstances of his absence to me. He informed me that he presently served as a secretary to Viscount Torrington, who was then His Majesty's ambassador in Brussels. His duties necessitated that he undertake frequent travel and so he had found himself regularly in Paris, Coblenz, Spa, Geneva and Turin.

'However,' he explained, 'my title is but a formality, for the role I am charged with is far more critical than this.' He then hardened his blue-eyed gaze upon me. 'You apprehend what has occurred in France? That a good many of the nobles, a good number of the court have abandoned their country since the fall of the Bastille?'

I nodded.

'Among those who have fled their country are the King's

brothers: the Comte d'Artois and the Comte de Provence; and his cousin, the Prince de Condé. They have gone to Coblenz, in Prussia, where they live as émigrés. It is from Coblenz that they seek to further a counter-revolution by raising an army. It remains in the interests of our King that relations are maintained between Britain and the émigré court, and it is my duty to ensure this. I have been made the emissary between our King and the supporters of the French King.'

Allenham said that this was a mission which required the utmost discretion and when he had taken his leave of England he had not been at liberty to inform so much as a soul of his departure. The position had been granted to him through the influence of his friends in government, and rewarded him with an income of which they understood him to be in need.

'I fear that my debts are vast,' he whispered to me, his brow heavy with sadness. 'Herberton and my lands have been mortgaged. The house in London has been let, and my resources are at present entirely spoken for.' He slowly shook his head before continuing in a low, apologetic tone: 'Henrietta, I have not the means to wed you, nor the means to support any children of our union. It is a predicament that has vexed me since the day we parted.'

I studied him, his dark hair and sharply formed features. His remorse was etched deeply into them. It was then I recognized from where his sorrow sprang and how I might soothe it.

'My dear love,' said I, 'you believe I have pursued you to France in the hope of marriage? Why, you know well enough that I abandoned such notions upon the very day I surrendered myself to you. I have been long reconciled to a life as your mistress. I am not such a fool as to think that a gentleman of title with little income is any more at liberty to marry according to his tastes than is the friendless and illegitimate daughter of an earl.'

He raised his eyes and appeared somewhat surprised to find a gentle smile upon my lips.

'I request no more of you than the constancy of your heart, which you have ever given to me freely,' I affirmed. 'It would be an honour if you would permit me to return to Brussels with you and there live quietly in some lodgings not far from your own.'

There was a moment of silence while he sat and contemplated my proposal. Then the corners of his mouth turned carefully upward, before he placed upon my lips the kiss that sealed his consent.

From that instant, I resolved to forsake all that I had become since venturing forth from Orchard Cottage. My finest watered silks, my tissues of gold thread and heavily plumed hats: those many articles of attire which served no purpose but to remind me of my bitter compromises were packed away. All of my banknotes, all of the riches I had received – the shoe buckles that glimmered with rubies and sapphires, the diamond eardrops and brooches, the collars of precious gems which formed the mainstay of my fortune – were consigned to a locked silver coffer within a sealed chest. So determined was I to rid myself of the souvenirs of my former existence that I even disposed of the silk-lined town coach in which I had made my escape from London. (That fetched me a handsome sum, to be sure.)

It was with the promise of a new life that Allenham and I proceeded to Brussels. There, he arranged for me a set of rooms upon the rue des Petits Carmes in the home of a widow by the name of Madame Vanderoi. Madame's late husband had done well by the linen-draping profession and left his wife a genteelly appointed house in the upper town. I had at my disposal a comfortable bed hung with emerald damask, several finely made cabinets of mahogany and a snug dressing room, which was warmed in the winter months by a tall blue and white enamelled stove.

I had been introduced to my landlady as Mrs Lightfoot, a young English lady, not long married and recently widowed. *Mr Allen*, my only relation, had paid for my passage to the Austrian Netherlands where he resided and conducted his business as a lace merchant. A fine tale indeed, and one as embroidered and perforated with holes as any piece in which *Mr Allen* purported to trade. However, Madame Vanderoi appeared contented enough with this sham, and ventured to ask no questions of my *concerned relation*.

I could not utter a single complaint while I sojourned beneath Madame's roof. There my life was a retired one, but I possessed all that I required. Allenham, who lived but a short stroll away at the Hôtel Duplessis, called upon me most days when he was not engaged with the business of his position. Although he found himself frequently abroad, I was relieved that his absences seldom lasted more than a fortnight. In that time I diverted myself well enough. I took my meals in the company of my amicable landlady and occasionally formed a fourth pair of hands at cards or accompanied her to the Théâtre de la Monnaie. I acquired a harp and took instruction upon it and, when not engaged in that pursuit, turned my attention to my box of watercolours. From the Egmont Palace gardens I would trace the broad vistas in shades of amber and rust. As autumn chilled into winter I copied the interiors of Madame's rooms; sketching her maids as they tended the grates with one suspicious eye upon me.

All the while I would await Allenham's certain return with a quiet contentment. The day never failed to arrive when I would be roused by the familiar deep tones of his voice upon the stair. When at last Madame's servants showed him into my company his arms would be far too burdened with packets or boxes to embrace me. Instead, he would set before me the modest collection of treasures he had gathered whilst abroad.

'Had I the means, I would not scruple to adorn you with jewels worthy of a sultan's bride,' he would apologize. 'But perhaps you will indulge the hapless fool who adores you and pretend to take pleasure in his pretty trifles?'

On each occasion I was presented with the most thoughtful of gifts. From Paris he brought delicate silk stockings, perfumes and eaux de toilette. There were scented gloves, embroidered shawls, and, from Geneva, a pretty white-faced watch upon whose gold case the words 'Constant, comme mon coeur' were engraved.

'A memento by which you might always recall the constancy of my love . . . particularly in my absence,' said he as his gentle fingers pressed it into my hand.

Although in my previous existence I had been decorated with diamond baubles and even granted the run of my own townhouse, these extravagances were but vanities masquerading as love. Unlike many ladies of my sort, I had learned what it was to own a heart and to give one in return. I understood well enough that whatever gifts were made to me on behalf of that tender organ were of the greatest value by far. Of those cherished objects Allenham bestowed upon me, none were dearer than those he set before me upon his return from a journey to Turin. Such a grand assortment it was: a parcel which contained not only a silver pen and ink, but a set of gouache pigments, brushes of silky sable hair, and three bound books of Italian paper. The largest of these was filled with sturdy sheets for painting, while the other two, bound in smooth red calfskin, were designed for use as pocketbooks.

'I fear I have been most inattentive as your patron,' said he with a teasing wag of his head.

I turned to him questioningly.

'Is it not my obligation to see that your talents are amply rewarded, if not nourished with regular encouragement?'

I sighed bashfully.

'I merely pretend at . . . dabbling . . . and . . .'

'You know very well that is false modesty.'

I attempted to defend my humble assertion but his lip had already curled into a smile. He took several swaggering steps towards me before placing a finger beneath my chin.

'You think I merely seek to flatter you, madam? You think my judgement has been overruled by my heart? That your beauty blinds me to your true absence of skill and I am left entirely bereft of discernment in your company? Is that what you imagine, eh?'

I could not prevent myself from laughing at his taunts, even as he covered my mouth with kisses. Like my father before him, it was Allenham who recognized and praised my early talents. My beloved had once purchased for me a table designed for my artistic endeavours, at which I sat by a window in Orchard Cottage and filled my hours painting in a contemplative reverie. I was no Angelica Kauffmann or Madame Vigée-Lebrun, but in those youthful days my burgeoning abilities displayed no small amount of promise. While most gentlemen would have taken but fleeting notice of my accomplishments, Allenham admired them. He never once condescended to me, and spoke as plainly with me upon matters of philosophy and politics as he might a member of his own sex. Our conversation turned as much upon the words of Monsieur Rousseau and Herr Goethe as it did upon whispered exchanges of love.

'My patron's gifts come to you with a condition,' announced he, once we had disentangled from our embrace. 'I should like you to practise your skills upon me, in taking my likeness.'

'A portrait?' I smiled.

'A miniature portrait. A keepsake . . . for you.'

'I have never tried my hand at painting visages . . .' I demurred.

'Then you might apply yourself to it, my love, for I reckon you will excel at it. You have subjects enough about you here. I dare say Madame Vanderoi would make an agreeable sitter, and her household . . .'

I contemplated his suggestion and resolved to make an attempt of it. I also decided that I would put to use one of his tightly bound pocketbooks. In his absence I would scribble an account of my days, my thoughts and bons mots on to its pages and amuse him with them upon his return. What delight I took in this: pouring forth the contents of my heart and mind and occasionally committing to ink my rather petty witticisms. However, commonsense and prior experience soon reminded me what trouble often came of laying one's thoughts bare for the discovery of servants. Although Madame Vanderoi possessed but a few words of English, it would require little more than that to learn the true nature of my relations with *Mr Allen*. Indeed, I believe her entire household had already guessed at it, and sniggered at the ignorance of their mistress. As my tenure there depended upon my pretence of discretion, I alighted upon the idea of recording my thoughts in a simple code and then took great pleasure in devising one. No person should ever again come to know my secrets, I determined. I had learned too much of the world to scatter my trust about so freely.

In the weeks that followed, I observed Madame Vanderoi and her household as much with my brushes as I did with my pen. I painted each of her maids and then their double-chinned mistress in her starched lace and linen cap. Only once I believed I had acquired an understanding of what it was to sketch a countenance did I attempt to take Allenham's likeness. Of course, my little portraits were not the elaborate works one might have commissioned from Mr Cosway or Mr Bone in Piccadilly. They were but simple drawings in pencil to which I applied a light wash of colour over the sitter's features. It was a convention very much à la mode at the time.

I recall the day in early spring when Allenham sat for me. The blackthorn blossoms were swelling upon the trees and the daylight had begun to shed its grey winter pallor and once again assume a hopeful brightness. He reclined against the back of the chair and conversed with me in an easy manner as I sketched the square outline of his handsome features and the full form of his mouth. He uttered compliments and teases, jesting that I was not taking his likeness at all, but painting the view from the window behind him. After a spell, his light chatter faded and his animated countenance fell still. As I worked, a distant, pensive expression gradually crept over his face.

'The Habsburg Emperor has died,' said he. His voice was quite flat. 'The advisors to his son talk of nothing but war with France. The French Queen is his aunt, you see . . .'

I raised my eyes to him.

'And what of it? Is there to be war between France and Austria?'

'It is likely,' he stated, dropping his gaze to his lap, where it lingered for what seemed a lengthy while. 'I am afraid I have been called to Paris, Hetty. I am to depart this week.'

My heart filled with heaviness. I sighed and rumpled my brow, but continued to sketch, pretending his words had not caused me disappointment. Instead, I pushed a smile on to my mouth.

'But now I shall have this keepsake to remind me of you. I shall have it set in a frame and will look upon it every day, until the original who inspired it makes his return.'

Allenham's expression lightened.

'Upon that day you may depend, my dear angel.'

I believed his journey to Paris would be much the same as any of his others. When he called again to bid me farewell, I did as I had ever done and began to count the days from the instant he vanished from my view. I imagined that it would require three days to arrive at Paris, and then a further handful more to transact his business there. He would write to me as often as time permitted and inform me when he was likely to take his leave for Brussels. Then I would begin to number the days until his return, quietly, hopefully, patiently.

A week had passed and no letter arrived. Several more days followed. When at last a packet was placed into my hand, I tore at the seal with such eagerness that I feared I would shred the very words I had so longed to read. However, what my eyes discovered written there disconcerted me greatly. It was not a lengthy missive detailing his days upon the road or his diversions abroad, but rather an officious, if not anxious scrawl:

I write in haste, my dearest Henrietta, to inform you of an alteration to my circumstances. I have been instructed that I am to remain here at Paris for the foreseeable time. While the unrest of previous months has subsided, the uncertainty of this nation's politics renders life precarious, if not perilous. Were it anything but, you might believe that I would not hesitate to summon you here, but as it appears that a war with Austria is imminent, the situation is certain to worsen. I have not the capacity to determine precisely when such an occurrence is likely to transpire, but suffice to say what upheaval may occur in Paris will be visited likewise upon Brussels. It is therefore that I write to urge you, my angel, to quit Brussels and remove yourself to London. I have ordered my effects currently at the Hôtel Duplessis to be transported from Zeebrugge to Dover upon the *Marchmont* Tuesday next. I very much wish you to make your passage back to England upon this vessel and have made arrangements for you to be received upon it by Captain Steele. I shall not rest soundly until I am certain of your safe arrival in England, and then shall not enjoy a moment's contentment until the occasion of our next reunion. Until that time, I would beg you not to fear for me nor question the constancy of he who ever signs himself as your adoring,

G.W.A.

Allenham's news was so unexpected I felt a curious chill begin to spread from the centre of my breast. A great many thoughts began to tumble through my clouded head, yet I could fix upon none of them. Was Allenham in some distress? Why, the letter seemed to suggest it. What intelligence did he withhold from me? The more I allowed my mind to contemplate these possibilities, the more vexed and agitated I grew. What lay between his lines, I could not fathom, no matter how many times I read through them. He affirmed that neither Paris nor Brussels offered me a place of safety, but London . . . *London*. My heart seemed to contract at the mere consideration of it. After liberating myself from the grip of a life I abhorred, an existence passed entirely in designing schemes for my escape, I wished never to return there again. For a moment, I imagined what it would be to appear once more in that city of my birth, to take up again the false mask of gaiety, to be made to wear like an old discarded gown a manner of life which I had forsworn. It sickened me.

Allenham claimed that he would not 'rest soundly' until he was certain of my safe arrival in England, but indeed how might I rest soundly when I knew nothing of his circumstances, nor who or what detained him? I would fret without end; I would fear for him, just as he had bid me not to do. My thoughts turned to Paris, and once they had alighted upon that notion, they stuck fast. Certainly, I might only assuage my concerns by making a journey there and observing his situation, and had he not written that 'the unrest of previous months has subsided'? Why, it could not be so perilous at present, no more so than Brussels. If I lived undisturbed in this city, might I not live equally unmolested in the French capital? While his concerns were noble ones, I concluded them to be unduly cautious. And should the Austrian army appear at the gates of Paris, I could not think they would seek to trouble an Englishwoman with their complaints.

And so upon that day it was decided. I resolved to take my leave of the safety and comfort of Madame Vanderoi's warm, wooden-panelled rooms and begin preparations for what I would later come to regard as an exceedingly ill-advised journey to Paris.

Chapter 3

At the sagacious age of nineteen years, I fancied myself an expert in all matters of foreign travel. My flight from London had taught me that I required the necessary passports, while my maid, Lucy Johnson, without whose assistance and advice I would have found myself quite lost, was fair enough at managing the affairs of packing and removing my effects. With Madame Vanderoi's assistance, I was able to hire a suitable remise, horses, a manservant and a coachman familiar with the roads that ran to Paris. This, and four volumes of Mr Nugent's *Grand Tour*, that indispensable friend to all English travellers, was what in total I supposed I required for my journey. Indeed, I might well have succeeded at it had Nature not possessed designs of her own.

Those of you who have never before ventured upon the roads from Brussels to Paris will not have much comprehension of their conditions. The land lies quite flat and regular; indeed, it is not so unlike the great fenlands and marshes of East Anglia. It is possible to see for many miles in all directions, so that the distant church spires with their bulbs and points appear to poke like pins into the horizon. Rivers and bridges cross here and there, and in the spring months the storms knead the ground between them into mud. The spring rains do not fall lightly in these parts, but blow in sodden sheets which smack and slap against carriages and windows, beasts and men.

In spite of these deplorable conditions, by the conclusion of our first day, we had progressed as far as Cambrai. There, a night was passed in a draughty but private room at the Dauphin, an inn described in Mr Nugent's book. All night the rain drummed upon the roof and poured through the chimney at such a rate as to extinguish the fire twice. By the following morning, much to my horror, it appeared as if the Paris road had swollen into a flowing brown river. However, my fearless coachman refused to be put off by the mere 'puddles' along our route. So, the team of horses plodded on steadily through the morass, throwing out a murky soup upon the carriage. I continued to glance uneasily through the filth-strewn windows as the coach lurched and shook and jumped. My concern increasingly turned to my boxes upon the roof, for there were a good number of them bearing down upon us as we sank and rose through the muck.

We had slowly rocked from side to side, like a ship upon the seas, until it came: a sudden, mighty jolt. I am only grateful that Lucy was sitting beside me, and not upon the bench opposite, for in one swift motion we were both pitched forward, and then amid our howls of terror dropped like two heavy stones upon the floor. I gasped for breath and, as I did so, noted that the entire cabin had tilted backward. It seemed to have fallen between its hind wheels and come to rest upon the ground.

'Are you well, madam? Have you an injury?' My maid's freckled face peered at me. I nodded at her, for I felt no pain, only shock.

'And you?' I enquired as we attempted to disentangle our skirts, books and scattered sewing boxes.

'I have had a fright, madam. That is all.'

At that moment the coachman threw wide the door, his expression a picture of anguish and fear at what he might discover. He seemed to take some relief at spying us, shaken but unharmed.

'It was the axletree,' he explained. 'The roads have broken it. We require another, but must wait here to be rescued. It is four miles to Saint-Quentin, to the first inn.' He then turned and shouted through the rain to the footman, ordering him to set forth immediately. 'It will be some hours before his return.' Water poured from the brim of his tricorn hat; his nose throbbed red. 'It is best if you remain within the cabin, mademoiselle. I shall stand upon the road, and perhaps, if God is considerate, he may deliver us assistance.'

We sat in silence upon the sunken bench, gazing upward at the curiously angled opposite wall and waited for deliverance to arrive. For some time there came nothing but the ceaseless patter of rain. The wind blew against our thin wooden walls and rattled the glass. I could hear the coachman cursing to himself in gruff *bruxellois* as he unhitched the horses and paced the road.

Perhaps a half an hour or so had passed before the noise of a beast and a vehicle was heard. Lucy and I hastily drew down the window. A man and his son were driving what appeared to be a two-wheeled cart of stacked logs in our direction. As soon as their eyes met sight of the spectacle they stopped. For some moments, our coachman stood in animated conversation with them. Shrugs were exchanged and arms flew about, before all three turned and approached us. They stared at us in our collapsed contraption, as one might gawp at two curious creatures in a cage. Gradually they removed their sodden felt hats and ventured to address us.

'Mesdames,' the eldest of the two began, 'it . . . it would be my pleasure to carry you to the Pot d'Étain in Saint-Quentin. If you will . . .'

I examined the cart behind them: a rickety tumbrel half filled with soaked wood and as spattered with mud as my own conveyance. I did not require more than common sense to determine that the solution he proposed would have caused me more discomfort than remaining upturned in my own carriage. I would have arrived at the inn, entirely drenched and certain to have caught my death. Lucy paid me a cautious look.

It was at that precise moment that our little cabin began to reverberate. The road beneath us moved to what seemed to be the beat of hooves and the roll of wheels. Lucy and I turned expectantly towards a bend where a copse shielded the view. From behind it emerged that for which I had been quietly praying: six chestnut horses pulling a wide Berlin carriage. For an instant it appeared so coated in mud that I believed it to be the *diligence*, but as it neared I could see this was no stagecoach, but rather the proudly owned possession of some person of quality, and if not a person of quality then certainly a person of means. Beneath the veil of filth could be spied red and gold painted wheels and a highly lacquered cabin. Though he wore his hat over his eyes, the driver was attired in a livery of blue wool and gold lacing and sat upon a handsome crimson-fringed hammercloth. He hastily drew back on the reins and slowed the charging team to a cantering halt. All three men approached this vehicle, and once the well-attired coachman was convinced it was not some ruse for a robbery, a liveried footman opened the carriage door.

Out on to the thick filth of the road stepped a pair of high black boots. Attached to them was a pair of neatly tailored doeskin breeches and a voluminous heather-coloured greatcoat. The traveller wore his high-crowned black hat set at a slight angle, so that one of his fair eyebrows could be seen, while the remainder of his long, pale face was hidden beneath a modishly alluring shadow. He held his nose aloft like a French courtier, and approached our wreck almost upon his toes. His coachman, footman and all of our party tripped anxiously behind him. It was only once he caught sight of my round blue eyes and pretty blond curls that his haughty look melted into one of pleasant surprise. He smiled boldly and then gave a gracious and slightly overblown bow.

'Mademoiselle,' he exclaimed. 'What inconvenience you have suffered here! I have been informed that you and your maid are unharmed but that your axletree has given way. I pledge to aid you in any manner required. Please, may I assist you and your woman from the carriage and into the comfort of my own?' He opened the door and extended a buff leather glove to me. Gingerly, I placed my half-boot upon the sludge, while lifting the hem of my brown riding habit. He then performed the same courtesy to my maid, simpering throughout, as if he had the pleasure of escorting a duchess through the muck.

'I am Monsieur Andrew Savill of Thornton Hall in the County of Hampshire in England,' said he, taking my arm and guiding me to his coach. 'And pray tell me, mademoiselle, into whose service have I the honour of placing myself?'

I did not hesitate.

'I am Lady Allenham, sir.'

At that, a ripple of amusement moved across his mouth. 'An Englishwoman! Travelling unaccompanied upon the roads of France!' he declared in our native tongue. His words were laced with an Irishman's brogue.

'Why yes, Mr Savill . . . and I must say, you sound like no Hampshire man I have ever chanced to meet.'

My rescuer's expression deepened into a cordial smile.

'You, my Lady Allenham, are most observant,' he teased as he assisted me and my maid into his Berlin. 'I herald from County Mayo, but have made my fortune in England. Breeding stock. Some of the finest champions to be found in Europe were bred in my stables. Why, I am presently en route to Paris from the court of the Duke of Württemberg, who has made a purchase of some stud. I fear I am ever upon the road . . . or else in the halls of the great courts.' He sighed theatrically, as if to convince me that such a life was a terrible imposition. 'My lady, will you permit me to remove you from the depredations of the road and this wretched climate to an inn at Saint-Quentin until your carriage is repaired? The Soleil d'Or keeps a table far superior to that of the other hostelries.'

To this offer I heartily agreed, though not without some reservation. I thought this man a curious specimen: part macaroni, part sportsman, part Irishman, part gentleman, part coxcomb, part toad-eater. Although I was most grateful to him, I could not deny that I studied him with a wary eye.

'Allenham?' questioned he, as the wheels of his coach were set into motion. 'I am unfamiliar with that family . . .'

'The Barons Allenham, of Herberton in Gloucestershire,' I announced.

'And his lordship . . . ?'

'His lordship is presently in Paris.'

Savill responded with an inquisitive arch of a brow.

'And he has summoned you there?'

'Yes,' I affirmed, straightening my head.

My inquisitor paused for a long beat, his smile not wavering for an instant. I recognized that my tale required further weight in order to fix it as truth in Andrew Savill's mind.

'We have been resident in Brussels for some time, where his lordship holds a position under Viscount Torrington, His Majesty's ambassador to the Austrian Netherlands.'

Mr Savill continued to gaze upon me and smile, as if not a single word of mine had penetrated his brain.

'Ah, Brussels,' sighed he at last. 'The casinos, the Théâtre de la Monnaie. It is all the same faces and dull beyond description. I dare say you will find Paris most diverting by comparison, the current troubles notwithstanding. And pray tell, my lady, where does his lordship reside in that fair city?'

'Where?' I echoed. Indeed, for an instant he had taken me entirely unawares. It was here, scarcely a handful of minutes into our acquaintance, when I feared my entire story would be torn upon this one sharp question. I had made no arrangements for my lodgings in Paris. Why, any hotel that featured among Mr Nugent's recommendations would have sufficed until I sent word of my arrival to Allenham at the embassy. 'His lordship resides with His Majesty's ambassador there.'

'At the home of Lord Gower and Lady Sutherland?'

'Indeed, sir. At the home of Lord Gower.' I swallowed.

My rescuer cocked his head as if he did not quite take my meaning. His expression had begun to arouse my anxiety. I drew in my breath, for I understood what was now required of me; in order to preserve my initial falsehood, I must lay another upon it. And then, undoubtedly, another upon that, so that in no time at all a veritable façade of brick would stand between the truth of my situation and this busybody.

I paused and then lowered my head. I shut my eyes tightly, as if forcing away some painful remembrance.

'Mr Savill,' I began in little better than a whisper, 'I confess, I . . . I am quite undone and find myself in the most dire of circumstances . . .'

The Irishman moved nearer to me upon the bench. His countenance had altered into an expression of genuine concern.

'You see, sir, his lordship has been away for some time – near to a month. When we parted he directed me to await his instructions, but I fear they have never arrived. I have not had a single letter from him, Mr Savill, and I know not what to think. Every day I have petitioned Lord Torrington and his secretary for intelligence of him, but they too are unable to account for his silence. They know only that he arrived in Paris but have heard no more . . .'

Mr Savill drew in closer still, rapt by the details of my story.

'My lady, such disappearances . . . they are not without precedent in these times.' He spoke in a grave tone. 'Imprisonment for . . . trifling offences . . . it is not uncommon . . .'

I met his gaze. There was unfeigned disquiet in it.

'. . . but it is also entirely possible that Viscount Torrington is not presently at liberty to reveal the nature of your husband's mission to Paris. I realize this possibility will do nothing to assuage your immediate concerns, either.' He then lifted my hand into his. 'My dear, dear Lady Allenham, what suffering you must have endured these past weeks, and I cannot but think this latest misfortune with your equipage will have taken a great toll upon your nerves.'

I bit my lip and nodded.

'Why, it is quite intolerable to contemplate, and I shall not permit you to pass another moment unassisted. By your leave, my lady, I shall endeavour to manage the entirety of this upon your behalf. It will be an honour to serve you in his lordship's absence. I insist that you complete your journey to Paris under my protection.'

This was not the response I had anticipated nor would I ever have solicited it. I wished no person to learn of my business, to question me, to examine my character (or my fibs) too closely.

'Mr Savill,' I began, 'while your feelings do you credit, sir, I would not wish to inconvenience you with such a matter as this . . . which I dare say will be easily remedied as soon as I arrive at Paris. Why, I anticipate that upon my arrival, Lord Gower will direct me to his lordship and I shall discover it all to be some . . . some . . . unfortunate misunderstanding.'

But my noble Irishman would not hear of it. The greater my protests the more he insisted. No, it would be 'the most considerable honour to facilitate a reunion between you and your beloved husband', Mr Savill declared, 'and furthermore, as I am possessed of many connections in the highest circles, it would please me vastly to make your introduction to them. Why, I shall begin by delivering you directly to Lord Gower,' he determined. And so the matter was fixed, as if set into the mortar of my lies.

I made a pretence at a smile, before slowly bowing my head in a show of gratitude. Unbeknownst to my rescuer, it was only then that my anxieties truly began to mount.

Chapter 4

I had no cause for concern, or rather, I ought not to have. When I had quit the comforts of life beneath Madame Vanderoi's roof and set out upon the road for Paris, it was in the belief that I was certain to meet with Allenham at the embassy in that city. As his business lay in matters of diplomacy, to where else might he have repaired?

I turned these thoughts over in my mind, repeating the words to myself like a silent rosary. When I took my leave of Brussels I possessed not a single apprehension as to the correctness of my course but, curiously, in encountering Mr Savill, a seed of doubt had been sown between my reason and my conviction. I had not even been acquainted with the ambassador's name until the Irishman offered it to me: Lord Gower, His Majesty's ambassador to France. All would be revealed upon my arrival there, when Allenham gazed upon me with the same bemused delight that he had displayed at our first reunion.

The hooves of Savill's six horses seemed to beat out his name as his coach shuddered along the road from Saint-Quentin to Noyon, from Noyon to Compiègne to Senlis to Paris. Lord Gower. Lord Gower. Lord Gower.

I held Mr Sterne's *Sentimental Journey* to my face as we travelled, but my galloping thoughts prevented me from turning little more than three or four pages. While at present I had succeeded in duping Mr Savill, I feared for the ending of my drama. I knew not for how long I may be forced to enact it, nor what pitfalls awaited me. Occasionally, my eyes crept over the top of my book and studied with trepidation the gentleman in whose coach I rode. His blond hair inclined to a reddish hue and seemed dressed with a great deal of orris-scented powder, most inappropriate for the road. Even when at rest, his expression appeared affected. His thin mouth was set in a smug simper at all times, as if he were enjoying some private jest. I was pleased to have Lucy beside me. We exchanged knowing glances as she diligently worked upon her tambour.

As I found Mr Savill inscrutable, so I could not say what he made of me either, for I sat erect with a haughty, priggish demeanour throughout. I refused to speak more than a handful of words to him. This was not because I did not welcome the company, but rather because I did not wish to provoke his enquiries. I feared my brain could not spin fibs as quickly as he would have demanded them. I counted the hours until he delivered me to the embassy, when this ordeal would be brought to a conclusion and Allenham would bid our meddlesome friend adieu. I did not trust him one jot, though I derived some comfort from his incessant bowing and flattery. So long as my deceit remained secure, so long as Mr Savill had no reason to think me anything other than a lady of consequence and breeding, I believed myself safe in his protection. Confirmation of this was offered to me at the Fleur-de-Lys in Noyon, where Mr Savill announced we would pass the night. As I had given up my hired equipage at Saint-Quentin, I was in no position to dispute his determination. Naturally, this suggestion gave me pause. There was but one straw bed at the inn, but not for a moment did the impeccably mannered Andrew Savill suggest we shared it. Rather, he gallantly slumbered upon the benches of his coach and awoke the next morning appearing much the worse for it.

It was from that day forward that my mistrust of him began to soften into mild suspicion, though to be sure, I found him a good deal irksome. His flattery could be as rich and thick as treacle pudding and his boasts equally excessive. He spoke of his 'numerous acquaintance' at the courts of Europe, from Catherine the Great to King Carlos of Spain. It was not until the end of our second day upon the road that I even learned he had a wife. Of course, she possessed 'the heart of an angel and the beauty of Helen of Troy', while his son displayed 'all the genius of Socrates'. He effused over the fields and meadows of Thornton Park, and spoke at great length about his many prized stallions and mares.

Reader, I shall be the first to concede that before I entered the barriers of the French capital, all I knew of that place had come to me through books, newspapers and the gossip of my friends, many of whom had never quit the shores of England. My acquaintance had talked of nothing but the extravagance of the French nobility: how their silk gowns, lace, dainty shoes and eau de parfum were of incomparable make. The ladies adorned themselves in scent; they smelled of civet and jasmine; they soaked their persons in asses' milk and rosewater. They wore more powder and rouge than even the actresses at Drury Lane. They dyed their hair the colour of cherries. There a mistress might live as a wife and a wife of title might live as a queen in her own apartments at Versailles. Every gentleman was a fop or a libertine or both, and not a single one among them married for love. The royal family was as profligate as the emperors of Rome and the people had come to loathe them . . . or so I had heard and read, and even repeated in conversation, as if I possessed some authority upon the matter.

As a girl I had pored over engravings of this place: this city of palaces and Gothic cathedrals, of aristocratic *hôtels particuliers* and perfectly clipped, symmetrical gardens hidden behind high walls. I imagined it was not so different from Brussels – perhaps somewhat larger, but similar in a fashion. There would be quiet squares and snarls of lesser streets, markets and shops whose fronts had been painted in bright shades of green and carnation and blue. I imagined that Allenham would find me lodgings in some location near to the place Vendôme or the Palais-Royal; perhaps a set of apartments in one of the more modest *hôtels particuliers*.

We jolted through the barriers with what I later learned was to be considered a minimum of fuss. The guards removed every box from Savill's coach, including my own. They ordered each one of them to be opened. They shouted and demanded their tax. They held our passports to their lanterns and peered at the spidery writing, enquiring of our business again and again. I sat back against my seat, observing and silent, as cowed as a child. And this before we had so much as turned on to the darkened streets.

In London I had seen my fair share of the grotesque: the screeching peddlers and swarms of children, the snapping stray dogs and the beggars with scarcely a scrap to cover their nakedness. However menacing these spectacles appeared in England, they seemed all the more terrible in Paris. Not one road or byway appeared in any manner familiar. Indeed, the city seemed to extend before us in an infinite twist of black streets, which turned and rolled into one another like writhing snakes. At other times, its thoroughfares appeared as broad as rivers, lined with illuminated stalls and shops. Here hung threadbare coats and stained silk mantuas; there were goldsmiths and pawnbrokers, dentists, broom-sellers and barber surgeons ready with their knives and bleeding bowls. We passed beneath an endless succession of low-hanging street lamps, half of which had blown out. What pavements could be seen crumbled into the grime-slickened roads. In places, the darkness consumed everything. Nothing was visible but a single candle here and there, glowing yellow through unshuttered windows. Then there were the faces, gaunt-cheeked or fat, painted or hungry, appearing apparition-like from beyond the carriage glass. I sat and observed these images as I might the projections from a magic lantern.

We moved slowly across a narrow bridge, squeezed tightly with shops, until we arrived upon the left bank. There, I moved the fog from the window and spied below me the inky, flowing Seine.

I had heard Mr Savill direct his coachman to the rue Jacob, in the neighbourhood of Saint-Germain-des-Prés. I knew this to be a salubrious address and now was most grateful to be repairing there. By the time we entered into the courtyard of the Hôtel l'Impératrice, I discovered my hands to be so tightly clenched together that they had turned entirely cold within my gloves.

Mr Savill, sensing my apprehension, had looked at me with what I took to be an expression of pity.

'My dear Lady Allenham,' he sighed, 'I believe you will find Madame Bonet's establishment among the most reputable in this quarter.' Then, to prove its credentials, he took from the box of books at his feet Mr Nugent's *Grand Tour* and pointed to the author's commendation of it. I peered up at the Hôtel l'Impératrice through the window. Although largely obscured by shadow, it seemed a tidy enough place; its whitewashed edifice was adorned with neat black shutters.

There seemed nothing irregular in the manner of its squat proprietress or in her army of footmen. She had come in a hurried manner to greet us, her chatelaine of keys bouncing at her hip. Immediately she fell into a curtsey worthy of the halls of Versailles.

'Madame Allenham,' she pronounced. 'Monsieur Savill sent

word from Saint-Quentin that you would be amongst his party.'

I cannot imagine what nonsense the Irishman had written to her of me. Whatever the case, she seemed as convinced of my rank as he, and for my clever deceit, I was now to pay dearly. With a gracious smile, Madame Bonet led me up one pair of stairs and I was ushered into the Hôtel l'Impératrice's finest set of apartments.

Each room was unlocked before me, like the drawers of a treasure cabinet. The footmen moved hastily about with their tapers, lowering chandeliers and setting light to the wall sconces. From beneath their light a wealth of riches was revealed. There were gilt furnishings and clocks, Sèvres porcelain, Chinese vases and vast canvases upon the walls: still lifes and Madonnas, and pious saints upon their knees. The proprietress continuously nodded and smiled, and occasionally searched my expression for approval. I offered her nothing in return but aloofness, which I hoped masked my disquiet.

I was shown two dressing rooms hung with Gobelin tapestries, a white-panelled dining room with ornate gold architraves in addition to two bedrooms and antechambers:

'For your maid, madame, and for your husband's valet . . . when Monsieur le baron Allenham joins you here.' Madame Bonet took me through each door and only once she was content that I had studied each gold pier table and gilt door handle did she turn to me. 'I do hope the rooms are to your taste, Madame Allenham?'

Mr Savill, who had stood beside me throughout, peered at me with anxious anticipation.

My expression did not move.

'Why yes, yes, madame. I thank you kindly.'

What other response might I have made? I was an impostor who had played for high stakes with a poor hand.

What sickness now began to fill my belly. How much this

extravagance would cost me, I could not fathom. There would be all manner of bills. The expense of the lodgings would be but one of them. No traveller resides at such an establishment without paying the most exorbitant amounts for victuals, laundry, candles, etc. While I possessed the funds to discharge these obligations, I recognized that my purse could not sustain such an assault for long. What then? Once my coffers were empty, what measures might I be made to take – or manner of life might I be forced to resume?

I rose early the following morning and was startled to find my Irish knight errant already in attendance and awaiting me in my dressing room. He leaped to his feet at my appearance, nearly splashing his buff silk coat with the coffee he had been sipping.

'My Lady Allenham' – he attempted a laugh – 'I would not wish you to think me remiss in escorting you upon this most pressing errand.' It was only as he led me to his coach that I learned he had taken rooms directly above me, so that I would 'never suffer inconvenience by his inattention'. I was not certain how to take this news, whether I should welcome his proximity or learn to abhor it. La, but it mattered not, I told myself, for I was about to meet with Allenham and bring this episode to a close.

We passed beneath the archway of the Hôtel l'Impératrice and out on to the streets, which by day seemed less daunting. This is not to suggest the roads were any more passable than they had been by night. Our progress was slow and laboured: a cabriolet driver argued upon the street with two fearsome women, riders wove their horses perilously in between carts and coaches, children ran into the road, while a lazy-eyed cow obstructed the thoroughfare. I gazed up at the high gates of *hôtels particuliers* and out at the dusty windows of shops, filled with gaudy-coloured goods. There was something of the carnival about this place: both gruesome and delightful, mysterious and threatening. I soon discovered that the Parisians had written the names of their streets upon corner buildings, and then began an anxious search for the rue Saint-Dominique, our destination.

When at last we arrived there, at the Hôtel de Monaco, I could scarcely contain my nerves. Savill assisted me from his vehicle and our names were given to an attendant who showed us up a pair of stairs to a vast mirrored salon thronged with waiting gentlemen. There I sat, attempting to compose myself, imagining with each moment that the curtain was about to fall upon this unfortunate piece of theatre. How would Allenham receive me? What awkwardness might I encounter with Mr Savill as my audience? An hour passed in this manner before a footman appeared.

Mr Savill had requested an audience with the ambassador, but instead we had been delivered to what seemed to be a library. The walls were lined with cases of books and tables stacked with ledgers. A young gentleman with curled hair and spectacles stepped from behind one and introduced himself as Mr Huskisson, secretary to Lord Gower.

Before I could speak a word, the Irishman launched upon my tale. He told it plainly enough, with all of its fibs attached. He explained that my husband, the Baron Allenham, had made for Paris about a month ago, and had not been heard from since. He then paused, before continuing:

'Lady Allenham is certain that he was received here, and resides with Lord Gower and Lady Sutherland . . .'

I felt my throat tighten and my heart leap.

Mr Huskisson examined me quizzically from over the rims of his spectacles.

'I . . . I am afraid your ladyship is mistaken. To my knowledge, his lordship has not been received by the ambassador, nor has he attempted to call upon him.'

For a moment, I was uncertain if I had heard his reply correctly.

I stood for a spell, not knowing how I might respond.

It was then the secretary unlocked a case of books behind him and laid two ledgers upon the table before us. The first of these he opened, and ran his finger down a lengthy column of neatly written names. He turned several pages and repeated his search, before shutting the book.

'I fear I am correct, Lady Allenham. Your husband has not paid call upon Lord Gower, nor any person at this embassy.'

I felt Andrew Savill's hard gaze pressing into me. I dared not meet his eye.

'But, Mr Huskisson, this is most peculiar . . . You see, he was, prior to coming to Paris, engaged with His Majesty's mission at Brussels, under the Viscount Torrington . . . I was of the understanding that he was to perform the same role here, but under the direction of Lord Gower.'

The secretary now appeared quite puzzled indeed. He rumpled his brow.

'If I may enquire, my lady, did he inform you as much?'

'Why . . . yes, yes . . . in a fashion. He . . . implied that he had received instructions to remain at Paris . . . Why, Mr Huskisson, from whom else might he have received such an order but Lord Gower?'

'Madam, if I may . . . I intend no disrespect to your ladyship but I am privy to all of Lord Gower's affairs and correspondence, and not once have I heard mention of Lord Allenham's name. You are certain he was at Brussels with Lord Torrington?' Mr Huskisson enquired.

'Of that I am most certain, sir, for I resided there with him,' I responded, my voice quivering. 'Why, I cannot believe it to be true . . . How could this be so . . . ?'

I stopped. All at once it occurred to me that the nature of Allenham's position at Brussels had not been an acknowledged one. It was possible that this explained the omission. I wondered: had he used his own name, or had he been known by some other? If this were the case, how might I ever locate him?

'Mr Huskisson, sir . . . might I enquire if Lord Gower has received *any* English visitors from Brussels . . . in the past month?'

'Brussels, no . . .' He shook his head. 'I am afraid not, madam.'

A coldness gripped me.

'I am truly sorry for your distress, my lady. If it will offer some comfort to you, I shall inscribe his lordship's name upon a list of His Majesty's subjects whose whereabouts are at present . . . unknown. Should my Lord Gower receive any intelligence concerning your husband, I would see to it that it is relayed to you directly,' said the secretary, a scant hint of sympathy showing through his officiousness.

As we returned to his coach, Mr Savill spoke softly to me, patting my hand all the while and drawing me nearer to his side.

'My lady, simply because his lordship has not called upon Lord Gower does not mean that he does not reside in Paris. Why, it is entirely likely that there has been some miscommunication, some letter which has gone astray. The post in Paris is no longer to be relied upon as it was once . . .' He continued to prattle: 'What a blow this has been to you, dear Lady Allenham, what a blow indeed. Well, I simply cannot account for this mystery. It is most irregular . . . but you must not despair, madam . . . Why, should it ease your troubled mind, I shall make enquiries with the authorities at the various section houses this afternoon . . .'

I bobbed my head absently. I had ceased to listen to him. It was as if a fog had settled over my senses.

'By your leave, my lady, I shall put this matter to my acquaintance. Yes, I shall write to them at once . . . as soon as we return to the Hôtel l'Impératrice . . . the Comte de Ségur, the Duc de Biron, the Comtesse de Coigny, the Bishop of Autun . . .' He paused and examined me again, hoping that the mention of these noble names would cause me to marvel. But I said nothing. I was scarcely able to form words until we drew into the courtyard of Madame Bonet's establishment.

'Mr Savill, if you will pardon me, I should like to retire. My nerves, sir . . . they are somewhat disordered.' I addressed him distractedly as I moved to step from the carriage.

'Why, but of course, madam,' he responded whilst shooing away the hotel's footman and handing me from the vehicle himself. 'Do you require a physician, my lady? Would you like me to summon one? I can assure you, I know one of incomparable reputation, Monsieur de Sancerre, physician to the Duc d'Aiguillon.' He hung upon my response with an eager grin.

'A physician is not necessary, Mr Savill, though I am grateful for your concern,' said I with a wave before fairly racing up the stair.

Once I had come through the entry and into my drawing room I wished I might have drawn a bolt across each glittering door. I wished I might have barricaded myself in there, behind a stack of ormolu chairs and boulle cabinets and sofas. I went to the window and pulled away the lengths of pink taffeta drapery so that I stood with my face but an inch from the glass.

I gazed down upon the rue Jacob, upon the crowns of hats, into buckets and baskets and carts, upon the moving flanks of horses. In the distance I could spy the spire of a church whose name was unknown to me. There was not a road adjacent to this one, or a house, or even a face beyond the courtyard of the Hôtel l'Impératrice that I would recognize. It was then I understood where I found myself: I had entered a labyrinth. I could not begin to fathom how I might navigate this confusion of streets, let alone where Allenham might dwell amongst them.

I confess, dear friends, I was most terribly frightened.

I began to pace about the room. I turned circles upon the parquetry. I squeezed my mind for some solution to this problem, but none came. After rendering myself dizzy, I retired to a chair where I laid my head against the back of the seat and shut my eyes.

When I opened them once more, I found myself staring at the spine of a book which Lucy had unpacked and laid upon a table. She understood well enough the significance of it. It was to me as precious as any memento, any set of paints or watch Allenham had given to me. Unlike these other objects, this one alone possessed the ability to soothe me in times of distress or weakness.

When I had been an awkward miss of sixteen, Allenham had bid me read this novel which he claimed had come to shape his understanding of the world and his own sensations of love. An edition of Mr Goethe's *Sorrows of Young Werther* was put into my hand at the time I had placed myself under his protection, nearly three years past. The little tome I took into my lap was not this same book, but rather Allenham's own. The sight of it brought an instant flow of tears to my eyes. I rubbed them from my cheeks as I began to idly thumb through the pages. My heart was too weary to read and so, with a sigh, I moved to shut it.

A curious thing then occurred. Indeed I cannot explain it except to credit Winged Fortuna for her intercession. The book slid from my hand and in grasping for it, it opened to the inside cover. There, pasted to the green and red marbled paper, was something of which I had never before taken note: a neatly engraved bookplate. Between two Corinthian columns sat a cartouche with the name, 'Jean-Baptiste Marie Mariot', and then the words, 'L'Académie royale des inscriptions et belles-lettres'.

I drew in my breath.

Monsieur Mariot had been Lord Allenham's bear leader, the tutor who had led him upon his Grand Tour as a boy of sixteen.

My beloved had been a devoted pupil and was given to reminiscing fondly about his travels with this eminent scholar of antiquity, who, he had instructed me, resided at Paris. It was Mariot who had first introduced Allenham to works of philosophy, both ancient and modern. Indeed that very edition of Mr Goethe's book had been a gift from his tutor's collection, the first English translation. His lordship had prized it and, in Brussels, bequeathed it to me.

I ran my finger across the name. 'Thank you, Fortuna,' I whispered, before rising to my feet in search of pen and paper.

Chapter 5

Upon that day, all that I possessed was a single hope of finding my beloved. I folded it into a sheet of paper and sealed it. How it should make its way to the recipient I could not say. Indeed, I had no notion if this Monsieur Mariot still lived, or if he had grown infirm or blind or mad, or if he had abandoned his country with so many others. All that providence permitted me was to dispatch a letter and wait.

Of course, my Irish protector claimed to have many more possibilities at his disposal. He returned to me later that afternoon to announce he had penned no fewer than eight letters to his acquaintance in Paris.

'There is the Princesse de Tarente, who presides at the centre of all gossip. I once had the great fortune of attending a dinner in her apartments at Versailles . . . before the current troubles, of course. She is certain to offer some intelligence. There is as well the Prince d'Aremberg who is an intimate associate of mine, a devotee of the turf . . . and the Marquis de Molleville, who once purchased a very fine white mare from my stables – I do believe he is privy to the whereabouts of most anyone.' Savill smirked and raised an eyebrow. 'Why, I would reckon that this unfortunate business will be concluded within no more than a week. In the meantime, my lady, I shall not permit you to pass your hours pining as if you were Penelope awaiting the return of your Odysseus. I insist that you accompany me tonight to the Théâtre Feydeau – that is, if your ears will tolerate a performance sung entirely in the French language?'

With some hesitation, I accepted Andrew Savill's invitation that evening and on other occasions as well. He would not have me 'sitting indoors all day now that the weather has grown so fine', I must come with him 'at once and take the air at the Jardins des Tuileries'. Naturally, having seen the delights of the Tuileries, 'one must compare them to the beauties of the Jardins du Luxembourg'. I was coaxed here and there; whisked through the Bois de Boulogne in a cabriolet and taken to 'glimpse the majesty of the Cathédrale de Notre-Dame'. I was in no position to refuse, for I had not a single legitimate excuse to make. There was no person upon whom I might call, no honest reason for absenting myself from his tiresome company.

In this manner a week had passed. Each morning, at an hour scarcely decent, the Irishman would appear in my dressing room as if he were attending my levee. 'Mr Savill awaits you,' Lucy had come to mutter as she parted my bed curtains.

'Then permit him to, for as long as I deem fit,' I had taken to answering. To be sure, I understood his game. I meant to prove to him that I was in no manner like the many French ladies of his acquaintance. I did not receive company whilst languishing in my bath, nor did I wish him to observe the intimacies of my toilette. I knew of many a respectable woman of that nation who thought nothing of entertaining gentleman callers in her chemise while dabbing her underarms with Hungary water.

As you might well have supposed, by this time my patience with Andrew Savill was sorely tried. There had been not so much as a mention of any replies to his letters. When I enquired after them he would offer some excuse or other: 'The Prince is not in town at present,' or, 'I understand that the Princess currently suffers with the dropsy and has not entertained a soul since February.' He would smile as he spoke, though his eyes remained as dead as those of a landed trout.

My champion may have been content to pass his days in idle amusement or pretending to transact business, but I was not. The true cost of this folly was mounting by the hour. By the conclusion of that week the thought of my expenses had come to preoccupy me. At the risk of giving Madame Bonet's cook offence, I refused to take any further meals from her kitchen, but rather sent Lucy to collect my victuals from a *traiteur*. My maid laundered my linens herself and I took to lighting no more than three candles upon any given night, leaving Madame's glittering chandeliers to hang in darkness. Needless to say, I did not succeed in currying favour amongst her household. Her housekeeper and footmen eyed me with disdain and I feared that they would soon share their suspicions with the proprietress. Daily I felt my thin lace of falsehoods stretch further and further. One day, quite soon, I knew it would snap.

Fearing that this occasion was close at hand and having no indication that my Irish protector had received even the briefest note from any of his 'numerous acquaintance', I resolved to confront him. I had cogitated a good while upon this and had begun to fear that Andrew Savill was as much a fraud as was I. During all of our excursions abroad, our visits to the theatre and constitutionals, not once had we encountered a soul who knew him. But for his banker, no one called upon him. Indeed, I could not even determine if his affairs of business were genuine, or if the horses he professed to trade in were any more real than the Pegasus.

I prepared myself to greet him that morning and found him in his usual chair, with his white-stocking-clad legs crossed and out-stretched. In his hands he held the same small dish of sweet tea or coffee he had supped upon day after day. He rose at once and offered a flourish of bows.

'My lady, how might I be of service to you today?' he said.

Reader, I fear I could bear it no longer.

'Mr Savill,' I began. 'When we first arrived in Paris more than a week ago, you assured me that you were possessed of many friends here who might offer me some assistance.'

'I did, my lady.'

I held his gaze. There came not a twitch of concern.

'Sir . . . I must confess, it strikes me as most curious that in all this time you have received not a single reply to your letters, that not one invitation has been made to you by the numerous acquaintance you profess to have in this city. Pray, Mr Savill, what explanation do you offer, for I fear I am unable to make any sense of it?'

The Irishman's expression remained quite still and steady.

'Well, my lady, you needn't make sense of it,' said he.

I rumpled my brow.

'I needn't, sir?'

'No, my dear Lady Allenham, for I have here in my pocket a letter from a most cherished friend who has invited us to dine with her this very afternoon.' He then slipped his fingers into his waistcoat and produced a neatly written note which he waved before me.

My eyes followed the folded sheet as he wafted it about. I could scarcely believe it.

'To . . . dine, sir?' I stammered.

'Yes, my Lady Allenham, to dine. Why, the moment this lady learned of your name she expressed a great wish to make your acquaintance.'

I studied his features, uncertain what to make of this. All at once I could feel the colour rising upon my cheeks.

'The invitation is for three o'clock and I shall attend you shortly before then, my lady.'

I smiled at him. It was a weak and contrite expression. Needless to say, upon spying me so humbled he instantly reached for my hand and, with a slightly triumphant glimmer in his eye, placed a lingering kiss upon it.

Shortly after two o'clock he appeared as promised and I emerged attired in my red and white sprigged silk gown. How the compliments dribbled from his mouth. He was in raptures over my beauty. The high-crowned green hat I wore set off my perfect golden curls; the rubies in my hat pin sparkled with the fire of my eyes. He was heavily perfumed with eau de bergamot. I permitted him to take my arm and lead me to his coach. There was a new hammercloth upon the coachman's seat, he explained, and new white feathers atop his horses' heads.

'The rue de Miromesnil,' I remember him instructing his footman. He could not recall the precise address, but: 'The initials G and E may be seen above the gate.' Then he handed me inside.

I had been so distracted by my angry passion and its unexpected resolution that I had not even thought to enquire after my hostess's name until our journey was underway. I put my question to him and he seemed to coo with delight.

'Oh, Lady Allenham, she is a Scotswoman and a most celebrated lady. Why, there is not a person of rank, not a gentleman of title she does not know. She is an intimate of the Duc d'Orléans and is acquainted with all his circle. Indeed, my lady, if there is one person in Paris who should know of your husband's whereabouts, it is she.'

I smiled to myself at this.

'And her name?' I enquired.

'Elliot,' responded he. 'She has recently been made a widow, but is neither elderly nor dull. She has seen a good deal of life, having lived much of it in London among *haute* society.'

'And what has brought her to Paris, so far from her native shore?' I pressed.

Mr Savill paused and regarded me, as if savouring a moment of expectation. Then, just as he drew breath and opened his mouth, his coach came to a sudden halt.

'Out of the road with you!' I heard Savill's driver shout, but the voices continued.

The Irishman pulled down his window, and I mine.

Ahead of us three rogues in red caps, their arms about one another, swayed in the road. They were very much in drink and were crying out what sounded like the verses of a song. I grimaced and drew up the window once more.

'There will be more of this to come, I fear,' he grumbled.

'And why is that?'

'Why? Because the French have declared war upon Austria, my dear. This very morning. Did you not hear the peal of bells? The tocsin? I cannot blame you if you did not. This city is constantly a-clatter with infernal ringing.'

I stared at Mr Savill. His indifference disquieted me nearly as much as did his announcement of war.

'But what is to occur now?'

A wry expression crept over his face. 'The French army will march as near to the border as the Austrian army will permit them and then there will be a battle, my dear,' said he, pressing my hand in his once more.

I scowled at his teases and pulled away. He merely laughed.

'My lady, you have no cause for alarm. We are in no danger of the Austrians appearing at the gates of Paris this afternoon and spoiling our dinner.' He gave a small snort. 'It is no concern of ours.'

But I was in no manner consoled. My thoughts turned immediately to Allenham, to the warnings he had written in his letter.
I had not heeded them. I was not in Brussels. I was not upon a
ship returning to England. No, contrary to his advice, I was in
Paris and he was nowhere to be found, and I could not conceive
of how I might locate him. My mood instantly fell into something
sombre and fretful.

After a spell, the coach resumed its course and I began to feel
my companion's eyes upon me.

'Scandal,' said Mr Savill, interrupting the silence.

At first I was not certain I had heard him correctly.

'Scandal?' I said, puzzled, turning to him. He bore a most curious expression, like a child who held a purloined sugar plum in
his mouth.

'Mmm, yes, my lady. Scandal. The usual reason a woman of
Mrs Elliot's sort would come to Paris. The French, as you know,
are far more forgiving of transgressions than are their English
cousins.'

I returned his look with faint bemusement.

'I . . . am afraid I do not take your meaning, sir?'

My companion's brow twitched playfully, as if to insinuate that
I did.

'Some years ago, she was found abed with Lord Valentia.
Frightful scandal. Her husband, Dr Elliot, a miserable old dog,
initiated proceedings for criminal conversation against him. Poor
Mrs Elliot was then cast adrift. She had only her lovers to support
her, but there were a fair many of those to keep her in ribbons.' He
snorted with a sort of debauched glee.

I stared at him. I could not move, for the shock of his revelation
had frozen me quite in place.

You see, the name Grace Dalrymple Elliot was not unknown to
me. While I had never made this lady's acquaintance, those of my

London circle had spoken of her frequently. She was to them an absent sister. 'Dally the Tall', as she was known, was a cherished companion of Mrs Mahon, a woman of the demi-monde who had been as a mother to me. Indeed, it was even said that Mrs Elliot had been an intimate of my true mother, Kitty Kennedy, before her demise.

It was not until that moment that I saw Savill for the villain he was. He had set a trap for me with such a light touch that I never once suspected him to be hard at work spinning his web. Now he hungered for my response. He veritably smacked his chops in anticipation. Like a butterfly with one fair leg stuck upon the spider's silk, I began to flutter and flap.

My friends, permit me to put this plainly to you: no virtuous young wife or girl delicately bred would have had any cause to know the name Grace Dalrymple Elliot. However, a woman of the town, a *femme galante*, a demi-mondaine, a *dame entretenue*, a gentleman's whore would. My Irishman's intentions were to lure me into the home of a courtesan, either to seduce and debauch me or to expose me. Whichever the course, it was a wicked scheme, and I would not stray willingly into this spider's snare.

He continued to search my face. Although I attempted to disguise my indignation, I sensed my cheeks burning hot. After a spell, I could scarcely breathe. Gently I lifted my hand and steadied myself against the carriage wall.

'Mr Savill,' I stated softly, 'I fear I am taken ill. I am ... I wish to return at once to my lodgings. Pray, sir, do call out to your driver. At once.'

But the Irishman did not move. Instead, he beamed at me.

'My dear Lady Allenham . . .' Then he laughed, shaking his head.

'Do not mock me, sir,' I snapped. 'I shall have a fit if you do not return me at once.'

How could I have deceived myself as to the designs of this scoundrel? I had scented the high note of duplicity upon his person, but I had believed the stink to emanate from his sham connections and embellished tales. I had believed this coxcomb to be no more than a harmless fibbing flea whose vanity had blinded him to my own fraudulence. I was as furious with myself as I was with him.

I took hold of the window and pushed it down before crying out to the driver that we were to return to the Hôtel l'Impératrice. When I resumed my seat, I found Savill reclining with folded arms.

'I do believe you have at last betrayed yourself, madam,' he announced.

I threw him a vexed look.

'I cannot think what you mean by that, sir.'

Savill gave a sniff.

'You are no more the wife of the Baron Allenham than am I. From the instant I laid eyes upon you in your ramshackle remise it was apparent to me what was your manner of life. You think yourself capable of aping the conduct of a virtuous wife merely by disguising your décolletage beneath a fichu?' He waved his hand over the gauze at my breast and laughed. 'No, madam, it is in your comportment. It is in your air. You have been so long in the company of demi-mondaines that they have left their indelible mark upon your conduct. You forget yourself. No lady of character would venture upon the road in a hired coach with no more than a maid to assist her. Not a single acquaintance of yours resides at Paris? Not a cousin of your husband's, not a friend of title from London of either sex? Hey? Why, it seems you are possessed of no society whatsoever but that of your *lord*,' he said. 'Why, *is* there a Lord Allenham, my lady? I dare say, if there is, he has jilted you.'

I clenched my jaw as I withstood his battery of insults.

'You abuse me, sir!' I railed at him. 'In all my life I have never been so ill used as this!'

The hateful rascal merely sighed.

'You may protest, Lady Allenham – or whoever you fashion yourself to be – but you wear the truth as plainly as you sport his lordship's silk gowns. To be sure, I have witnessed many feats of female gallantry, but your relentless pursuit of a lover who has abandoned you has proven the finest show I have seen to date. Why, I might write your tale for the stage: *La Pouffiasse galante.*' He roared with laughter. 'But now, the time has arrived for you to call off your quest and take to heart a lesson: if a gentleman has not made his whereabouts known to you, he does not wish to be found.' Savill surveyed me from top to toe. 'I shall say this much, the man who jilted you is either half-blind or half-witted. I have never beheld a finer piece in all my life, and the devil take me if I am not half in love with you.'

If ever I was persuaded to hold firm to a falsehood it was then, and I clutched it to me for dear life. When I at last found my voice it was surprisingly calm and measured.

'Sir, I would remind you that as an honourable and faithful wife, I withhold nothing from his lordship. I will not hesitate to inform him of this attack upon my character. I shall leave you to imagine what remedy he may seek.'

My words did not touch Savill's haughty look. It remained firmly in place.

'And I shall leave you to imagine, my lady, what it will be like to abandon your game and give yourself freely to a man who has made a considerable investment in catching you.'

I did not deign to respond.

When we returned to the Hôtel l'Impératrice, Mr Savill unceremoniously threw wide the door and stepped from the vehicle. He left me in his furious wake, to be assisted by Madame Bonet's footman. I could not say that his barbaric conduct startled me. He had sought to unmask me, but had only succeeded in revealing himself.

I lingered in the courtyard long enough to observe him ascend the stairs and disappear from my view for what I intended to be forever.

Chapter 6

As you might imagine, I returned to my apartments in a storm of indignation. I immediately resolved to alert Madame Bonet to my ill usage. All the baseness of Savill's character, his insinuations and insulting words would be repeated to her and I did not doubt that she would seek recourse. I had determined to have him thrown from the Hôtel l'Impératrice. I had summoned Lucy to me and was in the course of relating my tale to her when we were interrupted by the sound of the servants' door in the dining room.

'Madame Allenham?' called out the proprietress.

Anxiously, I advanced into the adjoining room, ready to pour forth my story, only to stop short. Madame stood before me, her face as hard as a blacksmith's anvil.

Before I could so much as begin my tale, she raised her chin. 'Madame,' she began, 'I shall make my point directly. Monsieur Savill has brought to my attention the true nature of your circumstances. He has made plain to me your scheme, and that you are not who you claim to be. I say to you now, madame, my establishment will not be known as a home to impostors and adventuresses who wish to make use of my rooms to perpetrate their crimes.

Neither shall I tolerate the abuse of my loyal patrons, Monsieur Savill being foremost among them. I would therefore have you settle your bill and quit my hotel at once.' She then attempted to hand to me a sheet of paper upon which a lengthy record of my expenses had been tabulated.

I did not take it. Instead, I stood fixed in place, staring at her incredulously.

'Madame Bonet,' I began, 'I fear you are under a grave misapprehension. Why, I was about to recount to you the insults I have received from Monsieur Savill when you—'

'I have heard enough of your falsehoods, madame,' she snapped. 'I shall instruct my housekeeper and footmen to pay close heed to every pin and jar your maid places into your boxes. The inventory will be examined and if so much as a spoon is found wanting, I shall have you dragged by your little head of curls to the section house.' She glowered at me, her once conciliating features now creased through with anger.

'But I have told no falsehoods . . . and I . . . I cannot think what lies Monsieur Savill has invented to suit his treachery. I tell you, madame, this is pure fabrication. It is he who is the villain and the impostor!'

Madame came a step nearer, as if to sniff me.

'I am under no illusions as to who and what you are. You have deceived him, a good and honest gentleman. You have enticed him to Paris under false pretences. You have taken this man's money and promised him favours from your husband . . . a husband who does not exist. You are no better than a thief, madame . . . and a common whore, and I shall not suffer you under my roof a night longer.' She folded her arms as if to make final her resolution. 'And these, my most costly rooms. In all the time you have occupied them I might have let them three times over!'

'I shall pay you, madame,' I insisted, but she shook her head and huffed and puffed. 'Whatever lies Monsieur Savill has told you, I possess the means to make good on all my debts, but I beg of you, Madame Bonet, you must permit me to make arrangements, for I have nowhere else to repair—'

'Whither you repair concerns me not, madame,' she remarked as she laid the bill upon a side table, 'so long as you discharge your obligations and take your leave immediately.'

Without so much as another word or even a look, she turned upon her heel and disappeared down the back stairs.

I took the note into my hand and saw, much as I had dreaded, a vast reckoning of all that I owed. There were not only fees for my rooms and meals, amounting to an exorbitant sum of twenty-one *livres*, but costs for the laundering of my linens and sheets, the use of candles and coal, costs for the water drawn for my bath and for any other purpose, expenses for the portering of my belongings to my apartments, even for the posting of a letter. This came to a further eight *livres*. I shut my eyes tightly and thought hard upon those measures which I might take. I knew of no English or even Austrian bankers in Paris who might make the exchange of my various banknotes, nor could I any longer call upon Savill to assist me in locating one.

How I detested that odious villain. No, it was more than simple disgust. Never before had I truly feared a man. My dear friend Mrs Mahon had once instructed me that in order to preserve myself, I must discover the weakness in every gentleman. Until that afternoon I believed that I had poised my sword against Savill's Achilles heel. He was as vain as a peacock, he was a braggart and a fibber. But he was far worse than this; he was also calculating and cruel.

I knew I must quit the Hôtel l'Impératrice with as much speed as I was able. I turned my mind to which of my jewels I might pawn to make up the sum I owed. I had scarcely regained my composure from that encounter when I heard the doors to my apartments open a second time. Fearing that Madame Bonet had returned to collect her debt, I charged forward to explain how I intended to satisfy it. But it was not the proprietress whom I met with, but the devil himself. My back stiffened.

But for the curious twist of his mouth, the expression he wore was entirely flat and placid. He appeared a perfect gentleman in his port-wine coat and breeches and his flawlessly pomaded curls.

'How dare you!' I could scarcely manage to spit the words at him. 'How dare you intrude here!'

Savill took several slow steps towards me.

'What do you mean by this? To have me thrown from my lodgings! To bear false witness to Madame Bonet! Leave here at once, I say!'

The monster did not reply. Instead, he continued his slow progress about the dining room. He paused to peer from the window; he ran his finger along the glass case of a rapidly ticking clock. Then, spying Madame Bonet's bill upon the pier table, he took it into his hands.

'I shall do no such thing,' stated he while inspecting it.

I took an uncertain step backward, towards the door.

After a moment, he looked up at me.

'You think me cruel? You are quite mistaken. You see, dear madam, I have come to relieve you of this burden.' He gestured to the tally of expenses and took several more cautious steps in my direction. 'I intend to dispatch this. I shall discharge your obligations and make an apology to Madame Bonet. I shall explain that it was all an unfortunate error on my part. All shall be made well – and, in return, I shall conclude that you have come to your senses and now agree to my proposal.' His tone was beguiling, as good-natured as the chidings of a lover.

The disgust rose into my throat.

'Proposal?' I said. 'Sir, you fancy that I am without means and therefore in your debt? Then it is you who are quite mistaken.'

Savill's eyes narrowed.

I would have done well to have said no more. It was never my intention to provoke him; I merely wished to make myself plain.

I lifted my chin and glared at him. 'Has it not become apparent to you that your trap has failed to ensnare me? You have lost the game, sir. I never wish to speak to you nor see you again, and if you do not leave me this instant, I shall cry murder.'

Andrew Savill remained fixed in place. The only part of him I observed moving was his upper lip, which had begun to twitch furiously.

'Damn you,' he seemed to mutter.

I took another step backward, but before I could remove myself from his range, he flung himself at me with a roar: 'Damn you! Insolent bitch!'

I screamed and raised my arms to repel him, but it was far too late. Mr Savill was too inflamed with rage. Down came his fist as hard as a hammer upon my left cheek. The blow came with such strength that it sent me tumbling. I fell against the mantel and, in doing so, unbalanced a porcelain urn, which smashed to the floor beside me. For a moment, I lay almost insensible, horrified and gasping, before attempting to clamber to my feet.

He stood over me, surveying the scene, like a filthy-faced boy gazing at the butterfly whose wings he had stripped. He straightened his waistcoat and ran his fingers down the gold buttons, which he claimed had been a gift from Queen Caroline of Naples. Then, without uttering a single syllable more, he stomped out of the room.

It was there, upon the floor of Madame Bonet's ornate dining room, that Lucy discovered me. She cried out in horror and gathered me into her arms, swearing like a Billingsgate fishwife and cursing Savill's blood. She moved me slowly from where I leaned against the wall, but my face throbbed so feverishly that I could scarcely see where I placed my steps. She assisted me to my dressing-room sofa and there laid me upon some cushions, before muttering that she would make up a compress for my injury. As she moved from me I grabbed for her hand.

'Lucy,' I whispered, 'do not trouble yourself . . . We have not the time. Madame Bonet wishes us to quit her hotel immediately. You must gather my possessions and pack them away. At once.'

My maid furrowed her brow.

'But . . . but where are we to go, madam?'

'I know not,' I responded. My eyes began to well with tears. 'I have not a friend in Paris.'

For an hour or so I lay upon the sofa. I stared at a small painting upon the opposite wall, but could see no more than a riot of pink and green and yellow. I shut my eyes and listened to Lucy's footsteps. After a time, these were joined by those of Madame Bonet's servants and housekeeper. I heard the billowing of sheets and linens, the brushing of clothes and rustle of papers, the rattling of keys and turning of locks, scuffling and shuffling and dragging, and the snap of orders being given. Madame Bonet's housekeeper commanded that my belongings be removed to the stables until directions were received to send them elsewhere.

I did not move. I could not. My head was so heavy from the day's events that I could scarcely lift it. But for the throb beating along my temple and eye, I felt nothing.

The green and gold Sèvres clock upon the mantel pinged six times. I knew the hour of our departure would be soon upon us, and so, with some discomfort, I raised myself from the sofa to make my peace with the Hôtel l'Impératrice's dragoness. I determined that I should offer her a pair of ruby eardrops in place of my expenses. Then, Lucy and I would take our chances upon the street and begin to seek out some other suitable accommodation – but where, I had not the slightest notion.

I retrieved the jewels from my coffer, which Lucy had already locked away tight and stowed within my sturdiest of brass-studded boxes. I wrapped the dainty red starbursts in a silk handkerchief and placed them into my pocket. 'I shall return shortly,' I announced to my maid, before making my way solemnly from my apartments on to the landing.

No sooner had the doors closed behind me than I heard a rattle from above. I stopped and listened. There came two or three quiet footsteps. My heart began to thud and I set off down the stair as quickly as I could fly.

'Lady Allenham!' Savill called out.

The sound of his voice struck me near dumb with terror. Indeed, that he had been lying in wait for me should not have come as a surprise. I dare say he had paid some informant amongst Madame's staff to observe my every movement.

I did not answer; instead, I hastened into the hall upon the ground floor. But for the candles glowing against their mirrors, all was still. Neither Madame Bonet nor any of her footmen were to be found.

'Madame?' I cried.

A quick march of feet came from behind me.

'What do you require, little creature?'

I turned to see Savill approaching me. His mouth had been shaped into a smile, but his eyes were as sharp as blades. He moved towards me with the slow menace of a gunship.

I backed towards the entry.

'Sir!' I cried. 'I bid you keep your distance or I shall scream.'

But he did not cease his advance.

I pushed through the door and down the steps into the court-yard. Savill followed me, his intent graven upon his features.

'Dear, dear angel,' he sang out. 'I can bring an end to your difficulties. Remember you that. You need only say the word.' He folded himself into one of his dissembling bows.

He must have thought me a dunce indeed to have offered such a sham display of contrition. I continued to move cautiously towards the gate which led on to the rue Jacob.

'I cannot think where you propose to hide,' he called. 'If you flee, I shall find you. When you return, I shall be here awaiting you. You see, this is a foolish sport. You would do well to give it up.'

Each step I took away from him was countered by one of his own, until I recognized that I had no option but to pass through the gate and on to the street. My belly tightened with dread. I could not think in which direction to turn. Night had already thrown its dark grey tint along the houses and shutters. A lamplighter, bearing his ladder and vessel of oil, crossed the road before me.

'I mean to pursue you, little minx!' he barked. 'You are in my debt and I intend to reap the rewards of my endeavour.'

At that I began to run, skidding and sliding upon the grimy cobbles.

'See how grand you are now, *Lady Allenham*!' he called as I stumbled.

I did not dare peer over my shoulder. I knew not if the beat of footsteps behind me belonged to him or some other. I scrambled as fast as my legs would carry me away from the rue Jacob, away from Saint-Germain-des-Prés.

Although my mind had never determined on my destination, my feet knew precisely where to lead me. They followed the route we had travelled earlier that day, across the river, down the rue Saint-Honoré, towards the rue de Miromesnil.

Chapter 7

I did not open my eyes immediately upon awakening. It required a moment or so before I could gather my sleep-burdened thoughts.

I knew myself to be at the home of Mrs Elliot, though I possessed no memory of the bed into which I had crawled or even of drifting into sleep. I remembered speaking at great length with my hostess, long into the night. The candles burned down to their nubs before a maid quietly came and replaced them. I recited my tale to her just as I have presented it to you and by the time I had completed it, I felt myself in a sort of delirium.

I stared upward at the hangings of the Turkish bed in which I now found myself. They were lustrous, the colour of coffee, and smelt of eau de rose. I listened for any noise, and as I heard none, parted the curtains. The room was dark and shuttered. I slid out of the alcove and, though dressed in nothing more than my chemise and one of Mrs Elliot's caps, crept to a window. There I parted the slats and was greeted by bold daylight. I recoiled and rubbed my eyes. A hint of sunlight bounced along the mirrored walls of the room, revealing its hidden beauties.

But for the bed, it was furnished entirely in the Roman style.

There was a petite white dressing table adorned with gold-painted swags and similar thin-legged chairs and side tables to match. I understood well enough the expense of such modish furnishings. They appeared entirely untouched: the chairs had never seen a pair of breeches upon them; the tabletops had been unmolested by anything more than dust.

It was then I heard a sound, as if a drawer had been opened nearby. I looked and saw that the bedchamber was adjoined to another room. A door had been left slightly ajar. I rapped upon it softly before pushing it wide. To my astonishment I was greeted by the sight of my possessions and a tall, plain-faced maid who was engaged in folding and sorting my linens. Upon seeing me there, she curtseyed and wished me good morning.

'My boxes!' I exclaimed. 'Why . . . however did they come here?'

'We retrieved them from the Hôtel l'Impératrice this morning, while you slept, mademoiselle,' she replied.

I smiled to myself.

'But . . . did Madame Elliot arrange for this?'

'Yes, mademoiselle. I accompanied Langlois, Madame Elliot's porter, to the hotel with a cart. We discovered your maid asleep in the stables keeping watch over your belongings.'

'And Lucy? Pray, where is she?' I demanded, greatly anxious for the welfare of my servant.

'She is presently with Langlois . . . at the Hôtel l'Impératrice.' The maid then hesitated. 'When the proprietress learned we had arrived with a cart to remove your boxes, she flew into a rage. By order of my mistress, Langlois has dispatched your debts to Madame Bonet, but . . . it seemed some other dispute had arisen. Langlois ordered that I return immediately with the cart and that he would follow on with your maid once the matter has been resolved.'

For a moment I found myself struck almost dumb at learning

of Mrs Elliot's act of generosity. That a lady who had never before laid eyes upon me, and who scarcely knew me, should fly to my defence so readily disquieted my conscience. My debt to Madame Bonet was no trifling sum and I instantly resolved to make amends.

'And . . . may I enquire as to your name, so I may apprise your mistress of your kindness to me?'

'I am Thérèse Bertrand,' she replied with a quick bob.

As she spoke, my eyes began to survey the small closet room throughout which she had diligently placed my belongings. A black Chinese clothes press on fat gold legs squatted with its doors spread. An assortment of my linens, petticoats and jackets had been tucked into it. My mind immediately went to work tabulating an inventory of that which lay before me: a green watered-silk gown over the back of a chair and, atop it, two muslin gaulle gowns. In an opened trunk, I spotted several overskirts and two redingotes, as well as a scattering of hats and slippers. Much of my attire and many objects of great worth were still absent. I drew in a long, anxious breath.

'I do hope Lucy arrives soon.'

On such occasions, I despaired that my character had grown so mercenary. I had never grasped the value of most things until circumstance forced me to live by my wits. The world is so hasty in its condemnation of ladies of my sort who it judges to be ever cogitating and counting the worth of this pair of bracelets or that patch box. How can it be otherwise when a woman such as I has not the advantages of either a banker or some male trustee to guard over her riches? She is left with no recourse but to sew her jewels into skirts, to hide her coffers up a chimney or bury them in a field. This is precisely the situation into which I had been cast. There had scarcely been a moment when I did not fear for my cache of worldly wealth. How simple it would have been for a servant with pilfering fingers to rummage through my baubles. How convenient it would have been for a spark from a fire to set it all ablaze, or for robbers upon the road to make off with my banknotes.

As I stood uneasily in the doorway I felt Thérèse studying me.

'Do you wish to be dressed, mademoiselle?' she enquired.

I nodded, but my thoughts were elsewhere, down some fetid alley where a gang of barefooted beggars hacked at my locks.

I splashed my face with water and washed my neck and thighs and hands. Thérèse removed my soiled chemise and pulled a fresh one over my head. I had scarcely finished tying my garters when there came a rap upon the door. Thérèse scurried across the room and opened it to reveal my hostess, along with a housemaid, bearing a silver chocolate pot and a set of dishes.

'Dear Miss Lightfoot, have you slept well?' she enquired with a bright smile. She seemed not the least bit disconcerted by my state of undress. Instead, she made her way to a chair beside the dressing table while waving her hand at her maid to set down the tray. 'You appear to have recovered your colour,' she said, making no mention of the lump still throbbing along my face.

'Madam, I have your exceeding kindness to thank for that.' I dipped my head to her.

'You need not thank me, child, for it is what any sensible Christian would do for another.' She smiled graciously.

The housemaid poured a sludge of chocolate into a dish and passed it to me as Thérèse tightened my stays.

'But you are too kind, Mrs Elliot,' I protested. 'To have fetched my belongings, sent for my maid . . . and dispatched my expenses . . . I—'

'Nonsense,' she clipped my words before pressing her dish to her mouth. 'You owe me nothing, Miss Lightfoot. You are known to my truest and dearest of companions in London and so it is my duty to claim you as a friend in kind. Had I been lost upon the streets of London, I would have expected no less of *you*, my dear.' She held my gaze, as if I were one of her admirers.

Somewhat ashamed of myself, I lowered my glance. Not a day before I had endeavoured to avoid making her acquaintance, and now I found myself very much indebted to her.

'But of course.' I blushed, unable to think of a single appropriate word to express my gratitude. Instead, I stood there, awkward and aware of Mrs Elliot's eyes as her maid tied on my skirts.

'Is that . . . is that the gentleman, Lord Allenham, of whom you spoke?' she asked, breaking the silence. I turned to her, startled by the mention of his name. She gestured to the miniature portrait which I supposed Thérèse had laid upon my dressing table, beside my boxes of pins and my *nécessaire*.

'Why yes, yes it is.' I took the small watercolour into my hand and passed it to her.

She gazed at it for a long while, smiling thoughtfully.

'He is most handsome. I can well imagine how he captured your heart.'

I shook my head and smiled bashfully.

'I fear I have not done his features justice, for he is far more handsome even than that . . .'

'You are too modest, Miss Lightfoot. Why, if this is by your own hand, you are most accomplished indeed. I should very much like to see what else your brushes have produced.'

I was about to dismiss this as polite flattery, but before I could protest, I noticed that my hostess had fixed her eye upon my folio of watercolours, which had been laid upon a nearby table.

'Is that not the very book of sketches which you described to me last night?' she enquired, before directing her housemaid to fetch it.

I felt my cheeks flush hot as she opened the cover. I had displayed my renderings to no one but Allenham, and even he was shown them with much reluctance. I observed her turn over each sheet of paper: the winter scenes taken from my window, the views from the Egmont Palace and the Parc de Bruxelles, the portraits of Madame Vanderoi and her servants, the interiors of my apartments.

'These are most charming,' she exclaimed with an expression of genuine delight.

I shrugged.

'It is but a diversion, though one I enjoy.'

'Every lady requires a diversion,' she announced, delicately shutting the folio. She then turned and beheld me with a gentle, almost pitying countenance. 'Miss Lightfoot,' she began, 'I should not wish you to think me unkind, but I feel I must speak plainly, out of the regard I have for you . . . You see, my dear, for one who is no stranger to the ways and manners of this world, your innocence where matters of the heart are concerned has struck me as . . . most uncommon in ladies of our experience.'

I regarded her, uncertain of her meaning.

'Last night, when you revealed your tale to me, my heart filled with such sadness for you, child. Why, if I possessed so much as a shred of intelligence about your beloved Lord Allenham's whereabouts, there is nothing I should not do to bring about a reunion. For you seem to believe that only he is worthy of filling your days, that you are incapable of knowing happiness in his absence.' She inclined her head and fixed her eyes firmly upon mine. 'My dear Henrietta . . . May I address you as such?'

I nodded.

She then reached for my hand and held it in hers. It seemed a curiously intimate gesture.

'I would bid you hear me, child, for I have learned much from experience in these matters: it is folly to attach your affections so completely to one man . . .'

I opened my mouth to remonstrate with her, but she continued.

'. . . Lord Allenham, for whatever reasons, was forced to part with you. Our role is not to pry or question men upon these matters, but merely to accept them as faits accomplis. My dear, if he had wished for you to accompany him to Paris, you would be with him at this very moment. You must take this to heart along with his pledge to return to you once more, when his business here is concluded. Until that day, you must attempt to forget your sorrows and make something of your existence in his absence.'

The firmness of her words surprised me. The night before, she had sat and listened to my tale and uttered not a single thought or judgement. Indeed, at the time I had believed her to be entirely sympathetic to it. I did not anticipate such a response as this. A certain disappointment settled upon me.

'You . . . you would advise me to quit Paris and return to England?' I whispered, unable to look at her.

'I would not dare,' said she, attempting to catch my eye. She offered me a tender smile. 'You have made your thoughts quite plain upon that matter, and if your lover failed to persuade you to do so, I do not anticipate enjoying much success at it. But if you have truly determined to remain upon these shores, then I would advise you not to pine away another hour. Nor should you permit yourself to become consumed in the fruitless pursuit of him. You must consider your lot as no different from that of a sea captain's wife. She does not think herself abandoned when her husband's frigate leaves port, for he has promised to return to her. It is not so dissimilar, is it, my dear?'

I contemplated her words. While her argument was a reasonable one, I was not so certain my heart wished to embrace it.

Mrs Elliot continued to peer at me with a hopeful look, as if she half expected me to give up my struggle that instant. I brightened my expression to please her.

'Come then,' she announced, rising from her chair. 'Now that you are dressed, we shall tend to your bruise.'

As my hostess led me from the room, I glanced at Thérèse, who had returned to the task of sorting my attire, and prayed for Lucy's swift return with my remaining boxes.

We passed through two sets of doors and across the black and white marble floor of the landing to her apartments. There she led me into her dressing room, which proved a marvellous spectacle: a veritable pageant of decoratively painted walls bearing ornate classical designs, lyres and staffs and vases in carnation pink, sea green and china blue. I had never spied a room so à la mode as this, with its Roman couches and tripod tables. She brought me to her dressing table, which was painted with scrolls of ivy and tiny colourful flowers. Upon it resided the greatest assortment of emulsions, powders, boxes, eaux de toilette and glass jars I had ever before seen.

'Poor lamb,' she sighed, leaning over me. 'Only a monster would attempt to make a pudding of a face so fair.' She then turned me towards the looking glass.

Until that moment, I had not possessed the courage to gaze upon myself, for I had imagined some great balloon of flesh to have risen from my left side. Instead, I was pleased to see only a black oblong bruise, encircled with burgundy, resting at the base of the cheekbone. I touched it lightly with my fingers, and then recoiled with pain. I could not think how long it would take to heal, nor how I might go about concealing it.

'Perhaps some ochre powder and rouge would disguise it?' Mrs Elliot mused while gathering pots and peeking beneath lids. As she did so, a small book-sized portrait, which sat beside her unctions and potions, caught my eye. Its subject was a young girl with a shy gaze. The ruffle of her linen cap sat low across her light-brown fringe, a lock of which had been plaited into the frame.

'I see you have discovered my Georgiana,' remarked my hostess.

'Yes.' I smiled. 'She is . . . your daughter?'

'Indeed. Miss Georgiana Seymour. She is nearly ten years of age and with her father, Lord Cholmondeley – and Lady Cholmondeley – in their nursery,' said Mrs Elliot, dropping a small silver teaspoon of hair pomade into a porcelain dish and opening a jar of yellow-tinted powder.

I observed her in the reflection. She seemed entirely unconcerned by that which she had revealed to me. Her countenance remained steady and pleasant. I returned my attention to the miniature portrait; the girl depicted in it could not have been much past her fourth birthday. She bore the look of a cornered mouse; her deep-set eyes and tight mouth seemed to beg for something. I could not but wonder at her life in her father's nursery, a child unwished-for but nonetheless delivered. A burden laid into servants' arms. Her expression was not unlike how I imagined mine to have been at that tender age, or indeed how I imagined the expression of another child, in another gentleman's nursery many hundreds of miles from Paris.

I am not certain how Mrs Elliot knew my thoughts. I suppose I wore my pain so boldly upon my face that she guessed at my troubles. She stopped, laid down the porcelain dish and placed a gentle hand at my shoulder. At her touch, my eyes grew wet. She spoke softly to me.

'You too have borne a child, Henrietta?'

I nodded and hastily rubbed the tears from my eyes.

'He lives with Lord Bolingbroke, in his nursery.'

'He is Bolingbroke's child?'

'No, madam.' I hesitated. 'His uncle, Mr St John, who took me

74

in when I found myself quite reduced, believes that little George is his.'

'You convinced him of this?'

'Yes,' I confessed, not daring to meet her gaze. 'But he belongs to Lord Allenham.'

Mrs Elliot gave a mild smile and a sigh before placing herself upon a chair beside me.

'You have lived as have I, dear child, upon the generosity of many gentlemen. You must not feel ashamed on account of that. The world is not a kind place for those who have fallen. We do as circumstance bids us.'

'But I only ever wished for the love of one man. There is no justice in the world's condemnation. Is there no means by which to lessen my sins?'

I knew the answer to my own foolish plea long before I watched her slowly wag her head.

'Your sins will never be lessened except when amongst your own kind.' She held her hand out to me. 'You must not feel shame for your deeds, but enjoy the liberties that have been bestowed upon you.'

I thought for a moment upon her words. That which she bid me do seemed too simple by far; I could not merely shrug away the heavy burden on my conscience.

'Allenham has no knowledge of his son. How I longed to inform him . . . but . . . but under Lord Bolingbroke's care the boy wants for nothing. Allenham . . . cannot provide for him . . .' My heart heaved as I spoke of my woes. 'Perhaps one day . . . it may be otherwise?' I gazed at her hopefully.

Mrs Elliot tipped her head and offered me a compassionate look.

'Perhaps. But Fate is not known for her generosity, my dear. You must reconcile yourself to that which is – to loving your child from afar. Letters can be the most cherished of gifts and your meetings will be filled with unparalleled joys.' She pressed my hands in hers once more. 'It is simply the way of the world. Take heart that you are no different from many of us, and that there has been no harm done to anyone by your deeds.' She smiled, but appeared to look beyond me as she did. When I turned, I noted that she was gazing at our reflections, united in the looking glass.

'Now,' she announced, rising to her feet and returning to her pots and boxes. 'Shall I restore you to your natural beauty?'

She waited for a hint of a smile from me before she set to work once more, moving her swan's neck from side to side. It was apparent that she was as aware of my gaze as I might have been of a man's upon me. Each lift of her chin, each tilt of her head was engineered to display her features in a more flattering light. I had never met a lady so practised in her manner that even a performance seemed artless. This is not to say that what flaws she possessed were invisible. No, she was of the age when paint and powder are no longer applied to augment beauty, but rather to disguise the withering of it. The small creases along her eyes glinted with pearl powder, and even the carmine upon her mouth failed to detract from the deepening grooves on either side of it.

'We must rid you of Mr Savill. He is a villain,' Mrs Elliot muttered as she stirred a measure of rouge into her preparation. She worked the mixture together, much as I would my colours upon a palette. Soon a fleshy-toned emulsion emerged. She examined my face again, and added a touch of white powder to her pot.

'You are not the first to suffer by his violence. There was a dancing girl several years ago. When she refused his advances, he came at her with a knife . . . Now, pray, turn to me . . .' Mrs Elliot dipped her finger into the paste and began to dab it along my bruise. 'The unfortunate creature was only saved by her maid, who screamed murder and alarmed the entire household. She was at the time kept by the Duc de Brissac. You might imagine how that gentleman received the news of this event,' she said. 'He sent a footman to thrash Savill with his own horsewhip, while Monsieur le duc looked on.'

I could not prevent myself. I gasped in unfeigned delight at this and then laughed with such force that Mrs Elliot was made to pause her work until I shook no longer.

'I should very much like to dispatch the rascal once and for all. I would be celebrated by every *femme galante* in Paris for performing such a merciful deed.' She sighed and reached for a jar of face powder. 'It is a misfortune that you ever met with him . . . but la, this *petit* souvenir of your association will soon be healed. Then you will be in as much demand as you ever were,' said she while dusting my face.

'But I do not wish to be in demand, Mrs Elliot. Nothing pleases me less.'

She lowered her marabou puff.

'Then what life do you intend for yourself, child?'

'A single life,' said I, holding my head firm. 'I shall not return to my former existence. I vow it.'

'But for how long? Until you are reunited with your beloved?' She raised one of her dark brows. I could not dispel the sense that she mocked me, for I believed I had expressed myself quite clearly to her.

'Why, yes. That is my intention.'

Her calm marble-blue eyes settled on mine.

'And how, pray, do you intend to divert yourself until the arrival of that day? Will you repel the advances of every gentleman who makes himself known to you? Will you don a widow's cap and pass every evening with your embroidery and a book of psalms?'

I found myself lowering my eyes into my lap.

'I do not intend to pine, if that is what you imply, but nor do I intend to lead a life of . . . variety . . . as I did once. For I found no solace in it.'

She sat in silence for a spell, observing me, before speaking in a soft voice.

'You understand, dear Henrietta, that the world will ever take you for what you have become. A young lady of manners, of deportment, and such beauty as yours . . . who lives without family, without a husband, or a father, or brother to care for her . . . Why, Mr Savill guessed it through the window of your coach! There is but one other sort of woman who lives as we do, and while at thirty-seven years I may pass for a widow, you, my dear, would not. Indeed, no person in full command of their sight would believe you had not one hundred offers of marriage the very instant your husband expired.' She laughed. 'How else can the world account for your single state and your finery, or for the manner in which you traverse the continent without a household or letters of introduction? Come, child, you know well enough that this cannot be. It is a flight of fancy. Who will defend your interests or make investments on your behalf? You require a protector with influence as much as you require diversion, and in Paris at the present time, this is most especially true.'

I listened to her sermon with polite patience, prepared to convince her that I required no assistance of any sort. I had earned enough by my previous existence to subsist comfortably without inconveniencing a soul, so long as I chose to live without extravagance. But a gentle rap upon the door curtailed my intentions.

A housemaid slipped in accompanied by Lucy, still wrapped in her cloak. My happy expression of relief lasted but an instant, for the look on my maid's flushed face was one which I had never before seen.

She stood with a lowered chin, her back nearly against the door. 'Lucy,' I called to her, rising to my feet. 'Lucy?'

At first she would not raise her eyes to mine, and when at last she did, they were wide with dread.

Chapter 8

I t was told to me like this:

My trunks had been laid, one by one, in the stables of the Hôtel l'Impératrice, where Lucy sat vigil over them all night and into the morning. 'It is possible,' she sniffed through her tears, 'that I fell into a doze, madam, but not before that brute Mr Savill accosted me, demanding to know your whereabouts. I told him the honest truth, that I had not the faintest notion where you had got to. To be sure, I had never been so a-feared in my life – he stomped about in the courtyard a good while and offered me a *livre* to inform him of your return, but I refused to have it.' My maid then claimed that the blackguard Savill went off in a passion, vowing to have his revenge. It was only in the morning, after Langlois and Thérèse had arrived to fetch her and my belongings, that Lucy noticed two trunks were absent. One contained summer attire and various fripperies, the other my jewels. In a storm of curses and fury, Langlois accused Madame Bonet and Mr Savill of conspiring at the theft. Mrs Elliot's porter promised to turn the Hôtel l'Impératrice upside down in search of those boxes, but the proprietress would not stand for such treatment. She threatened to denounce him and then set two of her footmen upon them so that Lucy and the heroic Langlois were sent fleeing into the road, just as I had been.

On hearing this news I remember that I stood very still, as if made of wood. I did not tremble or fall into hysterics; instead, I observed Lucy through insensible eyes. Not a sound could be heard beyond her bitter heaves and sobs, for she believed herself to be at fault and was certain I would dismiss her on to the perilous foreign streets. I ought to have behaved with the charity of a good mistress and consoled her, but I could scarcely bring myself to breathe, let alone speak.

Reader, lest you judge me to be cold of heart, I would beg you to consider the enormity of the blow I had suffered. You believe I grieved simply for the loss of my necklaces and baubles? That I now feared for the plainness of my unadorned ears and fingers? How mistaken you are. No, it was not the diamond brooches, circles of brilliants and aigrettes that I had lost. Nor was it the rubies and emeralds and sapphires and pearls set into buckles and eardrops and pendants and pairs of bracelets. That for which I mourned would not be the jewel-handled fans, the gold and amber and ivory patch boxes or even the silver purse which contained most of the sum I had acquired in selling my town coach. No. That which had been taken from me upon that day was far more precious than any of these trifles. It was my very liberty that had been spirited away. The box that had disappeared from my collection held the only means I possessed to forge an existence of my own design. The sacrifices I had made to acquire those sparkling gems and gleaming trinkets; the gentlemen with whom I had lain without love or honour; the falsehoods I had told; the tricks I had played: all now seemed for naught.

If any one person understood the grave consequences of this tragedy it was Mrs Elliot. As my incomprehension gave way to grief she took me into her arms. I wept against her willowy frame as if my entire life were at its end. She held me and hushed me, but I could not be calmed. I hiccoughed and gasped and wailed and quaked, as I have rarely done.

'Poor dear, dear lamb,' she repeated as she rocked me, as if she were consoling her little Georgiana. 'I shall make it well again. I vow it. I shall go with Langlois immediately to the *commissaire de police* in the Section des Quatre-Nations and make an accusation of theft against Madame Bonet and Andrew Savill. I shall not permit this to stand. We shall endeavour to retrieve your jewels from the villains . . . Oh my dear, dear girl, this is too much for you to bear . . .'

But no matter how gentle her words, I could not fathom how this might be accomplished, by her or by anyone. I was inconsolable.

A great fuss was made of laying me to rest upon a couch, for I had all but given in to a fit of misery. A glass containing a concoction of wild lettuce and poppy was produced, and soon my weeping fell away into a drowsy haze.

I could not find fault with Mrs Elliot's kindness. Over the next several days, she proved herself a nurse of unparalleled sensibility and insisted that I take rest and live 'very quiet and undisturbed' so I might recover my nerves. In that time, she assured me that she was engaged in writing letters and paying calls to the requisite officials. All manner of visitors came and went from her drawing room, and I was instructed daily on her progress. She comforted me that every possibility had been probed and every authority canvassed, but sadly, this was to no avail. Madame Bonet vehemently protested her innocence, and when Mr Savill's rooms were searched, not so much as a paste bead belonging to me was found. My heart sank at the words she dared not utter: that my trove of treasures was lost to me for ever.

Mrs Elliot remained tireless in her efforts to raise my spirits.

When she was not at the disposal of the Duc de Biron, who I learned was foremost among her paramours, she would come to me in the mornings as Lucy completed my toilette. It was the same upon most days; her arrival would be heralded by the appearance of Thérèse bearing a pot of chocolate or a kettle and tea. Soon after, her mistress would make her cheerful entrance in some length of pale muslin, her undressed hair concealed beneath a fashionably angled linen cap. There she would perch beside me, insisting that I make an attempt at a smile. She would reach for my hand and beg me for all the gossip of London: who were now the reigning beauties of the town? What plays were performed? What had I last heard of Mrs Armistead and Mrs Robinson and dear Gertrude Mahon, from whom she never received letters? Although I attempted to amuse her, my mood was entirely devoid of levity. When she retired from my poor company, I moped and wept and stared at some pages of a book before summoning Thérèse to fetch me another draught of wild lettuce and poppy. Then I would throw myself upon the coverlet of my bed and sleep once more.

Near to a week had passed in this manner, when one morning Mrs Elliot crept into my room before I had even been roused from my bed.

I heard the bed curtains part and, thinking I should see one of her housemaids, or Lucy, I turned. At spying me, her brows arched in surprise.

'You are awake, my dear,' said she softly. She then gathered her skirts and settled beside me upon the bed. 'My dear Henrietta, I have come to a resolution. I mean to make amends for the misfortune you have suffered.'

Beneath her large frilled cap she appeared particularly maternal. I calmly shut my heavy eyes and followed her words with my ears.

'From the very day you came to me and placed yourself under

my protection you clearly expressed a wish to lead an independent life. Your jewels: they were the means by which you hoped to secure your future. I take it that you are in possession of no other fortune?'

At the mention of my tragedy, I felt the tears begin to pool once more.

'No,' I said.

'Then what manner of friend would I be to permit a woman of our kind to suffer such a calamity? In London, it is not uncommon for subscriptions to be raised for a frail sister who has found herself beset by tragedy. If I am not mistaken I recall that your mother was once released from the Fleet on account of a sum collected by her friends.' She stroked my hand as she spoke. 'I cannot promise it will be a large amount, nor do I think it will adequately replace what was lost to you, but I hope that it will offer you some solace. Until that time, you need not trouble yourself as to the expenses of living. It would please me if you would accept my invitation to remain here as a member of my household until you see fit to quit it.'

I opened my eyes. Through the blur of my tears she appeared especially saint-like. Her sharp features and pronounced cheeks softened into an indistinct oval of warm flesh tones and dark hair.

I did not much care for the word charity. She had not spoken it directly, but nevertheless, this is what it was. It humbled me, it embarrassed me, but I could not think how else I might survive. I reached for both of her hands and pressed them with gratitude. I could not bring myself to say more, for my overbearing pride would not permit me.

'My dear, you cannot lie abed until you waste into nothing.' She smiled and sighed. 'Might I persuade you to accompany me to the Palais-Royal this morning? I am without a companion and . . .

I thought you might wish to admire the shops and the spectacle there. Have you never been?'

I shook my head.

'Ah!' She tutted. 'That anyone might come to Paris and not have seen it. It is a wonder. You will have never seen anything so diverting in all your life. Say you will accompany me, my dear.'

I was in no mood for amusements but I could scarcely refuse.

'Yes.' I tried a smile. 'I should like that very much.'

Of course, I had heard much about the colonnades and gardens of the Palais-Royal long before I had ever set foot in France. I had studied the engravings of it in a number of books and heard gentlemen who had visited Paris rave of its delights.

'The Duke of Orléans is a clever devil, to be sure,' Lord Barrymore had said to me, 'for he has spared himself the unpopularity of his cousin the King and sold his palace to the shopkeepers and whoremongers so they may conduct their business untroubled beneath his very windows.' At the time, I had been unable to conceive of that which was described to me: a space as long and broad as St James's Park, surrounded on four sides by the wings of a vast white palace. 'All along the colonnades are shops and restaurants, clubs, societies, gaming rooms and cafés of every description. By day it is peopled by titled ladies, and by night it is entirely given over to the basest sort of *filles de joie*,' he had whispered into my ear.

Although these words had coloured my thoughts about the place, I could not begin to fathom the marvels that awaited me. When Mrs Elliot guided me through the arch upon the rue de Richelieu, a veritable Xanadu unfolded before me.

At its centre could be found a vast pleasure garden replete with avenues of chestnut and cherry trees frothing with pink blossom. Statues and fountains, bowers and secluded seats were positioned amid a profusion of flowers. But these picturesque charms served merely as the backdrop for the circus which whirled all about us. There were tents arranged as a Turk's bazaar, there were amphitheatres, fire dancers and musicians who appeared to lurk behind every tree or column. There were menageries of beasts in gold collars as well as giants and fortune tellers. There were girls peddling sweet rolls and coloured ices, as well as firebrands in their *bonnets rouges* hollering at the crowds.

Never before in Paris had I surveyed such a broad field of humanity. They were of every rank and order, from the noble-born child with her nurse and satin-slippered *maman* to the threadbare old man in wooden sabots. And scattered throughout could be seen what seemed hundreds of tricolour rosettes. They bloomed upon lapels and hats and shoes. Some were as large as sunflowers, while others wilted like poppies. Beneath the mid-morning sun, Mrs Elliot led us on a slow, meandering path through this vibrant garden, pausing here to observe a jig dancer or there a harpist, before passing into the shade of the colonnades.

We moved through the rows of chairs and tables where gentlemen took their coffee and played at chess, or supped brandy. We strolled beyond the windows of countless cafés and wove our course along the shops. Such an emporium of wares I had never seen in all my life. Why, I was perfectly dazzled by the rows of booksellers and instrument-makers, purveyors of soaps and perfumes, of haberdashery, tobacco, carpets and jewels. As we progressed, the light spring breeze blew their scents of lavender and leather and dankness through the arcades.

My friend gently looped her arm through mine and drew me nearer to her side so that our skirts moved together with each step. She took me to this window and to that, admiring snuffboxes or gloves. When we arrived at the shop of a ribbon-seller, she led me through the low door. 'Come,' she insisted, 'I should like to purchase a gift for you.' Then, before I could protest, we stepped into a narrow space no larger than a kiosk which flowed with strips of silk and grosgrain in every colour. Here Mrs Elliot selected four finely sewn red, white and blue rosettes. They were dainty, and as ruffled as roses. Not a one was larger than the bottom of a teacup.

'It is necessary that you are seen to wear one, my dear,' she counselled me in a quiet voice as we moved away. 'It need not be sizeable. I wear one with discretion, often beneath my lapel.' She moved her fingers to the half-concealed circle at her jacket collar. 'I do not much care for the politics of this nation. However, if one wishes to make a life as we do, it is wise to display some measure of approval for the Revolution.'

I was somewhat intrigued by her comment, for I could not imagine what a freeborn Briton would find so objectionable in the notion of liberty.

'You do not approve of the Revolution, Mrs Elliot?' I whispered to her.

My companion tightened her lips and smiled. 'My politics conform to the politics of those gentlemen who offer me their hearts – and their purses, whether they be supporters of the King or of the Revolution.' She then nodded to a row of windows across the garden. 'For a time, my politics were those of the Duc d'Orléans, but as he seems to have given me up entirely, my loyalties have strayed elsewhere. What support I grudgingly profess for the Revolution is on account of Biron, who loves Orléans as a brother. But now there is war with Austria, I fear that association will soon be at its end.'

I did not take her meaning, and I expect she read the question upon my face.

'Biron will be leading the Army of the North, Henrietta, and will soon be departing for Valenciennes.' She raised an eyebrow at me. 'Gentlemen are not known to pine for the aged arms of old mistresses once they have abandoned them.'

I studied her, but as she had spoken her sharp words through a smile, I could not determine the true sentiments behind them. Neither would she permit me to contemplate them for too long but hastily turned my attention to other matters.

'Now,' she announced, tapping my elbow, 'see there. I shall scandalize you with Jacobin filth.' She nodded in the direction of a print-shop window.

Why she wished to draw my notice to such monstrous pictures completely eluded me. Nevertheless, she pulled me with great determination to a window smeared with what seemed a pomade of grease, ink and dust. Pasted over it was an assortment of images and pages of pamphlets, as disgusting to behold as the glass panes themselves. Here, in bold lettering, the immediate execution of the entire royal family was demanded. One engraver had seen fit to render the King and Queen stripped naked as a sans-culotte lashed them with a whip. Another depicted the Queen abed with one of her ladies-in-waiting, entangled in an embrace. 'You please me just as well as that bullock, my husband' read the words inscribed upon it.

I turned to Mrs Elliot to gasp over the audacity of such prints, but found that she seemed to be peering through the glass in the shop door. I stared at her a moment, until she noticed me there. She gestured for me to join her, and although somewhat puzzled, I approached her. She turned me to face the door.

'Can you see? Can you see within?' she demanded.

I hesitated. I was two heads smaller than her and from where I stood the glass was so gummed with grime that not an inch of it was transparent. 'No . . . I am afraid I cannot . . .'

At that she seemed to sigh.

'I mean to have a glimpse of those blackguards who peddle such tripe,' she muttered, pressing her face nearer. Then, all at once, she stopped and a satisfied glower spread over her countenance. 'Hmpf.' She sniffed and then tugged at my sleeve to come away.

'Did . . . did you see them?' I enquired as we continued along the colonnade.

'I saw all I cared to,' she announced. I had anticipated she would reveal more of her thoughts upon the matter, but she maintained her silence. 'My stars, what a pretty assortment of miniatures,' she said before I had an opportunity to pose any further questions.

She drew us to a halt before a bowed window where an assortment of little painted visages was displayed. Each was carefully set in a golden oval or a black square, or surrounded by pearls, garnets or plaited locks of silken hair. My friend leaned forward to study their detail more closely.

'These are not half so accomplished as the portraits you rendered,' said she.

'Oh!' I said. 'How you flatter, madam.'

'But no, no, Henrietta dear. You must not mistake my admiration for empty platitudes.' She addressed me firmly and her look was so earnest that it disarmed me. I shook my head and lowered my eyes.

'I am no miniaturist. My works are simply fine line sketches with a touch of wash. I have never learned to work on ivory. It . . . it is a skill—'

'Pshaw,' she dismissed me. 'Your protests only succeed in furthering my resolution.'

'Your resolution for what . . . ?'

'Why, to have you paint my portrait, dear child.'

I drew back and examined her, thinking this was some jest.

'Henrietta, you are exceedingly clever. You cannot know that I was considering sitting for a miniature when you appeared with your book of sketches and your handsome portrait of your Lord Allenham. And now, well, I am most taken with the notion. A pretty little sketch in watercolour will suffice. It need be no different from any of the other visages you have rendered.'

I smiled awkwardly, unable to determine whether this was a genuine expression of her regard or yet another display of her charity.

'No, my mind is quite set upon it. I shall not permit you to refuse me.' She turned to me with narrowed eyes and a deepness in her voice. 'Remember, my dear, you are in my debt.'

I beheld her, quite startled. For a fleeting moment it was as if my heart had stopped still. This was until a great clap of hilarity took hold of her.

Upon seeing this, I too burst into laughter, though on my account it was as much relief as amusement.

'Oh, my dear.' She placed her hand upon my shoulder. 'See how I have made you laugh!'

I touched my cheeks and felt the happiness rise upon them. What a curious sensation it was; one I had not known for many weeks.

'Please,' said she, presenting me with her arm. I rested mine atop it and together we stepped out into the brightness of the garden.

Chapter 9

After that day, I resolved to make every attempt to please her. She had displayed such generosity, such compassion, such a determination to lift my spirits, that I could think of nothing but returning that kindness. Indeed, the more I learned of her character, the more I saw about her person to admire.

Although I could never pretend she was a perfect beauty – her face was rather too triangular to be thought soft and her nose too hawk-like to be considered demure – she possessed many other winning traits that rendered these defects invisible. Her very movements were those of a dancer. The manner in which she held a dish, or descended a stair, or turned her fair head, was informed by a light elegance. She never stumbled upon the hem of her dress, or allowed her sash to come untied. Never did a comb or a feather tumble from her coiffure. Never did an inappropriate sentiment or an incomplete thought escape her lips. She was that very thing which her name suggested: grace.

I had never met a creature like her. Even amongst my companions in London there were none who bore the same degree of refinement. There was a certain unfinished quality to the women of my acquaintance. They bounced and bobbed and flirted in an artless manner. While they understood gentility and polite conduct, they were also known to laugh with shameless abandon or, in the case of Lady Lade, swear like the wife of a Billingsgate fishmonger. Such would be inconceivable for Mrs Elliot with her practised simpers and courteous air. Although she was no Madame du Barry and had never lived among the court, she had adopted the manners of those who had, and never once abandoned them – no matter the circumstance. And to think that I had succeeded in winning the favour of such a flawless being, that she had deigned to take me beneath her wing; well, I felt myself to be vastly honoured.

However, as my esteem for her grew, so too did my anxiety about taking her likeness. I was most anxious to render her miniature in a manner agreeable to her. Never before had my hands quivered at the prospect of holding a pencil, and yet upon that morning they shook mightily. My friend sensed my discomfort and immediately set about putting me at ease. She chattered and passed witty remarks until we both were giddy with giggles. By the time I presented the finished image to her, I had not the slightest doubt that it would meet with her approval, for my heart had been assured that it was not the execution that concerned her so much as the artist who had executed it. Nevertheless, she exclaimed exuberantly at my skill.

'Why, the likeness is such a fine one that I shall have it set into a frame of pearls and then have it delivered to the Duc de Biron in Valenciennes. That will remind him of the bedfellow he has left behind in Paris,' she declared.

Her compliments caused my breast to swell.

'And might I beg another favour of the paintrix?' She tilted her head.

'But of course, madam.'

'A self-portrait.'

92

'For you . . . ?' I was uncertain if I had understood her request.

'But of course, silly! And why should I not wish a portrait of my dear friend?'

That she should desire an image of me, perhaps to place beside that of her own cherished daughter, made my cheeks flush violently.

The attention which Mrs Elliot paid to me was unlike that which I had ever received from one of my own sex. I had known true love from Allenham, but here I had become the object of constant care and affection of the sort one might bestow upon a kinswoman. There seemed no gesture too generous, no deed too conciliatory. At times I felt as if Mrs Elliot were in my debt, rather than the contrary. I ruminated upon this, how it could come to pass that a person, once a perfect stranger, could demonstrate such heartfelt concern for another. My conclusion was that my friend was guided by her sense of remorse; to some degree she held herself accountable for the loss of my jewels.

This conviction was made firm to me shortly after I had completed our portraits. One morning, my friend announced that we were for the Comédie-Française that evening.

'It is *Le Bourreau bienfaisant* tonight. Monsieur Préville will be upon the boards,' said she, her features dancing with excitement. 'Madame de Flaghac, who is a friend most dear to me, has bid us accompany her. Her box is well situated, near enough to the stage, but with a fair view of the box of the Duc d'Orléans.'

It was not clear what she insinuated by this, but I continued to smile.

'What do you propose to wear, Hetty dear? The mode in Paris differs from that in London for such occasions. If you like, I shall advise you . . .'

'Why yes . . . yes please,' I stammered, quite flattered by her suggestion.

She asked that Lucy fetch my finest attire. So out came those lavish pieces, those flamboyant souvenirs of a past from which I once hid. Laid before me were my embroidered green silk open gown, another in pale lavender satin and a third of saffron stripes, with three voluminous red furbelows upon the skirts. The hats were retrieved too, every one of them purchased for me for lying upon my back, the vast bonnets with crowns arrayed in blue, pink and white feathers, and caps flounced with the richest lace. There was my hooded cape of ottoman silk, and another trimmed with Russian fur, and fichus of the thinnest gauze embroidered with pearls and delicate needlework. My satin and bright leather shoes were paraded before her, some with the soles scarcely scuffed by wear.

I observed her as she fingered each flounce and ruffle, admired the fabrics and colours, and held my shoes to the light to watch the purple-green taffeta shimmer. Anxiously, I awaited her judgement. I ached to hear her approval of my taste.

'This will do perfectly,' said she, holding out my saffron-striped gown. 'The colour draws the blush from your cheeks.' Her eyes then wandered to my throat and ears. 'And you need not concern yourself as to your adornments, Hetty, for my ruby necklace is perfectly suited. And you might make use of my diamond girdle buckle and shoe buckles as a complement to it. They were gifts to me from the Prince de Condé. How do you fancy that, eh?'

And so that afternoon Mrs Elliot's maid, Victoire, appeared, bearing two gold coffers inlaid with amber, which she placed upon my dressing table. Close behind her followed a thin little man, a *friseur* by the name of Monsieur Gris.

'Madame suggested you might wish to wear your hair à la Coblenz, as does she,' offered Victoire, turning to Monsieur, who had already begun to spread out his tools. 'It is best for displaying the jewels,' she added.

And so I sat beneath his fingers as he removed the curling papers and teased the crown of my hair upward before affixing it in place with a red swatch of silk. He then let lengths of my locks down my back and shoulders, smoothing them with pomade, so that only the ends retained their curl. Into the back of this construction was fastened one grand white ostrich feather. Only once this stage had been set, the curtains of hair drawn back and the background painted with rouge and powder, were the jewels permitted to appear upon it.

A short collar of square-cut rubies, each the size of my thumb-nail, was arrayed about my neck. The stones appeared so large that, had I not known better, I might have guessed them to be made of glass. Victoire then removed three vast circles of brilliants from a flat gold case. The shoe buckles were so broad, they fairly covered my toes and sat heavily upon the tops of my feet. The girdle buckle which she threaded through the band of scarlet satin at my waist was nearly the circumference of my palm.

I stared at myself in the looking glass, astounded by the mag-nificence that hung from me. No heir to a Barbadian sugar fortune, no son of the English gentry might have purchased such wonders. These were the fruits of an unimaginable wealth, grown from miles and miles of vines and fields and harvested for centuries. And to consider they represented but an insignificant thimbleful of what belonged to the royal Dukes and Princes of the Blood. For each necklace or buckle in Mrs Elliot's coffers, there were more elsewhere. There were other mistresses with other boxes, and wives and daughters and mothers and aunts and sisters all with caches of similar treasures. The thought fairly humbled me, that these men were each as wealthy as a king.

The jewels felt both an honour and a weight about my neck. Not only did I fear an accidental loss of these riches – a slip of a clasp, the loosening of a diamond – but my concern also began to grow that Mrs Elliot had selflessly adorned me in her most valued ornaments, and that her person would appear almost bare by comparison.

No sooner had I assumed my seat in her coach than I began to discreetly examine her apparel. She sat opposite me, resplendent in a pale blue watered-silk gown, her firm bosom raised into prominence by a compress bodice. Her hair was arranged into a grander, darker version of my own and decorated with a star-shaped aigrette and feather which tickled the ceiling of the cabin. A festoon diamond necklace dropped from her throat, while two round flowers of brilliants sat upon her earlobes. But these objects were mere pretty baubles, simple trifles by comparison to the *pièce de résistance* affixed to her bodice. Here, just at the edge of her powdered cleft, sat a single sapphire the size of a farthing. Were its size and deep blue hue not commanding enough, it lay encircled by two rings of diamonds, which radiated forth from it in an exquisite starburst.

Once I had spied that sublime stone, I could scarcely remove my attention from it. It dazzled me, as did Pharaoh's crown the infant Moses. My friend caught my eyes upon it and lifted her fingers to stroke the object.

'Is that a gift from the Duc de Biron?' I enquired gently, not wishing to appear green-eyed.

'Ah, no, it is also from the Prince de Condé. The necklace, the buckles: they were among the gifts he made to me for several months with him at Chantilly. But the sapphire, it is the most exceptional, is it not?' she said.

''Tis indeed! It looks fit to adorn a sultan's headdress.'

'It is most ancient and is rumoured to have belonged to the Empress Theodora,' she said, lowering her voice. 'And the worth of it, my dear, is considerable. Condé gave me no annuity, but I have *mon saphir*, which, were I to pawn it, would guarantee me no small share of future comfort.' She then placed a kiss upon her fingertips and pressed them to the brooch. 'You might equip yourself similarly, Hetty.'

I examined her uneasily. I did not wish to appear rude.

'I had once an entire coffer of treasures . . .'

'And you shall again, my dear!' said she, taking my hand. 'Such beauty as yours will not go unnoticed for long . . .

'Henrietta,' she continued after a spell, 'if you mean to make your life here in Paris, you must learn to do so with a certain cunning. Gifts and annuities, my child. One must take care to feather one's nest before all the golden geese in France are plucked. My hotel on the rue de Miromesnil, my house at Meudon and all of my furniture were from Orléans. This coach is from the Duc de Fitzjames. Biron, Condé and others have purchased for me my jewels, and many other luxuries besides. These suffice well enough, but none offer the security of an annuity. A *guaranteed* annuity, my dear, the promise of a regular income, a pension, like that received by any widow or housekeeper. A house and furniture may be burned and jewels stolen . . . but an income, if it is secured by law, is the very cushion which rests between comfort and destitution.' She sharpened her look upon me. 'You must hear me when I say, in Paris at the present time, it is most essential that one acquires friends of influence. Many of my protectors have fled; the others . . . well, I am too old to sustain their fancy for long, but you . . .' She raised her chin. 'You may rise to a great height.'

I attempted to return her warm, hopeful expression, but I suspect she may have spied my reservations through my limp smile. I had begun to fear that this lecture had been but the prelude to some well-intentioned mischief awaiting me at the Comédie-Française.

As we entered the theatre and progressed through the throng up the great stair, I eyed each person who approached Mrs Elliot.

Those who flew to her side were not the modish young bucks who tripped in my wake, but rather the portly, sunken-eyed roués of great wealth. They sported gems upon their fat fingers as glittering as that which sat at her breast. My friend deftly pushed me before them, offering me up to their wet lips like a sweet morsel. Some stood near enough to me to inhale the eau de orange blossom from behind my ears.

I was most relieved to be removed from this milieu by a liveried servant, who promptly delivered us to our box. He led us into a dim narrow corridor. All along the passageway observing eyes crawled over us like insects. My skirts brushed those of countesses and whores alike. We passed door upon embellished door, each heavy with golden scallop shells and fat-faced putti. When at last we arrived at ours, it was opened like the lid of a jewel box. At the centre of it, upon a velvet seat, resided a rare and curious treasure. She sat with her back to us, a small, thin creature enveloped within the voluminous folds of a cherry-coloured gown. Her hair, which she wore atop her head in the fashion of thirty years gone, was entirely grey and looked as if it had been spun from the finest silver thread. As for her face . . . well, as she turned to greet us, I might have sworn she was made of porcelain. It appeared entirely white but for her lips which were painted the gaudy hue of her skirts.

'Ah, *ma chère petite*,' she exclaimed, holding out her arms to Mrs Elliot, who towered like a heron above her. They exchanged kisses as affectionately as might a mother and daughter.

'Madame de Flaghac, may I present to you Mademoiselle Lightfoot, who is my relation from London.'

There was an exchange of curtseys, before the old woman squinted at me.

'Come into the light, my child.' She beckoned me with her closed black fan. 'Here, sit beside me, mademoiselle.' I followed her instruction. Then, quite without warning, she took my face into her hand. 'La, such pure, fresh beauty. Eyes like bluebells . . . and the cream of your neat skin . . .' she marvelled, her eyes but inches from mine. Her breath smelled of sweet liquorice-root lozenges. 'You must have many admirers, Mademoiselle Lightfoot.'

I wished to say I had no need for such things, but held my tongue.

'I was once as beautiful as you . . . when I danced upon the stage. It fades quickly, my child. One minute you are as radiant as summer, and then, alas, it is autumn.'

'Madame is too modest, Miss Lightfoot,' interjected Mrs Elliot from the opposite side of her matronly companion. 'Her summer was a long one. She was celebrated in her day, mistress to Louis XV and painted by Monsieur Boucher.'

'Ah, but now winter has come upon me and I am as decrepit as a felled oak.'

'But most fortunate in widowhood. A countess,' Mrs Elliot teased her. 'Pay no heed to the silly goose. She has been like a mother to me, a tutoress when I found myself in Paris.'

'You were in no need of a tutoress when we met, *ma chère,*' rejoined the old *dame.*

At that moment a great swell of music rose from below and extinguished their sparky banter. While the orchestra played the overture, I observed Madame de Flaghac survey the boxes. After a pause, she leaned towards Mrs Elliot.

'I see the Bishop of Autun sits with Madame de Flahaut again, in plain sight. She is as shameless as her sister. And look, there is her husband.' Madame de Flaghac gestured with her fan to the tier above. 'If ever there was an old fool . . .' She snorted. 'And there, another fool . . . see the American ambassador? The fat one beside Monsieur de Narbonne and Madame de Staël? He will never succeed with her . . .'

I studied Madame examining the audience, her eyes picking through each box, like a huckster's wife at a rag fair.

'Orléans has now appeared,' she muttered through the side of her mouth. There, in the box directly across but four, entered three shadowed figures, two men and a woman in a great peaked hat. The shortest gentleman I recognized to be the Duc de Lauzan, Biron's heir, but the other two silhouettes I did not know.

We both turned our gazes to Mrs Elliot. She did not move.

'She has seen them,' whispered Madame de Flaghac. 'And now her eyes are as sharp as bayonets upon Madame de Buffon.'

'Madame de Buffon?'

'Orléans's mistress.' The elderly lady regarded me with surprise, as if she could not fathom how I failed to recognize this name. 'Has *ma chère* not confided in you?'

'No.'

Madame moved her lips closer to my ear.

'Now, I shall inform you of this, but you must not betray to Madame Elliot that you have heard it, and certainly not from me.'

I nodded.

'There exists a great enmity between our Madame Elliot and La Buffon, and not without some justification. Before La Buffon's grip on Orléans was secured, he loved Madame Elliot, though briefly. La Buffon would not countenance another mistress and has since sought to remove our dear friend from Orléans's life entirely. Well, I shall tell you, mademoiselle, in this past year, La Buffon all but succeeded in her aims.' Her nostrils flared.

I leaned nearer to her, greatly intrigued by this news.

'You know Orléans and Madame Elliot are no more than friends?'

I nodded again.

'Why, their affection is that of brother and sister, but no, La Buffon will not countenance this. Orléans has been forbidden from calling upon Madame Elliot or from corresponding with her. Oh, but there is worse still.' Madame de Flaghac sucked in a great dose of air and then paused. She waited until she was certain that I hung upon her words before blowing them out. 'Since the Duke's separation from the Duchess of Orléans on account of . . . political differences, his finances are now approaching ruin – or so I hear. I understand that he has been forced to sell many of his possessions and to curtail his expenses. La Buffon has insisted that he cease to pay Madame Elliot's annuity, *which is a substantial one*.' She mouthed each syllable.

I stared at Madame de Flaghac for a moment, taking in the news she had conveyed.

'But poor Mrs Elliot,' I whispered. 'Why, she does not appear to suffer . . . she lives in a manner most luxurious.'

'No, not at present . . . but soon . . . I dread to think . . .'

'Well, what is to be done about it?' I asked with some alarm.

The old *dame* shrugged.

'One waits for La Buffon to fall from favour, but that may not occur for a great while – if ever. I have been led to believe that she and Orléans are very much in love. They live in a state of conjugal felicity, as might an Englishman and his wife.' She then made a grunt of disapproval. 'But do not mistake this simple domesticity as an indication of La Buffon's mild character. No, that woman is a true viper and not to be crossed.'

Although I did not intend it, my eyes widened with intrigue, which only served to encourage Madame. She was a fountain of gossip, one which bubbled and gurgled without pause.

'There is a lady now much out of favour amongst Orléans's circle. She is Madame Meyler, a compatriot of yours.' She then drew back and examined me. 'You tell me that Madame Elliot has never recounted this incident to you?'

I shook my head.

'Ah, your relation has been most neglectful.' She tutted. 'Madame Meyler is the very reason why La Buffon is now entirely bereft of female companionship and ladies no longer seek to win the attention of Orléans. *They are too frightened*, mademoiselle.'

'Why?' I asked, rapt by her masterful storytelling.

She lowered her head and peered into my eyes.

'They say La Buffon attempted to murder Madame Meyler when she suspected her to be with child by Orléans. They had been the most intimate of friends. Shortly after La Buffon heard of Madame Meyler's condition, there was what some call "a mysterious accident" while they were riding in the Bois de Boulogne. Madame Meyler was thrown and the infant came away. They have not spoken since.' Madame de Flaghac pursed her lips disapprovingly. 'She once lived in great elegance in the place Vendôme. She now has but two rooms up four flights of stairs upon the rue d'Enfer, behind the Opera House. Disgraceful.' My companion then turned her gaze across the playhouse. My eyes followed hers as they settled on the villainous subject of her tale.

But for the shape of the elaborate *chapeau à la Tarare* she wore, I could make out little of her through the shadows. She seemed of a slight build and regular in height. Her age was concealed by the darkness, but she moved with the quick spark of an excitable young woman. Occasionally she inclined her head to whisper something into Orléans's ear. As for the Duke, his appearance did not strike me as exceptional. From what I could discern, he was tall, but stout. His head seemed round and melon-like. For a moment or so, I studied them in their box, observing as two gentlemen entered and paid their regards.

'I shall tell you this much, girl,' continued the *grande dame* at my side, 'in spite of Orléans's current difficulties with regard to his purse, there are few who possess his influence. So long as the King and Queen are shut away in the Tuileries, and Danton and the Assembly are at liberty to do as they please, Orléans reigns over Paris, as if . . . as if *he* had been *appointed* king in his cousin's place. The King fears him like no other, that he feeds the rats who make this hateful Revolution—' She then broke off abruptly, as the great Préville stomped on to the stage to loud cries of approval. 'I should not like to speak of politics in this place,' she muttered, as the noise died away.

It was at that moment that she turned and looked over her shoulder. Much to my surprise, I found that a young man had crept up behind Madame de Flaghac's chair. He placed a kiss upon her hand and then another upon Mrs Elliot's before leaning to speaking into her ear. No sooner had he done that than she turned her gaze to me.

'Miss Lightfoot,' said she, addressing me in English, 'I should like to present to you Mr Drummond.'

I regarded the boyish-faced gentleman. He appeared to be not much older than me. His fawn-brown hair had been coiffed and curled and his person sewn into a plum-coloured coat and tight grey breeches.

'Miss Lightfoot.' He made a small bow and then, in a most irregular fashion, offered me his hand. I stared at it, before cautiously taking it into mine. Then, in one quick motion, he raised me to my feet.

'Miss Lightfoot, would you do me the honour of accompanying me upon a call?' he enquired.

I immediately threw Mrs Elliot a look of concern.

'That would depend entirely upon the nature of that call, sir,' I responded. 'I cannot think what manner of call would be made at such an hour.'

'Dear Miss Lightfoot,' began Mrs Elliot, 'you need have no uncertainties about the nature of this errand. Indeed, you will thank me upon its completion. It is in your interests to go at once with

Mr Drummond or I fear the opportunity will be lost,' said she, nodding to the young man.

My eyes darted between them, and then to Madame de Flaghac, who simply returned my look of question with a faint simper.

'Miss Lightfoot, if you will?' he implored, offering me his arm.

I fixed my uneasy gaze firmly on Mrs Elliot. I could not prevent myself from thinking that this was the scheme she had designed for me all along: that Drummond was intended as a paramour.

'My dear,' she now beseeched me, 'you must place your trust in me. Will you not grant me that honour? Will you not trust her who took you to her bosom, who has sheltered you for these many days?'

I hesitated. For an instant I considered resuming my seat once more and refusing to move. But what then? I could not risk offending my only friend; she who had preserved me from the streets of a foreign city, she who had spared me the abuses of a brute and healed my wounds.

'Miss Lightfoot.' She gestured with a nod of her head to the door. Her soft eyes entreated me with the kindness of a mother. 'Do trust me.'

I looked at Mr Drummond and took hold of his arm.

Chapter 10

Mr Drummond marched us through the corridor at a brisk pace. He pushed past a pair of intriguers pressed against the wall, whose courtship we interrupted. The man hissed at us, but my companion paid no heed. He fairly pulled me along beside him, down the empty stair and beyond the doors to the rue de Richelieu. There awaited his coach and valet at the ready.

'Sir,' I begged him, 'to where do we repair? What errand is this?'

'Ah,' he replied. 'You will soon learn, Lady Allenham.'

I started at the mention of that name. Indeed, I felt my mouth part in shock. Drummond roared with laughter.

I found no humour in this at all. Rather, I had grown quite agitated.

'Pray, Mr Drummond, do you intend to play me some . . . some trick?' I demanded.

'Indeed, madam, a trick shall be played, but not at your expense,' he said, his eyes fired with mischief. No sooner had he spoken those words than the vehicle began to roll forward.

Mr Drummond and his careless air had filled me with a great sense of dismay. For a moment I feared that Allenham was to be the subject of these high jinks. I could not determine whether this ruddy-cheeked beau wished to mock me or entrap me, or even, dare I venture, assist me. Perhaps, I began to wonder, my suspicions were unjust? Perhaps there was no menace to this scheme at all. Perhaps Mr Drummond was in fact leading me to my beloved . . .

The carriage moved decidedly southward, towards the Tuileries and then across the bridge in the direction of Saint-Germain-des-Prés. It did not require more than several moments before I recognized the route we followed; our destination could be none other than the rue Jacob.

'Mr Drummond, what do you mean by this?' I implored him.

The young gentleman sat, perfectly sanguine.

'Why, I mean to restore your honour, Miss Lightfoot.' He then paid me a wink.

I regarded him quizzically.

'And, pray, how do you propose to achieve that, sir?'

'Quite plainly through the application of fraud, madam,' he announced, slipping his fingers into the pocket of his waistcoat. He drew out a visiting card and placed it into my hand.

When at last a cast of light fell upon it, I could scarcely believe my eyes. It read:

The Baron Allenham
HÔTEL D'ESPAGNE, RUE DE SEINE

I looked at him, aghast.

'How did you come by this?' I cried.

Drummond laughed again, in that conceited manner so natural to young men of great fortune.

'Why, I had it printed for me this very evening, at Mrs Elliot's behest.'

'Mrs Elliot?'

'Your relation, Miss Lightfoot,' he said. 'She has arranged this entire affair.'

At that moment, we found ourselves at the gate of the Hôtel l'Impératrice. The mere sight of that dreaded place caused my belly to fold over. It was then I believe Drummond spied the alarm upon my face.

'I can assure you, Miss Lightfoot, you have nothing to fear from that blackguard.'

We passed through the arch and into the courtyard, the scene of my last encounter with Mr Savill, upon whom I had hoped never again to lay eyes. One of Madame Bonet's footmen hurried to the carriage and assisted Mr Drummond from it.

'I would have you remain here, concealed in the coach, madam. From that vantage you will not be seen, but it should allow you a fair view of events,' said he as the door was shut behind him. He then placed his card into the hand of the servant. 'Please deliver this to your resident, Mr Savill. Given the nature of this matter, I do not propose to be received by him in his rooms. I would have him attend upon me in the coach yard, this instant.'

I swallowed hard and observed as my champion stood, his arms folded in an impatient stance at the centre of the yard. Above him I noted a light in one window of the apartments I understood to belong to Mr Savill. Now the urgency of our visit became apparent to me; Mr Drummond had taken pains to learn that the offender was at home.

A moment or so passed. Then the light that had glowed in Savill's window was suddenly extinguished. That act of cowardice prompted my champion to look across his shoulder and exchange a knowing glance with me.

A further handful of minutes elapsed. Drummond removed his watch from his waistcoat, held it to the light, clapped the case shut and returned to the coach.

'Your whip, Dupont,' said he to his coachman. His servant handed over the instrument and the young man strode back to the centre of the courtyard.

'Andrew Savill, you niggardly dog!' he thundered. 'I have seen the light in your window, sir, and know that you cower from me.'

Drummond then paused for a moment and paced the coach yard, awaiting a response. There came none.

'For the gross offence you have paid me, for the dishonour you have done to my wife and for the theft of her property, I demand that you attend me here, this instant, to receive the punishment you have merited.' With that, the young man cracked his horsewhip with vigour. An electrifying snap reverberated through the enclosed space.

'A barbarian who sees fit to raise his hand to a lady should be prepared to pay in kind for his crimes. I propose to thrash you within an inch of your life, sir, to flay you for the beast you are!' He snapped his whip once more.

One by one, the shutters of Madame Bonet's establishment began to move. The faint glow of candles and curious faces appeared at the surrounding windows. Amongst them, I spied the proprietress herself, partially disguised behind the drapery and wearing a disquieted expression.

Seeing that his proposition met with silence, Drummond howled once more. 'Mr Savill, you damnable scoundrel! Villain! Coward! Come receive your dues! I shall not depart without some promise of satisfaction!'

This charade continued for the better part of a half-hour before the doors of the Hôtel l'Impératrice flew wide and out came a waiter bearing a note. The frightened lackey handed it to Mr Drummond, who tore it open, read it and threw it upon the ground.

'Very well then, sir!' the young man called out, pointing his whip at Savill's window. 'Prepare your second for two days hence and I shall meet you in the Bois de Boulogne at a time agreeable, whereupon your blood shall be let. And do not mistake me, sir, I am an excellent shot.'

With great composure, young Drummond then turned upon his heel, returned the whip to his coachman and quietly resumed his seat within the carriage. Only once we had begun to roll away did his expression shift. He clapped his hand upon his face and began to snigger. I studied him apprehensively. The snorting and snuffling grew louder until all at once he threw back his head and emitted a scream of laughter. At first, I was quite startled at this, but soon found myself carried along by his mirth. I began to tremble and then, like him, burst into uncontained levity.

It had been an audacious act, to be sure, but one which Andrew Savill had merited. I snorted at the thought of it, of his drawn, terrified visage. Mrs Elliot was a genius with her cunning, I concluded, before a sobering thought came upon me.

'But . . . but, Mr Drummond, I do hope you do not intend to see your challenge to Mr Savill to its conclusion?'

'I shall fight for your honour, Miss Lightfoot, if that is indeed what is required,' he replied with a smile.

'You cannot! No, I insist – you must not . . .'

But my concerns did no more than amuse him.

'Come, dear Miss Lightfoot, you must take a drink with me in celebration,' was his only riposte. 'I propose to show you the delights of the Café du Plaisir.'

I drew back from him uneasily. Although I was grateful for my champion's defence of me, I had no intention of extending our acquaintance. I was certain I knew Drummond's sort and had suffered my fair share of young men's antics. How many dreary hours I had passed in the company of Mayfair bucks and bloods as they rolled dice and emptied bottles, I would not venture to recount. Such was the lot of the fallen sisterhood: to play the cheerful companion to the drunkard; to whisper sweetly in his ear as he lost at cards, to titter merrily while bouncing upon his knee, to permit his cold, rough hand into a bodice, to sit beside him in a hackney cab as he vomited down his waistcoat. I studied Mr Drummond and sighed with resignation. I supposed he had earned his night of revels.

I had gritted my teeth in anticipation of what I was to discover at this Café du Plaisir at the Palais-Royal. However, much to my relief, the evening did not end as I had feared. I might have placed more trust in Mrs Elliot's judgement. This was no gambling hell or dark stinking bagnio, but rather a curious establishment more closely resembling a watchmaker's shop, where patrons were served refreshment through a mechanized system of pulleys and trapdoors. Mr Drummond slapped his knee with delight as he pulled upon levers and drew bottles of wine from the cellar through the hollow legs of a table. Alas, a good deal of this was imbibed, but as we were joined by a nephew of the Earl of Abercorn and his abstemious po-faced bear leader, the night did not prove so entirely disagreeable.

My champion returned me to the rue de Miromesnil in the last hour of darkness. He begged no more from me than a handful of innocent kisses, which I granted him. To this very day, I have never been asked to trade so little for so much male kindness.

I had believed myself the only soul awake as I returned to my rooms, but no sooner had I roused Lucy from her chair than there came a soft rap upon the door. Victoire stood in her night shift with a candle.

'Madame bids you to come,' she whispered.

I followed her along the corridor and across the house to Mrs Elliot's apartments. There I found my friend between the parted curtains of her Turkish bed. She sat with a single light and bright, eager eyes.

'Hetty, I have lain awake all night in anticipation of your return. Tell me, dear, what has become of Mr Savill?'

She gestured to the bed beside her and so I climbed upon it. There, I regaled her with all the details of Mr Drummond's performance, with tales of Savill's cowardice and the promise of a duel, the notion of which I claimed to abhor. At that, Mrs Elliot laughed.

'Child, you have nothing to fear on that account. It is well known that Mr Savill has been challenged no less than four times and has never once shown himself upon the field. At each occasion he made off long before the fateful day. He is notorious for it! Why, his name is not even Savill, but O'Mara. He had it altered by Royal licence when he married his wife, who, poor creature, had been an heiress. He posed as a gentleman and now has run through near all her fortune.' My friend shook her head. 'Indeed, I would venture that he is at this very moment upon the road to Calais!'

At this I laughed heartily and with relief. Mrs Elliot joined me, before sighing and bidding me to lay my head upon her shoulder.

'Do you know how I conceived of this trick we have played upon Mr Savill?' she began.

'No.'

'Gertrude Mahon and I once did the same to the Duke of Dorset.' She then embarked upon a well-spun narrative which drew me back to the streets of my birth, to Mayfair, to the theatres and to Vauxhall, to the faces and names of friends I had left behind in a previous lifetime. Her lilting voice with its vague trace of Scots rendered me drowsy and content. I could still smell the faint hint of her eau de musk as I curled beside her in the warm bed.

'I dare say our appearance at the play tonight has set tongues wagging,' said she as I was drifting into sleep.

I looked up at her through a haze. She wore a tired but roguish smile.

'They will formulate a story about you and me. They will suppose that you are my niece and have fled some scandal in London . . . or that you are in fact my daughter, the product of some youthful dalliance. Perhaps some will guess you are the very reason why my father married me to that old toad, Elliot, when I was younger than you.'

'But we look not at all alike,' I protested.

'Psh. That matters not. They will invent what amuses them.'

Silence settled into the room. I listened to the rise and fall of her breath and assumed she had given way to sleep.

'That would not be so disagreeable to you, would it?' she murmured. 'That you should be taken for my daughter?'

Her words hung in the air, begging for my heart to catch them. She understood how I had longed to hear such a thing uttered: 'my daughter'. *That you should be taken for my daughter.* How did she know I yearned for that thing more than any other? To call some gentle person 'Mamma', as I had never done.

'No,' I whispered at last. 'Not in the least.'

Chapter 11

Here, reader, I shall abandon my pretence. I shall confide to you this: I understood precisely the significance of my appearance with Mrs Elliot at the Comédie-Française. When I had accepted her invitation I had agreed to place myself once more at the centre of the demi-monde, that scene from which I had only lately escaped. Indeed, it was not without a good deal of contemplation that I arrived at my determination. You see, since the loss of my jewels, I did not believe I possessed any say in the matter. I knew well enough that my friend would never suffer me to make use of her *hôtel particulier* as might a nun in cloisters.

However, this is not to say that I was in any manner prepared to resume the *habits* of my former existence. Why, I might play the cold-kneed prude for as long as I desired, regardless of what the world assumed. While they regarded me as her protégée, I was introduced among her more intimate circle of friends as her 'relation'. The invitations that you might expect soon followed. I accompanied 'my relation' to the usual dinners, card parties, gatherings and visits to the theatre. There were the rides through the Bois de Boulogne and excursions upon the river, as well as a masquerade at the *petite maison* of the Marquis de Sillery, held in a sumptuous Turkish pavilion at the bottom of his pleasure garden. Although I willingly followed my friend to these places, I took care to remove hands from my bodice and to slide like a slippery fish from embraces. My actions were so discreet that I did not believe she was aware that I thwarted my admirers, when in fact my indifference to their approaches suited her grand scheme for me perfectly.

It was at about this time that I began to wonder what had become of the self-portrait she had requested from me. I had not spied it among her possessions since the day she dispatched it to be framed. I had searched for it upon the wall in her closet where hung several others, and had even peered amidst her collections of porcelain and geegaws, but to no avail. No sooner had I truly begun to fear that it had displeased her in some manner than the mystery was solved. One morning, Madame Laurent, an acquaintance of Mrs Elliot, came to call. Having been introduced, the visitor approached me and with great familiarity kissed me upon both cheeks before exclaiming: 'Ah, *la belle artiste anglaise*! Has there been a pair of hands into which Madame Elliot has not placed your fair portrait?' Then, much to my surprise, I received a commission upon the spot.

This was but the beginning. Within a handful of days, I had a letter from none other than the celebrated Mademoiselle Dervieux, an opera dancer in the highest of keeping who wished to have her likeness rendered. Later, I received a similar entreaty from Madame de Beauvert, the mistress to General Dumouriez. Gentlemen too learned that they might procure a private audience with me. There came the Chevalier de Jean, a young man with a face quite ruined by the smallpox, who lounged and flirted as if his success with me was assured, and the ancient Duc de Bouillon, who wore a lifetime of debauchery between his double chin and heavy-lidded eyes.

Much to the satisfaction of the sitters, each of these small sketches I completed in a matter of hours, during which time tea was taken and gossip exchanged in a pleasant manner. On occasions, Mrs Elliot played hostess and sat with me in the white-mirrored antechamber I had fashioned into a studio of a sort. She entertained with her bons mots and teased the gentlemen as I bent over my small easel. Afterwards she would gaze upon me and with the satisfied smile of a mother offer words of praise.

'See, my dear, how celebrated you are?'

I was, however, under no illusions. I did not believe for one instant that my patrons sought me out for my reputation, nor was I so deceived as to think they came of their own inclination. They had been encouraged and enticed. It was but another act of kindness, of charity, I had concluded, orchestrated by one who wished to demonstrate her affection for me. Her intention was to beat the fattest birds in Paris from the hedges in the hope that they would fly towards me. And indeed what better tool for this than to hand about a pretty portrait of the sweet young paintrix herself?

She had conceived of such a clever plan. It was genius, to be sure, for she had determined not only to set a fashion for my miniatures among the demi-monde and gentlemen of the *haut ton*, but to distract me from my woes. Whether or not she believed it to be possible, Mrs Elliot sought to convince me that I might earn an income through the practice of art rather than the practice of love. Her strategy succeeded, but only to a degree. I was not paid as might be an artist of any name or esteem, but rather rewarded in the manner of a *femme galante*. Bouillon sent me a gold filigree patch box, and from the Chevalier I received an ivory fan from Pondicherry into which had been folded some verses, 'On Beauty'.

I cannot relate to you the pleasure my friend seemed to derive from my improving spirits and contentment. Indeed, it appeared to me that nothing granted her greater happiness than to be of assistance to others in need. While I continued beneath her roof I bore witness to many acts of charity similar to that which she had extended to me. She had loaned money to Madame Meyler and had intervened in a dispute between Monsieur de Chalut and his former inamorata. Her hours were consumed in constant correspondence, assisting a former lover or even a rival in emigrating to London. She wrote letters on their behalf to solicitors and land agents and friends, hoping to ease their passages to a foreign land. Each morning, I listened to Thérèse's footsteps upon the back stairs as she set about delivering her mistress's messages. As I toiled over my sketches I could not have imagined that Mrs Elliot's correspondence would have ever come to concern me, but in the final week of June, it was revealed to me that it did.

One afternoon, when the weather had grown hot and rendered the rooms too close and damp for dining, Mrs Elliot insisted that we take our dinner in the garden. We sat beneath the shade of the cherry trees where a table had been laid and a breast of veal with some ragouts and tureens were brought to us. She said little to me throughout our meal, which at the time I thought curious. At the conclusion of it, she put down her fork and knife, straightened her back and fixed her gaze upon me.

'Henrietta', she began, 'I have this morning received a response to an enquiry. It appears that the apartments which once belonged to Madame de Chalmont in the Hôtel Blanquefort have become vacant. It seems she has quit Paris to join her son in London. She has left behind all of her furniture.' My friend smiled at me, hoping I might read her implication.

I did not.

'My dear, from the day you arrived here you made plain to me your desire for an independent life and your abhorrence for the existence you once led. The loss of your jewels was a cruel blow to that ambition and one for which I shall ever hold myself accountable—'

'Oh, but, madam, you must not . . .' I protested.

'We shall not speak of it, child,' she commanded. 'I wish you only to know that I have taken measures to repair the situation to the best of my abilities and have hired the apartments on your behalf.'

I regarded her with complete surprise. In truth, I could not think what response to make. Some part of me was uncertain if the wish I had expressed two months earlier was indeed that which my heart still desired.

'But . . . you . . . you have not the means . . . the Duc d'Orléans no longer pays your maintenance . . .'

Her face soured.

'And how did you come by such intelligence?'

'Madame de Flaghac informed me.'

'Of course,' my friend stated tersely. 'Although dear to my heart, La Flaghac will repeat any nonsense she hears.' She then sighed. 'That matter with the Duke has nothing to do with this. When your jewels were lost, I promised I should enquire among those of my acquaintance in Paris and raise a subscription to assist you. These are the proceeds of their benevolence. Additionally, I have arranged that you may call upon my credit at all the shops.'

I was rendered quite speechless. My mind was awash with confusion and contrary thoughts. This deed was generous beyond anything I might have reckoned, and yet I could not dismiss the sense that perhaps she had grown weary of my company and was eager to be rid of me.

'But . . . but I do not wish to live independently of you. Why, you are so very kind . . . your companionship . . . I should not like to lose it,' was the only remark I could think to make.

At that, she laughed.

'Oh, dearest Hetty, we are as fast as kin, are we not? Nothing will diminish that. The Hôtel Blanquefort is situated upon the rue du Faubourg Saint-Honoré, but several moments from here. We may visit each other daily, though privately.'

'Privately?' Her use of this word bemused me.

'Yes, *ma fille*. I know the notion of it is disagreeable to you, but I have spent some time meditating upon it. I do not doubt Madame de Flaghac has apprised you of my relations with Orléans?' She frowned so slightly.

I hesitated.

'Yes.'

'Then you understand that I am no longer in favour with the Duke or his set. Even my association with Biron has been a discreet one, which is to say it has been kept as far as possible from the ears of Madame de Buffon.' She studied me with a fond but almost sad look. 'My dear, I should not wish to be a hindrance to you, and that I shall be if our association remains a public one.'

'Oh, but I should hate that to be the truth of the matter!' I protested.

'But it is, Henrietta. With each month that passes my protectors in Paris are fewer. My most ardent admirers, those upon whose assistance I have relied, those who have remained most constant to me, are of the court. Their allegiance will ever be with the King. Honour binds me to them and their friendship, you understand.'

I regarded her, though did not offer a response.

'You, however, will not secure your future by forming associations among these aristocrats. It would be a cruelty on my part to impede your prospects in such a manner. You must be seen to have your own lodgings. You must demonstrate to the world that you are free of my influence. And should you still wish to follow an independent life, and to wait for the return of your beloved Allenham, you may do so.' Then, as if to make final her resolution, she knotted together her fingers and laid her hands upon the table. 'There is one further point upon which I would counsel you.' Her eyes met mine. 'Should fortune favour you with an introduction to the Duc d'Orléans, or one near to him, do not be so rash as to dismiss the connection. Never place matters of the heart before the wisdom of the head, *ma fille*. Allow yourself to be guided by reason alone. To do otherwise almost always proves ruinous.'

I searched her expression. There was not an ounce of levity within it and this, more than anything, impressed upon me the importance of her sentiments. I nodded and gave her my word, wishing above all to secure her affection.

And so this is how I came to live upon the rue du Faubourg Saint-Honoré in that summer of 1792. Although it saddened me to take my leave of the rue de Miromesnil and the contented existence I had known there, my apartments in the Hôtel Blanquefort proved a most agreeable consolation. They were neither grandiose nor without their comforts. In short, they suited my tastes precisely.

I had the use of a drawing room with silk chairs and sofas the colour of daffodils, as well as a dressing room and a fashionable round bedchamber. Adjoining this was a little mirrored closet which the French liked to call a *salle de bains*. Although I had heard of such curiosities, it was the first time I had seen a room of its sort, with its white-glazed stove and tub affixed inside a cabinet. There was even an antechamber used for dining, which was connected by a back stair to the kitchens in the court below. This, I was instructed, was a luxury in Paris, for it meant that the dishes laid upon my table would arrive still warm.

In addition to these extravagances, my lodgings were equipped with two chambers and an *entresol* for the use of my servants. The first of these rooms belonged to Lucy, but the second was to be occupied by a housemaid. Mrs Elliot suggested that this position be filled by Thérèse Bertrand, who might act as 'a faithful reminder of home'. Into my household also came a cook, Madame Vernet, and her son, Jean, who served as my footman.

I had scarcely been settled in my new residence for a day before the acquaintance I had formed began to call upon me there. Just as she had promised, my dear friend appeared with regularity in my apartments, and when she was not present, I could be found at the rue de Miromesnil in her drawing room or at her table. However, the visits to the theatre, the rides in her chariot and constitutionals along the Champs-Élysées and the colonnades of the Palais-Royal were no more. While the absence of her society saddened me, she was quick to spy my downturned look and upbraid me for it.

'It is for the best,' she would insist, smiling with a look of reassurance. 'Think on your prospects, *ma fille*.'

Mrs Elliot continued to do her best to further these and remained tireless in her efforts to puff my talents to all her associates. Requests for my miniature likenesses did not cease. Indeed, I believed it was her intention to drive every opera dancer, chanteuse and diamond-decorated mistress to my drawing room. Within a fortnight, I had sketched the countenances of the notorious La Clarion, an actress who lived with great extravagance, as well as her nimble-footed sister who danced and sang with the Comédie-Italienne. A Swede of Mrs Elliot's acquaintance, a ship-owner called Major Backman, came too, along with the tattle-tongued Madame de Flaghac in her elaborately flounced skirts.

She sat next to me in my sunlit drawing room, where I had

assembled an easel upon a small table. Like Mrs Elliot, I had acquired a fondness for this toy-like grand matron who arrived in attire far too formal for morning. A vast tucker of embroidered black gauze was crossed along the front of her plum-hued bodice. It reached to her very ears, which were covered with a starched balloon cap hung with a profusion of blue ribbons. I could scarcely spy her features between these frills and froths. Politely, I invited her to arrange the gauze. She responded by whipping away the garment.

'I am pleased to see Madame Elliot is not present,' she muttered as I traced my pencil across the sheet.

'And, pray, why is that so, madame?'

'So we can speak candidly, of course.'

'Upon what matters could we not speak freely before Madame Elliot?' I enquired, attempting to disguise the amusement as it curled over my mouth.

'Matters of the truth, my child,' she parried. 'Matters of love, of course.'

I let out a little laugh at her teasing.

'It is said that Madame Elliot intends you for the young Duc de Chartres . . .' she probed.

I did not so much as raise my eyes from my work.

'That is nonsense,' I replied, smiling.

At that moment, Thérèse entered the room bearing a tea tray and a kettle. However, it was only as she rested it on the table beside Madame de Flaghac that I noticed a small box and a letter perched upon it.

The old woman's black-painted eyebrows instantly rose into two intrigued arches.

'Why, mademoiselle,' she breathed, 'it seems you have received a gift from one of your admirers!'

I laid down my pencil and walked directly to where they sat.

It was all I could do to prevent the meddlesome Flaghac from pouncing upon the items herself. I rubbed the charcoal from my hands and examined the sealed packet and box of tooled Morocco leather. The script was unfamiliar to me, as was the seal, which bore no indication of the sender beyond a laurel wreath and the inscription 'Liberté, Égalité, Fraternité'.

'Who delivered these?' I enquired of Thérèse, who had turned to quit the room. She paused at the door.

'I am afraid I know not, mademoiselle. It was a boy. A messenger.'

I studied the objects again.

'You will never know whence they came if you do not open them, *ma chère*,' urged an impatient Madame de Flaghac.

At her behest, I broke the seal.

'Read it aloud, child, or I am likely to die away in a fit of anxiety!' my patroness commanded.

I had not anticipated what I found within. I dare say neither had Madame de Flaghac.

'Ma chère mademoiselle,' its author began.

As we have never enjoyed the good fortune of a regular introduction, I would beg you forgive me for the liberty I now take in addressing you.

You must know, chère mademoiselle, that you are much talked of amongst the officers at Valenciennes, who are most curious to make the acquaintance of this pretty English femme peintre. I am equally so, and would be greatly flattered should you consent to take my likeness.

I am presently at La Volière, a house I have taken near to Valenciennes, and should you agree to my commission, it would please me to dispatch my coach to you and arrange the necessary passport for your travels.

Likewise, it would do me a great honour to have your company at dinner Friday next, when Monsieur d'Orléans will be in attendance. Upon that occasion, you might wish to wear the enclosed gift. Until then, I shall remain your most impatient,

A. de Buffon

Madame de Flaghac sucked in her breath with such vigour that I feared she might indeed fall into a faint.

'How remarkable! La Buffon means to court you.' She exhaled in one. Her eyes widened. 'Why, she is scheming something. It is certain. There is some design at work here. You must consider it closely, child,' she babbled frantically. 'Ah, but Orléans. She wishes you to make his acquaintance. What will you do? How will you respond, *ma chère*?'

I did not answer the flustered Flaghac, but reached for the leather case and lifted the lid. An enamel miniature portrait of the Duc d'Orléans, set within a circle of pearls, stared back at me. It was no larger than a coin and had been threaded through with a red, white and blue grosgrain ribbon, so it might be worn as a bracelet. It was an exceptional gift, and one which would have cost the bearer a considerable sum. Such a prize would not be awarded without a good deal of calculated thought.

I handed the box to Madame, who pursed her lips. 'It is a fine piece. A costly one. She is most intent on making your acquaintance, Mademoiselle Lightfoot.'

I was in part flattered and yet at the same time somewhat wary and uneasy. I could not begin to think what the infamous Madame de Buffon desired of me, nor did I believe her solicitations to be entirely genuine.

'Surely Madame Elliot has not contrived this?' I looked to La Flaghac questioningly.

'Why ever should you think she would, *ma chère*? La Buffon is her most vicious rival.'

I searched the *grande dame*'s expression, now with greater puzzlement.

'Because . . . because . . . she has sent all of you to me. It is merely one of her charitable acts, so that I should earn back what I had lost when my jewels were stolen. You . . . All of her acquaintance have made a contribution so that I might live here and repair my fortune without the need to—'

There, I broke off, for Madame de Flaghac appeared entirely bemused.

'Contribution?' Her brow folded.

For a moment I believed my French had failed me. It was not without its flaws, in spite of my time upon the continent.

'Charity. A collection was made.'

Madame shook her head slowly. '*Ma chère mademoiselle*, I know nothing of a collection. Is this what Madame Elliot told to you?'

I stared at her.

'Yes.'

'Well, it is not the truth.' She settled against the back of the chair as if she required the support of it to convey her news. 'Madame Elliot has sold some jewels. A sapphire of great worth, I believe.'

At that, I gasped. I pressed my hand to my throat.

'But that cannot be! I would never have permitted it had I known . . .'

'Which is precisely why I suppose she did not inform you. It is her nature, *ma chère*. She would make any sacrifice for those people and causes she deems of value.'

I felt for the chair beside Madame de Flaghac and folded myself into it.

'It is too generous, madame. It is too much to accept. First she agreed to shelter me and nurse me and then drive off Mr Savill. She has encouraged me in this . . . endeavour . . .' I gestured to my easel. 'She has shown me nothing but the most Christian benevolence . . . but to sell her sapphire, which I knew to be her most treasured of possessions, to make up for my loss . . . How can I ever repay her?'

Madame de Flaghac reached for the letter on the table and held it in her lap for several moments.

'This,' said she. 'This is the means by which you can repay her kindness, mademoiselle.'

I exchanged an uncertain look with her. She nodded.

'Write to La Buffon. Accept her invitation.'

I did not comprehend the matron's reasoning. 'But you have warned me against her. Now you would have me embrace her in friendship?'

'Not embrace her, *ma chère*. An ambassador does not journey to a foreign court to embrace a king. He pays his respects. He ingratiates himself among the court, yet he remains the emissary of his queen. In this fashion he is able to effect good, to persuade the monarch against aggression, and all the while he is serving his own cause too. He is cultivating friends and connections and influence.' Her old brown eyes fixed themselves on mine.

I contemplated her advice, which struck me as reasonable, though calculated.

'Do you believe it possible for me to convince the Duc d'Orléans to restore Madame Elliot's allowance?'

'Mademoiselle, I believe you may attempt it.' She smiled at me hopefully. 'But you would do better to persuade Madame de Buffon that she has nothing to fear from her rival. I am given to understand that since the departure of Monsieur Laclos it is she more than any advisor who holds Orléans in thrall. He is a weak man and easily led . . . by women in particular.'

She handed me the letter and I received it hesitantly.

I sighed. I knew what I must do. Indeed, the more I considered it, the more my resolve began to gather, the more certain I became that this was the correct course of action to take.

'I shall write to Madame de Buffon,' I whispered. 'It is the very least I can do.'

Once I had pledged myself to this path, and composed my letter to La Buffon, my determination to execute my plan became unshakeable. In order to prevent Mrs Elliot from raising any objections, I resolved that I would only reveal my design to her upon the eve of my departure. And so I set about making preparations for my travels in secret, while securing the word of my entire household that they would not betray my plans to my friend.

On the Wednesday afternoon, as Mrs Elliot dressed for dinner, I called upon her and was most relieved to find her alone, but for Victoire and the *friseur* who was arranging her hair.

I resolved to tell her instantly, not to demur or gossip or complain about the heat which lay as heavy as a fur pelisse across Paris. I took my seat, drew in my breath and recounted the contents of Madame de Buffon's letter to her, before announcing my intentions. After I had said my piece, I sat with perfect stillness, anxiously awaiting her response.

At first she made no remark. Her mouth remained set. Her flinty eyes appeared as flat as a calm sea. Then a gentle smile raised her cheeks.

'*Ma fille*,' said she, 'this is the opportunity I had hoped for you . . . but I had not imagined it would come to pass so swiftly as this.'

'But it is on your behalf that I have agreed to assume this errand,' I attempted to correct her, wearing a bright, conciliatory smile of my own.

She lowered her gaze in a shy, grateful manner which I had not before witnessed. It was a moment more before she spoke.

'*Ma chère fille*, I am genuinely blessed to call you a friend.'

'It is I who is blessed to know such true kindness, as I have never before, my . . . *chère maman.*'

She lifted her gaze again and held her hands to me. I took them into mine, as if sealing the pact between us.

'You must write to me frequently.'

'But of course . . . I shall miss you every day!'

'Tell me everything. Tell me what poison La Buffon drips into his ear. Write to me of what Orléans says to you, of their conversations. I must consider how to make amends with him. You must not attempt it yourself, but allow me. I know the words to speak to him, how I might soften his heart. Do you understand, my dear?'

'Yes,' I agreed eagerly.

She pressed her hands in mine and beamed.

'You must make use of every advantage given to you, Hetty. Whatever is requested of you . . .'

My expression began to fall at what she insinuated.

'You understand, do you not? Ingratiate yourself and the rewards will be great.'

'Yes,' I said.

'Very well, then.' She sighed, and I rose from my chair.

We then embraced, as might a devoted mother and child, and bid each other tender farewells.

'Henrietta', she called out to me as I advanced towards the door. 'Do make certain not to leave your secrets exposed to La Buffon's prying. Direct your letters under cover to Thérèse. Instruct her to bring them to me here. La Buffon will be most suspicious of you. If you are seen to be corresponding with me you are likely to forfeit her trust.' Her face turned quite solemn. 'Proceed with great care, my dear.'

I offered her a deep, reverential curtsey and turned on my heel.

Chapter 12

I know your thoughts, reader.

You are shaking your head. You are knitting your brow. You fear for me. For certainly no happiness ever came of courting the good graces of a friend's rival. Well, I shall grant you this: when I set out upon the road to La Volière, which lay just north of Cambrai and less than an hour from the camp at Valenciennes, I understood that I placed my fate in the hands of Providence. I knew nothing of my destination and had heard not a single compliment uttered about my hostess. Yet I entered willingly into her capacious coach, with its green leather seats and gilded wheels. I did not relish the errand I was to undertake, but took special pride in placing myself at the disposal of one to whom I owed so very much.

As Madame de Buffon's coachman intended for us to arrive in the late hours of that night, we embarked shortly before dawn, when the air had still a freshness to it. The streets of the city were just rousing themselves into life. The ragged scavengers could be seen picking through the dust, while the servants emerged with their brooms and baskets and pails. The first carts and barrels were rolled into the lanes, and the drunkards and beggars removed from the doorways where they slumbered. There could be seen, too, another figure, a curious one amid this regular morning scene. He appeared in a blue uniform and cockade and made a slow progress down the centre of the road upon his horse. He read a proclamation as he did so, crying it out at the shuttered windows and locked doors. In those days, I paid but scant attention to such things. There was always some warning of trouble, ever some agitator or other upon a street corner spouting a promise of a bloody end for the King and Queen or the nation. So consumed was I in my own thoughts and machinations that I did not bother to take down the glass and listen, but instead turned to Lucy and sighed at the familiarity of this spectacle. I had begun to grow quite indifferent to these constant threats of danger, which never once manifested themselves as these harbingers would have the city believe.

I found the guard at the barrier who examined my passports no less determined to terrify me.

'You know there is war near to where you journey, mademoiselle? You know that the counter-revolutionaries prepare their armies? That there is likely to be an invasion?'

I nodded to each of his questions, although the third was not something of which I had been aware until that morning.

Seeing that he could not dissuade me from my travels, he grunted and offered back my documents. 'You are safer in the country than in Paris,' said he, before signalling to the coachman.

From that inauspicious beginning, my journey was not to improve. For the better part of it, the heat was intolerable. My maid and I baked like breads in an oven. To open the windows only drew in clouds of dust and insects, which swirled about and coated our damp faces in a fine brown powder. By evening, grey rumbling clouds pinched out the light before throwing torrents of rain upon us. The coarse road was pounded into a stew through which six sets of horses' hooves sucked and spat. La Buffon's liveried coachman and footman appeared as drowned as sailors, the very curls of their wigs unfurling in the gale.

On account of the poor weather, we lost several hours, so that by the time we stopped to change horses at an inn at Combles, it was near to midnight. It was here we were felled completely, as one of Madame's horses had injured its hoof. Greatly fatigued, we had no choice but to remain where fortune had deposited us, amid the inhospitable walls of the Fleur-de-Lys. After an execrable meal of eggs and stinking rabbit, Lucy and I were made to pass the night in one bed, which we discovered the following day had been home to a good many fleas.

Morning had ripened into early afternoon before a suitable replacement for the mare could be found. As you might imagine, I observed the sun rise in the sky with increasing agitation. Although I had dispatched a note to Madame de Buffon explaining our delay, this did not quell my anxiety. My fear of offending a woman who I suspected bore a natural antipathy towards me increased with each hour. As we joined the road to Valenciennes once more, I could think of nothing but her wrath, her face contorted with vengeance at my failure to appear. I supposed La Buffon would conclude I had played her some trick, that Mrs Elliot had connived with me to humiliate her. Worse still, I conjured a scene in my head where I would be forced to concede to my friend that I had not only failed to gain an introduction to Orléans, but succeeded in insulting him as well.

By the time we neared La Volière, the hour approached four o'clock. It was then well past dinner and I was overcome with dread. Quite without thinking, I took Lucy's hand for comfort as we passed through the gates of the château. It glowered at me at the end of a perfectly straight drive, a squat, wide building of rose and buff stone, with a low, sloping roof.

We were greeted by the appearance of Madame's *intendant*, a tall, droop-eyed servant, who assisted me from her coach.

The pallid hue of my countenance must have struck him for he immediately offered an apology for the state of the roads and the inconvenience of my journey.

'Madame awaits you in the salon,' said he, making no mention of my absence at her dinner table. As he led me through to the house, the hour upon the large white-faced clock above the entry read ten minutes past four. My belly instantly tightened. With a jumping heart, I followed him over the black and white flagstones of the hall and through the doors to a grand room where I was announced.

At first I saw no one in this space but a bespectacled gentleman in a blue army uniform. He raised his head from the letter he had been writing and regarded me briefly, before returning to his correspondence.

'Mademoiselle Lightfoot!' called out a soft, beguiling voice from behind me.

I turned and spied, in the corner, my hostess.

In my youth, the French were not in the habit of rising to greet visitors. Indeed, at times one was fortunate to be granted so much as a formal introduction. It was possible to pass an entire evening without ever knowing the name of the person with whom one conversed.

Madame de Buffon received me in such a fashion. She beheld me from where she reclined upon a sofa, her red-shod feet elevated upon a stool. In a chair beside her sat an older woman with a book, who I guessed to be near fifty. At her hem snuffled and yapped a pair of black and white Papillon spaniels, which the matron eyed with annoyance.

It was not the simple yet affected domesticity of this scene which surprised me, nor was I entirely taken aback by the absence of polite conduct. Rather I was struck by the unexpected appearance of Madame de Buffon.

She was as fair as I had imagined, and perhaps no more than five and twenty. Her pretty visage was a perfect heart shape with a pointed chin, around which fell her brown-gold tresses. Her lips were rather bee-stung, while her wide-set eyes conferred upon her a slightly feline look. But it was not this which captured my notice, so much as the mound which lay upon her middle. From its size, I reckoned her to be at least six months gone. Not so much as a word had been whispered to me of this, by any of my acquaintance. Indeed, I could not fathom how it had escaped the knowledge of Madame de Flaghac. La Buffon had succeeded in maintaining a perfect secret which was certain to scandalize society as soon as it was known.

'Oh, *ma chère* Mademoiselle Lightfoot, how delighted I am to see you.' She beamed at me; then she held out her arms and implored me to approach her. I did so uneasily. She leaned in to kiss me, leaving a trail of something like sandalwood and jasmine across my cheeks.

'Do sit beside me, do!' she commanded. 'Are you in need of refreshment? You must be quite famished, quite parched from the road. How hot it has been. Intolerably so. Romain! Romain!' she called out.

The tall *intendant* reappeared at the door.

'Bring some wine and fruit and sweetmeats for Mademoiselle Lightfoot.'

He nodded.

'So here is the pretty little paintrix about whom Monsieur de Biron speaks,' she sighed while examining me from top to toe. 'It was upon the request of Monsieur d'Orléans that I wrote to you. He admired your self-portrait, the one which you had sent to Monsieur de Biron.'

I moved to correct her that it was Mrs Elliot, not I, who had placed the miniature into Biron's possession, but thought better of it. To raise my friend's name so soon would have been imprudent, though I now saw quite plainly how this introduction had been engineered.

'Ah, but when I saw the portrait for myself and learned of you, I thought any English lady so accomplished and so fair I must have to entertain me at La Volière. You must know, mademoiselle, that Monsieur d'Orléans is a great admirer of your nation,' she said to me in perfect, though heavily accented English. 'I have visited it with him. Your native land is a most diverting place, though London has not the amusements of Paris. We formed many connections there and were regularly entertained by the Prince of Wales and Mrs Fitzherbert. Are you acquainted with the Prince and his lady, mademoiselle?'

'Yes, madame, I have had the honour of making their—'

'And Mr Fox entertained us, and Mrs Armistead, who are kind and genteel and *très* droll . . . but the English ladies, they are so formal, no? Everything is so . . . correct in England. It is as if they fear the displeasure of every person who gazes upon them. The English ladies, they say they are as cold as nuns' knees!' She laughed. 'Ah, but you are not. Why, you are far too beautiful and warm of heart and . . .' La Buffon's words were suddenly clipped by a violent eruption of growls and snaps. 'Fantouche! Moustache!' she scolded the twin Papillons. The pair had playfully launched themselves at her elderly companion's ankles.

'*Alors!*' cried the woman, gently kicking the dogs from her. 'Agnès, will you not command them?'

My hostess huffed, though whether her exasperation lay with her spaniels or her companion, I could not say.

'Madame, you know I can no more command them than I can you,' she answered haughtily.

The two women locked eyes with disdain before the elder of the two rose silently and removed herself from the room. Madame de Buffon observed each of her retreating footsteps as she crossed to the far side of the salon and passed through the door.

I sat awkwardly, too cowed by this scene to make any noise at all.

'She is most disagreeable, my aunt Laval. Full of vinegar,' La Buffon snorted after a spell. 'I have had quite enough of her, and I dare say she has had enough of me. She has acted as my *dame de compagnie*, to assist me in my condition while I am here. You know, that feather-head would emigrate if she had the means . . . but she is dependent upon me, which is to say she is here upon the sufferance of Monsieur d'Orléans, a circumstance which she can scarcely tolerate.' My hostess rolled her eyes in disgust. 'She will sit alone in her rooms now. She will not even return to greet the gentlemen for supper.' La Buffon fell quiet, her mouth pursed with displeasure.

'The . . . gentlemen?' I ventured to enquire, attempting to alter her temper.

'Yes, they have gone to race Monsieur d'Orléans's chargers.'

It was at that moment a footman arrived bearing wine and dishes of oranges and peaches and grapes, as well as nuts and chocolates and candied fruits. Much to the irritation of the gentleman who had been sitting at the table, La Buffon ordered the feast to be spread upon it.

'Monsieur Rotaux, you must join us,' she called to him, but the uniformed man declined, claiming that Monsieur d'Orléans's correspondence could not wait, before he graciously removed himself to another room.

La Buffon appeared quietly delighted at the secretary's departure and turned to me with wide eyes and a tight-lipped smile.

'Oh, mademoiselle, how pleased I am that you are arrived. How

I have longed for the companionship of one of my sex. Someone clever and accomplished, who is not such a dullard as my aunt. Do take my likeness, Mademoiselle Lightfoot. Yes, do paint me before the gentlemen return. I grow weary so easily. I fear I may drift into sleep as I sit here.' She giggled and rubbed her belly.

I had scarcely taken more than a handful of grapes and a sip of wine. There had been no suggestion of dressing for the evening or taking some rest from the road. I sat before her in my redingote, cloaked in dust as if I languished in a taproom at an inn. Hesitantly, I called for Lucy to bring my implements and paper.

Far from wearying, Madame did not cease her chatter. With great curiosity she asked to inspect my brushes, my charcoals, my pencils, my watercolours. Every piece within my box she studied with a keen eye. Where did I acquire such skills? she begged. Who had been my tutors? La Buffon absorbed each word before contributing opinions of her own. Did I know that Madame de Condorcet painted too?

'Oh, I do admire her so. I was invited to attend her Cercle Social . . . once. Orléans does not know. And when I was first married to Monsieur de Buffon I had the good fortune of attending Madame Le Brun's salon upon several occasions. It is a great pity she has emigrated. She is too much in love with her Queen and has been utterly ruined by all she glimpsed at Versailles.' She continued apace as I sketched her, her face brightly animated by conversation.

Madame de Buffon was not at all as I had imagined. I knew not what to make of her candour or her inquisitiveness. She was not the dragoness against whom I had been warned, but her strong-headed opinions gave me pause nonetheless.

Her talk soon turned to books. She mused on those she had read, which were a fair few in English: Mr Fielding, Mr Smollett, Mr Richardson and, most recently, Mrs Radcliffe. She enquired as to my thoughts upon their style and stories and claimed to favour Mr Fielding over Mr Richardson, though she preferred Rousseau's *Julie* to any novel in English.

'Monsieur Rousseau claims that nature did not intend women to live as do men, but designed them for entirely different roles in life. Do you believe that is so?' she pressed.

'I am not certain I know,' I replied as I sketched. 'While a woman's form differs from that of a man, I do not believe what lies within her head is so dissimilar. I do not believe myself incapable of reason, nor do I acquire knowledge in a mode unlike that of a man. But, as I have never been a man, I have no manner of determining whether my conclusions are correct.'

La Buffon clapped her hands together and laughed heartily at my response.

'How clever and witty you are, mademoiselle,' she exclaimed. 'Indeed, I cannot say for certain what lies within the mind of any of that sex.'

As she spoke I noticed her eye was drawn to something beyond the window. Her gaze then fixed itself quite intently, which rendered her features even more cat-like. I turned and observed two figures approaching arm in arm from across the garden. One appeared to be attired in the blue uniform of a high-ranking officer, while lilac muslin blew against the legs of the other. It was only when they appeared at the door that I recognized the stout gentleman beneath his crescent-shaped hat to be the Duc de Biron. La Buffon made not a sound, but stared impassively at the pair until they passed over the threshold.

Biron was not a little surprised to discover me there. Upon catching sight of me at that table with La Buffon, he gave an anxious laugh and greeted me with an awkwardness that spoke of a secret revealed. There was no contrition upon his face, nor upon that of his friend, who did not so much as tip her head in my direction. Her arm was entwined with his and she rested her cheek coyly upon his shoulder.

'Madame de Morency wishes to rest before supper,' he explained, avoiding my gaze. 'The others are not far behind.'

Madame de Buffon's sharp eyes followed them across the room, her expression hardening into that of a Medusa. Indeed, had she possessed the power of that mythic monster she might well have turned the unfortunate Morency to stone.

'It was not I who invited that woman here,' she muttered in the wake of their departure. 'Biron insisted, and Orléans denies his friend nothing.' She then turned to me with a scandalized look. 'Madame de Morency rode from Lille to Valenciennes to seduce him. I hear she paid Biron's servant to show her directly to his bed, though I would wager it was Orléans's she sought to warm. I dare say he is a bit envious of Biron's good fortune.' She let out an angry laugh, a sound which seemed to rouse Fantouche and Moustache into a frenzy of barks. 'Hush!' their mistress commanded them, but to no avail. The dogs scuttled excitedly towards the glass doors that led into the garden.

We heard the noise of the party's approach before catching sight of them. Their boisterous laughter blew through the windows upon a gust of early-evening breeze. They wound their path slowly through the row of trees, taking care to tread only in the shade. In their heavy boots they appeared weary from the heat; many carried their dark blue plumed hats beneath their arms.

Even at a distance, I recognized Orléans amidst his party of officers: bulky but possessed of a certain grace in his gait. He resembled very much the likeness La Buffon had sent me. His mouse-brown hair had begun to recede, which made his nose appear a bulbous shape, and his head seem somewhat wider than average. As they came through the doors, it struck me that had he been anything other than a Prince of the Blood, not a soul would have remarked upon his features. His visage was neither handsome nor entirely without merit. Nature had spared him from ugliness by bestowing upon him a truly fine pair of sleepy aquamarine eyes.

'The celebrated Mademoiselle Lightfoot,' he exclaimed as he crossed the salon to greet us.

I dropped into a deep, sober curtsey, but Orléans merely laughed at this formal display and took my hand to his lips.

'Your nation is most expert in its manufacture of female beauty and accomplishment,' he announced after paying me a thorough inspection. 'Have you amused my Fanny?'

La Buffon smiled brightly.

'We have not suffered a dull moment.'

The Duke leaned forward to examine my sketch, which was nearly complete but for the watercolour wash.

'Monsieur d'Orléans is a great connoisseur of art,' proclaimed Madame de Buffon.

'And ladies,' added one of the officers. This aroused much laughter.

'Hush, Courcy, you will offend my Fanny,' he teased, placing a kiss upon her forehead. 'My collection is complete with her.'

'Mademoiselle Lightfoot, I insist you paint Monsieur d'Orléans next,' my hostess commanded. Her voice seemed suddenly small and childlike in Orléans's company. Her lover wrapped an affectionate arm about her wide waist and drew her to him.

'There is time enough for that, *ma petite*. Now I should favour some wine and a game of *cavagnole*.' He sighed and turned from her.

For the briefest of instances I believed I might have a moment to refresh myself, but this was not to be. Orléans's place was instantly filled by a pair of eager, flirtatious young officers.

'Will you take my likeness, mademoiselle?'

'And mine?' said the other, with a broad grin.

'And mine?' called out a third from the window.

I smiled graciously, flattered though wearied at the prospect.

'But I fear we shall soon lose the light . . .' I attempted my protest. This, however, did not work for no sooner had I spoken it than two gentlemen came forward to transport my table beside a window and into a flood of summer evening light. I stifled my desire to sigh. The thought of my rumpled attire, my damp chemise and the grime upon my person made me wish for a moment's respite, for a basin and some Hungary water or at the very least a change of linens. I was permitted not even so much as an instant to fix upon my wrist the miniature portrait that my hostess had kindly given to me, and I feared she would notice its absence.

In order to meet the gentlemen's demands, I sketched more rapidly, anxiously endeavouring to capture all of their features as the last glow of day sank into the woods. They laughed and teased and made love to me with their praises. I set my mouth into a pleasant smile, my eyes so sore that any who had gazed upon me in earnest and not merely for their own pleasure might have observed my exhaustion. It occurred to me as they gathered around, peering over my shoulder, studying my progress and passing comment, that this was the very reason for my invitation. I existed to delight and amuse, to perform as might a musician or even a troupe of actors. As night fell, one of my attentive swains thought to assist me by placing a candelabrum on the edge of my table. My glass of wine was replenished and a dish of sugar plums laid at my elbow. It was only when supper was called, sometime after ten o'clock, that I relinquished my pencil and brushes. My hands were filthy with charcoal and pigment, and they trembled.

Madame de Buffon proudly fetched me from my corner and took my arm into hers. She sat me beside her at the dining table where there seemed no semblance of formality; men landed themselves wherever they pleased. Most were a good deal in drink by that hour, having emptied a punchbowl and countless bottles of wine. I was scarcely aware of what I ate. Some portions of cold fowl and lamb in unctuous sauces were offered to me and I took thoughtless, tired mouthfuls with few words in between. All that I heard was a din of noise. The company appeared no more than a blur of blues and white, the glinting gold lacings of their uniforms serving to outline their forms in the dimness. However, exhaustion had not entirely blinded me to the antics at the far end of the table, where Biron fed his lusty mistress oysters. What a performance they enacted. She unfurled her tongue and he slid on to it one wet prize after another, much to the uproarious delight of the gentlemen beside them. La Buffon, who sat with me, grew silent and stony. Eventually, having viewed enough of the spectacle, my hostess laid down her fork and knife and pushed herself unsteadily from her seat.

'Forgive me, for I am grown quite weary.' She smiled at me weakly before looking to Orléans and signalling her wish to retire. I rose from politeness, but she laid a hand upon my shoulder and bid me sit once more. '*Bonne nuit, ma petite Anglaise,*' she whispered into my ear and placed a kiss upon my cheek. 'You will endeavour to amuse Monsieur d'Orléans in my absence, will you not?'

I agreed, believing I understood perfectly her wishes; she hoped to enlist me as Orléans's chaperone.

She was scarcely gone but an instant when the object of her concern summoned me to assume her vacant chair. The Duke ordered a clean plate to be placed before me and replenished my glass of Madeira to its brim. He then commanded all the various dishes to be brought to him, one by one, whereupon he did me the honour of serving me. I sat somewhat awkwardly as the Prince of the Blood delighted in laying slices of duck, pickles, cheeses and oysters before me.

'The English have no taste for the food of our cooks. They complain of the sauces, that we are dishonest for disguising our meat,' he remarked as he dropped a piece of cold roast lamb on to my plate. 'But I should not hold it against your race, mademoiselle, for there are few qualities which I do not admire in Englishmen. You must eat, *mon petit oiseau*.' Orléans gestured to me. Hesitantly, I raised my fork, feeling his eyes upon me. He continued to study me as I nibbled, as if I were some creature brought to him beneath a glass.

'Has Madame de Buffon regaled you with her tales of our travels to London?'

'Yes, monseigneur. She has related some to me.'

'There are few places I love so well as your nation, Mademoiselle Lightfoot, for there a man of title possesses the liberty to live out his days as he pleases. He is not beholden to the King if he does not seek His Majesty's favour; he is not made to serve him. He may come and go at his own whim. He may live in quiet seclusion upon his lands, if that is his fancy. I should like such a life well enough,' he grunted.

'Then perhaps, monseigneur, you might wish to return there soon?' I offered in a spirit of true naivety.

A great laugh burst forth from him.

'Your advice differs little from that of your relation,' he declared, taking another mouthful of lamb.

I sat somewhat dumbfounded, not knowing if I had caused offence.

'You are not at all like her.' He leaned nearer to inspect me. There was a hint of teasing in his tone. 'You are accomplished and beautiful, as frail and sweet as a butterfly. She is majestic . . . and calculating.' He took a swallow from his glass. 'I can never abandon France, mademoiselle. I shall die here, on French soil, but it will not be in service to the army.'

I believe I must have given him a confounded look, for after staring at me for a heavy moment, he continued:

'Have you not wondered why I wear the uniform of a volunteer, mademoiselle? Why it is that my associates at this table, Monsieur de Biron, even my sons, Messieurs de Chartres and de Montpensier, are given ranks among the Army of the North and I suffer to wear a tunic no different from that of any broom-seller?' Orléans's lip curled, more with amusement than anger. 'The King will not offer me a commission. I do not serve in His Majesty's army because he has instructed me to do so, but rather on account of my allegiance to the nation.' He smirked. 'My cousin is a fool, and has always been poorly advised. What worse decision might he have made than to force the Champion of the People into the uniform of the people, *non*?' He raised his glass to me and sighed, deep and long.

I could not think of any appropriate words to offer and so alighted upon some other silly matter in the hope of distracting him from that which clearly vexed him.

'Pray, monseigneur, how is it that this house has come to be called La Volière?'

Orléans's expression instantly lifted.

'Has Madame not shown you?'

I shook my head.

'Then I shall remedy that this instant.'

Orléans called for a lantern and promptly removed it from the servant's hand. He turned to me and offered his arm.

Of course, you think me a fool to wander into some dark passage with a gentleman known for his predilection for debauchery? Well, Madame de Flaghac and Mrs Elliot had both reassured me that his character had been entirely reformed. And had I not seen great proof of his doting affection for Madame de Buffon? Indeed, it was not he who had engineered this stroll away from the company, but rather it had come at my behest. It was no more than an innocent request, spoken by a wearied but polite guest, who was very much bemused by the day's events.

I was somewhat relieved to find that we proceeded through no more than an antechamber before arriving at our destination: a set of green and gold apartments upon the ground floor. As the rooms were lit with but two or three candles, the spectacle along the walls would not have been visible had my companion not raised his light to it. From beneath the lantern's cast emerged a fantastic aviary. Painted peacocks with broadly fanned feathers, long-necked swans, goldfinches, pheasants and spotted starlings spread their wings across the panels. They held garlands aloft in their beaks and even soared into the sky-coloured ceiling, between puffs of thin white cloud. I marvelled aloud at the skill of such a master.

'But you have not yet seen the finest feature of La Volière,' said Orléans, opening the glass doors that led from the house.

I confess, here I hesitated for an instant.

'Mademoiselle, you cannot presume I wish to confound you in the darkness, like the prey of some wild beast?' said he with a playful look. 'Why, you are as nervous as a doe.'

'I am nothing of the sort, monseigneur.' I straightened myself, not a little piqued at his remark.

We strolled for a few moments in silence, taking in the redolent scent of warm damp earth and wet green.

'I was here when a child and still recall La Volière's charms with fondness. It belonged to the Comtes d'Aubry for many generations.'

'And what of the current Count?'

Orléans regarded me quizzically, as if he found my ignorance faintly amusing.

'Monsieur d'Aubry and his family have emigrated. He has forfeited his estate to the nation, mademoiselle.' There was a hint of sadness in his voice. 'As I understand it, he is at Coblenz. When I heard word that La Volière had been confiscated, I engaged it for *ma chère* Fanny in her confinement, so she might be near to me.' As he turned towards me, the lantern shone against half his face, so that his round countenance appeared particularly moon-like. 'The army will not have me on the battlefield, so I am fixed at Valenciennes, which is less than an hour's ride from here. It is a most idyllic spot, is it not?'

'Yes. Yes, most certainly, monseigneur,' I answered with eagerness.

'Ah, but you must see my house at Le Raincy or Monceau with its pleasure garden of follies. You will never observe anything of its kind in Paris, *non*, or even in the whole of France, mademoiselle. Have you never ridden upon a *jeu de bague*?' he enquired with a raised eyebrow.

'I cannot say I have, monseigneur.'

'It is what the English call a carousel, but mine is made of Chinese dragons. I have a minaret and a pyramid, temples and tents and a windmill.' He boasted like a boy. 'But I must concede, even at Monceau I possess nothing so singular and transporting as this,' said he, directing his sights to the path ahead of us.

We approached the silhouette of what I guessed to be some sort of Chinese or Indian pavilion. Its three triangular turrets rose starkly against the star-speckled background of sky. As we neared it, I could discern that it comprised two levels. A row of circular windows decorated its first floor, while below, a series of rectangular apertures were covered entirely by latticework. The Duke turned to me and smiled as he leaned upon the door. Once again, I hesitated before entering. It was only when Orléans held forth the lantern that I saw plainly where we stood.

All about us were arranged a variety of perches. Some, which had been set into glazed Chinese urns, resembled bare trees, while others, formed from ceramic, appeared to twist and grow from the mirrored walls. Upon them rested the sleepy occupants of this aviary, this fantastical *volière*. The sudden appearance of light roused a few of its inhabitants from their slumbers. Finches and canaries primped themselves. A white cockatoo examined us with a single open eye.

'It is remarkable!' I whispered.

'But there are further delights, mademoiselle,' said he, beckoning me through a second set of jade and gold doors. We mounted a stair that led into a set of three rooms, the largest of which was elaborately furnished with lacquered chairs and tables, cabinets and sofas, in a riot of reds and greens and blacks. Here, as in the house, the walls were decorated with a profusion of birds and blossoms, though they had been rendered in the Chinese style and painted on to gilt panels. As the lantern's glow fell upon them, they gleamed like a necklace of gems.

I cooed and marvelled as the Duke turned his light about the room. Then, all at once, I found his arms about me and his mouth buried against the side of my throat.

'Oh, Mademoiselle Lightfoot, what a game you play me,' he murmured. 'How I should like to devour you, like a little quail!'

How you laugh at me, reader. Indeed, how hindsight permits me to laugh at myself. This is what comes of believing a libertine capable of reformation. But, alas, a dog will ever be a dog. It matters not how well groomed or disciplined the creature, when presented with a plate of meat he will never fail to lick his jaws.

I struggled in his arms, greatly ashamed of myself, and once that emotion fell away, there came another: fear. It was not Orléans who inspired it, for he was no brute like Andrew Savill. Rather, I feared for myself. I feared Madame de Buffon.

This situation was not at all what I would have designed. I had not imagined it would have occurred so instantly as this. I had arrived at La Volière entirely unprepared. I had not conceived of a strategy, nor had I even contemplated what action I might have taken should I find myself the recipient of Orléans's overtures. When I had accepted Madame de Buffon's invitation, my concern was only to ingratiate myself with her. And now . . . now, well, all that had been spoken of Orléans's mistress, every sharp word, every warning throbbed in my head. I should incur her wrath in the same fashion as had Madame de Morency.

'No, monseigneur,' I commanded him, pulling away.

The Duke ceased. His look was one of utter bemusement, as if no person had ever spoken those two words to him.

It was then I committed a most grievous error. I flew from him, as might a bird through the open door of the aviary below. I fled in fear, but as I ran, I found no relief. Rather, the nearer I drew to the lights of the house, the greater those shadows grew. I thought first of Mrs Elliot and how I had failed my friend by spurning the attentions of the very patron I had promised to court. I could not think what would become of me now, of the insult I had done to Orléans, and yet I could not imagine what would have become of me had I remained. I feared La Buffon like no other.

I ran to the house, where I arrived breathless and begged to be shown to the privacy of my rooms. I wished for nothing more than to hide myself away, to cower quietly, but I had no sooner closed the door behind me than I recognized this to be an impossibility. There would be no solace for me, no refuge in the wake of this. I would not find that anywhere at La Volière, and certainly never again in Paris.

Chapter 13

I lay awake for the better part of the night, cogitating. I could not begin to fathom how I might extricate myself from this twisted web. It mattered not in which direction I turned, I believed myself dishonoured, if not damned.

At first light, I rose and with a tightly gripped pen attempted to write a letter to Mrs Elliot, laying forth all that had transpired. I crossed out so many words that I was forced to take a clean sheet and begin once more. I blotted the second also and then tore it into many pieces. I found my third endeavour no better, and for a moment bent over the paper and wept at the thought of my disgrace. I knew not how I might ever confess to her my failure, she who had vested such faith and kindness in me. Indeed, I felt my heart shrink when I imagined her downcast expression, and how I should suffer in her estimation. I could not bear to compose that letter. I resolved to undertake the task at some other time and instead commit to my journal, that book which I had begun in Brussels, a discreet record of my conversations with La Buffon and Orléans. I wrote out the details of these in the same coded hand that I had used when living beneath Madame

Vanderoi's roof, when I wished to keep my secrets guarded from her household. By the time I had completed my account, I guessed it to be mid-morning. I returned to my bed, as if taken ill, and drew the curtains about me.

I awoke some time later with Lucy standing over me.

'Madam,' she whispered. 'Are you unwell?' I squinted at her. Over her shoulder I glimpsed the figure of one of Madame de Buffon's maids wearing an anxious face.

'No, Lucy. I am well, but weary.'

'Madam, if you please, Madame de Buffon has been asking for you. It is after midday. She wishes to converse with you,' my maid informed me.

At the mention of this, my pulse leaped.

'Is . . . is there something the matter?' I enquired in French, gazing beyond her to La Buffon's servant.

'Madame has called for you. She wishes you to wait upon her in the Chinese aviary, mademoiselle.'

At that, I blanched. La Volière was filled with eyes, and many pairs of them had witnessed me quit the dining room with Orléans and not return again. But I could not imagine that gentlemen, officers no less, renowned for their feats of gallantry, would have acted with such indiscretion, with such malice. Then I recalled who else might have glimpsed me with the Duke as we disappeared into the dark, fragrant garden: Madame de Buffon's companion, Madame de Laval. If there had been a spy, it was almost certain to be her, waiting, watching from her windows for some transgression. I stared at La Buffon's maid, almost too frightened to move.

'Do you wish to be dressed, madam?' Lucy enquired.

Was I possessed of any other option, reader? It was an inevitability that I would be made to face my hostess, if not at that moment, then later in the day or upon the following one. And so, like a prisoner condemned, I consented, and rose from my bed to receive my sentence.

I felt myself sick with dread as I followed Madame's maid along that same path to the aviary. The full heat of the cloudless day bore down upon me, burning through the crown of my flat straw hat, dampening my muslin gown, and yet I shook, quivering as if in the grip of a fever. I had begun to spin words in my head as frantically as my mind would permit. I thought a plain but honest confession would best suit. If I informed her simply what had come to pass, that he had attempted to embrace me and that I had denied him, she might not blame me so harshly, though it was unlikely she would heed such a tale. La Buffon was more likely to believe Orléans. I would be to her no more than another scheming siren, a sister to Madame de Morency.

The Chinese pavilion appeared far more spectacular by daylight than when silhouetted by the moon. While obscured by night, its fanciful position at the end of a formal clipped garden, shaded by a veil of willows, had passed unnoticed by me. Its three triangular black and red roofs poked through the greenery, the dragons which adorned its top curling their tongues ferociously at those who dared approach it. Even the latticework of the aviary had been decorated with oriental scenes: blue lakes surrounded by forests and snow-tipped peaks; while the golden door handles were the shape of two pheasants in full flight. Had I not dreaded my encounter with that which lay within this cage, I might have stood gazing at it, entirely enchanted.

The door squealed ominously upon its hinges, causing many of its feathered inhabitants to scream and flutter. My breath came hard and fast as I was led above stairs and into the very room where the crime had been attempted. There Madame de Buffon rested upon a golden chair, like an empress. Fantouche and Moustache slumbered at her feet as might two imperial lions. She appeared curiously quiet and contained. A book lay open upon her mound, while the black-lacquered tripod beside her held a Chinese porcelain teapot and the dish from which she had been sipping. She smiled at me weakly and invited me to sit. I studied her cautiously and obeyed.

Her demeanour seemed entirely altered from the day before. That volatile spark, which had glowed and jumped and animated her, appeared absent. Instead, she sat with a pensive, almost melancholy air.

'You have passed the entire morning in your rooms, *chère mademoiselle*. Were you taken ill?' She spoke quietly and poured me a dish of tea, though without enquiring if I would take one.

I was uncertain if this were some trick.

'I felt myself for a spell . . . perhaps unwell but . . .'

'If you require him, I shall summon Monsieur Seiffert, Orléans's physician, from Valenciennes . . . They have all returned there, quite early this morning.' She held me in her gaze for a beat. I shifted anxiously.

'Oh no,' I demurred. 'I am quite recovered. It was merely a . . . passing complaint.'

La Buffon tilted her head and smiled at me. 'Henriette,' said she, 'may I address you by your Christian name?'

I swallowed.

'Yes.'

'You may call me Agnès, if you wish. Orléans calls me Fanny. I was christened Françoise Marguerite Agnès, you see . . . He began to call me Fanny when we were in England. Like an English lady.' She handed me my dish of tea, though she avoided meeting my eye. 'Henriette, do you know how my introduction to Monsieur d'Orléans came about?'

Once more, my heart began to gallop. 'I am afraid I do not, madame.'

'You have heard no gossip about me, Henriette?'

I shook my head, and without warning she burst into a hard, forced laugh.

'Now I am certain you are telling falsehoods! There is not a woman in Paris whose tongue does not begin to flap at the mere mention of my name.'

'Yes . . . yes . . .' I hastily corrected myself, 'I have heard some things, but not as much as you would suspect . . .'

She examined me with a wry expression, one which understood perfectly the fibs I offered.

'Then you do not know that I was introduced to him by my dear friend, Madame de Genlis, who was then his *maîtresse-en-titre*?'

This I did not know. I observed her eyes move rapidly back and forth, studying, calculating, taking in each twitch of my face.

'No, madame.'

'I was once the mistress of her husband, the Comte de Genlis, but I suspect you know nothing of that affair either. How soon the world forgets my past sins when I now commit greater ones by appearing with Orléans. You see, Henriette, in my country it is permissible for a married lady to take many lovers, so long as she does not part company with her husband, or cuckold him so boldly as to insult him. It is upon this point that I find the habits of your nation most hypocritical, for the English are less tolerant of such conduct, yet gallantry is as common in London as it is in Paris. I am certain your "relation", Madame Elliot, has much to say upon that matter.' She caught my gaze and simpered provocatively.

I did not respond, but maintained my mild, polite expression.

'You must understand, *ma petite*, we do not harbour those foolish romantic notions of marriage so adored by the English. I never loved my husband, the Comte de Buffon. Not a single moment of affection passed between us in the three years I was his wife. He was entirely devoid of wit and intelligence, which I might have come to forgive had he not also possessed such unnatural tastes. He recoiled from the female touch.' She took her dish to her lips. 'He preferred his valet to his wife. He passed no more than a handful of nights in my bed. I despaired of this at first, but soon learned that I had many admirers and that all the world laughed at the notion of fidelity to a husband.' A smile rose between her cheeks. 'It was Monsieur de Genlis with whom I first knew true love, and as I could no longer bear the depravity of my husband, I abandoned that life. Monsieur de Genlis kept me as his mistress, in my own *hôtel particulier*, away from that sodomite. That was when society turned from me, for the humiliation I had wrought upon Monsieur de Buffon and his family – his father, the renowned naturalist, so revered at court.' She rolled her eyes, but there could be heard a strain of regret in her voice. 'And so I was no longer a wife, but became to them a *femme galante*. Monsieur de Buffon took great pleasure in procuring a separation from me, so he might disgrace me as I had disgraced him.' Her gaze fell from mine and she sighed. 'But had it not come to pass, I might never have made the acquaintance of Madame de Genlis.'

I examined her with bemusement.

'But . . . you came to know your lover's wife?'

La Buffon laughed.

'But of course. I offered her relief, Henriette! She was most grateful for it, too. Madame de Genlis held no love for her husband. Why, she scarcely knew him before they were wed; the entire matter had been arranged by her father.' She seemed amused by my ignorance of the scandal. 'You do know that she was Orléans's mistress before me – for many years? She was governess to his children . . .'

I nodded.

'It was she who introduced me to Orléans, when she wished to . . . retire from her obligations to him. She had come to know me and love me as might a mother . . . or an elder sister.' La Buffon's eyes reached for mine again. 'There is no person who knows a man's desires, his preferences and inclinations, his taste in female beauty better than does his mistress . . .'

Her gaze fastened itself to mine so tightly that I found myself scarcely able to draw breath. As she held me there, the black circles within her eyes seemed to widen. It was as if I stared into the very barrel of a rifle. I awaited the first volley, stiffening with dread. But that hail of words which I expected to batter me did not come. Instead, she sat, her lips pressed together, her expression firm until quite unexpectedly her eyes began to flood. Large, wet pearls soon tumbled down her cheeks and then hung upon her trembling chin. I was so taken by surprise at this display that, for a moment, I knew not how I might comfort her.

'Oh, madame,' I said. 'Oh, forgive me. Forgive me, madame.'

With that, a sob broke free and La Buffon hastily clapped her hands to her mouth.

'I swear to you, upon my life, upon my honour—'

'You have no honour, mademoiselle!' she burst forth in what seemed a laugh within a sob. 'You are a *dame entretenue*! A gentleman's whore! That is what we are . . .'

'I swear to you I tell the truth when I say that I fled. I fled, madame . . . I would not permit him . . .'

'What manner of *femme galante* refuses Monsieur d'Orléans, a Prince of the Blood, a Bourbon?' she exclaimed in an almost horrified disbelief.

I set my jaw.

'A woman of honour, madame, who would not wish to risk offence to her hostess.'

Madame de Buffon's tears ceased. She stared hard at me and

then, quite without warning, she began to laugh. She wiped her tears against her white muslin sleeve in a most artless, girlish fashion.

'*Ma chère* Henriette, that is the very reason why I should wish it to be you.'

I regarded her uncomprehendingly.

'I had hoped he would try with you. I knew you were to his taste, his precise taste, mademoiselle, but I could not imagine you would refuse him.' She rubbed her eyes again and sniffed, before folding her hands over her belly. 'I had heard Biron speak of you and seen the miniature. I had heard the stories: that you were Madame Elliot's relation eloped with a lover who jilted you – an officer in the army; and that you were kept for some time by an Irish gentleman—'

'An officer? Is that what is said?' I echoed, most astonished to learn of this fabrication.

'A captain or some such.' She sighed and shrugged. 'I knew that Orléans was likely to be captivated by your charms and your beauty. Had you not refused him . . . it would have lessened my burden, Henriette,' she complained as if heartbroken.

I studied her, still entirely befuddled.

'But . . . he is your lover. You love him tenderly. He is devoted to you. I . . . I have seen proofs of it.'

She shook her head.

'That is not to be questioned . . . it is true. There is none I love so much as him and his love for me is absolute, but what he requires – what *I* require, *chère* Henriette, dear sister – is . . . respite.' She moved her hands along her belly and shut her eyes. 'From the day I discovered myself with his child, I have not permitted him to lie with me. It has been near four months since then . . . and he is near distracted with desire.' Her lips attempted a faint, fleeting smile. 'Henriette, this infant inside me . . . this child . . . he . . . It is possible he may be ruler of France . . .' She opened her eyes and gazed deeply into mine. I returned her look, unable to formulate my response, for what she claimed seemed to me nonsensical.

'But how, madame – if you will forgive me – I cannot understand . . .'

'At present, the Church has made divorce an impossibility. We are at liberty to separate, but are eternally joined. Orléans, although separated from his wife, remains locked in matrimony to her still, as do I with Monsieur de Buffon. But this soon will change, Henriette.' Her eyes began to glint as she spoke. 'It is proposed that the law be altered and divorce permitted, and with that comes the ability to marry. Orléans and I shall be married' – she smiled – 'and this child will be our first-born.'

'But what of Monsieur d'Orléans's other children? His heir, Monsieur de Chartres . . . or Messieurs de Montpensier and de Beaujolais?'

She waved her wrist in a dismissive manner.

'Orléans would never permit his children to suffer.'

I wished to smile, to share in her hopefulness, but somehow I simply could not. Perhaps I was too much of an Englishwoman in my sensibilities, or perhaps my rational mind could not conceive how such a conceit could come to pass so readily.

'You see now, do you not, Henriette? Why I so wish to preserve this infant within me? I have lost two before this one. The first came away after I permitted him to lie with me.' Her voice grew tremulous. 'I . . . cannot allow it again. Not . . . not at present . . . and yet Monsieur d'Orléans is a man of great passions and needs. He is not accustomed to living as if a monk.' She lowered her eyes and smiled. 'And there are many ladies who wish to conquer his heart . . . and not return it to me. Like that Morency creature.' La Buffon raised her brow at me. 'There are so many of her description, and notwithstanding such invitations, Orléans has been true to me, but I cannot expect his fidelity to endure when I do not perform the role of a mistress, mademoiselle.' She dropped her gaze once more. 'In France, among the Bourbons, it has been a tradition for a mistress to hand her lover to a woman whom she wishes to assume her role. One chooses one's replacement with care. To leave such matters to chance is unwise. It would be an honour to me if you would assume care for Orléans's needs until I am safely brought to bed and then recovered. It would give me pleasure to know to whose bed he goes and that I remain in possession of his heart. Do you understand that which I beg of you, Henriette?' She raised her chin.

I continued to hold her gaze, but made no sign or movement.

'He *shall* live to rule France. You will see it come to pass, mademoiselle. Of this I am certain, for they talk of it – his supporters. They talk of a constitutional monarch, a king who is ruled by the Assembly. The King and Queen will soon be sent into exile and all the court with them. You will see.' She grew quite animated, her face beaming with an almost beatific expression. 'Do not think that I should ever forget your kindness to me, Henriette.' She reached for my hand. 'Think what good you will effect, *ma petite Anglaise*. A good for the nation of France. For liberty, *ma chère*. For the new Republic and all the change that comes with it . . . and for womankind too, *ma soeur*.'

I did not venture to move. My mouth parted; my brow creased.

It was not Madame de Buffon's fierce love of liberty, or her convictions, or even her fantastic schemes for Orléans that unnerved me so. No, it was her proposal which succeeded in doing that. I have never comprehended the French. They are of a different order entirely from their English cousins. They possess no sense of delicacy; there is no refinement in their nature, not even among those of birth. I recall that upon a recent sojourn in Paris I bore witness to a respectable young beauty making use of her chamber pot before a room of adoring beaux. Not a soul present thought anything of it.

I continued to behold La Buffon, studying her sweet features, both hopeful and pleading. While her intention had been to honour me, I could not but feel a sense of mortification, as if my character had been dealt the most heinous of insults. Of course the truth of the matter was that Orléans's mistress saw me plainly. She regarded me in a manner no different from Mrs Elliot, and Mr Savill as well. She viewed me as Orléans had the night before, as did all who made my acquaintance. To the world I was a whore, and yet I would not countenance it. I would not answer to it. I still held fast to the notion that I possessed some ability to determine my fate. But I had been ruined and so long as I remained in the single state, I would never be restored to wholeness.

I rose to my feet as La Buffon stared up at me questioningly.

'Madame, you will forgive me, please . . . but I am in need of air . . .' I said and made a curtsey to her.

I stepped from the pavilion into the blaze of mid-afternoon and, with some determination, began to walk. I knew not what was my destination, only that I could not bear to stand idle so long as my mind ticked. I paced along the cut hedges of yew and box, through a *patte d'oie* decorated with white marble benches and statues of Apollo and Daphne and the goddess Diana, hiding her nakedness from the gaze of Actaeon. I strode between these clipped avenues, these channels so contained, so geometric and ordered, and longed for the open English fields of my father's estate at Melmouth. I strode in an aimless march, my breast filled with ire.

I did not wish to become mistress to the Duc d'Orléans. Never was I more certain of it than upon that afternoon. Yet I also understood the matter had already been determined. My indebtedness to Mrs Elliot's kindness had decided it, long before La Buffon had ever penned her letter to me. It was this, more than any other sacrifice, which I owed her; she who had given me so much, she to whom I had pledged my assistance, she who had called me daughter. I had passed the previous night stricken with grief at my failure to honour my promises. I could not have imagined fortune would have allowed me such a reprieve as this. My dear friend had longed for such an opportunity for me, and yet I would never have desired it for myself, for in accepting this prize I was finally admitting defeat.

The remainder of the day passed without event. There was nothing in La Buffon's manner to suggest we had spoken upon this matter and I made no further mention of it. La Volière was still and tranquil that afternoon. Flies gathered in the cool shade of the house and moved in slow circles about the rooms. The windows had been left wide open and the château swallowed and exhaled great gasps of warm evening wind.

I saw nothing of Orléans until supper when he arrived in his coach with Rotaux, his bespectacled secretary, and his valet, Mongot, from the camp at Valenciennes. With the sour-faced Madame de Laval looking on, we played several hands of whist and took some wine before retiring.

It was only upon returning to my rooms that I noticed what preparations had been made. Upon a side table sat several bowls of fruit, nuts and sweetmeats. A gold walnut cracker had been placed beside a decanter of wine and two glasses. For a moment, I puzzled over these items, as I had made no request for them. However, it was upon turning towards the bed that all was made plain to me. There, beside the alcove, had been placed two low, chair-shaped objects whose seats had been replaced by covered silver pans. One was smaller and daintier than the other. I went nearer to inspect it. It appeared to be an elaborate chamber pot, but when I lifted the lid I noted that it was full of water, heavily perfumed with some concoction of herbs. I recognized it to be a bidet and recalled that Mrs Elliot possessed one not unlike it. The French, I had been told, possessed a certain fondness for such apparatuses following the act of love.

Upon opening the tall compartment that formed its back, I discovered a sponge, a mirror, a small folded piece of linen and a hollowed half of a lime. I stood for a moment in contemplation. I had reconciled myself to this. It was for my dear Mrs Elliot and no one else that I consented to it. Indeed, that thought alone confirmed in my mind that the actions I would take were worthy ones. I would gain the ear of the Duke and secure the affection of La Buffon, I assured myself. My sacrifice was a noble one. I would assure the livelihood and happiness of my dearest of friends, my most devoted of protectors, *ma chère maman*.

La Buffon had discreetly arranged for this and I understood well enough the use she intended for the lime. I shut my eyes, not from the thought of the discomfort (of which there would be much) but from disdain for the deed I was about to commit and all that it represented to me. I lifted my skirts and pushed the lime inside of me, wincing until it found its natural resting place, covering my womb. I was then about to ring for Lucy to undress me when there came a faint rap upon my door. I did not call out an answer, but within a moment or so it cautiously squealed upon its hinges. Orléans stepped into the room, attired in his Turkish robe and nightcap, and bowed to me.

'You are not indisposed, mademoiselle?' he enquired gently.

I shook my head.

He approached me slowly, as if he feared I might dart away. When at last he stood before me, I came no higher than his chest. His round hill of a belly pressed into me as he reached slowly for my hands. His mouth lingered for a long while on the back of each one, in what seemed a polite display of gratitude. Then he took me by the chin and placed his lips on mine.

I would venture that he thought me cold and prudish, for I demonstrated no eagerness for his embrace. I did not reciprocate his hunger. I did not pretend to feel that spark of wanton desire men wish to believe is lit within the breast of every woman upon the instant of their touch.

Once he had sampled my kisses, his hands moved to the front of my bodice. Orléans had opened so many gowns that he knew precisely the mechanics of my attire. He understood how to unwrap me from its flat front, how the flaps crossed behind one another, held by disguised buttons within. He made no enquiries. He fumbled over nothing. He turned to my sash and untied it. I lifted my arms without resisting as if he were Lucy preparing me for bed. No words passed between us as he continued to perform the role of my maid: untying my skirts, and unlacing my stays. He bid me sit upon the edge of the bed so he might unbuckle my shoes before running his hands above my knees to untie my garters and remove my stockings. Only once this had been accomplished did he push me back against the cushions and begin to roll his lips across my flesh. His mouth was firm and his hands soft, flabby and moist. He sighed, exclaiming at the yielding creaminess of my skin, the roundness of my breasts and thighs before placing his hand upon the seat of Venus.

Like a man who enjoys the delights of the table, the Duke seemed intent on sampling every dish before gorging upon the roast. There was not a spot upon my person he did not stroke or kiss or examine, breathing praises for all of which he partook. He was most considerate in his explorations and keenly studied my expression, as if hoping to find some evidence of approval. Then, at long last, he heaved his mass upon me. Beneath his girth, I felt myself pressed like a flower amid a stack of books. I reached my arms backward to brace myself against the bed frame and shut my eyes tightly.

He was a big and heavy man and his thrusts came with force, pushing the air from my lungs in what sounded like grunting expressions of pleasure. When at last he came to completion, my fingers ached from their grip. He had produced a long braying exhalation before rolling from me on to his side. It was then that I opened my eyes and stared at the inside of the saffron hangings.

I would come to know the routine of this, I comforted myself. It would be just as it had been with the others. I would learn to predict his actions, the sounds he emitted, his warm spiced scent of amber and civet. It would soon grow familiar and consistent and therefore not as unpleasant.

Orléans sat up and smiled at me, before begging a kiss. I had expected he would depart, but he did not. Instead, he ambled to the corner of the room, poured two glasses of wine and removed a large orange from the porcelain bowl of fruit. From there he gestured to the bidet.

'You may make use of it,' he said to me. 'You do not need my leave.' He laughed.

I removed myself from where we had pressed the feathered mattress flat, and crept to the stand beside the bed. With my soiled chemise still hanging from my shoulders, I mounted it. It required some feat of imagination as to how I might best employ it. I soaked the sponge in the scented water and as I applied it to that hidden place, I noted Orléans's eyes observing this performance with an amused smile. Without thinking what I did, and perhaps even to spite myself, I raised the short hem of my linen shift and exposed my temple of delight. Noting that his eyes had fixed upon it, I reached within myself and, contorting my face, retrieved the lime. This caused Orléans to roar with laughter.

'You are not at all of her blood!' he exclaimed, shaking his head.

I could not help but look at him with amusement.

'I have heard it said that she is your mother. A monstrous false-hood! I knew from the instant I looked upon you that you were no relation to Madame Elliot. Why, there is not so much as a hair upon your person which is like hers. Your temperaments are as dissimilar as those of a peacock and a goldfinch. Come . . .' He raised his arms to me, offering me a warm smile. He then tapped the spot beside him on the edge of the bed and began to peel his orange. 'For sharing with me your sweetness, Henriette,' said he, pulling apart the sections of the fruit and handing me a portion of it. He placed one slice into his mouth and smiled as he ob-served me do the same. He then touched my cheek with a certain tender fondness. 'You have raised my spirits immensely, *ma petite Anglaise.*'

'I am pleased for that, monseigneur.' My reply brought another orange-flavoured kiss.

'In my present circumstances, such moments as this, when I can enjoy simple pleasures, prove most restorative to me. In that regard, I suppose you are not so unlike Madame Elliot, who was most accomplished at distracting me from my cares.' His brow creased slightly. 'There are many more of them now than before.'

I nodded slightly. I wished to demonstrate sympathy, but I also recognized that an opportunity had presented itself.

'She . . . Madame Elliot, she fears you forget her—'

'Bah!' Orléans dismissed me. He continued to gaze at me with a playful look. This was not the response I had anticipated.

'She fears that your friends persuade you against her, that Madame de Buffon does not care for her . . .' I continued, though anxious not to provoke him or say more than I ought.

Orléans sighed as if he had heard this refrain before. 'Mademoi-selle, I shall tell you this: all of Paris believes that I am at the command of my mistresses – first Madame de Genlis and now my Fanny. Although I am devoted to her every desire, I am not a slave to the fantasies and whims of women. I am guided by men of intellect and my own convictions. At present, I cannot see Madame Elliot because she is a royalist and favours the King. I am at odds with the King, as you know, and I am most unlikely to be persuaded from that position . . . by any person.' He touched my cheek again and gently moved the strands of my hair from it. 'But I should never dream of disowning her. She is as dear as a sister to me and she knows that well enough.'

I opened my mouth, wishing to make some defence of Mrs Elliot and the reduction of her settlement, but before I could, he raised his finger to my lips.

'Hush. I will hear no more complaints.' He kissed me once more. 'Only pleasures.'

With that, he rose and stretched by placing his hands at the small of his back. His nightcap had fallen from his head during our exertions and his once fashionably curled hair stood out like a lion's mane on either side of his head.

'I will have returned to Valenciennes by the time you wake to-morrow,' said he, moving to make use of his bidet. I lowered my eyes in a show of modesty. 'But I dare say I shall return to you in fine health by evening. They will never permit me beyond the cannons. I am of far more value to the nation alive than dead.' There was a wryness in the Duke's tone, which seemed to mask a certain weariness beneath it.

Upon his departure, La Volière was enveloped by a night silence. I listened for his footsteps shuffling their retreat before I turned and went to the chair upon which my attire had been discarded. I rummaged amidst my effects for my pair of pockets and withdrew that one object which I never failed to carry upon my person. I unlatched the etched gold case of the watch Allenham had given me in Brussels and admired its handsome white face, feeling its steady pulse in my hand. 'Constant, comme mon coeur', it read. My little companion had travelled with me upon that long night when I had fled the Hôtel l'Impératrice, ticking all the while like a furiously beating heart.

I returned to my dishevelled bed and, with the watch against my breast, curled myself into the twisted sheets, tight and small, until sleep arrived at last and deadened me.

Chapter 14

Never had I been more aware of my constant friend concealed in my pocket than I had been in the course of those three weeks. The routine of my life seemed to move with the regularity of that device, tapping out the hours.

In the mornings, I was at liberty to do as I pleased and quite happily occupied my time with my paints or books or in tending to my journal. At midday I might expect Madame de Buffon to enquire after me. Shortly thereafter we would set out to take the air, accompanied by our noisy companions, Fantouche and Moustache. Dinner would be had, with or without the company of the silent, wretched-faced Madame de Laval, and following this sombre affair, La Buffon would take to her bed. As the infant grew, so her limbs weakened, she complained. Upon rising, she would then insist that I read to her. Much to my surprise, I discovered an entire trove of English books in her dressing room which she had had delivered from London.

'I wish to improve my English,' she begged while handing me Mrs Radcliffe's *Romance of the Forest*. She would listen intently, mouthing the words which were unknown to her and pausing to enquire as to their meanings.

Several times a week we were joined in the evenings by Orléans. Often he brought with him a handful of officers destined for the battlefields of Flanders. There would be supper, wine and cards. At the conclusion of this entertainment, I would withdraw to my rooms and await Orléans. He would appear with absolute regularity, take his pleasure with me in precisely the same fashion as he had upon our first encounter and then retire to his mistress's bed. And so the mechanism would be rewound and the entire course of events repeated the following day.

It was during those undisturbed hours of the morning that I would undertake my duty to Mrs Elliot. As I have described, it required some time before I gathered the courage to pen her a letter. When at last I accomplished this and dispatched it under cover to Thérèse, I was fraught with anxiety. I feared it might be intercepted, that she might not receive it, or that its contents would fail to please her.

A week or more elapsed before I received a response, which arrived along with two additional letters from Mademoiselle Devries, an opera dancer, and the great Madame du Barry requesting that I take their likenesses. Upon first glance, this first packet appeared to me as a letter from Thérèse. The hand which wrote it seemed a poor one, and the seal was no more than a blot of wax. It was only as I read it that I recognized the genius of its disguise. In order to evade suspicion, Mrs Elliot had dictated the contents to my housemaid, who had scribbled it in her uneven script and inferior spelling. For the most part, it read as might one's correspondence with a housekeeper. There were mentions of the purchase of candles and soap and a recitation of all the shopkeeper's bills, amid snippets of gossip. Initially, I could make no sense of this, but then the logic of it emerged through the ink.

'I have learned that Beaumont has closed the shop and departed for England . . .' she wrote, and then again about our friend

La Flaghac: 'The ancient printer of news and intelligence upon the rue de Richelieu was most delighted to hear that you had gone into the country and begs many questions as to your return . . .'

Imagine how I laughed at her cunning and wit! Think how I exclaimed at her cleverness in hiding its true contents from the long nose of any of Madame de Buffon's servants! But nothing pleased me so much as the postscript, which read simply:

Your neighbour begs me to express her pleasure at your most fortunate news and to remind you that she is most grateful for any word you may find the time to send to her. She says to me that your absence is dearly felt, and adds only that she is ever mindful of your well-being and entreats you to conduct yourself with care and consideration in all matters.

I did not hesitate to heed her warning and burned the letter almost as soon as I had consumed it.

In the days that followed, her words acted like a balm upon my heart. A certain sadness had settled there after my capitulation to the Duke, but her reassurances lessened the ache. With her sanction, my sacrifice felt an even nobler deed and my resolution to effect good was only strengthened.

But, reader, I would not have you believe that my existence at La Volière was that of an unhappy prisoner. It is true, my situation beneath Madame de Buffon's roof would never have been of my choosing, but I would not wish to suggest that I found nothing of merit in my hostess's company. Indeed, I was surprised if not amused to discover an affinity between us.

When I first experienced these sensations, I was mystified. I had been led to believe that La Buffon was possessed of not a single redeeming quality, but found this quite to the contrary. I came to admire her character, and indeed grew rather fond of her.

She was not the shrieking, long-clawed harpy of my fears, but rather a gentle, pensive soul. Unlike most ladies of my acquaintance, there seemed no artifice about her whatsoever. She spoke her mind freely upon every subject and appeared unconcerned as to whether she gave offence. As for her opinions, I shall not pretend that many of them were not objectionable. Her attachment to the principles of revolution was fierce and – dare I say? – it soon grew apparent to me how she had won so many detractors. Unfortunately, while at La Volière, her aunt seemed to show herself as being foremost among them.

Never had I witnessed a kind word or look pass between them. One vexed the other so incessantly that I fear the break which eventually occurred was inevitable. The particulars of their disagreement were never entirely made known to me, but I heard from Lucy that it concerned Madame de Laval's refusal to wear a rosette. There were fits of tears from both and, within a few hours, the injured Laval's coach was prepared for departure.

'She has no understanding of me, nor I of her. She wishes to emigrate and I cannot prevent her from dashing herself upon the rocks,' my hostess explained to me as we took our dinner. There seemed something sorrowful in her resignation, as if she had grown accustomed to such rifts and betrayals. She turned over a thin piece of trout upon her plate and sulked like a child.

There were times when I wondered if I was the only woman in France to glimpse her true character, or indeed if any person of compassion spied the loneliness in her. The tenor of her politics concerned me very little, and neither did it matter to me whom she took to her bed, revolutionary or royalist. Others would judge her for this, but I believe my affection for her took root precisely because I did not. I was an Englishwoman and regarded Madame de Buffon with the good sense of one of my nation. But one stone rattled in my shoe: the enmity she harboured for Mrs Elliot. I could not abide it, but resolved that it was in my means to correct it through our growing friendship. Once I had determined on that, I felt myself more at ease.

Until that time in my life, I do not believe I ever enjoyed the company of a female companion so similar in age and disposition to me. I had borne a natural affection for my sister, Lady Catherine, and a deep and enduring admiration for Mrs Mahon, but neither shared my interests or temperament. Even Mrs Elliot felt more to me a mother than a friend. Unlike these ladies, Agnès de Buffon's mind whirred like a waterwheel. She contemplated and cogitated; she devoured works of philosophy and debated their merits. Although an incorrigible coquette, she did not clutter her head with tales of gossip and scandal. It was she who first placed into my hand Madame de Gouges's *Declaration of the Rights of Woman* as well as that work upon a similar subject by Mrs Wollstonecraft.

'I do not agree with all she advocates. Indeed, I think Mrs Wollstonecraft most priggish at times,' she remarked. 'I should never wish Orléans to think I subscribed to such notions. Madame de Genlis counselled me to maintain my silence, to master the appearance of stupidity and charm, or else I should become suspect in the eyes of all Orléans's associates. The more clever appears the mistress, the more foolish appears the lover, she cautioned me.' La Buffon laughed. 'It was that very quality – cleverness – which undid Madame de Genlis. She did not wish me to suffer as she had.'

We continued to stroll through the cool, shadowed wood that bordered La Volière, listening to the wind shaking the many millions of leaves.

'I shall tell you a secret,' La Buffon began with a mischievous look. 'I have begun to write a novel. It is an allegory of a noblewoman who travels to a foreign land where her title is of no consequence and where the sexes are born equal. I write in private, in the mornings. I have told no one of this but you. Promise me that you will not speak of it to Orléans . . . or anyone.'

Of course I promised, and of course that promise was broken almost as instantly. I said nothing to the Duke, but rather disclosed the details to Mrs Elliot, though not without some sharp pricks of conscience.

My entire sojourn at La Volière seemed to follow in that vein: a sequence of unexpected pleasures tinged with private disquiet. Dishonesty and trust walked hand in hand unbeknownst to one another. Although I greatly enjoyed Madame's society, some part of me prayed that my time there would soon be brought to a conclusion.

If I have learned anything in the course of my varied life, it is that one must take great care with prayers. They are often answered, but in a manner most unanticipated.

That for which I had hoped came, quite without warning, on a night in early August. A rider arrived from the camp at Valenciennes with an urgent message for La Buffon.

'The King has commanded that Orléans return to Paris. He fears that Orléans is stirring dissent among the troops!' she exclaimed with an angry laugh.

'When?' I enquired.

Her eyes rolled down the letter.

'With immediate effect. Tomorrow morning at first light.'

That night, all the lamps were lit and the house was packed up in a frenzy. I retired to the sound of heels clacking back and forth upon the stairs and the distant stir of horses and carts from the stables. What slumber I enjoyed was interrupted at dawn, when Lucy shook me awake. Like children roused from their beds, Madame de Buffon and I boarded her carriage whilst still rubbing the sleep from our eyes. Orléans and the remainder of his household joined us in a princely train of four coaches which also ferried his young son Monsieur de Beaujolais and his tutor Monsieur Barrois, his physician Monsieur Seiffert, and Monsieur Rotaux. Romain and the other servants belonging to the Palais-Royal had been sent on ahead before daybreak.

I had been told nothing more about the circumstances of our departure other than that which La Buffon revealed to me the night before. It was not until we were upon the road that I mustered the courage to beg further details of the events which had prompted our hasty return. I sat observing Orléans's agitation and restlessness with quiet dismay. With each stop we made, he sprang from his coach and moved into another. He rode with us and then with his son before returning once more for our company.

'I am sorely in need of comfort,' he sighed to Madame de Buffon as he sank upon the opposite bench. His face was haggard from a lack of sleep.

'May I enquire', I ventured to La Buffon under my breath when it looked as if Orléans slumbered, 'what has brought this about?'

'The Duke of Brunswick, the commander of the Prussian army at Coblenz, has sent a letter addressed to the people of Paris. He does not approve of the King and Queen being held as prisoners in the Tuileries Palace and has now threatened that he will raze the city should any harm come to them.' She scowled. 'But the worst of it, Henriette, is that the Duke and the King have been conspiring in this. The King has been conspiring against his own people.'

I held her gaze.

'Certainly the people of Paris will not abide such a thing.'

'No, *ma petite*, that much is certain,' said Orléans gently, opening his eyes. 'I have been informed that Paris is now filled with volunteers who have come from across France to defend their capital. The people fear that an invasion is imminent.'

'And is it, monseigneur?' I pressed, now truly concerned.

The Duke lifted a single eyebrow in what seemed a careworn gesture.

'I cannot say.'

Not one of us spoke. The closed coach swayed from side to side, sucking dust through her windows. La Buffon sat, absently caressing Moustache. It was a moment before she drew breath to speak.

'Are you alarmed, monseigneur? Are you in fear of the émigré army? Of the Austrians and Prussians?'

Orléans lifted his head and examined her, as if uncertain how he should respond.

'You should not be. You should not be alarmed, monseigneur,' she insisted. 'The people will rise. We are greater in strength and number than the Austrians and the Prussians and the émigré armies. The men *and the women* will fight for France, for the Revolution, for all that is right. Do not underestimate the fervour of your brothers and sisters, *mon cher* Orléans. They venerate you and they love liberty. They adore their freedom from tyranny and they will die before it is wrenched from them.' She smiled and reached for his hand.

My eyes moved between the pair of them. Orléans considered each word she uttered and soon an expression of adoration and gratitude filled his countenance. It was the sort of humble look infrequently found upon a proud man of influence. That he loved her absolutely was unquestionable, and that she reciprocated could never be denied.

She was also not incorrect in her assessment of the people's sentiments; they adored Orléans. Indeed, my first encounter with this came while we were upon the road to Paris. Wherever our train came to a halt, whichever inn served as our place of refreshment suddenly came alive. Word of our arrival spread rapidly, and then it seemed all the population rushed forward to glimpse him. They ran from the fields; they came from the houses and shops and encircled the carriages as we sat inside taking our meals or wine or beer. They stroked the horses; they pressed their faces to the glass until we pulled down the shades. Madame de Buffon would then release them once more.

'You must permit them to look upon you, monseigneur,' she scolded him. 'They must see you are not the King, that you wear the uniform of a volunteer of the Army of the North. You are a hero. They believe you have fought at Courtrai. You must allow them to!' she would remind him. Orléans would then step from the coach and go out among them.

'*Vive Orléans!*' the cries would rise up. '*Vive Orléans! Vive la nation!*'

Weathered hands, both young and old, ungloved, hardened from work with scythes or brushes, stained with grime, would reach out and touch him. Sometimes they would handle his tunic or hold out a lame child, hoping that his touch, the touch of the Bourbons, the touch of monarchy (which they professed to abhor), would cure it. These simple creatures still yearned for kings and magic and talismans, though they would be loath to confess to it. I observed as one man with a small blade crept beside Orléans's coach and silently set to work removing two or three golden tassels from the hammercloth. He held his relics to his lips before pushing them deep into his pocket.

But for our sojourn that night at Chantilly, we rarely remained for more than half an hour at any one hostelry. These spectacles were brief affairs, short dramas enacted on a rural stage, and afterwards, the coachmen and footmen would mount their perches and the crowds would part to cries of '*Vive Orléans!*' Only once did they shout something other than that.

As we quit the small town of Verberie, an angry old man stepped into the road. I caught his eye as we flew past. His jaw was jutted and his hand clenched some piece of filth from the fields. 'Aristocrat!' he roared from his gut as he hurled his clod. I thought it odd that I was the only one amongst us to gasp as it struck the back of our coach. I turned and watched him through the rear window, shaking his fist at our trail of dust.

Chapter 15

We arrived at the barrier de Clichy before the city walls by late morning the following day. All along the road from Chantilly, the sun had pressed heavily upon the roof of our vehicle. Neither our fans nor the open windows succeeded in cooling us and Fantouche and Moustache panted and whimpered like two colicky infants.

At the time, I recall thinking there was something curious about our approach to Paris: the road leading from the city was all but deserted. The longer we were upon it, the fewer carts and Berlins we encountered, so that when we appeared at last before the barrier, it did not come as a surprise to discover it shut fast and overrun with National Guardsmen.

Orléans rode with us in Madame's coach and as it drew to a halt at the imposing columns of the tollhouse we found ourselves encircled. Without the armorial markings upon the door, the soldiers were at a loss to determine who sat within. La Buffon's coachman hastily explained that he had the great fortune to be conveying Monsieur d'Orléans back to the Palais-Royal. There seemed a good deal of confusion before some officer in a hat with a red plume stepped forward. I watched as, in the distance,

Orléans's valet, Mongot, presented him with our passports and spoke with him at some length. The officer then approached.

'Monsieur, it does me a great honour to deliver to you the news of the King's abdication,' said the commander.

The Duke's expression remained still. 'When did this event occur, Commandant?'

'Early this morning, monsieur. The King and his family have thrown themselves upon the mercy of the Legislative Assembly, where they currently reside.'

'They reside inside the Manège? In the Assembly itself?' Orléans's voice was puzzled, rising somewhat in pitch. 'And what will become of them? Has blood been spilled?'

The officer straightened himself.

'The King and Queen have not been harmed, but the Tuileries Palace is under siege. The Swiss Guard have fired upon the people, and our forces and the Fédérés have come to the aid of the citizens of Paris, monsieur.'

Orléans sat, taking in this news. After a beat, he gave a nod.

'The day we have much anticipated has arrived,' he stated with a sanguine tone. He did not wish to appear troubled but those who sat opposite him in Madame's coach could read the meaning of the creases which had appeared upon his forehead.

The commander brightened. 'It is a great day for the nation, monsieur.' He then hesitated. 'However, there is at present a degree of upheaval. All barriers to the city have been ordered shut. Many of the palace guard are at large and searches have been ordered of all homes. There are some sympathetic to the King who would harbour these traitors.' His hard eyes fell upon mine and Madame de Buffon's. He wished to frighten us and, indeed, he succeeded. 'I would warn you, messieurs-dames, there is unrest in all sections, but it would be a great honour for me to dispatch a detachment of my men to escort your party to the Palais-Royal in safety.'

Orléans glanced about the coach. His look was touched with faint unease. 'As you will, Commandant,' he agreed.

As the officer turned to rally his men, Madame de Buffon laid her hand upon her lover's arm. '*Mon cher*, you must ride at the head of the procession in your coach with Beaujolais. It would not do to have the Champion of the People seen returning to Paris in his mistress's conveyance.'

The Duke consented and took his place at the front of our train. Accordingly, La Buffon insisted that we travel at the end of it, before a small group of National Guardsmen. The gate was then heaved wide and our considerable parade, headed by the commander and his men, was permitted ingress.

We progressed at a cautious pace along the roads. Neither I nor Madame uttered so much as a syllable as her chariot rolled us along the thoroughfares. Our eyes were rapt by the scenes beyond the windows. I had not inhabited Paris for more than a handful of months, and yet I understood what constituted the city's regular pulse: a steady movement of cabriolets and carthorses, children spilling into the streets and shopkeepers reclining in their door-ways making idle chat with their passing neighbours. All this was absent. Doors were barred and shutters pulled across nearly every set of windows we passed. Here and there, blue-uniformed guards pounded upon them, demanding entry. But for this racket, nothing stirred. It seemed every street held its breath.

Deeper into the desolate city we penetrated, the acrid scent of smoke filling and then choking the air. It rolled like a fog in dark sooty clouds through the narrow streets. 'They are burning the palace,' La Buffon muttered. I was uncertain if it was wonderment or horror that she expressed. Without thinking, she wrapped her arms about her belly. As we neared the boulevard Cerutti men in sagging *bonnets rouges*, citizens it seemed, some with rifles and others with knives and brickbats, began to appear along the thoroughfares. They rested against doorways and beneath arches, halting their conversations and removing their pipes as they studied our procession with narrow, menacing eyes. Never have I been more reassured by the presence of soldiers than I was upon that occasion, for otherwise I was certain they would have fallen upon us like feral dogs.

Alarm would not permit me to remove my gaze from the window, lest some attack or accident befell us. I felt my heart thud heavily in my breast with each revolution of the wheels. Indeed, we seemed to move with such trying slowness. I imagined what relief I should feel to enter the courtyard of the Palais-Royal and observe the gates shut behind us. I studied intently each figure along our route: men in brown fustian coats, others in a better make of blue or grey, some simply in waistcoats, some stained with blood. Then there were the two who lay in the road.

The mind cannot conceive of death upon first glance. There is ever some explanation for a prone body: sleep, inebriation, even injury. It is not in the human condition to assume instantly that life has fled. I looked and then stared at the pair of Swiss Guard, one face downwards in the black filth, his white breeches saturated with blood, the other with a throat slit wide and a crimson crust obscuring his once animated features. It was only once we had passed that I cried out in horror. My friend pulled me to her with great force.

I feared I might be sick, but she held me and nuzzled her face into my hair.

'Do not think on it, Henriette, do not let it set in your memory,' she whispered and kissed my temple. 'Think on liberty. Think on liberty, *ma soeur*.' She held me close and tight until I felt I could draw air again. It was only once I had composed myself that I realized the coach had drawn to a complete halt.

We were upon the corner of the rue Neuve-des-Petits-Champs.

'Why do we pause?' enquired La Buffon. She rose up and peered through the rear window at the guardsmen, attempting to reassure herself of their presence. There appeared to be some disturbance ahead of us in the road. We could hear shouts and frantic noise but could perceive nothing from where we sat. Madame's horses snorted and shifted. The coachman called out in an attempt to soothe them. I felt once more my heart begin to pound. I could not sit still and pulled down the window to survey the scene before us. Much to my alarm I discovered that we had been separated from the other vehicles in the procession. We sat at a crossing, the centre of which was occupied by a gathering of some forty or fifty men in plain attire bearing rifles and assorted arms: pikes and axes, even the long scissors of a tailor.

'The road is overrun with volunteers,' I reported to La Buffon. 'They appear to be waiting for something . . . or someone. I cannot see the other coaches. They seem to have passed through before the crowd closed—'

Just then, the noise swelled. The mob turned. There was pointing and frenzied shouting in our direction where it seemed two men in Swiss uniform were fleeing for their lives. With a great roar the volunteers set off at a charge in pursuit of them, barrelling like a stampede towards us.

'Dear God!' I cried as I pulled up the window. 'They come this way!'

The guardsmen at our rear then surged forward, moving beside Madame's coach in an attempt to corner the fugitives. The horses shrieked and reared; the cabin shook as bodies collided with it.

'We shall be overturned!' screamed La Buffon, clutching me. I reached to let down the shade on the window, but we bounced and jumped so that I could not get a purchase on it. *'Mon Dieu! We shall die here!'* despaired my friend. I was cold with terror, for I too believed that I might meet with my end. There was a scuffle outside my window. I saw only a blur of blue guard uniforms and black hats. A pike clattered against the door and then came the most dreadful sound ever to pierce my ears: the dull thud of an axe against a man. A perfect arc of blood was thrown across the glass pane as the howls of the dying were joined by our shrill wails of horror.

Madame's coachman did not delay another instant. We broke free from the fracas at a gallop which sent us and the two terrified, yelping canines tumbling backward against the bench. We did not stop but drove at a maddened pace down the rue Neuve-des-Petits-Champs to the far side of the Palais-Royal, along the passage de Valois, passing similar scenes of chaos and disorder as we flew. All the while La Buffon clung to me, and I to her. Words had been stripped from us so that we could do little more than weep in unison.

Madame and I were still very much a-tremble as we stopped before an archway at the side of the Palais-Royal and were handed from her coach. From here, we were escorted up a modest, marble stairway which led on to a broad landing aglow with daylight. A set of gold painted doors were opened and we were admitted to what I learned were the Petits Appartements, the Duke's private residence within his formal palace.

I could not at first take in much of the magnificence of what passed before my eyes, for alarm had come over my senses like a veil. La Buffon had not let hold of my arm the entire time, nor had her tears dried. We swept through one gilded, mirrored chamber after another, one furnished with yellow silk and another in marine blue. Her stride grew ever more rapid as we progressed towards a destination unknown to me. When at last we arrived at a final set of doors and were announced, she tore free from me and fled to Orléans.

He stood at the centre of a white, mirrored salon, surrounded by dismayed and harried gentlemen, gesticulating and arguing furiously amongst themselves. Upon catching sight of her, his fretful expression was instantly transformed. Relief lifted his eyes and mouth. Mindful of the audience, he reached for her hands and pressed them tightly, then laid kisses upon both cheeks while whispering assurances to her.

A great fuss was then raised. We were seated upon the sofas and brought brandy to soothe our nerves while La Buffon recounted our ordeal. The Duke, his son, Messieurs Rotaux, Barrois, Seiffert and several politicians from the Hôtel de Ville gathered about us exclaiming and solemnly shaking their heads while offering praise for our bravery. It was from them that we discovered the Royal Family's fate had not yet been determined. No one within that room knew what would become of them. A few supposed it would be exile, another whispered death. It would be several days still before King and Queen, along with their children and a number of their loyal servants, were removed to the Temple Prison.

The gentlemen rambled anxiously about the massacre. *The massacre*, they called it, speaking the word over and over. They informed us that many hundreds of Swiss Guards had been killed, along with hundreds more among the royal household. I listened with silent incredulity that such an atrocity could have befallen the King and those loyal to him. It was beyond conception. Irrespective of how well they claimed to love their Revolution, there was not a pair of eyes within that room that did not display some look of dread or shock. Indeed, Orléans's countenance was flushed pink with heat and fury. Never before had I witnessed him in such a passion.

'It is complete disorder!' he fumed. 'Who do you propose should contain it, now that the commander of the National Guard is murdered?'

'They are attempting to contain it presently, monsieur. Searches have been ordered of all houses for Swiss Guards who have failed to lay down their arms. They have pledged to fight for the King and they must be brought to heel,' replied one of the gentlemen.

'There are corpses strewn about the roads, monsieur. The barracks at the Tuileries are in flames . . . Why, the city has been rendered a very picture of hell!' the Duke railed.

The shouts came, volley upon volley, the echoes rising to the ceiling like smoke from the cannons. I sat and observed, as passive as La Buffon's dogs listening to the noise. The words they spoke, the names they accused: they were meaningless to me, as if I comprehended not a word of French. With every flutter of my lids my memory turned over once more the images embossed upon it: the lifeless waxwork-like men I had glimpsed, the throat torn wide open like a ripped sack. I stared at my hands, my shaking fingers. I considered my arms. How easily they might be detached from my whole; how readily a body might be torn apart like a roast quail. I took another swallow of my brandy and felt its heat in my mouth. Where was Mrs Elliot? Where was Allenham?

La Buffon took my hand in hers and drew me back from my nightmare. I regarded her soft blue eyes.

'I do not wish you to take your leave of me. It is not safe to do so.'

I nodded at her. I certainly possessed no wish to venture abroad.

'You must remain here . . . for a while longer. Please, Henriette.' She spoke quietly while the gentlemen's conversation continued to rage at the centre of the room. 'I mean to say . . . you would do me a great honour if you consented to live here – as a part of the household. I am certain Orléans would assent to it.' A faint hopeful smile spread across her mouth. 'Since the departure of Madame d'Orléans the formality of life here is no more. There is no more court, as in the past. There are no longer public days or private days or grand suppers. The routine of life is simple, modest – not unlike our existence at La Volière. The formal apartments lie vacant. We live quite without grandeur, without pretence to the old conventions and practices, and although propriety forbids me from receiving guests, I can continue to do so at my residence upon the rue Bleue. You could do the same, should you wish. You need not give up your apartments at the Hôtel Blanquefort, though I believe you would prefer our society here to that of a solitary existence . . .' She inclined her head coyly. 'May I beg you, *ma chère* Henriette? It would please Orléans for you to continue amongst us. You have demonstrated such kindness to him . . . and to me, in particular. You have rendered my life not so bereft of female acquaintance as it has become of late.'

Her expression was so gentle, so pleading and conciliatory. When I had accepted her invitation to La Volière I could never have foreseen that events would have spiralled in such a direction as this, ever winding about me and binding me nearer to Agnès de Buffon. I knew what Mrs Elliot would have me do.

'Dear Agnès,' said I, raising my eyes to her humbly. 'At such a time as this, nothing would please me more.'

Chapter 16

The disturbances continued all day and night. From the windows of Madame's apartments I could hear them crying the verses of a song I had not before heard. They sang of 'children of the fatherland' rising against tyranny and 'cutting the throats of sons and women'. After that which I had glimpsed upon the streets, these words sickened me, these refrains of what I would learn was called 'La Marseillaise'. I feared for my household. I feared for Allenham and whether he remained in Paris or was in some other place, removed from harm. I feared for Mrs Elliot; indeed I found myself entirely preoccupied by thoughts of her welfare. That afternoon, contrary to my better judgement and at great risk, I penned her a note informing her of my return to Paris and of my situation at the Palais-Royal. I added that I might be met with the following morning at the Hôtel Blanquefort, where I intended to confirm the well-being of my household and tend to several errands. I begged that she would send me a line or two assuring me of her safety, but the day passed and then the morning came, and I received no reply. I prayed for her.

On the morning of the 11th August, Madame insisted that

I make use of Orléans's carriage and a porter to escort me and my maid to the rue du Faubourg Saint-Honoré unharmed. How the city reeked of ash and heat, I shall never forget. The sky had turned a curious brown, and a thick haze covered the sun. Apart from the troops of the National Guard, the streets were all but empty. Here and there could be found groups of citizens who had gathered in the squares to affix their ropes to statues of kings. They tugged and heaved at the bronze cast of Louis XIII which stood in the place Royale. As I passed I watched them rip it from its pediment, as if it were a rotten tooth.

I was deposited at the Hôtel Blanquefort and mounted the stairs to my apartment with some trepidation. All was silent. The neighbours, it seemed, were too frightened to stir. Here or there, a shutter was opened, but most were sealed fast.

I was greeted with great relief by my household, who claimed that they now jumped at the slightest rattle of a door. Madame Vernet informed me that the guards had come last night in search of conspirators, as they were now known.

'They requested that I unlock every door. They made a search in each room. They even lifted the mattress from your bed, madame,' Thérèse explained, her eyes quite round. To be sure, she appeared to me most terrified.

'And they are satisfied to have found none harboured here?'

She swallowed and nodded.

I was content to hear that no harm had come to those beneath my roof and to discover that my effects remained undisturbed, for pilfering was not uncommon in the course of such visits. I surveyed my rooms and ordered Lucy to gather a few pieces of attire and effects which I wished to have sent to the Palais-Royal. It was while I was engaged in this business that Jean Vernet approached me on tentative feet. He was a quiet, heedful young man and I was certain would one day prove to be a loyal valet to some gentleman. He held a letter in his hands as he stood before me, his eyes slightly averted.

'Please, mademoiselle,' he began uneasily, 'this arrived for you in your absence, but as I was uncertain if it was correctly addressed, I did not hand it to Thérèse to be forwarded.'

Though puzzled by his words, I took it from him.

'Monsieur Langlois, Madame Elliot's porter, said he received it directly from a messenger at the Hôtel l'Impératrice, where you were once resident.' He hesitated for an instant. 'He assured me the name was correct . . .'

I looked down at the packet, which was a filthy, battered thing, and read 'Lady Allenham' upon it. My heart fairly stopped. The seal, which bore the profile of a Roman philosopher or poet, offered no clue as to the letter's sender. Eagerly I broke it open, anxious to learn who would address me by that name. What I discovered within both astonished and intrigued me.

The letter was lengthy and came from the pen of one whom I had all but forgotten: Jean-Baptiste Mariot, Allenham's former tutor. A good deal of the page was taken up in an effusive apology for the belatedness of his reply. He cited this distemper and that illness before asserting he had made a full return to health. His words then rambled into fond remembrances of 'a most cherished pupil', before finally expressing his regret that he had heard nothing of Allenham in several years beyond his last letter 'which conveyed the news of his impending nuptials with the daughter of an English earl, which I conclude to be you, Lady Allenham'. He then continued:

As for any knowledge of his current circumstances or whereabouts, I must concede I am at a loss, though I feel I cannot in good faith close my letter without making mention of a curious coincidence. Not long ago, an acquaintance of mine, Monsieur DuLac, who once served as Lord Allenham's tutor of mathematics, remarked that he had seen a man quite similar in appearance to his former pupil at the Café de la Cloche at the Palais-Royal. Although bearing a most striking resemblance, his manner and speech were unlike that of an English lord. I am afraid I know no more than that, and I fear I have troubled you too much with these irrelevant scribbles. Should you wish to enquire of Monsieur DuLac, he and I are frequently to be met with in the afternoons at the Café de la Cloche, where it would be my great pleasure to receive any correspondence your ladyship should condescend to direct to your servant,

Jean-Baptiste Mariot

At first I knew not what to make of Monsieur Mariot's tardy response. Upon my arrival in Paris I might have mortgaged my soul to have received such intelligence, yet now my head seemed incapable of fathoming it. I stood for a moment simply staring at the words, knitting my brows together. What precisely did the author of this news wish to imply? I read it once more as I paced a circle about the floor. *Nonsense*, I concluded, abruptly folding it and thrusting it into my pocket. The information offered was so scant, so faint, so flimsy as to be deemed absurd. I felt myself quite irked by it. I attempted to carry on with my tasks, but found myself fastened firmly in place. The letter's implications began to seep steadily into my mind. You see, friends, once they had been aired, once the gate had been opened to this possibility, I knew I would be incapable of shutting it behind me. I simply could not dismiss it as a mere anecdote, never to be pondered again.

I chewed upon my lip and allowed my hand to creep back inside my pocket and retrieve the curious packet. I considered it. Perhaps this encounter was not so incidental as Monsieur Mariot had supposed, but contained some further germ of information?

Indeed, perhaps this Monsieur DuLac was half-blind or -deaf and failed to see or hear correctly. Furthermore, if this stranger was met with at the Café de la Cloche once before, was there not some possibility that he might be discovered there again? Might I not determine the truth with my own eyes and ears?

My thoughts were so consumed by this mystery that I was scarcely aware of the approaching footsteps in the drawing room. When I lifted my head I was most surprised to discover Mrs Elliot standing in the open door, with Jean about to announce her. At first I did not recognize her for she wore a plain blue riding habit and a heavy veil over her black hat, which she lifted upon greeting me. I hastily pushed the letter into my pocket and hurried to embrace her.

'My dear child!' she exclaimed. Her expression held delight but also anxiety.

'Oh, madam, I have been consumed by my fears for you . . . and when I had no reply to my letter . . . I have never witnessed such horrors . . . the soldiers . . .'

My friend hastily placed her finger to her lips to silence me. She then laid a gentle hand upon my shoulder. 'Hetty,' she began, almost beneath her breath, 'I am not at liberty to linger for long—'

'Oh, and I am most grateful that you have called upon me!'

'No, my dear, you mistake me.' She spoke hurriedly, her tongue flying over her words. 'I cannot remain in Paris. I am taking my leave for my house in Meudon, which is near Sèvres, just beyond the walls.'

'But the barriers have all been shut.'

She touched my cheek with her grey glove. 'I must get away. It is far too hazardous to remain here as a supporter of the King. I mean to go to Meudon on foot. There is a means of passing through the wall. Langlois has told me of a breach in it . . .'

'But it is far too dangerous,' I protested. She hushed me again.

'If I remain, I shall be harassed day and night. There are many in my section who do not regard me fondly. Perhaps unwisely, I have never sought to hide my convictions. Now that I am no longer in favour with Orléans, I have few protectors from those who would seek to accuse me,' she whispered, her eyes anxiously studying mine. 'Now, Henrietta, I bid you hear me. I feel it is my duty to inform you that the embassies are to shut. I have had word that Lord Gower intends to quit France immediately. If it is your wish to take your leave and return to London there will soon be no passports issued and no means of departing. Do you wish to return to London, *ma chère fille*?' she asked earnestly, taking my hands into hers.

I beheld her, and her apprehensive look. She seemed to await my answer with bated breath; her marble blue eyes were fixed directly upon me. I glimpsed then in her face what appeared to be the shadow of true fear. She depended upon me, just as I did her. I felt my heart tug with a certain gladness. Although this news disquieted me, it had not altered my resolution to remain in Paris, not when I had begun to effect such good with Orléans, not when I felt myself possessed of a true friend such as her, a true mother to me. I felt the sharp edge of Monsieur Mariot's letter through my pocket reminding me that I now possessed hope, no matter how small the quantity of it.

I shook my head. 'It is my intention to remain.'

Such a look of relief came over her. A smile spread between her cheeks, even the corners of her eyes turned upward.

'You do me a great honour, child,' said she, planting a kiss upon my forehead. 'I can fault your character for nothing. You have the courage of Bellona, my dear . . . as must I have now.'

I gripped her arm.

'I shall think of nothing but your safe arrival at Meudon.'

'Then do not neglect to write to me. Your letters give me

such pleasure and your presence with Orléans and Madame de Buffon has not been without reward.' She raised an eyebrow. 'I have received a letter from him. It is no more than a kind note of friendship, but nonetheless, it is an enquiry, and I have had none from him in near to two years.'

At this my face brightened.

'It is on account of you, *ma chère fille*, and for this I am more grateful than words can express.' She pressed my hands in hers again. 'Remain near to Orléans and Madame de Buffon. At present you are safer in his protection at the Palais-Royal than at any other place in Paris. It will provide me with great comfort to know that you are there.' She paused and then regarded me as if she were a proud mamma examining her charge. 'I dare say, if you continue as you have, you will secure your own fortune as well as mine. Now, I must take my leave of you. I fear it is unwise for us to meet again while you live beneath Orléans's roof.'

We embraced tenderly and then, with much reluctance, I summoned Thérèse to escort my cherished friend to the door. It was here she hesitated and drew her veil about her face.

'For reasons of discretion, I should prefer to take my leave by the servants' entrance,' she insisted, addressing my maid. I moved to follow them, but Mrs Elliot motioned for me to remain before blowing a kiss through the thin gauze.

I moved to the window and watched for her cabriolet to turn out of the arch and into the road. As it did so, I slipped an anxious hand into my pocket and felt for that secret square of paper. I did not intend for another moment to escape me.

I left my household to their tasks and made my way to Orléans's coach below. There, I informed the porter who had accompanied me that I wished to go immediately to the Café de la Cloche. He paused for an instant as if he had misheard my instruction.

'The Café de la Cloche, mademoiselle? Near to the puppet theatre at the back of the Palais-Royal?'

I hesitated before affirming I believed that was the very one. He rumpled his brow slightly, as if he could not conceive of my reasons for choosing such a destination. Nevertheless, he conveyed my orders to the driver, who spirited us away through the curiously quiet streets to the rue de Beaujolais. Here, beside the arch which led to the gardens and colonnades, he drew to a halt. I paused before stepping from the coach. The eerie stillness of this usually vibrant temple of diversions unnerved me. There were but a handful of chairmen and drivers standing about beside their empty chairs and cabriolets, whistling and waiting for passing trade. The well-attired bourgeois messieurs and mesdames who regularly strolled at this hour were nowhere to be seen. I took the footman's hand and looked about me. Orléans's porter came instantly to my side. I thanked him for his vigilance but insisted that I required no attendant.

'I am merely to meet briefly with an acquaintance,' I attempted to explain, but was greeted with a look of bemusement. And with that, I did not tarry.

I had no notion of where precisely this Café de la Cloche was to be found. I passed beneath the archway and looked left and then right down the colonnade. Spying the puppet theatre, I turned in that direction and marched hastily past the windows of fan-makers and booksellers, purveyors of trinkets and ices, some of them shuttered fast at midday. It was then that I glimpsed what appeared to be a sign painted with a large church bell, half hidden behind a column. I raced to the entry, my feet fairly tripping over themselves as I did so. It was only when I stood before this hostelry that I understood the porter's puzzled expression. This was a dingy, tired place, and certainly not one of the fashionable establishments to which ladies repaired. I stepped cautiously across the threshold and surveyed the interior. Here and there were arranged a collection of faded green chairs and tables and painted walls whose golden griffins and swags of flowers had been turned a dull yellow from pipe smoke. But for a knot of three thin-faced men engrossed in reading a single newspaper, the café was deserted. I approached a waiter, whose eyes had been upon me from the moment I had entered, and enquired of a Monsieur Mariot, or his associate, a Monsieur DuLac. He ran his fingers beneath his brown frizzed wig as if trying to recall their faces.

'Well, they are not here today, mademoiselle,' he replied, screwing up his face as if I were mad to have ventured out on such an errand. 'You might return tomorrow or upon any following afternoon, though you are unlikely to find them here before dinner.'

I nodded at him. I cannot say that I believed I would have found them there upon my first attempt, but I had hoped.

'Might I leave a letter for Monsieur Mariot here?' I begged. The waiter smirked and produced paper and a pen before promptly demanding two sous for it. Then he stood over me, reading across my shoulder as I scrawled my note. In it, I explained that I wished to make his acquaintance and that of Monsieur DuLac, and enquired when they next proposed to meet at the café. I apologized that, for reasons I could not reveal, I was unable to receive them at my lodgings and instructed him to leave his reply for me at the café. Then, with an ounce of daring, I signed my name in a manner I had not for some time, as Lady Allenham.

I know not if the meddlesome creature behind me was capable of reading so much as a word, but he took my folded sheet from me with an air of suspicion, while promising to deliver it to the gentleman in question. I could do no more than wait.

I crossed the quiet gardens, strewn with flecks of grey ash. A lone fiddler played a solemn tune where usually a cacophony of sounds competed. At a corner, a man bellowed out before a small crowd his hellfire curses on all aristocrats, on all counter-revolutionaries, on all those Swiss who hid in the garrets.

'We shall tear your limbs from you, we shall carry your heads about the streets for all to see and learn and know how Paris deals with those who fight to preserve tyranny . . .'

I strode briskly onward towards Orléans's palace, towards this promised haven of safety.

Chapter 17

Here, I feel obliged to say something of my position at the Palais-Royal. Do not mistake me, had the upheaval of the Revolution not prevailed and altered everything about the routine of existence within those walls, one with a name as humble as mine would never have been permitted to reside there. At the time when my belongings were carried into my rooms, the Palais-Royal was but a shadow of its former glory and a palace in name only. One might have likened it to a commodious St James's townhouse occupied by a nobleman whose finances and character were in a state of decline. Curiously, this reduced mode of life seemed to suit Orléans's ambitions to appear always the 'Champion of the People'. Madame de Buffon too was quite content to live amongst its empty state rooms and preside, where appropriate, as its informal hostess. It was this, more than anything, which gave fuel to her detractors. How incensed were those friends of the former Duchesse d'Orléans to learn that La Buffon had situated herself in her lover's wife's rooms. To those royalists such as Madame de Flaghac and others of Mrs Elliot's acquaintance, there were now few places so corrupted, so depraved and devoid of decency as the Petits Appartements of the Palais-Royal. It was here where I was invited to live.

In accordance with Madame de Buffon's wishes, I was granted a set of apartments across a landing, near to hers. They were as gilt-touched as you might imagine. The walls were decorated with pilasters of gold, the ceilings painted with floating gods; Mercury and Venus ascended like balloons into a cloud-strewn cerulean heaven. Every wall winked with mirrors so that the daylight blazed from the windows into each corner. I cannot well describe the impression these rooms left upon me, for, in spite of their luxury – the perfumed bed of fringed crimson damask, the dressing table whose looking glass was held aloft by golden putti, the altar-like marble mantels which rose nearly to the glittering squares of the architraves – they seemed the most desolate place on earth. I could not ignore the ghostly rectangular outlines that appeared upon the walls in nearly every room. Week upon week, Orléans's creditors claimed another of his treasures. The splendid Arcadian scenes by Claude and Poussin or the portraits of double-chinned Bourbons seemed to vanish without remark. Indian ivory cabinets disappeared, as did towering blue Chinese vases. It was as if the objects of the palace were gradually abandoning the Duke in the manner of the courtiers who had once lived in it.

For the better part of a year, the Palais-Royal had been in-habited only by a modest band of servants and those assorted members of Orléans's household whom I had met at La Volière. Where once the clack of hundreds of heels of nobles and ladies, of maids and valets, would have been regularly heard upon the parquetry floors, there now came scarcely a sound: not the trill of laughter from an adjoining set of rooms, not the plucked song of a harp through the walls. There came nothing but the forlorn moan of a persistent draught. Lucy and I rattled in my apartments like two small beads forgotten at the bottom of a coffer.

To live among these deserted spaces was to move in silence

along enfilades of rooms. Echoes followed footsteps, while the reverberation of a shutting of a door might be felt in the shake of a cabinet or a piece of glass. At night, a glance at the adjoining wing offered nothing but a view of row upon row of blackened windows. Neither the illumination of chandeliers nor any number of candles dispelled this sense of emptiness. There was but one remedy for it: company.

Almost as soon as I arrived at the Petits Appartements, I understood absolutely La Buffon's sense of isolation and why she had begged me to remain with her. As she had made plain to me, she was not permitted to receive callers of her own in the Duchess's former home. Orléans did away with most conventions, but he understood that to flout this final stricture would be to add insult to his wife's injury and to render all the worse his relations with his furious father-in-law, the erstwhile Duc de Penthièvre. Madame had no female society of which to speak. True, she made occasional visits to her house upon the rue Bleue and called on one or two ladies of her acquaintance, but she was never received warmly, nor encouraged to remain for long. It was me upon whom she relied for diversion, for consolation, for assistance and, most of all, for companionship. I soon found myself almost never out of her company, which was precisely as both she and Mrs Elliot would have had it, but I fear it did not suit my schemes at all.

No one but Lucy knew of the letter I had received from Monsieur Mariot, nor of the secret hopes I concealed. As Madame and I took our slow perambulations about the gardens and colonnades, I looked longingly in the direction of the sign of the bell, wondering all the while if a note awaited me there. On several occasions I dispatched Lucy to enquire after any correspondence but, much to my dismay, she never failed to return empty-handed. It was not merely a reply for which I longed, but to be permitted the liberty of attending the café and studying its patrons. I hungered not only to put my questions directly to Monsieur DuLac, but to apply my own eyes to the figure of this mysterious gentleman. There were but a scant handful of opportunities to engage in such a clandestine activity and when they presented themselves, I did not delay in grabbing at them.

Just as she had at La Volière, Madame often grew weary after dinner and took to her bed for an hour or so of rest. The very instant she took her leave of me I pretended to return to my rooms, but instead stole away like a mischievous maid, down the stairs leading to the passage de Valois and then across the gardens. I never failed to arrive at the Café de la Cloche breathless, my hand atop my hat to steady it in place. I cannot think what that mean-mouthed waiter made of me. Upon each instance he would wag his head, ruefully announcing the absence of a reply and, I suppose, mocking me. After making a slow examination of each of the patrons, I would then take my leave. Only one sort of woman would have lingered in such a place, and I had no wish to be mistaken for a common man's whore.

The days ticked past and this trick was repeated for just over a week, during which Lucy and I took our turn calling in at the Café de la Cloche unbeknownst to Madame de Buffon. Then, at last, upon the eighth day, Lucy returned to me with a wide-faced grin. She slipped the note into my hand and I tore at it.

Monsieur Mariot gave a brief response and stated that he and Monsieur DuLac could be met with upon Thursday afternoon when they would eagerly await my appearance. A smile swelled between my cheeks and then just as hastily dropped. How was I to keep such an appointment with La Buffon ever at my side? Our afternoons were filled with all manner of distraction: with drives through the Jardins du Luxembourg and visits to listen to the debates at the Legislative Assembly. What excuse could I possibly invent without arousing her suspicions? I soon began to fret, to nibble my nails, to gaze aimlessly out of my window, until a plan presented itself to me. It was as if Mercury had reached down from the ceiling and touched my head with his staff.

Upon the following day, Madame insisted that we attend the Hôtel de Ville, where the Commune sat.

'The greatest orations are to be heard there,' La Buffon explained, adding that she was most impatient to hear Monsieur Danton speak that afternoon upon the matter of defending Paris against conspirators. This concern had quite come to prepossess her; indeed, since the attack upon the Tuileries there now seemed to be ceaseless talk of counter-revolutionaries and their wicked strategies to rise and massacre all the republicans in France. We took our seats among the crowded benches in the gallery. The air was thick and stifling and Madame's face soon turned as red as the cushion her maid, Rosalie, had brought for her mistress's comfort. We fanned ourselves frantically, dampening our muslin gowns as Danton roared and raged, throwing his fists about as he called the nation to arms. The Austrians would soon be at the gates with their cannons, he warned, and a great number of royalists would turn upon their neighbours in revenge for what had been committed at the Tuileries. Statesman upon statesman joined him in offering similar sentiments. I watched as the thin, bespectacled Robespierre took to the floor and argued that the guillotine placed in the Carrousel outside the now ravaged Tuileries Palace should be put to good use in removing the heads of all the royalist courtiers who cluttered the prisons.

It was a sobering spectacle to behold and one which only succeeded in further disconcerting La Buffon.

'I confess it, Henriette,' said she to me upon our journey back to the Palais-Royal, 'although I would never admit as much to Orléans, it frightens me vastly, for it is he they will come for before anyone.'

'I cannot imagine how such a situation should ever come to pass, for certainly most who are loyal to the King have fled abroad or languish in the prisons,' I replied, attempting to displace her fears with reason.

'There are many who will always hold with the King, for it is the only manner of life they have ever known and an existence without such riches and privileges seems anathema to them. Like your relation, Madame Elliot, for instance.'

I gave her a sudden look. It was the first time in a great while that she had mentioned Mrs Elliot's name and I felt compelled to defend her.

'She has explained her convictions to me, that she has been rewarded handsomely by those royalists and feels a sympathy for them . . .'

'She has been rewarded handsomely by Orléans. Does she not feel a sympathy for him?' La Buffon peaked her eyebrow at me.

'Why of course, she cares for him greatly—' I began, but Madame wrinkled her nose.

'I am not convinced by it for one moment, Henriette. Her friends are dangerous ones, devoted royalists and, no doubt, conspirators against the Revolution. This is why I have forbidden him from meeting with her.'

'You think that she would murder him, Agnès?' I shot, somewhat offended by her suggestion.

'I do not think it impossible that he may come to some harm by her hand . . . and I should die if that fate befell him, or anyone whom I held dear. Why, are you a counter-revolutionary, Henriette?' She stared hard at me for a moment, so hard that it felt as if she levelled an accusation at me. I started, for I wondered if she had known about my visit with Mrs Elliot not a fortnight earlier. She then burst into laughter. 'I know you are not. You are an Englishwoman, a lover of Rousseau, a reader of Condorcet;

your heart and mind are guided by the principles of a new world.'

And yet, at that moment, as I was receiving her compliments and trust, I was contemplating how I might betray it.

I pretended at a smile and lowered my eyes.

'Agnès,' I began timidly, altering the subject of our conversation. 'You know that I have refused three commissions to paint likenesses on account of my sojourn at La Volière – why, one from Madame du Barry . . .'

She rolled her eyes at the mention of that aged former mistress of Louis XV.

'But . . . but . . . I have had another request: a letter . . . from Madame Talma—'

'Madame Talma?' Her face suddenly illuminated. She sat up as well as she could support herself against the coach bench.

All at once I feared I had fabricated the wrong patroness, for surely if La Buffon admired this actress so much, she would demand to accompany me. I hesitated.

'Yes.'

'And you wish to paint her?'

'Yes.'

'When?'

'Thursday . . . afternoon.'

'Well then. You must!'

I could scarcely believe it had been so simple to deceive her.

It rendered me quite sick.

And so I had set the wheels in motion and prepared to embark upon my secret excursion. On Thursday, shortly after dinner, I made my excuses and set out. In order to lend credence to my tale, Lucy accompanied me with my box of paints and implements, as well as my folio of paper. Anxiety rattled my nerves all that day and grew worse with every step I took from the Petits Appartements. I could not prevent myself from glancing back at those rows of windows as I turned, not into the courtyard where Madame had arranged for a coach to convey me, but between the columns of the galerie de Valois. I lingered in the shade as Lucy ran to dismiss the coachman before rejoining me. I know not why, but I could not dispel the sense that La Buffon had her eye upon me. As we carefully proceeded down the colonnade and out of view, I frequently looked up until I was convinced that there was no figure watching from her window.

However, my heart was as much a-gallop as it had been that entire day. I had prepared a great number of questions I wished to put to this Monsieur DuLac: what was this man's height? Was his hair dark like mahogany? Were his eyes bright as aquamarine? Was he exceptionally handsome? What distinguishing marks did he bear, if any? What was the mode of his conversation? Of what did he speak? I rehearsed these in my head again and again as we hurried to the café.

Upon entering, the waiter who had so vexed me in the past greeted me in an entirely different manner. He gave me a conciliatory nod of his head and gestured for me to follow him. This I did and he escorted me to a back table between two slightly blackened mirrors where sat a pair of elderly gentlemen, one thin and the other quite portly. They immediately rose to their feet and bowed in the old courtly manner.

'I am Monsieur Mariot, Milady Allenham,' said the slighter of the two in perfect English. He wore a short close wig, which I supposed he had possessed for the better part of thirty years. He then introduced his florid, puff-cheeked companion as Monsieur DuLac.

'Please, my lady, will you not join us?' Mariot smiled, rather abashedly. 'It . . . it is not common for . . . English ladies to visit a café so . . .'

'. . . humble,' added Monsieur DuLac.

'I care not so much for the formalities of old, messieurs,' I replied as if La Buffon had fed me the very words.

'Indeed.' Mariot cleared his throat and then glanced briefly down, as if to ensure his rosette was visible.

A small glass was brought to the table, along with a bottle of brandy, which was poured before me. The meeting in such an environment was an awkward one to be sure, and we sat for a moment shifting in silence before I saw fit to speak.

'Monsieur Mariot,' I began, 'I am so much obliged to you for replying to my letter. However trifling you believed your anecdote, I can assure you that it was not trifling to me.'

Here I launched upon a fanciful tale which I sprinkled with some true details of Allenham's disappearance and many false ones with regard to my invented marriage and my name, for Mariot believed me to be my departed half-sister, Lady Catherine. They listened and tutted and hung their heads. They apologized for my terrible misfortune and expressed their true and earnest concern for his lordship's well-being, 'especially in the wake of these atrocities . . .' lamented Monsieur DuLac. Mariot hushed him and glanced about anxiously.

'As you might imagine, Monsieur DuLac, I wished to interrogate you upon the subject of the stranger you saw here, whom you believed to be the image of my husband.'

DuLac took a hearty swallow of his brandy.

'The truth, madame . . . the truth is . . . it was dark, and my eyesight is not as it once was.'

I stared at him. He hesitated and gazed down at his glass.

'But if I am not mistaken, Monsieur DuLac, Monsieur Mariot implied you believed he bore a resemblance to Lord Allenham, with whom you had some acquaintance when he was your pupil?'

Mariot cast his friend an inquisitive look, but DuLac did not meet it.

'That is correct, madame, but it was . . . some time ago and I am certain your husband no longer resembles the boy I once knew. Human physiognomy possesses a great capacity for alteration over the years.' He gave an awkward laugh.

Although I attempted to politely conceal it, my brow furrowed with mounting frustration.

'Do you mean to say, monsieur, that you are now uncertain if this stranger bore any resemblance at all to my husband?'

'With all due respect, madame, I have since concluded it most unlikely. This gentleman with whom I spoke heralded from America, a native of Boston. He was a printer and had come to Paris to practise his loathsome art, if that indeed is what it might be called. He espoused such seditious notions on the nature of liberty and the French nation that I found him quite odious.'

I sat for a spell. This was not what I had anticipated I would hear.

'I am a good deal sorry to have disappointed you, madame, for I suspect your travails have been terrible ones. I take it that you have tried all avenues and applied even to your King's emissary in Paris? And that too has failed to offer you any satisfaction?'

I nodded. I feared that my desperation was now growing most apparent upon my face.

'But you must describe to me, monsieur, something of his appearance,' said I in a voice almost pleading, 'for my husband is unmistakable for that . . .'

DuLac sat for a spell twisting his mouth in contemplation. 'He did indeed look as I recalled my dear pupil. He possessed dark hair and eyes as exquisite as gems. He was an exceptionally handsome boy, even at sixteen. Eh, but this man . . . well, I suppose even the devil can sport a handsome disguise.' He sniffed and reached for his glass.

'And his name, Monsieur DuLac?'

'His name, madame?'

'Yes, did he not introduce himself to you?'

'Why yes, but his name was not Allenham.' He laughed and wagged his head.

'Then, I beg you, monsieur, what name did he give?'

DuLac had begun to appear weary. He exhaled loudly through his mouth.

'I am afraid . . . I am afraid I do not recall, madame.'

'Pray, monsieur, do attempt it – for a poor wife who has endured such terrible travails as I?'

As I held the plump man in my gaze, I contemplated what measures I might employ to cause him to recall this one critical detail. Perhaps a show of tears might shake his brain enough, I thought, before deciding better of it. I exchanged looks with Monsieur Mariot, whose wispy eyebrows were raised in what seemed to me an expression of apology.

DuLac squinted and balled up his features, as if he were attempting to produce an egg. At last he sighed and shook his head.

'It . . . it will come to me, madame,' he assured me. 'I shall write it in a letter if it does . . . but to where might I address . . . ?'

'Here,' I shot back with scarcely a moment's pause. 'My lodgings are not far and I send my maid into the colonnades near every day on some errand or another.'

Indeed, my answer was so suspect that I cannot but wonder what portion of my story Messieurs DuLac and Mariot had swallowed, if any of it. However, I did not like to dwell upon such uncertainties and thought it better that I take my leave at that very moment rather than risk subjecting myself to any awkward enquiries. I thanked them cordially for their assistance and impressed upon them the urgency of my situation: that I hoped to receive word from Monsieur DuLac soon; then I bid them farewell and flounced from the Café de la Cloche.

Following that interview my spirits were not high. I sighed and repeated my conversation with the gentlemen to Lucy.

She regarded me through sympathetic eyes. 'All is not yet lost, madam,' she offered to me. She was ever kind and encouraging, my maid.

As I did not wish to reappear at the Petits Appartements too soon, we wended our way slowly back along the passage de Montpensier. We stopped to gawp at the paste brooches and horn sewing boxes, lengths of silk and fustian, and were assailed by a colourfully adorned fortune teller who waved a card bearing a picture of a pregnant empress at me. I spoke very little and lost myself amidst the fog of my thoughts and doubts.

I made my way up the stairs and had no sooner entered my rooms than Rosalie appeared before me. She indicated that her mistress wished to speak with me.

'Is she well, Rosalie?' I enquired, but Madame's servant made no reply. I followed her through the doors and to La Buffon's airy drawing room. There she sat upon a wide gilt chair, her hands resting atop her maternal form, her face like a slab of stone. At the sight of this, I stopped.

'You have not been to paint Madame Talma, have you, Henriette?' she asked flatly.

I opened my mouth and grasped for words.

'Is your name Henriette?' She cocked her head. 'Or is it Lady Allenham?'

My throat closed, as if all my capacities for speech had abandoned me. I observed her expression grow harder, her eyes hotter.

'I should hate to think you have betrayed me . . .' She forced a smile which appeared so menacing that I immediately called to mind all of Mrs Elliot's warnings. 'You see, Henriette, I had you followed. Rosalie had confided to me that upon several occasions when I took to my bed, you seemed most eager to get away . . . On this instance, I sent a boy from the kitchens to spy upon you. He has reported everything to me.' She moved her head forward, like a serpent. 'Who are you, mademoiselle?'

At that moment I could not think of a single word to speak or action to take. I stood mesmerized with fear, held entirely captive by the power of my own dread.

Perhaps by that point in my young life, I had in fact managed to acquire some true sense. I can offer no other explanation for it, for how I understood that in some circumstances it is far better to present the truth than a falsehood. I suppose I had come to learn that lesson when I threw myself upon Mrs Elliot's mercy and having had success at that, determined that I should attempt that same defence once more. So, reader, I told her. I revealed my tale to Madame de Buffon, without so much as a hint of shame.

I informed her of my parentage and of my short but happy existence with Allenham. I presented her with the story of my fall and my time in London as well as my reunion with my beloved. While I was careful to omit the details of Allenham's role in Brussels, I recounted to her the unfortunate circumstances that had brought me to Paris. I explained about my correspondence with Monsieur Mariot. However, my wellspring of truth flowed dry when I spoke of Mrs Elliot and my obligations to her. Instead, I claimed, as I had always, that she was my relation: my mother's cousin, my mother who had been a whore, a *femme galante*, a *dame entretenue*, just like Mrs Elliot, just like me, just like her.

She observed me in silence as I spoke. Not a hint of her thoughts was visible in her expression. Then, at the conclusion of my sorrowful song, I bowed my head. I was uncertain what she had made of it, or if it had proven the correct medicine to soothe away her sense of betrayal. I fretted as to what she would make of me: no longer the fashionable pretty English paintrix, whose reputation had been touched by scandal, but rather a foolish, reckless adventuress.

'Henriette.' She spoke my name softly.

I raised my eyes to hers, fearful of what I might find there. They were calm like the sea following a storm. Then there came the sunlight: a smile.

'We shall find him together, *ma chère soeur*,' said she in a gentle voice. 'And what pleasure it will give me to see you reunited.'

Chapter 18

'Do you reckon that this stranger might have gone by the name of Mr Allen?' pressed my friend, her expression bright with intrigue. 'Do you think it possible that your lover has come to Paris in support of the Revolution? Why, so many have, it is not implausible to consider . . .' she conjectured as we rounded a fountain at the centre of the gardens. 'Mr Paine is an Englishman and he is a great supporter of our Revolution. Is Monsieur Allenham a friend of Thomas Paine?' She paused, but only for a fleeting instant. 'Perhaps he *has* taken another name. Perhaps he wishes to throw off the yoke of his noble ancestors . . . he wishes to appear as an American . . . but how curious that is, Henriette. Has Monsieur Allenham visited America?' La Buffon continued, allowing every thought that danced through her brain to take flight from her tongue. Indeed, I had not seen her so animated since our return to Paris. In presenting her with my dilemma, I had handed her the very distraction from her troubles for which she most yearned. 'You are like Monsieur Rousseau's Julie,' she exclaimed, 'and we must find your Saint-Preux and return him to you!'

Day upon day, this endeavour came to consume her, displacing all other cares. She spoke no more of her fears of counter-revolution, of assassins among Orléans's servants or of arsenic dropped into her wine. Rather she chose to fashion herself into my scrupulous inquisitor. She demanded details of Allenham's family and connections, of all his passions and interests, about Herberton, about his income, about his education, tutors and his manner of life. She enquired as to his taste in theatre and in books and asked which amongst them were most favoured. She listened with rapt attention to each answer and anecdote, and when I at last revealed to her the miniature portrait I had painted of him, she sighed, 'Ah, *ma petite*, we must find him!'

It was she who insisted we undertake daily excursions through the arcades to the Café de la Cloche. We set out each afternoon, at an hour when the fashionable set had made their retreat from the colonnades. The crowds mainly comprised the working sort: petty merchants, clerks and grisettes taking coffee and wine and listening to the shouted arguments of men in tricolour sashes.

'He is certain to be amongst them. We will discover him here, if not today then tomorrow . . .' Madame assured me as we strode purposefully to the sign of the bell. We would then wait at a respectable distance beside the door and dispatch Lucy or Rosalie to enquire within for Monsieur DuLac's much anticipated reply. La Buffon would take my gloved hand in hers and squeeze it impatiently as we waited. On the reappearance of a maid she would never fail to give a slight start and a mild gasp before sighting that their hands were empty.

'Oh, *ma petite*,' she would sigh, a moue upon her face, and touch my cheek. 'Tomorrow, yes, tomorrow. We shall call again.'

After a spell, she would take my arm in hers and convey her now vast girth to a position in the shade. We would sit in some bower beneath the cherry trees, or at a modish establishment which afforded us a view of the Café de la Cloche, so we might observe discreetly those who passed through its doors.

'It is not so inconceivable that he should return to the very place where your friends discovered him, Henriette. Why, you have said so yourself,' she would attempt to encourage me between sips from her beaker of ass's milk or some other such tonic prescribed for the maternal condition. However well intentioned her words, they never succeeded in raising my spirits.

'Henriette, you appear so low, *ma chère.*' She squinted at me through the afternoon sun. 'It seems to me as if your heart has been so injured that it no longer possesses the capacity for hope. You must permit me to do so on your account, will you not?'

I regarded her gently and with a look of appreciation. But I found myself greatly distracted. At the time, I could not fathom why this might be. I could not give a name to what it was that I felt, beyond a sense of apprehension. I could not discern whether it was on account of the constant warnings we received that the conspirators would rise and murder us in our beds, that soon Paris would fall to the enemy and all would be lost. I could not tell whether the guarded glances of everyone we met, or the silent *hôtels particuliers* and vacant theatre boxes were responsible for my unease. I could not determine if it was because I fretted for Mrs Elliot and her safety or for myself, scrawling my letters in the early hours of the morning, engaged in this constant dance of deception. All about me were the signs of change: Madame's growing belly; the dappling of brown and yellow upon the leaves of the chestnut trees. The season was approaching its turning. The world, my world, would not remain as it was for long. Somehow, I understood this.

But for a rare, cooling breeze, the heat continued to hold us in its firm fist. It rendered me quite dizzy at times. I was certain the heat had caused me to swell: my ankles, my bosom. I remonstrated with Lucy that she pulled my laces too tightly. After several instances of this, she paid me a cautious, sidelong glance, the meaning of which I did not take.

'They are fattening me for the slaughter,' I huffed as my bosom pushed over the edge of my bodice.

This agitation only grew worse. I found my mind unable to hold a single thought for more than several moments. It fluttered about like a butterfly. My eyes could scarcely take in the words of books or the suits of cards I held. Figures and sights passed before me like stripes of colour. Music pierced my ears like noise and conversation faded into babble. I felt myself a-tremble. It was on account of the talk. Of this, I was certain, for it was incessant, urgent and bellicose. It came from the mouths of those men whose names have been most blackened in the annals of history: Messieurs Danton, Desmoulins, Marat, Vergniaud, Hébert and even the tyrant Robespierre. Yes, friends, these villains became my constant companions at Orléans's modestly dressed table.

You might well imagine how it was to sit in the company of the frog-featured Danton, or beside Marat whose neck and countenance was enflamed with a bright rash. I attempted to turn my eyes from it as he rubbed and scratched at himself throughout our meal. He smelled of tar and sulphur. Although she argued that he was a genius and she hungrily consumed every edition of his newspaper, *L'Ami du Peuple*, even Madame could scarcely abide the stench of him.

It was a singular experience indeed to sit so near to these monsters, before they had shown the full horror of themselves to the world. I listened, hardly daring so much as to breathe while they aired their schemes. Why, it seemed as if revolution coursed through their very veins and pumped their hearts full of life. They frightened me a good deal, for they spoke rapidly and vehemently of murder and sacrifice. They raised their glasses to the guillotine. They weighed the merits of placing weapons in the hands of every citizen of Paris. Even Orléans fell silent as they argued these propositions. The more passionate they grew, the less he offered by way of his own opinion. He nodded and praised them, and agreed where necessary, but at times appeared almost as a bemused spectator at his own dinner. The footmen, of which there were but two, delicately handed about the dishes of carp and fried capons and breast of lamb, as if they feared disrupting the oration. More than any of the others, it was Danton who could hold an entire table in his thrall, like a magician.

'The Austrians move nearer to Paris with each day. Our armies are disadvantaged and cannot hold them for long at Verdun. And you know what deed they will commit the very instant they breach the barriers of this city?' He spoke each word with slow deliberation to La Buffon, who sat beside him, her eyes fixed like pins to his face. 'They will throw open the gates of the prisons and herd into the streets every enemy of liberty who languishes within! All those interned, all those taken from the Tuileries Palace, who clung to the skirts of the Queen, every lover of despotic kings, every oppressor of the people, every ignorant clergyman, will be armed with muskets and pikes and swords and knives to take vengeance upon us.' He paused for effect, his bloated cheeks and darting pupils coming to a momentary rest. Orléans's mistress was mesmerized, as indeed were all of us. Danton then raised his chin. 'But you have no need to fear, madame. The citizenry of Paris will never permit it. Before that day arrives, the nation will rise. The impure blood of traitors will be let by the hands of your very brothers and sisters.' He then raised his glass of Burgundy to Orléans. '*Vive la nation.*'

Those at the table reached for theirs and echoed his toast, '*Vive la nation.*'

I observed the deep, ruby claret roll about the vessel as I held it aloft. It coated the glass with a substance thick and viscous and seemed to reek of iron and rot. All at once my belly lurched. I pressed my hand to my mouth and ran hastily from the room for a chamber pot.

It is perhaps on account of that incident that I recall the final days of August so clearly. I remember early September too, and one night in particular. I had returned to my apartments that evening to discover several of the paintings stripped from the walls. Most notable for its absence was a vibrant image of St Cecilia in saffron and lavender robes which had hung near to the door of my bedchamber. I wondered if Orléans had determined which of his objects were to be removed or if he simply ordered Monsieur Rotaux to perform this loathsome task, to run his finger down an inventory of pictures and objets d'art and make his selection. The Duke seemed neither to notice nor care, though it must be said that I have never known a gentleman of great rank to bemoan his financial ruin to his mistress. In fact, to all appearances, Orléans continued to live as he ever did with regard to luxuries. While he made a good display of modesty to the world, he acted very much the part of the munificent protector in private.

The proof of this lay inside my bidet that night.

Over the weeks I had accustomed myself to learning the signals of Orléans's impending visits to me. In my bedchamber there would appear wine and other refreshments laid out, along with two bidets arranged near to the bed. One of these, an elaborate cabinet inlaid with ivory and bearing a bowl of gold, had been his gift to me. I learned there was a great tradition of such things in France. That night, as I approached this lavish commode and lifted its lid in order to prepare myself, my eyes were greeted by the winking facets of diamonds. There, submerged beneath the vinegar water, lay a brooch. It was as wide as my palm and fashioned into the shape of a basket cascading forth with flowers. Atop it, a cluster of emeralds had been fashioned into the form of a bird. It was an extraordinary thing, with so many squares and pears and circles as to confound the eye, and – as if the bearer did not believe this mere bauble sufficient – on either side of it was arranged a pair of brilliant earrings: two hanging baskets of sparkling blossoms. I could not begin to fathom the worth of these treasures and stood gaping at them.

I concede that, since consenting to Madame de Buffon's proposition, I had received a good many gifts: tokens of gratitude due to a woman of my sort. As a display of her affection, she had presented me with a set of diamond-star hair pins and two of her shimmering gowns of pompadour and tabby silk, which she had once worn at court. Orléans, too, had not neglected to equip me with gifts suited to a mistress, albeit not the official *maîtresse-en-titre*, worthy of her own furnished *hôtel particulier*, the position occupied by La Buffon, but a favoured one nonetheless. Therefore I was presented with an assortment of exquisite trinkets and treasures: embroidered silk shoes from Genoa with gold buckles; a necessary whose neat little box was hewn from amber; a fan whose handle was set with diamonds; and the daintiest of sapphire and emerald eardrops. I had made a gracious show of accepting these objects, all the while recalling the words of Mrs Elliot and how I had battled them in my heart. For as much as I was devoted to my dearest of teachers, my patroness, my *chère maman*, I loathed that she had been correct, that I might do better in my life by enacting a performance of love than by any other means. The painting of a hundred miniature portraits might procure me but one of Orléans's diamond eardrops, I mused. Indeed, while my character was muddied by my mode of life, while my associates remained *femmes galantes* and roués, no patron would consider my skill with paint a true accomplishment; rather it would be seen as a novel and charming manner of amusing him during a dance of seduction. I gazed at the magnificent jewels in my bidet and preferred to believe I had acquired them through my noble service as a forger of peace, as a maker of amends, as an ambassador, than simply through being what I had ever been: a whore.

As I stood there, bent and quizzically peering beneath the golden lid of this contraption, I heard the jib door open. Orléans emerged and upon beholding me let out a roar of delight. I beheld him with surprise, which only encouraged his hilarity.

'I have played a good trick on you, have I not?' He sighed and coughed and mopped his bald pate.

'Indeed you have!'

'Are they to your taste, *ma petite*?' he then enquired with a certain courtly deference.

I assured him they were sublime, for that was indeed the truth. Then, with a pretty smile and an enraptured gaze, I assumed the role he demanded of me upon the occasion of his visits: that of the adoring mistress.

I have often been grateful for my short stint upon the stage while in London. The performance of love upon which Mrs Elliot advised my future was best secured was greatly enhanced by the lessons I acquired there. I learned how to shape myself into the guise of another, how to make the appropriate expressions and gestures, how to pretend at anything. In my private hours with Orléans, it had grown plain that he wished me to play the role of besotted inamorata; one who regarded him with such affection that he might believe her soul would melt at his merest glance. This pleased him mightily and in return he played the part of the gallant lover who preferred no other embrace but mine. Both he and I understood well enough what was the truth. Once he had completed his caressing and unlacing and pushing me upon my back, once he had grunted his final pleasure and I made my soft mews of false reciprocation, we resumed our association as friends. Then there came the ritual of cleansing and taking of refreshment and making of frivolous conversation.

'It pleases me to make such gifts to you, *ma chère* Henriette,' he stated as he moved to pour two glasses of wine. He wore nothing but his soiled chemise which rose over his belly and scarcely covered his hanging manhood. 'For what is a Prince of the Blood if he does not still have some ability to grant favours to those deserving of them, hey?'

I was very startled to hear him name himself as such. In those days one did not make such references to the conventions of the former era, and especially not one who supped with half the Paris Commune. I examined his features for some hint of humour, but found none.

'But I am no longer in possession of that title, nor most of the extravagances of the past,' said he, glancing at where the picture of St Cecilia once hung. He furrowed his brow and tipped his head, as if attempting to determine which of his treasures had been removed. 'It is for the best. It is for the nation, for the Republic.' He then shrugged and drained the contents of his glass in two deep swallows. 'Why, I should rather live in an empty palace than in the Temple Prison eating sprats and crusts of bread beside my sobbing queen.' He handed me a glass as I sat mounted upon my bidet and then sighed to himself. Lately, Orléans's tone had seemed one of resignation. He had ever devoted himself to wine, but recently he had taken to imbibing copious amounts, though somehow managed never to lose complete command of himself. On that night, I sensed that he drank to quiet his concerns, but instead he merely gave voice to them. As they rattled off his tongue I was not certain if he was addressing me, or simply speaking his mind to the nearly bare walls.

'My cousin and I have ever been at odds, long before the outset of this Revolution,' he continued. 'It is natural that current politics should render matters worse between us. Over the years, I have made many attempts at reconciliation, and each one has been perceived as a sort of insult by the Queen. I offered my daughter's hand to the Duc d'Angoulême and it was Antoinette who would not countenance it.' He sniffed and lowered his head. 'The King is as stubborn as an ass and as stupid as a brick. If he possesses neither the wit nor the wherewithal to preserve himself, then . . . the devil take him. ' He refilled his glass with impatience and hastily imbibed the contents. 'At present, the Assembly cannot agree on what will become of him, but wherever his fate lies, I must honour their decision.' Orléans turned to me. 'I was never formed for politics, Henriette, and yet now I find it as necessary to my existence as the air I breathe. I am a man of pleasure and it is the pursuit of that which I understand best. I cannot say what the future holds any more than I am able to lay a winning wager upon a horse. I can study the form or guess at it and yet I may still find myself incorrect, but where the King is concerned, I do not believe the circumstances favour him . . . or, indeed, me.'

He fell silent, his gaze hanging upon mine. His eyes seemed to sag with weariness. It was a look which inspired me with nothing but apprehension for the future.

All of this was most irregular. Orléans usually demanded that we did not squander our time engaged in the discussion of political matters. In the past, when I attempted to raise such subjects he would instantly dismiss my attempts with a wave of his hand.

'Oh, that my ears could be free of such noise for but an hour!' he would protest. Why he should now choose to spread his troubles before his mistress perplexed me. Nevertheless, I spied before me an opportunity, and if I did not grasp it, I might never see the like of it again.

'Monseigneur,' I began, 'I would beg you to spare a thought for a much-loved acquaintance of yours who would not hesitate to offer you friendship at such a time as this.'

He raised his eyes to me.

'You know of whom I speak.'

He gave a small snort.

'Madame Elliot cares for you a great deal, monseigneur. She is quite alone and . . . without the resources she requires to ensure that her future is a comfortable one. That you will not see her is the cause of much of her unhappiness. I beg of you, monseigneur, she has assured me that she merely wishes to continue on a footing of friendship with you. She bears no ill will towards you or Madame de Buffon. Her heart is breaking, monseigneur, and you would do well to reconcile with her . . . for none of us know what the future is to bring . . .'

He sat himself on the edge of the bed and regarded me for a moment. His expression was fixed and still and full of thought.

'Argh! I am worn down by the demands of women!' he then groaned, before swooping me into his arms and placing me upon his knee. 'How happy you make me, *petit oiseau*, the little bird I snared at La Volière. You are a friend to everyone.' He kissed my neck. 'This is why you have jewels and gifts, just like that long-necked heron who took you into her nest.' He jiggled me about and laughed to himself. After a moment, he moved his hands about my belly and my bubbies, and began to knead and squeeze the flesh. Having thoroughly satisfied himself, he gave my neck a final few kisses. He then rose, placed me upon the mattress and wrapped himself in his Turkish robe.

'You are breeding, Henriette,' he said with a playful wag of his finger.

I stared at him, aghast.

'Yes, *ma petite*, you are. Do not pretend to ignorance. I would wager this is not the first occasion in your life that you have found yourself in such a condition. Why, I have felt enough women in fruit to know all the signs.' He smirked. 'In these six weeks I have not once been inconvenienced by your bleeding. One need not have received the education of a physician to understand such things, you know.'

I cannot imagine what expression I wore. I can only think it was one so contorted with shock that Orléans believed I was teasing him. He whooped with amusement at it. He laughed as he fumbled with the strings on his robe, this man so unaccustomed to dressing himself. He laughed as if he could not contain himself, the hilarity bursting forth from him. He laughed so loudly that once he had opened my door and passed through it, the noise carried down the enfilade of deserted rooms, filling each one, however briefly, with the sound of his emptiness.

Chapter 19

I shall not pretend to you that I did not suspect that which Orléans discovered. Indeed, what woman cannot correctly guess at her condition before proof of it stirs within her? The truth of the matter was that I had chosen not to see it, for its implications were too terrible to contemplate by far.

I had taken every precaution. I had made diligent use of the halves of lemon and lime that had been placed in my bidet cabinet. I had laved myself with the astringent waters until my privies smarted. I could not fathom how it came to pass, but Nature forces herself upon the fair sex in often miraculous ways.

There was nothing I desired less on earth than to find myself in such a predicament. While Mrs Elliot would have viewed this turn of events as a triumph, I did not doubt that La Buffon would conceive of it as a betrayal. Why, it was she who had arranged for my bidet to be equipped with those preventative devices. On many occasions she had peered into my eyes and enquired earnestly if I 'had employed the conveniences with care'. I took pains to assure her that I had.

'I have no more desire to bear Orléans a child than I have designs upon his affections,' I vowed to her repeatedly. 'You know my heart has been claimed by another, Agnès. I wish only for a future with him, and do not seek to make my fortune by filling Orléans's nursery.'

By God, truer words than those I had never spoken. I had once carried a child, placed inside me by a spark of love. I had pushed him through me as death held my hand. I had nurtured him and watched him grow fat on milk before a man determined that he was not mine to keep. He was snatched from my arms, never to be returned. This, beyond any other pain, I could not endure again.

There were means by which I might avoid this fate. Though prone to their own discomforts – sweats and aches and blood – they were far less injurious to the heart. I knew what manner of herbs to procure to induce it and how I might concoct them into a tisane. I would force it and its many woes from me as soon as I was able. However, I could scarcely perform this task in secret. There is not a woman of apprehension, whether married or debauched, who would not recognize the steeping scent of pennyroyal and her sister leaves. There is not a servant who would not understand the meaning of sodden scarlet linens. There was not a nose or a pair of eyes in the Petits Appartements who would not sense these irregularities and fail to hold their tongues. Madame La Buffon would learn of it, and it was best that she heard my confession before the tattle reached her ears. I could only pray that Orléans would permit common sense to command him and refrain from speaking of it. I would put it to her in the morning, I instructed myself, and then pulled my bedding close and tight and waited for sleep.

It was the sound of bells which roused me first. I was uncertain of the time, for the curtains still sealed me into where I slept. They clanged incessantly, wild and discordant and vaguely muffled from within the drapery. It is the tocsin, I thought, and then sat up straight.

'Lucy!' I called out, pushing my head between the lengths of silk, but my maid did not respond. The shutters and drapery were still closed and the room was as dark as a tomb.

'Lucy!' I cried, opening the door which led to my dressing room.

With my maid nowhere to be found, I threw wide the window coverings and was assailed by a blaze of morning light.

There came a sudden patter of footsteps from some corner of my apartments.

'I did not know you were awake, madam,' she called out in apology. Her expression was harried and almost entirely stripped of its colour.

'Lucy, what is the matter? Why is the tocsin sounding?'

'There has been a disturbance this morning, madam.' She seemed to tremble as she spoke. 'Monsieur Romain informed us. There has been an uprising at one of the prisons. The royalist prisoners . . . the counter-revolutionaries . . . But I am told it has been put down. There are many soldiers and citizens with arms still upon the streets—' She broke off and turned from me abruptly, intent on setting about her task of dressing me.

I waited for her further explanation but curiously, she made none. My eyes followed her about as she moved, darting and anxious as a mouse, shaking out my petticoats and mantua, collecting my linens from drawers. Her agitation alarmed me nearly as much as the news she had delivered.

'Lucy!' I commanded. She stopped instantly. 'Monsieur d'Orléans and Madame de Buffon? They are here and well? And no harm has come to any member of the household?'

'Yes, madam, they are here and well. There is no disruption within the Palais-Royal,' she said, though her voice quivered.

'Well then,' I concluded. 'We must accustom ourselves to such upheavals and not take fright at every disturbance. So long as the

Austrians have not arrived at the gates of Paris, we have nothing to fear.' I smiled at her, but this appeared to do nothing to calm her. Her hands remained unsteady as she dressed me. Hurried and shaking, she could not tie my garters without assistance, nor fasten the buckles upon my shoes.

'Lucy?' I spoke again, though softly and without reprimand. 'Whatever troubles you, girl?'

It was then she raised her gaze to me. It was wide and staring. She shook her head and then placed her hand to her mouth.

'There are bodies, madam,' she whispered. 'I saw them this morning. The prisoners' bodies, madam, they carry them through the streets. They carry them on pikes. There was . . . a head . . .' She stopped and her eyes began to fill.

I reached for her hand. I scarcely thought what I did, but I gripped it, I suppose out of fear. I recalled too well those scenes to which I had been subjected not a month earlier. I recalled what it was to witness murder and shut my eyes hard against the memory of it. She paused and regarded me, as if quite startled by my gesture.

'Lucy, you are safe here, more so than anywhere else,' I attempted to reassure her. I employed the very words Mrs Elliot had spoken to me, but I could not say that I derived any comfort from uttering them.

It was then I heard a soft rustling and looked to discover La Buffon standing awkwardly in the open door. All at once, my belly turned. Lucy's news had, for a short spell, succeeded in displacing my own grave concerns, but Madame's appearance there brought them back to me once more.

'Henriette.' She spoke softly, as if in a haze. Her moon-like mound protruded through her yellow sprigged gown. The golden curls which framed her face bestowed upon her the look of a disconcerted child. I was uncertain how long she had been lingering there, and what she had observed of my maid's distress.

'You have heard what has occurred?' she enquired gently, glancing at Lucy and then back to me.

'Yes . . . some . . . Tell me . . . ?'

'Monsieur Brissot has been here with Orléans,' she said, slowly lowering her girth into a chair. 'The counter-revolutionaries have attempted to break from the prisons. It is just as everyone warned. The people have gone to put down the rebellion, and they have succeeded, but . . . but . . . I have heard dreadful tales, Henriette.' She rumpled her brow, as if her head could not make sense of what lay within it.

'What have you heard, Agnès?' I begged, now greatly anxious.

'I know not what to believe, nor what to think, for I could never have imagined this . . .'

'What?'

'Monsieur Brissot called upon Orléans to inform him. It seems . . . it seems they have murdered all of the Queen's women: Madame de Tourzel . . . Madame de Lamballe . . . Madame de Saint-Brice . . .' My friend stopped upon that final name, as if it had stuck in her throat. She clapped her hands to her mouth. '*Mon Dieu!*' she cried, her eyes filling with a sort of wild panic. She shook her head as tears began to stream forth. 'I knew them! Madame de Lamballe was a friend . . . before . . . She was Orléans's sister-in-law, you know. She was so innocent.' La Buffon now fell into sobs. 'And others are dead . . . so many others . . . Madame de Lamballe was no counter-revolutionary! The others, I cannot say, but it does not seem just . . .' Madame searched my face, her expression imploring me to her side.

I moved to her and took her hands in mine, just as I had Lucy's. I listened to her great wails against the quiet of the dressing room. The pain of loss and remorse which they contained was so brutal that I felt them reverberate within me too. Although I had not yet spied the scenes that Lucy had described or heard directly the accounts that La Buffon conveyed, I could not but conclude that a calamity greater than those events of August or indeed any of which I could conceive was transpiring beyond my walls. Such a chill passed through me, a dread the like of which I had never known, cold and sickening and smothering.

'What does Orléans command us to do?' I begged, my voice weak and frightened.

La Buffon steadied herself and sniffed, attempting to contain her tears. 'He . . . would have us continue our day as if we are unconcerned by these events. They should not disturb our peace,' she announced with resolve. 'Those were his instructions to me, and they are wise.'

As she spoke, there was a rap upon the door and the tall figure of Romain entered. Upon seeing him, Madame rose and smoothed her gown over her belly. 'Monsieur d'Orléans has bid us to join him at breakfast. He entertains Mr Boyd and Mr Kerly, his bankers from England. That had been my intention in calling upon you . . . before . . .'

'Yes,' I responded, taking her hand again.

We proceeded through the Petits Appartements, our shoes tapping out a march against the polished floors. La Buffon's hand, cold and damp, still grasped mine. When we arrived at the breakfast room, that intimate wood-panelled salon which presented the illusion of bourgeois simplicity to which Orléans so aspired, we found the gentlemen already at their meal. The English, who had no true understanding of the manners of Frenchmen, stood and made their greetings to us. Orléans preferred to remain seated, lounging with as much indifference as a fat caliph at his court. However, upon spying us, he swiftly rubbed a look of polite pleasure across his sober countenance.

No one in that room sat with as much awkwardness as did

the immaculately attired Mr Kerly and Mr Boyd in their buff and yellow coats, their hair perfectly frizzed for the occasion. The former clutched the rim of his small dish of coffee as if his fingers had cramped upon it, while the latter picked at a single roll upon his plate. Not a soul at that table could ignore the events of that terrible day, and yet we set about enacting that charade. This was rendered especially difficult in the face of the chanting and singing from passage de Valois below, which swelled and died away in waves. The bankers shifted anxiously in their chairs as the bloody lyrics filled the pauses in our conversation.

> 'Ah! ça ira, ça ira, ça ira
> Aristocrats to the lamp-post!
> Ah! ça ira, ça ira, ça ira
> The aristocrats, we will hang them!
> If we do not hang them, we will break them
> If we do not break them, we will burn them . . .'

We listened, but did not remark. Why, it was as if we sat amicably in a box at the play while the performance continued below.

'I recall very well, monseigneur, that fine mare we examined at your stables last winter. She ran like no other I have had the pleasure of observing,' began Mr Kerly from between his set teeth.

'Calliope, I believe she was called,' interjected Mr Boyd.

'Yes, Calliope,' his associate continued. 'Have you bred her, monseigneur?'

'I regret to say that she has been sold, along with most of the beasts in my stables at Raincy, messieurs,' Orléans answered tersely.

Gradually, the noise from outside the windows began to increase in volume. It seemed as if further voices had been added to this angry choir. Jeers and cries of '*Vive la nation*' battled with the dissonant strains of song. I could sense from Orléans's tight expression that he was growing ever more agitated.

'Orléans!' came a shout from below. 'Orléans!' called out another.

'Monsieur d'Orléans has not been to Raincy since the spring, since the war was declared. It is best that he remains in Paris, here at the Palais-Royal, at the centre of life,' offered La Buffon graciously. A faint flicker of appreciation crossed Orléans's mouth as their eyes met.

'Orléans! Orléans! Orléans!' The cries came steadily. 'Orléans! Orléans! Orléans!' The chorus rose, now filling the room.

He remained rigid in his seat. The entire table had fallen silent.

'Come to your window! Come to your window, Prince of the Blood! We have brought you a prize! We have brought you a prize from La Force! Come give the Princess a kiss!' they cried.

Every gaze was upon him. Not a breath was drawn by any person in that room.

'My apologies,' said he, eventually rising to his feet.

The company clumsily followed suit, anxiously pushing back their chairs. Then, cautiously, Orléans proceeded to the window. Unable to contain their curiosity, both Kerly and Boyd joined him there.

I, on the other hand, found myself unable to move. Dread fixed me firmly in place. I did not wish to set my eyes upon that macabre spectacle which I guessed he might glimpse floating amongst the crowd. Instead, I found myself transfixed by the cast of the Duke's face. It was utterly flat and calm; I followed it while he moved aside the drapery. I waited for him to discover what I was certain lay beyond the window. My heart drummed furiously in my ears. I waited. I waited. And then his face dropped with the sudden heaviness of a stone.

'*Mon Dieu*,' he muttered. '*Oh, mon Dieu. Mon Dieu.*'

The gentlemen beside him seemed frozen in place, too mesmerized by that which they beheld to move or even to gasp.

'What has happened? What has occurred?' La Buffon cried out. A bright flush had begun to spread from her panting breast along her neck. 'Messieurs! What is it you see?'

It was at that instant that Orléans chose to open the windows on to a small balcony over the passage de Valois. A vast cheer blew in like a rush of wind. '*Vive la nation! Vive la nation!*' he called out to them, raising his arms like a musical conductor. His face bore the same mask he had applied when greeting us: his eyes were entirely void of life, while his mouth wore a victorious smile.

I had been so consumed in my study of Orléans that I had failed to notice my friend beside me, boiling herself into a stew of impatience.

'Monsieur!' She beckoned to him, but he did not respond. She heaved herself from the table and made her way towards Orléans with angry determination.

'No, madame!' he ordered her, putting out his hand. But La Buffon was not one suited to taking commands.

'Madame!' I called out as if I might stop her where her beloved Orléans had failed. But I fear it was then far too late.

Her cries brought the entire household to her side. They were of a sort I had never before known: echoing forth as if they emanated from the pages of Mrs Radcliffe's dark tales; as if they were issued from some dungeon, from a lunatic in chains. The horror of it – why, it seemed almost indecorous to gaze upon her while in the grip of this hysteria.

Orléans rushed to support her, and then Messrs Boyd and Kerly. There was such shouting and commotion. Two footmen and Romain came up behind them and struggled to place her back upon a chair. The table, gentlemen and servants barred my path to her and so I pressed in towards her, moving towards the windows. That is when I looked.

I cannot say why. Some animal passion drove me to it, perhaps. Some prurient curiosity, some part of me that wished to know the demon in human nature and to see its face drawn plain.

It was a head, but one so bloodied, so rolled in filth, that it was scarcely recognizable as such but for its long red curls. It had been stuck on a pike like a lump of bread upon a toasting fork. Behind it, at some distance, came the remainder of the person; the body, stripped naked in the most indecent manner conceivable. Several men alternately held it aloft or dragged it along the cobbles, its bowels left to trail behind it on the street like a tangle of wet, grey ribbons.

I returned my attention to La Buffon, who now held out her hand for me to take. She sobbed without end, her face as red as a cherry. I expect that mine was as white as snow.

'It is Madame de Lamballe! Oh, *mon Dieu*! That will be my head there one day!' she wailed. I attempted to hush her, but she could not be consoled. Her eyes began to flutter before she slumped motionless in her chair.

Orléans cried out to Romain, 'Fetch Seiffert! Where is the physician? Bring him immediately!' One of the footmen went running for hartshorn and salts, the other to locate Rosalie.

'Madame? Madame,' I called to her, tapping at her cheeks in an effort to revive her. 'Agnès, please, Agnès . . .'

All at once she gasped and opened her eyes wide. Two blue stones blinked at me.

'Agnès,' I breathed. For a moment, her countenance appeared calm, as if the storm had passed. I beamed at her and touched her damp, cold face, but as I did so her features contracted and she let out a sudden roar of pain. She clutched at her belly and then at her back.

'The child . . .' she breathed, desperately attempting to speak. She reached up for Orléans's arm. 'Oh, Philippe, it is too soon!' she cried. 'It is too soon!' Then she groaned in pain.

By then the breakfast room was crowded with servants. Near to fifteen sets of eyes looked on, awaiting Orléans's command. He appeared stricken, almost dumbfounded. 'Put her to bed! Now!' he barked suddenly, before muttering, 'Oh, dear God, what has this come to?'

I do not believe anyone heard him, but for me. I looked up to see his bright gem-like eyes full of trepidation.

'Henriette,' he said, almost inaudibly, and rested his hand upon my shoulder.

As we looked on, three footmen slowly raised the breakfast chair in which she languished and spirited her as hastily as they could manage through antechambers and drawing rooms and salons to her apartments. A great flustered procession of Orléans's household followed closely behind. Once through the doors of her rooms we were met by a winded Monsieur Seiffert, who assisted in laying his patient upon the bed. Orléans lingered at the edge of the bedchamber, shifting his weight from foot to foot, folding his arms and then pacing about, while servants spun around like wasps, circling the bed, moving in and out of the room. They came with bowls and water and wadding for the childbed. I attempted to go to La Buffon in the midst of this confusion, but found myself shunted away by Rosalie, who tutted and fretted as she tended to her mistress, waving her arms about and pecking hen-like at anyone who ventured too near. I found myself pushed backward into the tangle of spectators, and then into a corner beside a window.

My heart ached for my friend, for no one had suffered as had she. To have so nearly reached her natural time of lying-in, only to find herself tripped by the tips of Fortuna's wings was cruel.

Indeed, from all I had learned of late, it struck me that the goddess's favourite trick was to inspire hope before snatching it away. How furious I became at this, at the whimsy of life. I uttered a silent prayer. I willed that this infant should be spared and Madame might live to see it thrive. I shut my eyes as I did so, for the noise and disorder inside seemed to twist seamlessly into the commotion beyond the Petits Appartements. Upon completing my private communion, I turned contemplatively to the window.

My eyes did not fall upon anything at first. I swept a weary gaze across the figures gathering in the gardens and colonnades, before it stuck fast. I spied something. I drew in my breath. I placed my hand against the glass in shock.

It was Allenham.

I had seen him cross the garden, a man in a sage-coloured coat who moved with an unmistakable bearing. He had ventured slowly through a crowd of the curious towards the archway that led to the passage de Valois. However, it was only once he had stopped to gawp in horror at the spectacle before him that I knew for certain. He had removed his round black hat and revealed a countenance whose features I recognized even at a distance.

So consumed had I been in cursing Fortuna that I had nearly missed her pass before my nose. I did not hesitate for one moment, but dashed from the room. I heard Orléans exclaim in surprise, but I did not pause, I did not wait or alter my course, for I understood too well what would be the price of that. My feet fairly tripped across the floor, skidding and sailing upon my silk slippers. I gathered my skirts into my arms and flew down several sets of stairs which led to the passage de Valois. Out into the street I spilled, startling the porters who stood at the entry to the Petits Appartements.

The road was a sea of heads and shoulders, afloat with weathered *bonnets rouges* and linen caps, tricorns and straw hats adorned with rosettes. Pikes and swords tinted brown with drying blood bobbed through the mass. Several women in tricolour sashes linked arms and danced the Carmagnole as they continued up the passage de Valois, towards the colonnades. I stood upon my toes and attempted to see above the throng, but failed to catch sight of him. It was then, no more than several feet from me, they raised it, the great distorted head of Madame de Lamballe, like a flag upon a mast. The mouth hung slack, void of a tongue, and where the pretty light lashes had once framed her eyes there was to be seen nothing but two red-crusted hollows. The horror of it. I could scarcely mask my revulsion, not only on account of the atrocity which it represented, but because it stank of death.

'That is an abomination!' shot the voice of a man behind me. I turned abruptly to see who would dare utter such a thing. Two young men, finely clothed, their arms folded across their chests, looked on in disgust.

'You will rot in hell for this! You think a nation will be born from murdering innocents and women?' echoed his companion.

I felt a bristle of indignation roll through the crowd. A few halted their progress. Sensing danger, I hastily attempted to re-move myself from this group and swim forward through the morass, searching all the while. I turned frantically this way and that. Then, for an instant, I believed I had caught sight of him: his dark head appeared briefly above a wave. My heart leaped as I squeezed myself between a father and his young son.

'We should have your head upon there instead, aristocrat!' came a shout from behind me.

'That will be your head, traitor!' cried a second man, whose bloodied coat sleeve dragged against mine.

With fear swelling within me, I pushed away, but the crowd surged towards me. In an act of desperation I shouted out over their heads, 'Allenham!' I cupped my hands about my mouth: 'George Allenham! My Lord Allenham!'

Then something quite miraculous occurred. Almost as if it had been decreed by Fortuna herself, the sea before me parted.

At the end of this channel, he stood. Although his back was turned, I knew it to be him. I was as certain of it as I was of my own name.

'Allenham!' I cried again, his name flowing from me on an ebullient stream of incredulous laughter.

I observed him stop and make what seemed a cautious move of his head. I watched him slowly bring his gaze in the direction of my calls; those sharp eyes of aquamarine lifted and looked.

His expression was blank. He regarded me for no more than an instant, as if he had heard a strange sound but saw nothing more than a shadow.

'Allenham!' I cried once more, uncertain if he had spied me at all. But that was impossible, I reasoned, for he had stared directly at my face. I took several strides towards him, when, quite unexpectedly, he turned his shoulder to me and moved into the crowd. I could scarcely believe it. I might have stood there in shock for some time had I not felt myself suddenly shoved. A large brutish man shaped like a sack of corn pushed his chest into me.

'Eh! Royalists! I shall cut out your hearts and roast them before this day is through!' He jammed his finger in the direction of the two dissenting gentlemen. I had believed they were across the road, but started to find that in fact one of them stood beside me.

The well-attired man raised a disparaging eyebrow at his assailant.

'This is what I make of your Revolution,' he sneered and then, quite without warning, spat in the face of the beast against me.

It occurred with such swiftness that to this day I cannot recall all that came to pass, or in what order. I remember only that a war cry, a yelp of fury, went up from the ox-like creature at my side. There was a flash of a filthy reddish blade and screams and exclamations and curses. I attempted to recoil, but the crowd seemed to fold in on me. A stone was hurled and then another, which landed near my foot. I was tumbled and crushed. A knee collided with my thigh, an elbow came down upon my nose and then I felt the knife pierce my flesh in one swift motion along my arm. I cried out in agony and holy terror, certain that I was about to meet my death. I turned my eyes heavenward to find not deliverance falling from the sky, but rather a vast grey lump of stone. That was the last I saw of daylight. The rest was black.

Chapter 20

The pain was like nothing I have ever known. It thundered forth from my head and down my arm to the very tip of my hand. I was cognizant of no sensations beyond it. It was as if my entire skull had been split wide-open like a walnut. I could not open my eyes. I could not even determine if I was possessed of eyes. There was only agony. I tried them, but some dried matter kept them sealed. I recall moaning, and then, once I had discovered my mouth, howling. That was when my lids loosened, when the blood that had stuck them fast gave way.

Four, perhaps five figures loomed over me in the haze. One I came to recognize as Monsieur Seiffert, his brow furrowed anxiously, his eyes travelling swiftly between my face and my arm and back again. I moved my gaze to where his fell. There seemed some misshapen piece of meat beside me; some lump from a butcher's block, white and blue and leaking blood. Standing over it was a younger man in an apron streaked with scarlet, making nimble work with a needle and thread. I watched through dull, pounding eyes. How curious, thought I. How absurd to see a gentleman sew. He stuck the pointed end into the loin and then brought it out again. He sews meat, I recall thinking.

'Monsieur Seiffert,' he said. 'Would you assist me in holding the wound together?' I observed the physician place his hands on either side of this small joint and push. That was when I screamed. I screamed until the blackness came again.

I am afraid I retain no memory of the events which followed. I can say only that I remember finding Seiffert before me once more. He peered at me quizzically, his small, triangular nose and long, angled eyebrows bestowing on him the look of an owl. He widened my eyes between his two fingers and seemed to search for something within them.

'You have taken a blow to the head, mademoiselle,' he explained in his German-accented French. 'Your shoulder and arm have been punctured and cut by a knife. The wound is deep but the surgeon has stitched it shut. I believe you will live, though the crowd would have trampled you had you not been pulled from beneath their heels.'

I attempted to speak, but could only moan.

'You have narrowly escaped death, mademoiselle. Three others were not as fortunate as you.' There was a note of chastisement in his tone.

'Madame?' I muttered feebly.

'She is still in labour. I must return to her. She has called for you but I have told her you have met with an accident.' He paused. 'You should not have been upon the street, Mademoiselle Lightfoot. Monsieur d'Orléans cannot imagine what lunacy possessed you.'

I shut my eyes. I felt some cold poultice drying in my hair. My arm was tightly bound.

'Here,' said Seiffert, raising me. Lucy pressed a glass to my lips. 'It is laudanum.'

I recall no more than its warm, honeyed sensation in my throat before I sank into a lengthy spell of heaviness and dreams.

Banners of red billowed in my visions, wafting above fountains which ran with blood. The head of a Medusa with long skeins of hair floated at the base of one. I could smell sage. There were hedges of green, twisted bracken which tore at my arms as I struggled in search of someone. There were cries of the tortured. Briefly I believed that I had awakened and some angel brushed the hair from my forehead, but when I glanced downward, I spied two horned demons twisting my skirts about my waist. They turned and tightened them, compressing my hips together until I begged for mercy. At some point in the midst of this ordeal I grew aware of Lucy raising me in the bed. I was entirely unaware of the hour or the day and was somewhat startled to see daylight as I fluttered my eyes.

'I have not been murdered,' was all I could think to say to my maid. My tongue was so dry I could scarcely move it. She smiled at me, undoubtedly thinking my words to be mere laudanum-laced ramblings.

'No, madam,' said she, sliding something from between my legs before pausing to touch my forehead. 'You are powerful warm.'

I felt heavy, as if my limbs had been built of brick. The pain from my head had seemed to travel into my belly and down through my arm, which now throbbed and stung. I looked at her from slow, stunned eyes.

'It has come away, madam,' she whispered to me as she pulled the fresh bedding around me.

'What has?' I uttered through my parched lips.

'That . . . that which had begun to grow inside of you, madam,' she ventured, uncertain if I had ever been aware of my condition. 'It has come away of its own. On account of the fright you had and the injury, I expect,' she said softly.

Then I remembered. Remarkably, the urgency of that problem had all but vanished from my mind in the face of the shock and the discomfort I had undergone. I breathed a sort of sigh.

'I have dispatched the sheets and the soiled linens, so you need not fear . . .'

Lucy was a skilled nurse, and settled herself beside me before angling me forward to feed me a restorative broth and milk and bread.

'You are powerful hot,' she repeated as she laid me down again, her brow rumpled with concern.

I fell into a deep sleep from which I was later roused by the appearance of Seiffert, who jabbed at my swollen arm until I groaned with pain. There was much head-shaking, and binding and rebinding of the wound. A vein upon my other arm was opened, till I felt my strength, what little of it remained, emptied ounce by ounce into the porcelain dish. Scarcely able to move, I sensed Lucy press a cup to my lips several times. I knew from its sweet taste what relief the heady opiate would bring – relief, but no cure. Indeed, I was far from recovered. What trials and suffering I had endured until that point were mere trifles by comparison to the ordeal upon which I next embarked. My limbs were taken with the most violent shaking and tremors. My extremities contracted, my fingers balled into fists, my toes cramped and bent, even my jaw constricted so that I could scarcely drink or eat. My back arched and I writhed as if the devil had strung me up and danced me as his puppet. I could do nothing about it. I could make no utterances other than moans of anguish, for the tightening and flailing and throwing myself in fits was as excruciating as it was terrifying. Lucy and Monsieur Seiffert, along with several maids, took their turn at my sickbed, holding me down as I quaked. I was lowered into warm baths and cold. Camphor was applied to my trembling arms and legs and I was doused with opium, until I lay still and pliable and water, cordial and broth could be dribbled down my throat.

I do not believe I have ever approached so near to death as I did in those weeks. My maid's face confirmed this to me, for while I spasmed and sweated, her round eyes would fix upon me as if she were speaking her farewells. I existed only for the sound of the spoon tinkling in the glass and the respite it brought. Eventually, however, the heavy thumping of my pulse subsided and my fever burned away. I slept for what seemed months.

When at last I awakened, I was told that I had suffered from opisthotonus, brought on by tetanus. Indeed, my sufferings were such that Seiffert had believed I was not long for this earth.

'I own, mademoiselle, I am most astonished by your recovery, though it will require some time yet before you are entirely restored to health,' he confided. It cost me a great effort even to hear him, but I listened and took each of his words in slowly, as I had my teaspoons of nourishment. I attempted to recall those incidents that had transpired prior to my misfortune. I reached through the haze.

'Madame de Buffon?' I enquired. 'Has . . . has she delivered safely?'

'Yes.' The physician nodded. 'Some time ago, near to a month, now. She has been brought to bed of a boy. It was a difficult labour, but she has recovered. The infant is small, but well.'

'I pray to God that he will thrive.'

'I shall inform her of your sentiments,' he replied, smiling gently.

It had been some time since I had spoken with any person in Monsieur d'Orléans's household beyond Seiffert and those maids who had ministered to me. Although my illness had ravaged me and rendered me as limp and thin as a candlewick, I longed very much for company. Monsieur Seiffert had prohibited La Buffon from nursing me for fear that she might communicate some disease to her child. He advised against her visiting me until I presented at least a semblance of health. However, this did not prevent me from receiving others.

Orléans appeared at my bedside regularly and displayed such proofs of tenderness and concern that whatever doubts I had possessed in the past about the sincerity of his character were soon dispelled. He kissed me upon the brow as if I were a sickly relation and hung about my thin, pale neck a pendant of emeralds. He delivered to me books in my native tongue: Mr Boswell's *Life of Samuel Johnson* and a novel by Mrs Smith, which he instructed Monsieur Barrois, young Beaujolais's tutor, and the boy, to read to me. These two unlikely well-wishers came frequently to my bedchamber and from them I discovered a great many things. Barrois described in some detail those terrible events which had transpired in the prisons, how the people had broken their way inside and slaughtered thousands. I listened with awful disbelief at what he recounted to me: how parents were murdered before their children; how bodies were dismembered and paraded about the city for days on end. They had piled the corpses outside the prisons, where the sun heated them and created an intolerable stink. When he concluded his account, I lay in a state of shock. I could not conceive of how such things could have occurred in the name of revolution and told him as much.

'Ah, mademoiselle, revolutions are dreadful for those who live through them, but their benefits are immeasurable for future generations. It is those to whom we must turn our minds, rather than the unfortunate dead who dwelt in a world of the past.'

'I cannot imagine that any good should come from such wicked deeds,' I protested.

Barrois moved awkwardly in his seat, as if uncertain how to contend with such royalist sentiments. 'One may be inclined to conclude this in the face of the disaster, mademoiselle, but I would have you consider what has also come to pass. A National

Convention has been elected by all Frenchmen over the age of twenty-five. All men have been granted the right to vote. Is that not remarkable? The members have abolished monarchy from France. We are a true republic. Is that not worth the sacrifice of some? To bring liberty for all?'

In truth, I did not believe these principles so abhorrent, but I wondered at the price of them; however, I chose to say not a word to the contrary. To be sure, a good deal had transpired in the world as I had languished in death's parlour and much of it did not strike me as especially fortuitous.

'Papa has a seat in the new Convention,' interjected Beaujolais, who sat like a fully fledged gentleman in his white breeches and royal blue coat. A large, proud rosette bloomed from his lapel.

'But not as Monsieur d'Orléans,' corrected Barrois, with a gently piqued brow. 'The members have chosen for him a name less . . . obnoxious to the sensibilities of the nation. He is now to be known as Philippe Égalité.'

'I am Monsieur Beaujolais Égalité,' chimed the boy.

'The others . . . Monsieur de Chartres has become General Égalité . . . and Montpensier—'

'—is Monsieur Montpensier Égalité,' added Beaujolais. 'And Mademoiselle Lightfoot, it is my duty to inform you that you no longer inhabit the Palais-Royal.'

I cocked my head teasingly at him.

'This is the Maison Égalité,' he announced. 'The gardens are now Les Jardins de la Révolution.'

I was quite taken aback. I could not conceive that Monsieur d'Orléans would consent to such measures. To suffer the name Bourbon to be all but rubbed from his history would have rankled with his pride, for certain. Philippe Égalité, thought I. Why, it has the sound of a character in a comic opera. I might have laughed aloud at this absurdity, had I not thought I would give offence. To be sure, the expressions of my visitors showed no levity whatsoever. Whatever the nature of Orléans's true thoughts upon the matter, he knew better than to protest. Everyone about him from his friends to his household was fiercely Jacobin and I soon reminded myself by whose sufferance I remained there.

It is a curious thing to be an invalid. It has never suited me to be indisposed for great lengths of time. I have always despised a complete dependency upon the kindness of servants or the condescension of friends. During the time of my convalescence, I could scarcely hold a pen or sit upright in a chair. It was some many weeks before I could walk of my own accord. I lay abed every day, apart from those times when I was carried to a sofa, or a bath, and then returned again. As you might imagine, I passed many hours of solitude with nothing for company but the sounds within my head and, to be sure, the noise there grew more irksome by the day. There was one matter which vexed me more than anything else and it blared like a trumpet between my ears: the memory of my encounter with Lord Allenham.

I ruminated over every moment of that incident. I studied each of his movements. I examined the vacant expression upon his face when he caught sight of me and I shuddered again and again to watch him turn his back. The misery these remembrances precipitated is almost inexpressible here. I shed a good many tears in contemplating them, but once my sorrow was spent, it gave way to something else entirely.

At first it was a sense of confusion. No matter how I studied these events, they failed to join together into anything rational. I meditated upon the circumstances of our parting and I recounted each of his pledges of love. In the light of his actions these now appeared remarkably flimsy. I wondered if he had witnessed my injury or knew of my suffering. Why, when he heard the cries and shouts of the riot, did love not compel him back to the spot where he had last seen me so as to ensure my safety? Indeed, had he spied me lying prone upon the street would he not have rushed to my aid? Yet, if he had assisted me, surely I would have awoken in his arms rather than in the Petits Appartements? The more I permitted my mind to stray along this path, the more crooked and bleak it became.

It required but a few days of reflection for confusion to ripen into anger and anger to darken into remorse. Was it this that Mrs Elliott had wished me to see? She had been too kind, too gentle to assail me with the truth. She understood that my weak and foolish heart had not yet acquired the ability to apprehend it, and yet there, in my invalid's bed, I embraced it entirely: Allenham had abandoned me. I had been ruthlessly deceived by a man who cared no more for me than a pair of worn-through shoes. Was this not the very fact of the matter?

To think that I had chosen to remain in this place of bloodshed and war in the hope that we should be reunited, that he would return to me. Why, I no more belonged here than I did in the Palace of Troy! My head raged and ranted. What a fool was I! And to consider how Mrs Elliot had attempted to alert me to my own errors, how she had sought to disabuse me of my romantic notions, and how I had struggled against her. Why, I felt blessed for such guidance. Had she and my many other friends in London not cautioned me against loving a man so entirely? For in such absolute affection the heart may be ruined. That which held true above all other things was the friendship of women, and only that. How correct they had been. I should never be so ridiculous as to ignore this truth again, and how I wept at its recognition.

It was as I laboured under the heavy weight of my depressed spirits that La Buffon at last made her appearance at my bedside. She came to me, overcome with emotion, enacting all the histrionics of the playhouse. How she sobbed at sighting me, exclaiming in horror over my wan features and dull eyes. She took both of my hands and kissed them before doing the same to my cheeks.

'Oh, *ma chère* Henriette,' she cried, 'I prayed for you every hour! I could not bear to think of your agony, or that I could not serve you in your hour of need! Why, Monsieur Seiffert scolded me that I should have even considered it. They believed you would not survive and . . . I . . . could not endure the idea of losing you!' she bleated with streaming eyes.

I regarded her standing before me with not an ounce of artifice about her, her cheeks streaked with tears. There was something so gentle and honest in her demeanour, in her unpainted face and plain yellow muslin gown, that I was moved greatly. Here was a true friend, I thought, and I could not begin to express how pleased I was to greet her again. It brought a smile to my cheeks for the first time in many weeks.

Madame threw herself into the chair beside my bed and eagerly took my hand into hers. She held it firmly, pressing my thin bones into her soft palm. She said nothing, but sniffled and stared across the room for a moment, before the door opened. Through it came a nurse bearing a tiny infant in a white gown. Its mother eagerly reached out her arms, beckoning for the servant to fill them with the gurgling bundle. I observed her face brighten with love. It was a sentiment I had once known well when I had cradled my own little Georgie to me.

'He is called Victor Leclerc de Buffon,' said she, bouncing him lightly against her. 'He must have my husband's odious name, but only for propriety's sake, and only until . . . You have been told, have you not?' She turned her eyes to me. There was a twinkle of delight there.

'Told of what, Agnès?'

'The Convention has made divorce legal. There will be divorce in France, is it not extraordinary? Of course, Orléans must continue to return his wife's dowry and then . . . after a spell, I imagine we shall be free to marry. It is *everything* I have hoped for, Henriette.' She beamed. 'Then Victor will be recognized. A legitimate heir. Here,' said she, 'you must hold him, Henriette.' My friend offered her child to me, and I warmly welcomed him into my arms. He gave a yawn and then gazed at me with his glassy dark blue eyes. At that moment my heart yearned for my own infant, the boy whom I had not pressed to my breast in two years. I did not wish to ruin our happy moment by giving in to sorrow and so hastily turned my gaze to his mother. Agnès de Buffon returned my contented look with an expression of what I could only describe as adoration.

'You must know, you are my truest friend, Henriette. I had no sisters when I was a child. My brothers and mother died when I was young. Most of my girlhood was passed in a convent, which I loathed. I had some friends there, but never did I feel any true attachment to them,' she mused. 'It was not until after my marriage that I came to enjoy the society of women. Apart from you, I have possessed only one other cherished friend in the past. I do not doubt you have learned all about the scandal. Madame Meyler?'

At the mention of that lady's name, I froze. I was uncertain what response to make, but tried a nod.

'I am certain what you have heard are falsehoods. My life has been vexed by rumours. I have often said to you that the world looks for reasons to disdain me and so they will invent anything to please themselves. It is unfortunate that Madame Meyler fell from her horse when she was with child, but that was nothing to do with me. And I dare say you have heard it was Orléans's infant that she carried at the time?'

I looked away shamefacedly as she said that. I could not respond.

'That is what they all said, but I know for certain it was not Orléans's, rather, it was Monsieur de Lauzan's. They were much in love and I was privy to all their confidences. Jealousy played no role in it whatsoever. No, Henriette, the reason I ended my association with her was because she was a spy. She was dishonest, unfaithful and mendacious. No one had been dearer to me than her. I trusted her with my secrets and she betrayed me. This is what comes of too great a fondness for cards, eh?'

I did not follow her tale.

'Cards?' I enquired. This I had never heard mentioned before.

'Yes. She was grievously in debt,' La Buffon affirmed with vehemence. 'The former Duc de Penthièvre, Madame d'Orléans's father, wished to know the intimacies of my relations with his son-in-law and so offered Madame Meyler a considerable sum to purloin my correspondence. It was then circulated and all the *beau monde*, the court, all of Paris, they have made good sport from reading it and ridiculing me for years. All that I wrote in confidence has been devoured by those ladies and gentlemen I derided – for who does not write their opinions of others freely in their private letters?' she exclaimed, mildly outraged. 'I lost half my acquaintance when Monsieur de Buffon procured a separation from me, and the other half by this cruel trick. All that is said of me is unjust. They call me viperous, a cold-hearted snake, a murderess! Imagine!' La Buffon snorted. 'But Madame Meyler has suffered too, for which I *am* pleased. She has gambled away all that she received for her foul deeds and now lives in penury. She is no more tolerated or received than am I.'

When Madame concluded her tale, she sat with her arms folded. I could not take my eyes from her. I was in a state of astonishment. To be sure, it all made perfect sense. Of course I had never once questioned the gossip I had consumed. I had never considered that the stories Madame de Flaghac, Madame Laurent and Mrs Elliot had repeated were anything but the truth. But therein lies the true danger of listening to scandal, my friends. There is always another telling of the tale, and that is the version which most often goes unheard.

Madame de Buffon's account of events made more sense to me than any of the others. I had come to know her well enough to understand her true nature. The vicious creature I failed to glimpse in her never appeared because, quite simply, she did not exist. It caused me no end of shame to count the days I had spent in dread of her violence, fearing that I should be struck down by her lightning bolts of wrath. How cruel the world had been to her, and to believe I had played some role in that saddened me.

'Do you not think his eyes resemble those of his father?' she enquired, leaning in to gaze upon her child.

'Yes,' I agreed. 'He is possessed of his father's head as well.'

At that she laughed loudly and then sighed.

'The barriers are open once more. Tomorrow he is to be taken out to nurse at Raincy. I am forced to part with him, but only for a short while, I should hope. They cannot have Philippe Égalité's bastard and whore living in the Maison Égalité,' said she, now addressing her son. 'See, my child, this is what comes of arriving without warning and far too early. I might have been in the country were it not for the King and his obstinacy. But you will be well tended at Raincy, with many nursemaids to do your bidding, and where no one will know of your existence until the appropriate time arrives.' I saw the seeds of tears appear in her eyes once more. 'You will not have to wait long for that, *mon petit*. Maman promises you.'

I lifted Victor as best as my injured arm permitted and returned him to his devoted mother. As she accepted him, she looked down at me.

'Henriette, whatever possessed you to go on to the street that day?'

I paused, taken aback by her question. I had not considered what justification I would offer for my unaccountable actions.

'I . . . I believed I had seen him, Allenham, there amongst the crowds.'

My friend opened wide her eyes.

'And you went after him?'

'Yes.'

'And did you find him?' she fairly gasped.

'No,' I stated flatly. 'I had hoped too much. I fear that in the end it was no more than my imagination.' I shook my head. 'And what price I have paid for that mistake.'

Chapter 21

Reader, I dare say the scales have fallen from your eyes as swiftly as they had from mine. You have seen the truth as I viewed it from my invalid's bed and, having experienced such an epiphany, I understood that the course of my life must now be altered. If I was to forswear Allenham, so the entire axis of my existence must also shift. This great movement of the stars, this realignment of the planets caused all manner of disturbance in my heart and mind. With upheaval comes confusion and in the midst of it I was made to acknowledge another truth: I could no longer bear to live at the centre of deception. That I should betray the trust of Madame de Buffon had now become utterly repugnant to my sensibilities. The mere contemplation of my actions, the secret aide-memoire I had kept, the coded notes I had scrawled in there, the devious means I had employed to send Mrs Elliot my letters, and especially the delight I had once derived in making my reports to her, all disgusted me. Never had I believed myself capable of such treachery, such unspeakable ill-usage of a friend. Every day when La Buffon came to me, as she wrapped her arm about my waist to assist me to the window or the sofa, or later to the dining table, as she read to me from the pages of *Les Voyages de Madame Égalitine*, the novel she had written, or conversed with me about the debates at the National Convention, there was a part of me which recoiled at myself, at the thought of my deeds. I came to wish I had never agreed to Mrs Elliot's request. But you see, the recognition of my sentiments only resulted in a further predicament, for I could no longer conceive of how I might prove myself a devoted friend to both.

My accident and illness had caused me to all but give up my correspondence with the lady I had come to call my *chère maman*. Of course, this was not by calculation, but rather necessity. By the time I was again able to stand unassisted, the winter had plucked the trees free of their leaves. It required further weeks still before I was again able to hold a pen steadily in my hand. While this proved inconvenient, I confess it suited my inclinations perfectly, for the prospect of engaging in my former practice had become intolerable to me. Mrs Elliot remained a constant correspondent throughout my illness, though Lucy possessed the sense to conceal the packets amongst her own effects until my recovery. It was with some trepidation that I unfolded the first of these letters, which was by then more than two months old.

'Madam,' it began in its usual guise of Thérèse's handwriting.

I cannot convey to you the distress of your household in learning of your accident, which arrived today by *a messenger from the Palais-Royal*. I wept when he informed me of your grave state of health and more bitterly so that I had no means of assisting you in your distress. Upon receiving this news I made plans to return immediately to the rue de Miromesnil, where I currently reside. I have requested that the messenger, who you will be surprised and pleased to learn is none other than *Our Friend*, dispatch to me a regular account of your condition. He has promised to deliver this in person, whenever the occasion permits. Dear Madam, I shall make daily prayers for your recovery and think of nothing else until it is achieved.

Orléans had called upon Mrs Elliot. I straightened myself in my chair. I had hoped but not imagined that my entreaties to him would have yielded such success. Encouraged by what I had read, I hastened to open the next letter, which I discovered to be written in a curious fashion. There were but a few lines penned on an otherwise blank sheet.

Madam, today *the messenger* delivered the confirmation of your recovery for which we have long prayed. All the household sighed and wept to hear of it. That you shall not be taken from us is a blessing indeed, for which I sign myself ever grateful,
Thérèse Bertrand
P.S. Madam, I mean not to trouble you further, but with regard to the paper you bid me purchase, I would beg you to examine the watermark upon this sheet and instruct me as to the quantity you require of it.

I furrowed my brow and read the words once more. Most of Mrs Elliot's references were not so obscure as this one. Purchase of paper? I puzzled. I could not conjecture her meaning. Greatly bemused, I held the letter to a candle in search of its stamp. It was then I saw it.

As I held the paper near to the flame, I beheld no watermark upon it, but rather faint, browning sentences. As the heat took them they emerged through the grain. I could scarcely believe it, but as I moved the sheet about before the candle, an entire secret letter penned in an invisible ink materialized in my hands.

'My dear Henrietta,' the salutation burned itself upon the page:

Late events have now rendered it necessary for me to resort to a more clandestine method of correspondence. My home on the rue de Miromesnil is now subject to frequent searches by the guards who harass me with such regularity that when the barriers open, I intend to make for my house at Meudon once more.

O— now calls upon me regularly to ensure my well-being. Ma chère fille, it is to you that I owe this, for he has confided to me that it was you who altered his mind upon the matter. Although I have been unsuccessful in my attempts to disabuse him of his political convictions, I have been able to persuade him to restore my annuity and safeguard those assets which I possess in France, through the means of his banker in London. I cannot express to you the reassurance such a gesture confers upon me, and for this, my dear child, I am truly obliged to you. Now it only remains for me to offer you my most ardent prayers for your swift return to health and bid you not to neglect your correspondence with one who signs herself ever as your chère maman,

G.E.

What joy her lines inspired in me! How grateful was I to learn that all of my sacrifices, my efforts and suffering had not been in vain. To consider that I had been the author of my friend's turn of fortune inspired in me the greatest happiness I had known since arriving in Paris. I pressed the letter to my breast, wishing I might embrace Mrs Elliot in its place. However, as I did so, I was not so ignorant of those other sentiments rising within me. I felt myself to some degree discharged of my obligation and, as I had come to discover, there is nothing which so taxes the spirit as a sense of indebtedness to a friend.

There were further letters which I then proceeded to open. Each of them had been written as the last, containing a scribble from Thérèse on some household matter or other: a wax chandler's bill or Madame Vernet's toothache. Below that the sheet was blank. I held each to a candle and was as delighted as a child to observe the words bake brown upon it. She wrote:

Ma chère fille, my heart grows despondent at your silence. O— has sent me word of your improving health and I yearn to receive a note from you and learn of your news. I have quit Paris and am at my house in Meudon. I can only suppose my last letter or yours has gone astray.

And then in another:

I cannot think why you have not lifted your pen to write, dear Henrietta, to a woman who adores you as might a mother . . . My concerns for O— continue for I am given to understand from a gentleman of my acquaintance that he approaches ruin, that near everything of value in his possession has been sold or mortgaged. I hear that he has more than ever become the creature of those scoundrels in the Convention who intend to place the King on trial. Heaven preserve us from such an abomination. That O— should be forced to vote upon the fate of his cousin is a notion so insupportable that I can scarcely ponder it. I know him to be no champion of Monsieur Robespierre, but he will not speak a word against him, nor contradict the will of those blackguards who surround him. Now I read that Monsieur Marat has requested 30,000 louis from *Our Friend* to finance the aims of the Revolution. I pray to God he does not encourage the base designs of his vile companions from his own purse, for it seems he presents himself as a treasury to be pillaged by every rogue in France! Does Mme de B— confide in you upon such matters? Is it her persuasions which lie at the heart of his deeds? I understand her to be among the fiercest of Jacobins. I do not doubt her poison to be a potent one. Beware, ma chère fille. Your heart is such an open one that I fear you may expose it to her tricks and darts if you do not remain wary. Dear child, I implore you to respond to one who remains your chère maman . . .

No sooner had my heart rejoiced than it fell into despair once more. I sighed and examined my pen from across the room. It lay in its porcelain tray, as innocent as a knife before a murder. Slowly, I rose upon my weary limbs and then hesitated. I could not fathom what I should write to her, yet I understood I could not prevaricate without causing her greater agitation. I drew a long breath and then wrote a hasty scrawl begging her forgiveness. I gave a lengthy description of my sufferings and mentioned that Madame had been brought to bed of a boy, intelligence which I trusted Orléans had already delivered to her. I wrote nothing of politics, for in that December no one spoke of anything but the King's trial, the thought of which was so abhorrent that I wished to clap my hands upon my ears at its very mention. I sealed it and gave it to Lucy to send. In the days that followed, I was plagued by the thought of what I had written, or rather what I had omitted. I bit my lip as I imagined her reading down the single page and finding nothing there of interest to her. I dreaded the reply, yet I knew it would arrive, stinging with remonstrances and injury.

It did not come until the New Year, on the day the bells rang declaring 1793 as Year II of the Republic. I recall that week with much vividness, for in it I had taken my first strides across the frozen Jardins de la Révolution on strong legs. I had inhaled the crisp, sweet, smoke-laced air of winter without shortness of breath, nor the slightest touch of dizziness. I felt the thin light of January cross my cheek as if a gentle finger had stroked it. My health had returned to me by degrees, as slowly as my first steps. I had felt the steadiness return to my back and neck and the fullness to my face. Over the weeks I had learned to hold my paints and brushes again with ease. But as my youthful vigour was restored to me, so it brought with it a sense of uncertainty as to my future.

I did not belong in the Palais-Royal, nor did I wish to resume the role I had once filled in Orléans's life. I could not imagine how I should continue there, ever wearing two faces, one which I showed to La Buffon, whom I adored as I might have my own sister, and the other to Mrs Elliot, to whom I owed my life. The terrors of Paris had been made real to me and had succeeded in dousing the city in blood, so that one could admire nothing of it without recalling the sight of death or the scent of cannon fire, the cries of barbarism and the wails of injury. And Allenham, my dear Allenham, now lost to me. I would ever remember this place for its tragedies and great disappointments, and that in itself caused me to wish I might turn my back upon it, as he had upon me. Indeed, it occurred to me that I remained there on account of one person alone: Grace Elliot.

I did not appreciate this until I received her reply, the reply I had dreaded. I read it carefully and with much consideration.

Ma chère fille, you are so guarded in your letter to me that I cannot but conclude you have fallen prey to one of Mme de B—'s schemes, or are else unable to write freely of your thoughts. This latter problem may be remedied by making resort to the same precautions as have I, with regard to your ink. I shall have Thérèse send you a receipt for some immediately. I would strongly advise this, as the authorities at the post offices are now in the habit of opening letters, in particular those packets bearing the names of suspected royalists, which they know me to be. Although I have quit Paris for Meudon, my Jacobin neighbours are no less concerned with the nature of my politics than they were within the walls of the city. You might guess at the inconvenience and distress this causes me.

I would not like to conjecture that the brevity of your last letter is on account of the former reason. I would hope you have learned enough of the world to see through the artful deceits of those who can only pretend at friendship. Indeed, my heart would break to believe you have been so duped. But, my dear child, my intuition is that my anxieties in this respect are not founded ones and that I will hear from you directly upon all the usual matters, and you might then put your chère maman's troubled mind to rest.

I confess, the situation of the dear King vexes me most. I am of late given to thinking that I may not wish to continue in a nation whose politicians descend to the level of butchers. That they will find him guilty is a certainty and his death near guaranteed. But for some divine intercession from the heavens, I cannot see a conclusion to this tale which ends in any other fashion. O— has claimed he will abstain from casting his vote, but I have heard otherwise. I do not doubt the talk within the Petits Appartements is of nothing else and those he entertains there will offer further opinions. I cannot imagine Mme de B— permitting him to abstain. Does she make her thoughts known upon the matter?

My dear Hetty, I beseech you to disclose to me as much of this as you are able, for I should like to plan for the days and weeks ahead and make whatever preparations are necessary to ensure I am safe from harm. It falls to you, my cherished girl, to secure the happiness of your own chère maman,

    G.E.

Although many years have passed since I read that letter, and age has since dimmed my faculties, I recall perfectly the impression it left upon me. To my eyes, there was no ambiguity in her words: Mrs Elliot's intentions were to quit France. Her suggestion was like a seed laid into the ready-ploughed furrow of my mind. It took quite naturally and began to grow into something much larger.

I began to permit my fanciful brain to imagine a life entirely different from one which I had previously known. In this reverie, I returned to London with Mrs Elliot, who was to me as near as I could ever conceive a blood relation. If Orléans had made a provision for her – and for me as well – then we should never have cause to fear for our income. We might live tidily and quietly in some house in Marylebone or Paddington. With enough attention to economy, I might retire upon this annuity alone. I would never again be made to entertain the advances of a gentleman my heart did not desire. Perhaps, too, I might even prevail upon my former lover, St John, and be permitted to pay visits to Georgie. These thoughts gathered in my head, piece by piece, until they formed into a shape and then into a pleasing panorama. What happiness this would bring me. When once I could not see contentment without Allenham, now I understood that I might find a true home, a place of comfort with my *chère maman*.

I saw clearly what I must do. I would go to Mrs Elliot immediately, as soon as I was able, and plead my case to her. I would confess all. I would tell her that while her noble sacrifices had secured my duty and love, I no longer had it in my heart to practise such duplicity upon Madame de Buffon, who had also proven herself a gentle, generous friend. I would explain to her what I had learned of La Buffon, that she was no murderess, no scheming minx, but a lonesome, maligned creature, entirely unworthy of contempt. Why, thought I, Mrs Elliot is herself so good-natured that she is certain to take to heart my entreaty and see what anguish I suffer by prolonging this deception. I would then present to her my thoughts of a better life in London and beg that I should be permitted to accompany her on her return there. However, I knew these sentiments could not be conveyed so effectively in a letter as they might be in person. I understood as well that time was not in my favour and that I must go to her at Meudon immediately.

But to fulfil this task I required one thing of vital importance: a passport, and in those desperate months following the massacres, there were few items more elusive. Passports were as difficult to procure as hen's teeth and even once acquired they did not guarantee certain passage. I had heard terrible tales of guards at the barriers tearing apart wagons and carriages in search of counter-revolutionaries. I had been told that they had even rifled through the skirts of a high-born woman suspected of being royalist. They had nearly stripped her bare while laughing that they had seen many an aristocrat smuggled out between the legs of such harlots. Not a soul passed through the gates if they did not countenance it. Even the papers and visages of the most trusted Jacobins were subject to close enquiry.

I knew not how to obtain such papers, nor how I might do so without alerting the entire household, and Madame in particular, to my intentions. I began by discreetly approaching Monsieur Rotaux, who simply laughed at my enquiry.

'You wish me to issue a passport for you?' he cried. 'You believe I am some magician, mademoiselle? Why, even Monsieur Égalité has not it in his power to grant one! You must enquire amongst his friends – which is to say, his particular friends in the Convention.'

At the time, this caused me no end of despondency, as I could not possibly fathom how that task might be accomplished. I feared greatly that with each day that passed, so too diminished my opportunities to make my flight with Mrs Elliott. I was certain she was planning it, and no matter how closely I considered the words in her letter, I could not determine when she proposed it, or indeed how far she had succeeded with her preparations. I knew only that it was imperative that I acquire a passport and go to her, by any means permitting. In the end, desperation overcame me and I resolved to approach the one person from whom I had never before requested anything.

If ever I was moved to feel pity for Orléans it was in the early months of winter. In the short time during which I had been acquainted with him, I had seen him give in to occasional low spirits. The darkness would come and go like storm clouds, rolling across his expression for a day or so before clearing into something lighter. However, with the commencement of the King's trial in December a thick grey mist had settled upon him and demonstrated no signs of parting. To lift his mood, he took to attending the opera and theatre; indeed, his passion for it became a mania. He wished to go most every evening, for I believe, and La Buffon concurred, that he could not bear the emptiness of the Palais-Royal, for it reminded him that he had now acquired more enemies than he had friends and of those he trusted but a scant handful. More than any one person, it was General Biron who remained foremost among the true. It was on account of his reappearance in Paris before departing to join his regiment in Provence that Orléans insisted I accompany them to the opera for a performance of *Iphigénie*.

Friends, had you the opportunity to sit in any theatre in Paris in those days, your English senses would have been as assailed as were mine. I had been astonished to discover that while I lay in my sickbed, the daily rituals of life had undergone a transformation, the like of which I have never witnessed since. There was not a public space or centre of amusement untouched by expressions of patriotism and a fervent love of the Republic. The entire interior of every playhouse and opera was swathed in red, white and blue. Tricolour banners hung from each box, while the corners of the stage were decorated with vast busts representing Liberté, Égalité and Fraternité. This was, however, but the half of it. No evening of entertainment was complete without some elaborate homage enacted to the Republic. The spectacle was regularly performed in the interval between the end of the opera and the commencement of the ballet. The orchestra would swell into a rendition of the 'Marseillaise', while a great statue representing the nation, a beautiful Marianne with her spear in hand, sporting the *bonnet rouge* and bedecked in garlands, would be lowered upon the stage. Around her would gather a chorus of singers, covered in their tricolour ribbons, to sing verse upon verse of the anthem. This was a sober occasion. Salutes would be offered by the National Guard and the army, and not a single person who attended would dare remain seated or silent as the lyrics were cried out. On the first occasion I encountered this show, I found it so peculiar that I screwed up my face in bemusement. Madame de Buffon examined me from the corner of her eye like a censorious governess and, following that, I never once failed to sing as if my life depended upon it. For I soon came to understand that it did.

Upon that particular night, she was seated between me and Orléans. The chorus had just completed their final verse when she turned to me and pleaded a headache, before taking her leave. But for Biron, Beaujolais and Montpensier in front of us, this left me alone for the first occasion in several days with Orléans. I saw this opportunity for what it was and snatched at it. Discreetly, I moved to the seat nearest to him. Observing my approach, he wasted no time before leaning into my ear.

'Are you now restored to health, *mon petit oiseau*?'

I was not certain what further enquiry might be couched within that question.

'Yes, monseigneur, I believe my strength has returned.'

Orléans took that as a cue to lay his hand in my lap and stroke my thigh through my skirts.

'I should like to come to you tonight, if you will permit it.'

I swallowed. It had not been my intention to imply this, nor did I wish to resume this role. Now that Madame had been safely brought to bed and was past her period of lying-in I could not imagine she would countenance it.

'Monseigneur, if you will forgive me, I do not believe myself strong enough to bear that . . . Why, I fear it is sure to kill me . . . in my current weakened state.'

There was a hint of disappointment in his expression, and he gently removed his hand.

'But . . .' I began, seizing the opportunity, 'I should like, if you will allow, to make a request of you . . .'

Orléans raised an intrigued eyebrow.

'I wish to pay a call upon Mrs Elliot, in Meudon. It has been a great while since I have seen her. Madame de Buffon would not approve if she were to know . . . and for this short journey, as you well know, I require a passport.'

Orléans continued to regard me, his expression unaltered.

'And you would have me procure one for you?'

'If . . . I may beg one, monseigneur,' I replied, my eyes turned downward.

He let out a long sigh.

'You know I have it not in my power to grant such things. My influence is not . . . recognized for such matters.'

'But you are a friend to those who *do* have it within their authority.'

'I am,' he said with caution. He studied me for a spell through weary, sad eyes. For a moment, I feared he would have me barter for this privilege. I drew an anxious breath.

'I shall return to you,' I whispered, 'fully restored to health.'

At that he laughed, so loudly in fact that Biron, Beaujolais and Montpensier each turned their heads to look.

Orléans patted my knee lightly, with a jesting but reassuring hand. It was not the touch of a lover. Rather, it was a gesture exchanged between two intimate friends who understood what the future held, and that the day of their parting had arrived.

Chapter 22

It was on the following night, as Lucy was about to undress me, that there came a rap upon my dressing-room door. The instant I heard it I froze, for such a sound at that hour regularly signified but one thing: the appearance of Orléans. However, I was both relieved and surprised to find Romain standing before me. He paid me a bow.

'Monsieur Égalité has instructed me to present you with this,' said he, removing a letter from his waistcoat pocket and placing it in my hand.

'He has procured a passport!' I cried in astonishment.

'Yes, mademoiselle, for tomorrow morning.'

'Tomorrow?' I echoed. This was as sudden as it had been unexpected, but it presented me with an opportunity I could not well refuse. So long as I remained uncertain of Mrs Elliot's plans, I could not hazard delaying a single day more.

'You are fortunate that this opportunity has arisen at all, mademoiselle,' said he, lifting an eyebrow. 'It was only through happenstance that Monsieur Égalité encountered Monsieur Valentin at the Café de Chartres. In the course of conversation, this gentleman mentioned that he was to visit his sister in Sèvres the following day. Monsieur Valentin is master of the orchestra at the Théâtre de la République. Monsieur Égalité is greatly fond of him and had been a . . . particular acquaintance of his sister when she used to sing at the theatre. Valentin is very much in his debt.'

I curtseyed to Romain.

'I am most grateful to Monsieur Égalité.'

'Monsieur Valentin has agreed for you to accompany him and his daughters in his coach. He will escort you as far as Meudon. You must prepare for departure at nine o'clock.'

'Dear Romain—' I began to gush with gratitude, before he interrupted.

'Mademoiselle, permit me to say to you this: it is necessary at this time to take precautions with all things. It will behove you not to make any mention of your true destination, nor of the person whom you propose to visit. Monsieur Égalité informs me that Madame Elliot's sympathies are notorious in her district. Though there has been no proof of it, she has been rumoured to have given shelter to returned émigrés and counter-revolutionaries. Anyone who is found to be visiting her will come under equal suspicion. You are to travel as a guest of Monsieur Valentin, and he will describe you as such to the guards at the barriers and any soldiers with whom you may have the misfortune to meet. Do you take my meaning, mademoiselle?'

I nodded.

He studied me for a moment.

'Monsieur Égalité also bid me to remind you of the dangers upon the road. You have read of these barbarities? Anyone whom the soldiers or the people suspect of being a counter-revolutionary is likely to be robbed, beaten or murdered. These are not idle servants' tales, so take care not to dismiss them as such. The newspapers are filled with such stories as ladies forced to endure the ripping of earrings from their lobes and gentlemen suffering their fingers to be sliced from their hands for the rings upon them. Pay heed, mademoiselle, and travel safely. That is what Monsieur Égalité wishes most for you.'

As you might gather, I was exceedingly grateful to find that my request was to be fulfilled so instantly, but also somewhat disordered by the circumstances. You see, I had not yet decided how I was to put my proposed journey to Madame de Buffon. To make matters worse, the trial of the King at the National Convention was approaching its conclusion and the vote which would determine his fate was due to be called imminently. My friend had insisted that we attend the following day so as to hear the speeches. She had impressed upon me the importance of this, for she confessed that Orléans was 'labouring under the worst torments of his conscience and I must offer solace to him at such a time'.

I paced the cold, draught-swept room, fretfully knitting my fingers together as I contemplated how I might approach this unpleasant errand. It required very little time to conclude that it would be impossible for me to reveal the truth to her. I could not very well confess that the visit I proposed was in order to formulate plans for my departure from France, and certainly not upon the eve of such a critical event. La Buffon had been entirely distracted by this and by her fears that should Orléans abstain, he would send a message to all the nation that he was not the patriot he professed to be. I shrank at the thought of abandoning her at such a moment. I shuddered that I should be made to fib yet again. I shut my eyes. How might I remain true to one friend without being false to the other? Certainly, I consoled myself, after I had paid Mrs Elliot this call, I should never be forced to tell untruths or betray either of them again. I would be at liberty to make decisions in accordance with my heart's dictates, and was this not worth the spinning of one final lie, so that I might live in peace with myself thereafter?

I settled beside the low fire in my hearth and with my fur pulled about me began to construct this piece of fabrication. I would inform her that Mrs Elliot was unwell, gravely so. I would embellish this by claiming that she had called for me to come to her bedside and, as her relation, I could not deny such a request. Likewise, I would explain to La Buffon that as Mrs Elliot and I were of a different opinion on matters political, I would not entertain any talk of such affairs. Neither would I tolerate any abuse of Madame's name. This would be a time of forgiveness and farewells, for should it occur, I would not wish her to depart this world without having received these things from me.

Once I had tied all of my knots and fixed my tale, I examined it. This was a work of ugliness, to be sure. I knew I should loathe to feel it come out of my mouth. My hope was for a swift conclusion to our interview; that she would simply take the lie from me and embrace it. I prayed that she would not question it or remonstrate with me, for it was certain to prove excruciating. As the night was much advanced, I determined that I would put it to her the following morning, shortly before I took my leave.

I awoke to darkness. What morning light presented itself was screened by the frozen, dull mist of January. Not wishing to draw attention to my person, I determined that I would attire myself as modestly as possible for my journey. Lucy assisted me into a plain brown riding habit adorned with a tricolour rosette the size of a sunflower. I chose to sport nothing more upon my head than a plain dark blue hat, ornamented only with a silk band of red, white and blue. My maid dressed me in silence. I trembled, though the touch of her hands, tugging upon my sleeves and adjusting my skirts, offered me comfort. In truth, it was not the journey that caused me such agitation, but the knowledge that I must pass through La Buffon's gates before I took my leave. I informed Lucy that she might expect me that evening, or the following morning, if the weather turned. Then I steadied myself and made for Madame de Buffon's apartments.

As it was still early, I was uncertain if La Buffon had arisen. I approached her dressing room on light toes and then rapped upon the door so faintly that I feared I would not be heard. Within an instant, Rosalie opened it to me and revealed Madame standing at the centre of the room in her stays and underskirts. No sooner had I stepped inside than she pounced upon me.

'Orléans will cast his vote,' she announced with what appeared to be a triumphant, if not relieved smile.

I was taken aback by this.

'He laid bare to me the contents of his head last night and deliberated for many hours. His situation is a terrible one, to be sure, for all eyes will be upon him.'

'And what determination has he made? Pray, will he vote for his cousin's deliverance?' I ventured.

La Buffon lowered her head and shook it ruefully.

'Henriette, he cannot. The King is guilty of conspiring against his own nation, of inviting the Austrians and Prussians to do battle against his own subjects. If the King is sent into exile, he will gather further armies about him. Should these forces succeed, Orléans, his sons and all who have been friends to him will perish.'

'But certainly were he to abstain—'

'*Ma chère*, whether he absented himself from the vote or displayed any mercy whatsoever, it would appear the same to the people. They have begun to suspect his sympathies already, for he shares his blood with the King.' La Buffon slowly met my gaze. 'If Orléans does not vote for the King's death, he will be voting instead for his own . . . and for ours.'

I stood entirely still, as did she. I recalled Orléans's words to me, that he was never formed for politics. He no more enjoyed this sport than did a reluctant huntsman at the kill, but to be asked to deliver a fatal blow – why, this must have wrenched his heart into pieces. There is no knowledge more intolerable to the human condition than that one's own survival is determined by the condemnation of another.

'You must speak to no one on this matter, Henriette. No one is to know of it. Not even your maid.'

'No.' I shook my head vehemently, before remembering that which I had come to inform her. She would be certain to suspect me.

She then tipped her head to the side.

'You are dressed early, *ma petite*?'

'Yes . . . yes . . .' I stiffened. 'Dear Agnès, I fear you will not care much for what I am about to tell you.' I rattled out my words. 'I am afraid . . . I am afraid that Mrs Elliot . . . my relation, is . . . gravely ill at her house at Meudon. Yesterday I received a letter. She has summoned me to her—'

Madame began to wag her head at once.

'She has chosen this moment deliberately. It is a trick.'

'No, it is not, Agnès, it is true.'

'How can such a thing be true?' she said. 'She is artful and deceitful and dangerous! This is some trap for you . . . for Orléans . . .'

'She is ill, madame,' I insisted, my face contracting with the pain of speaking such lies, of feeling myself drawn more deeply into the wretchedness of my deception.

'I have confided in you!'

'I swear an oath upon my life, Agnès, that I shall breathe not a word to her upon the matter about which we have just spoken. I shall take it to my very grave. I love you as a sister and would never deceive . . .' With that, my words choked me and I sobbed as they stuck in my throat.

My friend simply stared at me in horror.

'Madame' – I attempted to command myself – 'I must see her. She is . . . dying. I swear to you, my sister, that it will be but a short visit.'

She narrowed her eyes.

'You cannot propose to go there at the present time, Henriette. Perhaps after the trial is concluded, after the sentence . . .'

I raised my wet eyes to her.

'The passport has been issued for today.'

'Today?' She regarded me with incredulity. 'Today? Why . . . How did you manage to come by a passport?'

'Orléans offered to assist me.' Of all the falsehoods I had fed to her, I knew that upon this one point I could not fib. There was no other person to whom I might have applied, and she would have concluded as much in an instant. I observed her lips part in astonishment and her round blue-grey eyes open wider still. Slowly, she raised her hand towards her mouth, but then stopped and instead laid it upon her heart.

'Why would he do such a thing?' she whispered. 'Why would he wish to send you to her, when he knows the perils? He promised me that he would never speak to her again, nor call upon her, and now, now he would put you in that place of danger?' Her gaze tightened upon me and as it did, tears began to form. 'Why has he not informed me of this? Do you not understand, Henriette? She is a royalist, an aristocrat! Her friends despise Orléans; they despise me. They would have us on trial rather than the King.' She frowned and vigorously shook her head. 'No, you cannot go to her. I will not countenance it!'

I own that from the very first instance that Agnès de Buffon had called me friend, I had come to dread this day. My heart had hoped it would never come to pass, but it was inevitable, was it not? In the end, it was certain that I would be made to choose between them.

I was never so deluded as to suppose that my residence at the Palais-Royal was anything more than a temporary situation, but my friendship with this most cherished of kindred spirits I had believed unyielding and eternal. That such affection had managed to blossom was a thing both remarkable and delightful to me, but I understood as well what it would mean for my association with Mrs Elliot. She was the one to whom I owed everything. She, like me, was a stranger in this land, a fellow countrywoman who would one day wish to return to the shores of her birth, as would I.

I pressed my lips together so as to prevent my chin from quivering. The tears left straight, wet trails down my cheeks.

'I must,' I breathed.

As I turned from her, she snatched my hand.

'I beg you, Henriette, do not be a fool! Can you not understand? You will be seen with her, with a royalist! You cannot hazard it, not at a time such as this, for you will be taken for one too and then . . .' She paused. 'Then I cannot hazard to be seen with *you*! Why, you will bring suspicion upon all of us, like a disease! I will not be able to know you, *ma chère*!' She tugged more forcibly at me, determined to fix me in place. 'Do you not perceive what is to come, my dear sister? Is it not plain to you? After the King is brought to justice, those who have supported him will also go beneath the guillotine. The finger will soon come to point at Madame Elliot, and I could not bear to behold you there beside her.' Her eyes grew round with desperation. 'Not even Orléans would be able to preserve you.'

'I shall not suffer myself to be seen by anyone, Agnès, I swear it to you,' was the only assurance I could offer. It was a feeble one, and she recognized that as well as I.

It was with great reluctance that I pulled away from her, my heart breaking as I did.

'You are no different from her,' La Buffon snapped at me. 'Dorothea. Madame Meyler. You are the same.'

My back was turned to her as that dart pierced me. She could not observe that my features were twisted with pain.

'Henriette!' she cried after me. 'Henriette, you betray me, sister! Henriette!' She wept as I passed through her dressing-room doors and down the long, empty enfilade of rooms. 'Henriette!' she wailed until I could bear it no longer. I clapped my hands over my ears and fled. I ran from her like the coward I was.

Chapter 23

I cannot think how I must have appeared when I boarded Monsieur Valentin's coach in the courtyard of the Palais-Royal. The sting of the act I had committed was so fresh that I could scarcely gather the words to speak. I was incapable of pleasantries, or even polite greetings. All the warmth had been hollowed from my heart and it sat cold and dead within my breast. For the entire journey to Meudon, which was two hours beyond the barriers, my head was filled with nothing but the sound of my friend's sobs. I cut such a melancholy figure that I am certain Monsieur Valentin and his two young daughters thought me poor company indeed.

Valentin himself was a somewhat puffed-up man of great show-iness, who, beneath his plum-coloured greatcoat, wore long lace ruffles at his wrists. His daughters, who could have been no older than ten and twelve, by contrast had a timid and glum air about them. They sat, quietly stitching samplers, almost too frightened to glance at me. Eventually, one whispered to the other and then, in an act of bravery, ventured to speak.

'Mademoiselle,' said the eldest in the voice of a mouse, 'my sister wishes to convey her compliments upon your English gown.'

I smiled weakly at them, before hanging my head once more

in despair and heartache. We continued in this manner as our carriage wound up the streets beyond Saint-Germain towards the southernmost wall of the city and the barrier Vaugirard. Here our vehicle was drawn to a halt and a soldier, much in need of a razor and soap, came to address Monsieur Valentin, who presented our passports. The guard picked his teeth as he read through them.

'Monsieur Valentin, master of the orchestra at the Théâtre de la République?' The guard smiled with what seemed an air of reverence for the man before him. 'And these are your daughters?'

'Yes, captain.'

He then shuffled through the documents and drew forth mine.

'And Mademoiselle Lightfoot . . . an Englishwoman?'

'Yes, captain,' replied Valentin on my behalf. 'She is a singer, come from London.'

The guard nodded approvingly.

'And you are for Sèvres?'

'Yes. We are to visit my sister.'

'Pray, citizen, is your sister not the famous Mademoiselle Valentin, also of the Théâtre de la République?'

Valentin seemed to puff out his chest.

'Indeed she is, captain, but she has lately been married to Monsieur LeRoy, who is *intendant* of the Théâtre du Marais.' Valentin laughed gently to himself. 'It was a fortuitous union of musical families . . .'

'Ah! She has made a good dowry but is wise to be finished with those other admirers, those debauched aristocrats, *non*?' the captain exclaimed with good humour.

'Indeed, captain,' Valentin agreed with him unsteadily.

'Very well, citizen, you may pass, and I bid you and your family and Mademoiselle Lightfoot well.' The captain, grinning broadly, leaned forward to return the documents, but then stopped short. 'Eh! But before you depart, Mademoiselle Lightfoot must favour us with a song!' he announced, turning to his fellow guards. The two behind him stepped forward, cheering their agreement.

'"La Marseillaise"? Or "Ça Ira"? Yes, that one . . . "Ça Ira", citizeness.'

Monsieur Valentin turned to me, his smile growing wider still.

'Do you sing, mademoiselle?' he asked me from between his teeth.

'No!' I breathed in terror. Nor did I know the words to 'Ça Ira'. My heart began to pound. 'What should I do?' I hissed beside his ear.

The guard still had in his possession our passports, without which we were captive.

'You must try,' he grunted, clenching his teeth.

'But I cannot! Monsieur, I cannot carry a tune.'

'What is the matter, citizen?' enquired the guard.

'Mademoiselle Lightfoot wishes to save her voice for this evening, when she sings with my sister.'

'Ah! She sings with Madame LeRoy? What a performance that promises to be!' the captain cried. 'Why, Sèvres is but a short ride from here! I have long admired your sister's fine voice. I shall never forget when she sang Joset in *Les Deux Petits Savoyards*. Ah! Well, citizen, I should like to attend tonight!'

'No, no, it is a private musical party . . . at her home.' Valentin was now fibbing wildly, stringing one lie into the next, like a net in which to entangle himself.

That statement came down upon the guard's demeanour like a great iron door. His expression changed instantly from one of lightness into something dark and vexed. He lowered his tone.

'But certainly, Citizeness LeRoy would welcome a captain of the National Guard in her salon, *non*?' He was now glaring at Monsieur Valentin, as if to challenge him.

'I am afraid I could not say, captain,' responded Valentin, his voice strained.

'Are Citizen LeRoy and his wife not friends of the Revolution? I hear the King still possesses many devoted friends in Sèvres . . .'

Valentin's face was now the cast of bleached linen. 'Yes, why yes . . . captain. My brother LeRoy is a proud member of the Jacobin Club.'

'Very well, then,' said he, handing back the documents. 'When you arrive, you must tell her to expect another guest this evening, Captain Lestrange. I cannot think it would be much bother to entertain another at the house of Citizen LeRoy, a man of such means, eh, citizen?' The guard then ruthlessly slapped the flank of the horse nearest to him so that the beast fairly bridled. Had the brake not been applied, we and the entire apparatus would have taken off at a charge. 'Until this evening, citizen!' hailed the captain as we rode away.

It was at that moment Valentin, his forehead beaded with sweat, turned to me with a scowl so fierce as to terrify me.

'What am I to do now, eh? This guard and his companions will come to the home of my sister and when they find there is no musical party, they will turn the house upside down and accuse us of unspeakable things! Oh, *mon Dieu*! What am I to do? What will become of my daughters!' Valentin cried in a rage, waving his hands about as if he were conducting an orchestra. All at once he let out an angry grunt and clapped his hand to his face. His two daughters looked on in horror, sitting petrified against the back of the seat. I too was afraid to move. For a spell, he went still. Then: 'You must come with us to Sèvres. I insist upon it,' he resolved.

I squinted at this absurd man and his preposterous suggestion.

'But I cannot sing, monsieur.'

'It does not matter one jot that you cannot sing, mademoiselle, so long as you are present. We can pretend you have taken ill . . .

that you have a fever . . . you are faint. Yes, that will suffice . . .' he rambled.

'But, I cannot, monsieur, I am to call upon my friend at Meudon—'

'Damn your friend!' he thundered. 'What of my sister and Monsieur LeRoy? Their infant son? What of them, eh? Oh, what trouble that cursed Égalité has brought upon me with his whores. It is ever the same with him. I knew I should never have accepted to undertake such a thing as . . . as this!' he said with a disgusted gesture of his hand to me.

I carefully considered the insult I had been dealt and raised my chin.

'Monsieur,' said I in a voice calm and sober, 'I would have you know that I owe my life to the lady to whom I pay this call. She has already suffered much at the hands of these soldiers who you fear will harass your brother LeRoy and your sister. I have but one opportunity of seeing to her welfare before she departs for England, and if you deprive me of that obligation, you will create a further injustice in your attempt to prevent one.'

Valentin examined me through one eye, as if measuring the reason within my words. He sniffed.

'No. You will come to Sèvres.'

I locked my gaze upon his. This cruel imposition I would not bear, not in light of my scene with Madame de Buffon. I was absolutely determined that I had not endured the agony of that confrontation with her to be carried to Sèvres and away from a resolution to my troubles. Others had shackled me against my will on so many occasions and I would not tolerate one more such inconvenience.

'No, monsieur, I will not stand for it. I will not! If you do not take me to Meudon as promised I shall go there on foot,' I commanded.

Valentin rolled his eyes heavenward, as if he were shrugging off the tearful demands of one of his daughters. How his disregard provoked me. In a storm of a huff, I moved to take down the window and call to the coachman, but Valentin sprang to intercede. He took hold of me by the shoulders and pulled me back with all of his strength.

'No!' I cried out. 'Let hold of me! Free me at once, I say! Coachman! Coachman! *Arrêtez-vous!*' I howled as I tussled with Valentin. The entire carriage shook with my endeavours to free myself from this scoundrel's grasp, while the demoiselles Valentin wailed at the horrific spectacle of their beloved father manhandling a defenceless lady.

'No, Papa! Please stop! Stop! You will murder her!' shrieked the eldest, courageously reaching forward to disentangle us. Something in her expression suggested that this was not the first occasion in which she had intervened. Once wrenched apart, we four sat in silence, panting, shamefaced and shaken. All that could be heard were the sniffles of the youngest Valentin as we continued to roll along the road.

After a spell, Monsieur spoke under his breath.

'I shall deliver you to Meudon, mademoiselle, but prepare to be collected at six o'clock. At this time my carriage will return for you whereupon you shall be conveyed to my sister's house and this charade shall be enacted, whether you will it to be or not. You have been the cause of this debacle, mademoiselle, and I mean to have you extricate us from it.'

I understood that this was no idle threat, though my contempt for Monsieur Valentin was such that I made no reply. I would not even deign to lift my eyes to him. Instead, I sat and listened to the rumble of the wheels along that stony, rutted road and contemplated my pleasure in arriving at the end of it.

Chapter 24

The frozen mist lay so heavily upon the road that day that when we approached Mrs Elliot's dark green painted gate, I could scarcely discern it from the stone wall which ran beside it. Valentin uttered not a word to me as I stepped from his vehicle. No sooner had I been deposited than he gave the coachman the order to drive away, abandoning me to my fate in the most ruthless fashion.

I pulled upon the bell cord and listened for the sound of footfall. Indeed, I waited some time, and with each moment that passed I began to fear that I had arrived too late. My head began to paint fanciful pictures of my friend's sudden departure. I imagined that her coach had been loaded and that she had already arrived at Calais. I feared that there was now a letter awaiting me at the Palais-Royal explaining all, and informing me that I was too late. I rang again, this time with more urgency. I had no sooner begun to curse myself, to fretfully twist my hands, when Langlois, Mrs Elliot's porter, peered from behind the gate.

'Mademoiselle Lightfoot?' said he with an air of surprise, before pulling back the doors.

What relief it was to behold his familiar hulking figure there!

'I fear Madame Elliot is not expecting me. Is she at home?' I apologized as I stepped through the gate.

'Yes, mademoiselle,' said he, 'and I should think she will be pleased to learn that it is not the guard returned again to make trouble.'

I smiled and emitted a soft sigh to hear that my anxieties were unfounded. It was only then that I permitted my heart to fill with the anticipation of a reunion with a friend I had not seen in many months.

'They come so frequently now that the rumour has been put about,' said Langlois as we proceeded down the short drive lined with skeletal trees, in which clung the odd cluster of white-berried mistletoe.

'What rumour is that?' I enquired with curiosity.

'That she assists counter-revolutionaries. That she takes in émigrés who wish to return and procures papers for those who wish to flee. Last month the entire section house from Sèvres came to search for Monsieur de Chansenets, who was once governor of the Tuileries and a conspirator. They had received word from the Section de la République in Paris that Madame had been seen with him.' He tutted. 'It is plainly absurd. I have seen no such man here or at her *hôtel*. To have hidden him would have been an impossibility. Time and time again they make their searches, here and in Paris, and still they find no proof for these accusations. No, mademoiselle, my mistress is disliked by many and they will say anything to blacken her name.'

I gazed at Langlois with admiration. His loyalty to his mistress was a credit to him and, I believed, a testimony to the natural affection Mrs Elliot inspired in all who knew her. Although I had never before ventured to Meudon, in seeing her porter and listening to his words, I felt at once the familiarity of a home-coming.

The grey was so dense about us that I could not make out Mrs Elliot's house till I nearly stood before it. It was not as I had expected. Orléans's great gift to her was a rectangular structure from the previous century with a sloping slate roof and no more than a small cupola atop it for ornamentation. It was set around a modest courtyard and hewn from a cream-coloured stone, much stained by the elements. It was no larger in size than her town-house on the rue de Miromesnil, yet with its tall windows it gave the impression of quiet stateliness.

Langlois led me through the entry and into an airy hall of white-painted panels and a marble floor. A low fire crackled with wet kindling. Even at this hour, the mist had rendered the house so dark that candles were lit all about. This was a place for summer and not the chill of winter.

'Pray, mademoiselle,' said Langlois, beckoning me to follow him. We passed through a succession of uninhabited rooms, painted in the hues of a box of pastel chalks. In the cold, their pale colours rendered them more frigid than inviting. At last we arrived in a sitting room of moss green, a shade not improved by the dim light which seemed to cast a type of sickly glow about it. Mrs Elliot's porter then disappeared to fetch his mistress.

I waited, somewhat impatiently, fidgeting before the fire and smiling to myself. I listened anxiously for her footfall, and at last heard its hasty approach from the distance.

I greeted her with a bright expression, but hers which met me was one of dismay and distress, not unlike the harried countenance she had borne upon the night of our very first acquaintance.

'Henrietta! Dear child,' she exclaimed. 'What has occurred? Has some tragedy befallen Orléans? Has there been some upheaval?'

'Oh. No, there has been nothing of the sort, madam,' I answered with a fleeting smile.

'Then what, girl? Whatever has brought you here? How did you arrive?' She rumpled her brow.

'It was with Orléans's assistance that I have been able to call upon you,' I offered demurely.

My friend continued to regard me, a look of suspicion or incomprehension forming upon her face. I could not decide which.

'And Madame de Buffon? She was content to have you call upon me here?'

I lowered my eyes, but knew not how I might answer. On spying my uneasiness, Mrs Elliot sat herself down upon a green-striped chair and gestured for me to do the same.

'You see, dear Mrs Elliot . . . it is on account of her that I have come,' I began, mustering my courage. I had rehearsed my lines to her a good many times before this, but still found my heart pounding with fear at the thought of speaking my piece. 'Madam, you know that you are to me as a mother, and I pray that I shall forever remain worthy of that name which you have called me: *votre chère fille.*' I glanced fleetingly at her and then away. 'But I beg that you hear me upon this subject, one which has caused my mind no inconsiderable torment. I would not wish to contradict you, *ma chère maman*, but you must accept that in the months I have lived with Madame de Buffon I have come to observe many qualities in her character which are not known to you. Indeed, I do not believe them known to most. She has been much maligned and the victim of gossip. Her break with Mrs Meyler was not on account of jealousy – and she is no murderess, to be sure,' I added with a light laugh and again glanced at my friend. Her head was tilted and an indentation had grown between her two dark eyebrows. She did not smile.

'I have seen in her heart great kindness and truth, much as I have beheld in yours. I have wished that you might be reconciled, for my sake as much as for yours. I have attempted to effect this, to speak favourably of you to her, and now of her to you, but I fear I am incapable of mending such a rift as this, for the Revolution and your opposing convictions render it deep. As you might imagine, I presently find myself in a position most disagreeable to my sensibilities. I can no longer bear to practise such a deceit upon a lady whom I have come to cherish as a friend. I pray that I have succeeded in assisting you, dear, dear Mrs Elliot. It has afforded me no small amount of satisfaction to learn that your friendship with Orléans has been restored and he has arranged to secure your allowance, but now that that matter is amicably concluded, I wish to bring an end to our clandestine correspondence, for it is a cause of anguish to me.' I paused and ventured to gaze upon her.

She sat forward in her chair and wore such a curious expression that it instantly filled me with unease. The crease between her brows had grown into something resembling a scowl. It seemed a strained look, as if she had failed to hear me.

'It is . . . it is my intention to quit my apartments at the Palais-Royal and return temporarily to my lodgings in the Hôtel Blanquefort. If you would permit me, I beg your leave to return with you to England, as soon as you wish to make your departure.'

Mrs Elliot's face was fixed. Not even the conclusion of my discourse succeeded in shifting it. I awaited some movement, even the briefest nod of approval, but nothing came. After a moment had passed, she leaned back into her seat.

'Henrietta', she began, 'while your sentiments do you credit, they are misguided.' She then sighed. 'I am afraid you are not at liberty to make such decisions, nor is it in my interests for you to quit the Palais-Royal.'

I could not believe that my entreaties had failed to persuade her. 'Madam, I wish not to remonstrate with you upon this point, but I beg you to consider—'

'I have considered a great deal, Henrietta. How much so, you cannot begin to conceive,' she clipped me. There was not an ounce of levity in her tone, not a hint of warmth, and I could not but conclude I had displeased her in some way.

'I am . . . afraid that I do not apprehend your meaning, madam,' I murmured gently.

'You would not.' Her marble-grey eyes searched mine. 'Truly, it had been my wish to avoid conversing upon this matter. However, as you have seen fit to come here and heedlessly abandon the position in which I laboured long to establish you, the situation must be made plain.' She inhaled and rose from her chair before crossing the room to peer behind one door and then the other. She shut each of them securely and glided almost noiselessly back to her seat. She leaned towards me. 'Child, you must believe me when I say that it saddens me to reveal this to you.' She spoke softly. 'I am quite uncertain how to put it. You see, much of what you believe to be true is nothing but a fiction. Indeed, much of the existence you have come to know in Paris is a sham.' She placed her hand upon mine, a brief touch over the leather of my glove. 'For this I am truly sorry, but you must be made to understand that it was necessary.'

I studied her features, searching for some greater explanation in them, but found nothing of any sense.

'You must not believe that I lay in wait for you like a spider, weaving some elaborate trap. No, this, all of this, came about quite by chance, from your arrival at my gate to . . .' She paused and looked away, carefully selecting her words. 'I will concede that I was most intrigued by the letter Mr Savill sent me, announcing that he wished to introduce me to a Lady Allenham . . . but all was made clear to me when you recounted your story. Indeed, as you sat in my drawing room I fairly marvelled at my good fortune. It was as if the heavens had parted and the angels had delivered you to me on their very wings. Why, Venus could not have invented a creature more perfectly formed to Orléans's tastes: such youthful beauty, sweet and ruined, trusting . . . and English. I knew I was certain to succeed with you.' She caught my eye, and gave me the only smile she had offered since my arrival. It was a curious one, of almost menacing delight. 'However, when you began to speak of your intentions to locate your beloved Allenham, I recognized that it was necessary to formulate a plan at once.'

I listened, but there seemed nothing in her words which amounted to any sense. I wondered if I had failed to apprehend some part of her story.

'I am afraid I did what circumstances demanded to keep you beneath my roof and under my watch. Your jewels were not stolen. I arranged for it to appear so, but I kept them in my possession until it became necessary to establish you in separate lodgings.'

It was then that a great gust of astonishment swept me to my feet. There I stood, rendered quite mute by the shock. Remarkably, she seemed unmoved by my distress. She merely tipped her head coquettishly, as she might have with any of her admirers.

'My dear, I spent your fortune in the very manner you would have wished. You expressed a desire to live by your own means, and so I enabled you to do so. Your household expenses have been paid from your own purse . . .'

'But . . . my apartments . . . you told me that a subscription had been raised . . . Madame de Flaghac said your finances were much disordered, that Orléans did not pay your annuity and then . . . why, she confessed to me that you had sold your sapphire on account of my troubles . . .' I gibbered, confounded by the pieces of a tale which no longer fit together.

'Yes, what was said with regard to my annuity from Orléans was true, but as for the rest . . .' She moved her head slowly from side to side. 'I am afraid not. I told La Flaghac that I had sold my sapphire, for I guessed she would repeat the story.' Mrs Elliot ran her hand along her lengthy neck and sighed.

I stood gazing at her in disbelief. Indeed, I did not think my brain capable of fathoming this.

'Why ever would you contrive such a scheme?' The words blew through my mouth.

The tall, heron-like creature shifted in her seat. She seemed almost to shrug as she did so.

'Henrietta, I could not very well reveal what it was that I wished you to accomplish for me. It was necessary for you to believe that you were in my debt. Ladies of our description who still cling to the vestiges of honour, who believe in duty and in love above all things, lay themselves bare to the world. You live by a code which does not apply in the demi-monde.' She raised her chin imperiously. 'Had I not convinced you that you were in my debt, you would never have ventured into Orléans's bed, nor befriended Madame de Buffon. Your sense of duty commanded you to make the sacrifices you did, and in doing so you have made yourself invaluable to me. You are a source of intelligence which cannot be replaced.'

I could not have felt more mortified if she had struck me across the face. The injury I felt, the shock at what had been delivered, was as severe. As I stood fuming and incredulous, I began to wonder what other falsehoods she had tied over my eyes.

'And Allenham . . . ?' I whispered, almost too frightened to hear her response.

She lowered her head. Whether it was a gesture of remorse or something which appeared like it, I could not say.

'Yes. I have known his whereabouts from the beginning.'

A gasp escaped me, as if my heart had been punctured and all the air released from it. My jaw began to tremble and I clenched it tightly.

'That first occasion when I brought you to the Palais-Royal, do you not recall it? I drew your attention to a print-shop window: Henry Tyrone, a purveyor of Jacobin slander and filth. Your paramour poses as one of two American gentlemen who are known by this name, father and son. More ardent lovers of the Revolution you will not find. Oh, they play their roles exceptionally well. There is no club or society to which they are not admitted. They sit at the table of Marat, Vergniaud, Danton and Robespierre – why, that scoundrel venerates your beloved.' She laughed. 'I made certain to catch his eye that day when we passed before the shop window. Lord Allenham observed you with me. I wished him to know that you were in Paris, to warn him.' She raised her gaze to mine and her smile retracted. 'Henrietta, he is a spy for His Majesty King George. As are you.'

This blow fell hard upon me, perhaps with more force than all the others combined. I have mused upon it over the years and concluded that there is no suffering in life worse than a sacrifice made in vain. It sickened me to retrace my steps through the twisted tangle of deceits, to consider each decision I had formulated and each deed I had committed in the hope of rendering myself worthy of her affection, of honouring a debt which never existed. To have abandoned my principles, to have lain with a man I did not desire, to have betrayed a true friend, to have nearly lost my life, all on account of falsehoods. It was unspeakable, unconscionable, cruel.

My eyes spilled forth their tears and still she sat, impassive, with a stare as cold as a cat's.

'My dear, the intelligence with which you have provided me has succeeded in winning me great favour with His Majesty's Government. Until I had made your acquaintance I had relied solely upon my own wits in gathering such information, but Orléans ceased to confide in me and Mrs Meyler did the bidding of whomever paid her the most handsome sum. Child, there are spies everywhere in Paris. They work for everyone, from our King to King Louis, from the Austrians to the police and the Jacobin Clubs. There is not a corner in all of France free of infestation. This nation daily talks of its new-found liberty, but still tyranny prevails.'

She then rose from her chair and moved across the room to an escritoire with a locked glass bookcase atop it. She removed the key from a dainty chatelaine at her waist and opened it, taking into her hands the book-sized portrait of her young daughter, Georgiana.

'You wish to know what role I have played in this?' she enquired, and then without pausing for my response pulled the backing from the portrait and revealed a secret compartment. Inside it were three letters, arranged like eggs in a nest of satin. 'My correspondents are abroad, mostly in Coblenz and London. I convey intelligence to all parts. Thérèse Bertrand assists in this task. Some letters come in code, others in an invisible ink.' She then pieced the frame together once more and returned it to the locked cabinet. 'His Majesty's Government desires to know Orléans's designs and convictions; if he aspires to the throne. Mr Pitt wishes to know the dangers presented by those of Orléans's acquaintance, if Madame de Buffon encourages him in his radical notions, and if he continues to empty what remains of his purse to fund the Revolution. He wishes to know if Orléans will vote for his cousin's death . . .' She aimed her gaze directly at me.

I might have told her, reader. I might have offered up to her that morsel of intelligence she most desired, but instead I held it firmly in my mouth. It was the only thing of my own which I felt I possessed.

Although I wept, I held her stare. I met her eye and did not waver.

'It is imperative that you return to the Palais-Royal at once,' she commanded me. 'That you should choose to take your leave of Orléans on a day so critical as this . . .' She shut her eyes and inhaled. 'You shame me. You shame me before our King.'

I could make no reply, for I had no words but those of fury and anguish and shock. I nodded, almost imperceptibly, before I remembered.

'Monsieur Valentin,' I said. 'He is in possession of my passport.' Then, much to my chagrin I was forced to describe that scene which had transpired upon the road to Meudon, and how Monsieur Valentin had promised to return for me that evening.

She sighed and looked away. 'This will not do,' said she with growing agitation. 'This Valentin – I shall order him away. I shall have to tell him you . . .' She pressed her hand to her mouth as she cogitated on a lie. '. . . you ran off . . . that it was all a sham, a scheme to meet a lover . . . that even I know not where you have gone to . . .'

I regarded her with some uncertainty.

'I do not think he will be inclined to believe you,' I offered quietly.

'Well, I dare say I shall not suffer him here!' she snapped. I had never before heard her voice raised to such a pitch. Indeed it struck me then that her falsehoods and deceptions had been so thick and knotted, so intricately woven, as to have completely obscured her true character from me. I recognized that I understood nothing of this woman, not even if she had ever been a friend.

'This will bring the guards, I am certain of it. All the house will be torn apart again . . .' she muttered anxiously.

I observed her as she began to pace and fret. In her disquieted state, she seemed oddly pitiable to me.

'You know that you are widely suspected,' I ventured cautiously. 'You cannot pretend that your allegiances are unknown, that the world does not take you for a royalist. It is only natural that they should assume you are a counter-revolutionary as well. You cannot expect to continue here as you have, madam. You hazard your life. You would do well to quit this place for England, as I believed you had intended . . .'

She stopped and turned to me. Her eyes glinted like two dark stones.

'Why ever should I return to England?' She wagged her head and emitted a short, angry laugh. 'What have I to gain by abandoning all in my possession? By closing up my houses which I am certain never to see again? All that I have procured from the existence I have led – all that I have toiled for – will be gone. I am no longer a young miss of twenty years who may gather wealthy admirers like wildflowers from a field,' she shot at me. 'Those noblemen who support the King, those who have fled to Coblenz, it is upon their purses as much as upon Orléans's which my existence depends. The Comte de Langeron, the Comte d'Artois, the Prince de Condé . . . I have managed their correspondence and attempted where possible to safeguard their interests whilst they are in exile. I must remain in their good favour, or I am lost. If I flee, I shall be forgotten as readily as the victuals which they last consumed. Nothing would compel me to abandon France. My insinuation that I would was merely to persuade you to write to me, not to incite you to throw yourself upon me!' she grumbled, her expression growing more cross and stormy by the moment. 'Madam, you labour under the illusion that you have acquired a certain understanding of the world and its ways. Your hubris has inclined you to believe that you will never again be played for a dupe, but you have failed to apprehend that lesson which all women of our sort must drive into our hearts like shards of ice. Dear little child,' she tutted, the disgust ripe upon her lips, 'it is trust that weakens us. If you do not learn to give it up, you will die a martyr to it.'

She stood over me, her long neck poised downward to make a close study of my features. She awaited my response, but I gave her none. I stared directly ahead of me through my silent tears.

'There is a means by which you can return to Paris without the need for a passport. Langlois knows of a breach in the wall near to the Military School at Invalides, not five miles from here. I have made use of it myself. He will guide you to it, but I would bid you to act with great caution. Do not suffer yourself to be seen passing into the city by this unlawful channel or you will imperil your life. There are soldiers, thieves and ruffians at every turn upon the roads, many of whom will think nothing of reporting you. Take pains to avoid them. Now, I will bid you adieu for you must depart at once.'

She turned abruptly from me to summon her porter. I listened to the hasty slap of her slippers upon the floorboards, and the sweep of her skirts. I heard doors open and her voice call out the names of those servants whom I had come to regard almost as my own. I listened but I did not look. I could no more bear to gaze upon her than I could the cruellest, most remorseless Judas.

Chapter 25

When I quit her house, I did not look back. I lowered my head and followed Langlois as he led us through a side passage and into a yard. From there we strode out into the thick folds of mist. We turned away from the road and wove a passage through the woods where we were less likely to meet with soldiers. As Mrs Elliott's house was at the top of a hill, this route was a treacherous one, a damp slide of black mouldering leaves, through which I could see little further than my outstretched hand. Langlois offered me his large, steady arm and guided me gently down into a forest of spindly beeches and oaks.

I said nothing to him as we progressed, listening only to the constant sound of our feet shifting the loose ground beneath us. I studied my toes, encased in their black half-boots, emerging from the bottom of my drab skirts as I walked. My face stung with tears and cold and shame. I kept my neck bent, occasionally blotting my nose and eyes as they ran.

I cannot say for how long we continued through this forlorn landscape; two or maybe three hours passed. In walking, I found the turmoil in my heart eventually loosened and spread like an ailment into my head. It began to throb with my troubles. It played out the scene with Mrs Elliot until I had committed each one of her sharp words to memory, until every barbed deception lodged itself deep into my heart. Oh how they pricked when I considered my errors and misunderstandings, my blindness to that which lay all about me. To think how Mrs Elliott had tricked and used me so ill. Not one assurance had been real, not one endearment spoken without artifice, not one pledge uttered without self-interest. How I ached to think of that which had been perpetrated upon me, and how easily I had fallen prey to her falsehoods, how apparent were my weaknesses. What bitter loathing I felt for her, as well as for myself. Madame de Buffon would berate me for my foolishness, to be sure.

Oh, Agnès, Agnès! My heart wept. *My dear friend! My one true friend.* I could scarcely bear to contemplate how she had cried out to me as I had abandoned her. I would return to her. Yes, I would beg her forgiveness. I would denounce the coldness of my 'relation'. I would say she refused to see me on account of my association with her and Orléans. Grace Elliot was a cruel and spiteful woman, I would confess to La Buffon. I would assure her that she had been correct all along and I had been the fool. *Oh, Agnès, forgive me or I shall never forgive myself.*

If there was one engine which compelled me along that path, it was that singular thought. My legs could not drive me rapidly enough back to the Palais-Royal.

I began to quicken my pace, which caused Langlois to glance at me.

'It is not much further,' said he, muttering the first words that had passed between us in several hours.

It was not long after that when we arrived at a small stone wall and a gate, over which Langlois assisted me. From there we found ourselves in the open, upon the plain of Vaugirard. The fog had begun to thin and I could see a road and the walls of the city coming into view.

'We must move with haste now,' said he, 'for there are guards upon this road and all manner of villains. Do not meet the gaze of anyone, no matter how genteel they may seem.'

No sooner had he said that than two women wrapped in grey cloaks came upon the path singing loud, lewd songs about the Queen.

'Good afternoon, citizens,' one cried out in a warbling, drunken voice. 'Will you buy my eels?' said she, lifting her basket unsteadily.

'Or are you a generous fellow who might buy us some brandy?' her companion hollered at Langlois. 'Oh, we are in much need of warming . . .'

They cackled at their bawdiness.

'Hussies! Do your husbands know you drank away their money on marketing days?' Langlois bellowed back at them.

The women laughed at his banter as they passed us by.

I inhaled, grateful for his presence, but also suddenly aware that I would not have it on the other side of the city walls.

Now that we had joined the road, faces passed us with regularity. A rider upon a horse emerged through the haze. He saluted us and carried on, the clip of his mount's hooves echoing through the grey space. A cabriolet passed us in haste; an ass bearing a cart of sacks moved steadily towards us and then beyond. We walked in silence through the gloom.

'It is just ahead,' said Langlois eventually, breaking the stillness. He nodded towards the horizon, where the road bent and rose. 'There,' he muttered as we approached. His voice had grown suddenly tighter and more anxious. 'The wall is hidden beneath a growth of vines. Three trees stand before it.'

Indeed, I looked along the road and spied three sets of skeletal branches intertwined in a wintery dance.

'Hurry . . . but do not run to it . . .' he warned as we had started towards the spot. My heart quickened with my steps. I could hear it thumping in my head.

We were no more than fifty yards from the spot when all at once the sound of a horse and rider approached us from behind.

'Citizens!' came a cry from over our shoulders.

We immediately halted our steps.

I cannot say why I thought it so, but upon first hearing his call there seemed something familiar in it. My alarm was then instantly increased when Langlois muttered to me from the side of his mouth, 'A soldier.'

'Good afternoon, captain,' said the porter.

There was a silence and then the most terrific of fears gripped me: Captain Lestrange, the man who had bid me sing for him at the Vaugirard barrier. We could not have been more than a short distance from that place. I felt every limb stiffen with dread.

'Citizen,' said he again, 'in which direction do you go?'

Langlois swallowed hard. I kept my head bowed, my heart pounding. The more I inclined my ear to the cadence and pitch of this man's voice, the more certain I grew that he was Lestrange. I began to shake.

'We are for Auteuil, captain.'

There was a thoughtful pause before he responded.

'Do you live close by, citizen?'

'Not far, captain.'

'Then, certainly, citizen, you would know of an inn near to here, the Lyon d'Or? I am from Nantes and know nothing of these parts. I fear I have taken the wrong road.'

I heard Langlois draw a deep breath into his lungs. 'No, citizen, you are on the correct road, it is but a mile from here, if you continue ahead.'

The guard saluted him and it seemed for a moment that he was about to kick his horse, when he paused.

'Citizeness?' said he, attempting to peer beneath my hat.

I did not move, but raised my eyes enough to see his boot, his breeches and the bottom of the cape he wore about his shoulders.

Then all at once a face appeared before me. He had leaned to the side and tipped his head so he might peep under the brim of my hat. A queue of mouse-brown hair fell against his shoulder, and then the pock-marked boy of no more than eighteen winked at me. He let out a roar of a laugh as he charged away at a gallop.

I eyed Langlois, who appeared as relieved as I. Together we stood in place and waited for the young man to disappear into the distance, before the servant pushed me forward. 'Now,' he commanded, 'we must be quick!'

Darting behind the trees, he approached the wall and began tearing at the vines. They came away so easily into our hands that I could only assume they had been placed there intentionally by those who passed regularly through the opening. Eventually, Langlois uncovered what appeared to be a Y-shaped breach. There were loose stones at the top which looked as though they might be easily removed, while a section towards the bottom appeared just wide enough to accommodate a child or a woman.

'My mistress was too tall to pass through this. She had to mount the wall and climb over, but you may squeeze through it like a rabbit.' He pulled out some loose stones and I unpinned the hat from my head. 'Look before you pass through,' said he, gripping my arm and addressing me firmly. 'There are guards on the opposite side as well. Take heed!'

This I did. As I peered through I could see nothing but what seemed to be a kitchen garden, and six large cabbages before me.

'You must not delay, mademoiselle!' he urged me forward, for we both could hear the approach of horses somewhere along the road. I bent down and pushed my head through first. My arms followed next and then my shoulders, before I drew through my torso and legs. Once I had risen to my feet, Langlois threw my hat over the wall. It fell upon the cabbages with a thud. Scarcely had I caught my breath before I heard him begin to fill in the breach once more.

'*À bientôt! Adieu, adieu, mademoiselle!* May you go safely,' he cried in a loud whisper from behind the stones. 'I will pray for you.'

'And I you,' I replied. 'And I you!'

Once beyond the city wall, my fear of discovery abandoned me and was replaced by a sensation of greater urgency: that I must make for the Palais-Royal, that every moment the ill consequences of my misguided deeds grew more grave.

I made my way across the garden, along rows of potatoes and onion shoots, the January soil hard beneath my feet. When I emerged I knew not in which direction to turn, for all I could see were the backs of cottages, small barns, hen houses and lean-tos. Cows stood in fields and, beneath the falling dusk, a flock of geese pecked along barren furrows. Hurriedly, I pressed through this patchwork of smallholdings, until I spied a passage that led into a wider thoroughfare. Beyond an old well which sat in the middle of the road, I beheld the spire of Les Invalides and strode purposefully towards it.

The mist had begun to smother the last remaining afternoon light. Darkness spread rapidly before me and without Langlois's Herculean figure at my side, I began to fear for my safety. After the barbarity to which I had been exposed, I had vowed I would never again venture forth upon the streets of Paris unaccompanied. I touched my shoulder, now with its red, tender scar hidden below my garments.

Was there no true kindness in the world? I recall thinking as I trod onward. *Was there not one heart untouched by baseness or corrupted by venality?* For the first time in a great while my mind alighted upon the memory of those conversations I had shared with Allenham, he who had believed with such passion in the gentleness of mankind. We were, all of us, rich or poor, high-born or low-, *tabulae rasae*. Our natural state was one of goodness, not evil, he had said to me. Did he still hold firm to those principles now, I wondered, or had the bloody spectacle of murder and the animal rages of those upon the streets turned him from them? Allenham, whom Mrs Elliot had kept from me. Allenham: how my heart wished to open once more to him, but pain had sealed it shut. Now I saw plainly the error of my ways. My heedless, strong-willed, foolish pride had driven me to Paris, rather than back to London as he had directed me. Mrs Elliot had been correct; in order to survive in this world, one must extinguish within one-self the urge to trust. Dear reader, if there was a single lesson I drew from my time in Paris, it was this. From that day forward, it was burned upon my heart like a brand from an iron, so that, like any thief, I might be reminded of my folly for the rest of my days. Never have I forgotten it since.

All about me, lamps were lit. Candles were placed beside small windows. The streets grew menacing. Malingering men in clogs sang and smoked and spat. Brash beggar children followed me with blackened open palms. Women called out between the windows, and threw showers of grey water on to my passage. The cobbles gave way under my feet. Cabriolets and barrels rolled in and out of my path. But still I walked, determined, my jaw set in angry dismay. My stockings and skirts grew ever more filthy as I traversed the seam of muck that ran through the road. The streets stank of foetid, putrid ruin, of excrement and, in places, of death.

As I approached Saint-Germain-des-Prés, a finely dressed gentleman had the misfortune to accost me. He stepped from a door and tugged upon my sleeve while making some lascivious noise. I turned on him with a jerk of violence. Some dark creature I did not know reared up from within me and shrieked that I would tear out his eyes if he laid so much as a finger upon me. He recoiled in terror. I am ashamed to confess it, but it pleased me greatly to witness the horror in his expression.

I sobbed freely as I approached the pont Royal. My hands trembled as I wiped my face with the backs of them. As I gazed out across the river, I recalled the night when I embarked upon this same journey to the rue de Miromesnil, believing I might find some solace there. Now I turned my eyes towards the dark and ghostly Tuileries Palace, and then beyond in the direction of the Palais-Royal, where I hoped to make amends. As I neared it from the rue Saint-Honoré, my heart, like a bellows, gave a sudden, fulsome heave. How I longed to be returned to my apartments there and to feel the warmth of their fires, to rest my tortured feet, to beg my cherished friend's forgiveness at last.

I entered through the passage de Valois, that set of stairs down which I had flown in pursuit of Allenham, only months before. What might have become of him had I revealed my lover as a spy to all the world? I have often had cause to reflect upon that. Surely the man who nearly took my life upon that day had also done a great service in preserving Allenham's.

Once inside, nothing within the corridors of the Petits Appartements struck me as out of the ordinary, and indeed its familiarity and its illumination welcomed me. Orléans's servants passed silently, obligingly averting their eyes as I moved beyond them, along the sconce-lit route to my rooms. Such hunger and exhaustion I had never known, as if all my body were melting like wax. I moved to open the doors to my sitting room, but was surprised to find them locked. I tried another set, and that too I found bolted.

'Where is Lucy? Where is my maid?' I enquired of a footman,

who claimed he did not know. 'Bring me Romain,' I called after him, knowing that Orléans's *intendant* would be better placed to assist me in this matter. A short while later, Romain arrived wearing a harried expression.

'What is the meaning of this?' I enquired in a somewhat indignant voice. Romain held his head high, but hesitated before speaking.

'Mademoiselle,' said he, 'I regret to inform you that shortly after you quit the Palais-Royal this morning, Madame de Buffon requested that your belongings be removed and returned to your apartments at the Hôtel Blanquefort.'

I stared at him. Perhaps I had been too fraught with exhaustion to have understood his words entirely.

'But, Monsieur Romain, why would she have done such a thing as that?'

Romain returned my gaze with a questioning air, as if bemused that I could not fathom the answer for myself.

'I am afraid she has spoken with Monsieur Égalité and insisted upon your removal.' Romain then turned his eyes from me. 'I understand you have displeased her, mademoiselle.'

'No,' I breathed in disbelief. 'How could that be, Romain? Why, she loves me like a sister. Monsieur Égalité . . . is greatly fond of me . . . How could this come to pass? There was a disagreement of a sort, but . . . that . . . but . . . I did not believe she . . .' All at once I felt a faintness coming upon me.

'I apologize, mademoiselle,' replied Orléans's *intendant* in a gentle tone.

'Why . . . why, where is she? Where is Madame de Buffon? I should like to see her. Now. Take me to her, Romain. Instantly, I beg of you.'

Without waiting for Romain's response, I set off down the corridor, past the varnished portraits of Bourbon cousins and grandmothers bedecked in the ribbons of Louis XIV's court, past ormolu mirrors shimmering with reflected candlelight. Romain chased after me. He knew whither I went. I flew to the doors of Madame's apartments and pushed them wide. They were silent and empty but for the embers of the fires, slowly burning out.

'Monsieur Égalité and Madame de Buffon are at Monceau this evening. They have retired there following the vote at the Convention.'

I turned and held the servant's gaze. I felt my eyes begin to well with tears. Of all that had occurred today, of all of my tragedies, this final calamity felled me entirely. My chin began to shake and I pressed my hand to my mouth.

'What am I to do?' I said. 'Oh, Romain, what am I to do . . . ?'

The old servant approached me and, as might a gentleman, offered me his handkerchief.

'May I suggest, Mademoiselle Lightfoot, that you return to the rue du Faubourg Saint-Honoré, where you will find your maid, and attempt to make your amends with Madame de Buffon tomorrow.'

So overcome with grief was I that I could make no reply. Romain, in the free manner of many French servants, insisted on taking my arm and gently escorting me into the courtyard, where a cabriolet was brought and I delivered into it. No sooner had I sat upon the leather seat of the carriage, indeed the first seat I had taken since fleeing Meudon, than I found myself near insensible with grief. Upon returning to my apartments at the Hôtel Blanquefort Lucy flew to my assistance. Had she not done so I fear I might have collapsed there, at the foot of the great stair.

'Madam,' she cried, supporting me against her. 'I was in such a fear for you. I knew not when you would return!' I rested my head against her shoulder and in that instant it felt to me like the softest pillow my cheek had ever touched. 'Oh, madam, what misery, what crimes were committed today!' she exclaimed. At first I believed she referred to my expulsion from the Palais-Royal, but then she continued breathlessly, 'The Convention has voted for the King's death. Monsieur d'Orléans has condemned his cousin! Oh, what horrors!' she gasped. Her voice echoed through the passage until I hushed her, frantically.

Beyond that, beyond falling upon my bed, I recall nothing more. Indeed, were it possible to tear free that entire day from my memory like a page, I would not hesitate to do it. I would commit all I heard and sensed to the flames, and watch it turn to ash. For in doing so, I believe it would have cauterized the wound in my soul and prevented its spread.

Chapter 26

I cannot say when precisely I became sensible of the noise beyond my bedchamber. I heard, at first, loud banging from some distant place. As the bed curtains had not yet been parted, I was unaware of the time. I lay there for some moments before I heard the door open and Lucy whisper to me:

'Madam, pray, are you waked?'

'Yes,' I replied. 'What is the matter?'

'We must dress you, madam. There are guards come.'

I sat up at once, my heart racing. Lucy drew wide the curtains. There I beheld for the first time my assortment of boxes and baskets ranged about the room. So fraught with exhaustion had I been that I had failed to perceive them the night before. My maid moved about between them as she assisted me off with my nightshift and dressed me in haste.

'Why are they here? Did they tell you?'

'Yes,' she replied anxiously. 'They have come to make a search.'

Immediately I began to think what there might be to incriminate my household. I had not been present here since August, the day when I met with Mrs Elliot. Certainly, I thought, I had nothing of any consequence to hide.

'Thérèse has said they have come before . . .'

'Thérèse!' I exclaimed, remembering all at once what Mrs Elliot had revealed to me. She had had the audacity to place a spy beneath my very roof. I turned to Lucy with a fearful look. She had been pulling my stays tight around me but paused when she caught sight of my expression.

'They never find anything, madam,' she continued uneasily.

Heavy footsteps could be heard throughout my apartments. Keys rattled and doors were opened and shut. Though I could not make out her words, I could hear Thérèse's soft but anxious voice addressing them in the adjacent room. With every moment that passed, I grew more unnerved, scarcely able to stand still long enough to have my gown buttoned over my petticoat. Still greatly dishevelled, I threw open my bedchamber doors to find near a dozen of them, rifles hanging from their shoulders, in my dressing room. One had been pulling at the drawers of a clothes press, while the others stood puzzling over several locked boxes recently returned from the Palais. From their careless manner and slouch, they seemed to me rough men. Two of them were consuming part of a sausage which they cut insolently with a knife as they regarded me. The victuals, I took it, were from my kitchens.

For a moment, I gaped incoherently at the scene. From the surrounding rooms I could hear the sounds of boots, of quick fingers turning and tipping my possessions.

'Citizeness, we would have you open these boxes directly,' ordered the most senior of the group, without so much as a nod of greeting.

'Guard, may I enquire what has brought on the need for a visit such as this? I have done no wrong nor committed any crime.'

'We are here to determine that, citizeness, for we have had reports concerning your household from some people in your section.'

'Pray, sir, what manner of reports have you—'

'Yesterday we received word that you had been to visit a friend in the country. This lady is a royalist and suspected in both the Sections de la République and de Sèvres of counter-revolutionary sympathies.'

I was startled by this, for I could not imagine how the guards had come by such information. My stomach turned over to consider that my friend Agnès de Buffon should be the source of it. My friend. It could not be. I shut my eyes tightly.

'If you please . . . it is true I have returned from a visit, but I know nothing of her sympathies. I had heard she was unwell . . . I went to call upon her. Who informed you of this?'

'Citizeness,' said he, addressing me squarely, 'the boxes, if you will . . . and the keys for the locked compartments to all of your furniture.'

'Yes . . . yes, certainly, captain.' I spoke in an anxious fluster. 'My maid is in possession of these . . .' I gestured to Lucy, who took them from her pocket. 'Please fetch Thérèse,' I then instructed her.

The guards began to unlock the portmanteaus which lay about my dressing room. Some of the boxes I did not recognize and I could not help but think of the haste with which Lucy had been made to fill them in my absence. I knew not what any of them contained, so that opening them was as much a revelation to me as it proved to the guards. All five were unsealed at once and I watched how the soldiers' interested hands rifled through my goods: my bandboxes and shoes, handkerchiefs, linens, feathers, ribbons, and then assorted books, papers, writing implements, paints, brushes and necessaries, jars, wax . . . I grimaced at the indelicacy of this intrusion. How they delighted in fingering the fine lace trim of the sleeves I wore upon my flesh, the bandeaus of silk which ran through my hair, the stockings that held my calves. Soon, all was a disorder, my effects strewn upon the floor in a litter. I remarked to myself how clever I had been in never saving one of Mrs Elliot's letters to me, and then it occurred to me. All at once my face ran white.

'Madam,' Lucy called to me, bereft of breath, 'Thérèse cannot be found. She is not in the kitchens nor in the courtyard . . .'

As Lucy spoke, I raised my eyes to see that the guards had alighted upon just that which I had recalled. They drew forth my three small pocketbooks, those aides-memoires into which I had scribbled for more than twelve months. In them I had recorded not only my own thoughts, deeds and actions, but importantly those of Madame de Buffon. Her private hopes and personal confessions, my discussions with Orléans and those of his household, in addition to my interactions with Mrs Elliot and my note of Allenham's travels from Brussels all lay within, concealed in careful code. My mouth fell wide with horror as I observed them thumb through the pages.

After a spell, the captain addressed me. 'Pray, citizeness, what are these books?'

'They are no more than my diaries, captain.'

'These words are not French.'

'I am an Englishwoman.'

The guard examined me and then the pocketbooks with a hard eye.

'Where is your correspondence, citizeness? Your letters from England, from your friends.'

'I do . . . not keep a regular correspondence . . . with anyone, captain.'

He laughed at this.

'Where do you keep your correspondence?'

'I do . . . not know . . . I do not keep letters, captain. I dispose of them . . .'

The captain did not make a single movement but, like a toad

following a fly, held me in his unflinching gaze.

It was this, dear friends, this omission more than the note-books themselves which undid me. What lady does not keep correspondence? What traveller does not receive letters from abroad, detailing all the doings of those whom they miss? What person of breeding or rank has not a friend in the world with whom they share their thoughts and secrets? Had I no family, no sweetheart, no parent who cared for me? What, dear reader, would be cause for more suspicion than this? For, although it was the truth, it seemed to them so peculiar as to raise the alarm.

I was taken from my home to the section house. They marched me through the streets at the centre of what seemed an entire battalion of men who had come to search my home. They permitted me to throw no more than a cloak about my shoulders to preserve me from the cold. My head reeled with all that had occurred in those two days. I wondered what would be the consequences of my arrest for the others. I dreaded that it should lead to the exposure of Mrs Elliot and then of Allenham, that these men should unpick the code of my diary and use my innocent scrawls against La Buffon, or even Orléans. I could not fathom what was to become of them or of me. I could not think what stories I should offer in an attempt to plead my innocence.

As I was escorted through the streets I was subjected to the vexatious looks of the people who were my neighbours. They paused to stare and hiss and shout that I was for the guillotine. I recall the cries of one woman, a perfect stranger to me, who stood with her three children and pointed, 'There, *mes petites*, there goes an aristocrat whore and a traitor to her death.'

I knew not what the officials proposed for me. I was seated upon a bench in a room with bars upon the door. There was one other prisoner for company, a gentleman quite haggard and in a soiled shirt, who would not look me in the eye, nor address me out of fear. The only warmth came from a low fire which burned in the adjoining guards' room where my captors played dice, swore, smoked their pipes and taunted me with the grossest insults.

'Citizen Capet shall lose his head tomorrow,' they teased. 'What think you of that, *ma jolie*?'

'We shall see if the little royalist weeps for the tyrant!' another jibbed.

'I am no lover of the King,' I protested.

'Why, *ma petite*? Would Louis Capet's cock not crow for you?' questioned another with a sad moue. With that, they fell about in hilarity. One guard then unbuttoned his white breeches and held out his yard to me.

'Did it look like this one, but smaller?' The laughter reverberated through the small, smoke-filled room. He then took hold of the chamberpot and began to fill it, not several feet from the door. 'Eh, do I give you offence, citizeness?' He raised his dark eyes to me in sinister fashion. 'You think you pass for an honest woman? Shall we see what offence it gives you to be made good use of?'

Their laughter and jeers continued until eventually they tired of their sport and returned to their games of chance. I passed much of the day too terrified to so much as raise my head, lest I should draw their notice. It was only when the captain who had made my arrest returned to my cell that I dared move. Upon hearing his voice I jumped to my feet. He came directly to me and for a moment I believed I was to be released.

'Your maid Thérèse Bertrand has run off, citizeness,' said he. 'Can you think why?'

I shook my head vigorously, for this news gave me a shock and I was now more frightened than ever of recriminations.

He regarded me through narrowed eyes.

'She has not been dispatched on some urgent errand for you?'

'No, captain! I swear I know not what is the cause of her flight,' I protested, my throat tight.

'To pretend to ignorance will be of no assistance to you when you are brought to trial, citizeness. It is best to confess all you know. You spare no one by your protests. You are to be brought to the Mairie, where you will be examined and your fate decided.'

'Pray, monsieur, you take me for something I am not. I am no conspirator! I am a friend to Citizen Égalité,' I cried in a thin, quavering tone. 'Pray, captain, pray you alert him to this injustice, for I am innocent. I know no royalists or émigrés. You cannot accuse me of such a thing! Why, I am a friend to your Revolution. Can you not see it in my dress?' I stroked my wilted rosette. 'I implore you, captain, I must send a message to Monsieur Égalité with whom I am most intimate. I have lived with him, in the Palais-Royal, where I am well known to all his household. If you would but bring me pen and paper,' I begged.

He laughed. 'Do you not think that every whore in the precincts of the Palais-Royal has not cried the very words you have uttered, citizeness? I am an intimate of Monsieur Égalité!' He ridiculed me in a high-pitched voice. 'Tell me, *ma mignonne*, have you a sou upon your pretty person to pay for your pen and paper?' Then he showed me a mocking smile while wagging his head. 'I did not think so. You see, there is a price for every pleasure. Have you yourself not uttered those words? *Non?*' He finished with a wink.

At that, dear friends, I recoiled in defeat. My interrogator, this monster, promptly turned upon his heel, abandoning me to my fate.

Chapter 27

I was committed to the Prison de l'Abbaye on the very day of the execution of Louis XVI. As for that treacherous event, I was grateful to be spared the sight of it, even if it was on account of my incarceration.

I had passed a sleepless night in the section house cell, wide awake and in mortal terror that the guards would commit upon me the violence they had promised earlier. For hours I had listened to their swearing and songs and speculation as to how the King's head might fall. They laid wagers upon the colour of his blood. One ruffian claimed that the monarch was certain to bleed purple for he had been told as much as a boy.

At near to mid-morning I heard the echo of artillery fire which I was told announced that the blade in the place Louis XV had fallen. The grim work had been done. This was later confirmed by the wife of one of the guards, who appeared bearing a blood-soaked handkerchief which she held up before their marvelling eyes. Each one of the men fingered the sodden crimson linen with what seemed reverence and incredulity, as if they could not determine whether this scrap of cloth represented a triumph or some shameful deed. I stared, awe-struck at the horror of what I beheld.

For all the talk of it, some part of me did not believe that such an abomination should ever come to pass. My thoughts upon that occasion were not the same as those of most. While many feared for the nation or wept for the Queen and her children, I could think of no one but Orléans and those nearest to him. I knew that the disquiet in his heart would be intolerable. My breast heaved with sadness, for myself as much as for the friends who I feared were lost to me for ever.

The monarch's blood had not yet been washed from the cobbles when I was conveyed to the Mairie and examined by the mayor. Here, I learned that Thérèse's disappearance had placed me in the most perilous of positions. What suspicion had fallen on the activities of my household was now redoubled. As the evidence they had confiscated from my apartments had yet to be examined, it was decided that I should be interned.

It is a curious circumstance that my sojourn in Paris should both begin and conclude in Saint-Germain-des-Prés, scarcely a moment's stroll from the rue Jacob and the dreaded Hôtel l'Impératrice. Had the Abbaye proven as hospitable as the rooms of that luxurious prison, I would not have uttered a single complaint. But, as a matter of course, they were not. From its exterior, the prison appeared more akin to a workhouse than a dungeon. Squat and turreted, it was neither large nor imposing, but that was where its catalogue of charms ended. Within, it was a place of damp grey stone and wretchedness.

The prospect of crossing the threshold of the Abbaye terrified me to my very bones so that I could not prevent them from quaking. I could not conceive of the terrors and depredations with which I should meet, nor if I would ever again know liberty. Oh, reader, how I attempted to make a display of courage, but soon found it near to impossible.

The room to which I was led appeared much like a servants'

hall in an ancient house. It was of a similar size, with stone floors and walls. Three barred and unglazed windows near to the ceiling permitted in both light and the cold. To my relief, I spied a vast hearth, large enough in which to roast a pig, but unfortunately even this convenience failed to dispel the ever-present chill. Arrayed about this space were no less than eight trestle beds, each of which had been manoeuvred into corners or at angles which seemed to provide the occupants with an attempt at privacy. There were no bed curtains, no screens to shield one's modesty anywhere to be seen. Instead, portmanteaus and rickety chairs were set about as if to divide the room. Atop these items of furniture were balanced various objects: a mirror, a sewing box and an assortment of the earthenware jugs and basins which each inmate was granted. These were to be my lodgings.

I was greeted at once by five of my sister prisoners who showed me the greatest sympathy upon my arrival. They made their curtseys and took my hand in such a genteel manner that it caused my eyes to flow. This, Madame Hubert, who had once been a mother superior, explained was a natural response.

'Not a one amongst us has entered this place without tears, *ma chère*. You will cease to shed them with time, but for the odd occasion.' With that, she turned her gaze upon another lady with reddish tresses that nearly matched the colour of her nose and eyes. Madame Crozier sniffled her apologies that the news of the King's murder had brought her quite low.

'It has had that effect upon all of us,' added Madame Desenfants, who stood beside her sullen-faced daughter of not more than sixteen years.

I was under no illusion as to the allegiances of those about me. I need not have even learned their stories: that Madame Desenfants and her daughter were returned émigrés; that Madame Crozier had pledged money to some conspirators led by the Marquis de la Rouërie; that elderly Madame de Vollet had attempted to unlawfully sell all of her silver abroad; or that Mesdames Hubert and Fourçon had been sisters of the Benedictine order who had by some miracle survived the prison massacres of September. I understood only that my existence would be one of less discomfort and unhappiness if I courted their good graces. They were royalists and I would not utter a syllable as to whose company I had kept prior to my arrival there.

In my first several days I did not trust a soul about me, no matter how affable her appearance, for I had learned the price of sincerity. I sat alone upon my bed, my head in my hands, awash with sorrows and racked with fears. I knew nothing of the consequences of my arrest and fretted endlessly that I had somehow imperilled Allenham. I had no means of discovering his fate or even that of Mrs Elliot, for to so much as breathe their names would cause them to become suspect. I knew the prisons to be filled with spies and that the guards would listen carefully to all conversation, so I resolved to speak to no one.

I continued in this reserved manner for two, perhaps three days until a box of my belongings arrived along with a note from Lucy. This served to raise my spirits, if only temporarily. I discovered that my apartments in the Hôtel Blanquefort had been sealed. But for this assortment of basic attire and necessaries, which my maid had been directed to assemble, all of my remaining possessions had been confiscated. Furthermore, as my lodgings formally belonged to Madame de Chalmont, who had now been pronounced an émigré, her property and all her furniture had been seized by the Republic. After a formidable inquisition by the guards, Lucy, Madame Vernet and Jean were turned out of my home, but I was relieved to learn that my maid had been taken in by my cook at the home of her sister. As my heart took in this news, I sat and sighed sadly to myself before turning my attention to my portmanteau.

No sooner had I begun to rummage through it and inspect what pieces of apparel had been delivered to me than I caught sight of the elderly Madame de Vollet. She advanced towards me with a slow, laboured limp before making a thorough examination of my items through her pair of lorgnettes.

'Mademoiselle, you must be certain to set aside your finest gown and laced cap,' she pronounced after a spell. 'Keep them folded and preserved from the damp and the vermin.'

I regarded her with an indifferent air.

'But why, madame?'

'For your trial, *ma chère*. It is so you may go to your death attired with dignity.' She raised her head and I stared at her in silence. Her eyes were crisp blue set within a multitude of pale folds and creases. She returned my unflinching look with one of equal defiance.

'If your time arrives before mine, I shall assist you, as will the others. That is our practice here. Each one among us has set aside our attire for that day. We prepare one another for the inevitable, *ma petite*. It is only kindness.' She lifted one of her faint eyebrows gently. 'Should the occasion of my trial arrive before yours, may I call upon your assistance too, mademoiselle?'

I felt shame stain my cheeks.

'But of course, madame,' I whispered.

From that instant, Madame de Vollet, who acted as the grand matron of our small circle of lady prisoners, maintained a tender watch over me. I have never witnessed such displays of civility, charity and fortitude as those I observed amongst my companions at the Abbaye. Each soul assisted the other; the young tended the old; the strong saved their bread and watered wine for those who fell ill. In the hours of daylight we were permitted to make use of a common room for dining which led into an enclosed courtyard with a well. Each morning we filled our pitchers here and made our ablutions by the fire, though we had no means of heating the water and the bite of winter was strong. We dined together with the men, of which there were a considerable number. Many of them had been priests or printers of royalist tracts or true counter-revolutionaries who made no secret of their abhorrence of the Convention. Together we shared quiet conversation and our meagre repasts: cabbage and eggs and a thin soup called *bouli*, which often rendered us quite ill. Our bread was brown and coarse and frequently full of stones, upon which it was not unknown to break a tooth.

At meals we affected a pretence of congeniality, though the turnkeys kept close watch over their prisoners and did not look fondly upon flirtation between them. Still, Madame Desenfants pinched her daughter's cheeks and fussed with her cap, as if the poor girl had some hope of ensnaring a former count or marquis for a husband. At all other times we attempted cheerfulness, though often without much success. At night our door was bolted at ten o'clock. We were then commanded to extinguish the single spitting candle we had each been allocated. No sooner had the darkness and silence sealed us into our frozen beds than the weeping began. At times the sobs were loud and alarming, but mostly the women pressed their faces to their flat straw pillows and wetted them. They cried for their children, for their husbands, their parents and siblings, many of whom languished in some other forlorn cell or had already met their fate upon the scaffold. Others wept with fear, for daylight never failed to bring a guard with a list of names who might swoop down upon any of the prisoners, as unannounced as the angel of death.

As the weeks passed, my spirits continued to sink like a stone dropped to the bottom of a well. In a fit of desperation I attempted to dispatch letters to the Maison Égalité by bribing one of the guards with a small enamel box of scant worth. I pleaded for

Madame de Buffon's forgiveness and Orléans's intercession, but as I received neither a reply nor a release I assumed my entreaties had never arrived at their intended destination. I did not wish to consider that they had, but had gone unanswered, or, worse still, that I resided precisely where my erstwhile friend intended. I called to mind many times her final words to me, that she could not hazard to be associated with one regarded as a royalist. I grew listless and, I confess, on occasions began to wish for death, that I might awaken that morning or the next to hear my name bellowed out for judgement. Despair had seduced me so thoroughly that I had begun to wish I had never abandoned my father's home, but embraced the fate he had designed for me. As for love, I eschewed that as no better than a phial of poison.

I did not know March when it arrived. I had long ceased to count days and weeks. The ice still hung in the air; my breath came in clouds even as I lay in my bed. Then one afternoon, as I scrubbed my chemises and stockings in a basin of frigid water, I was summoned into the presence of Monsieur Brudeau, the prison keeper.

'Your servant who absconded upon the day of your arrest, she was Thérèse Bertrand?' the short, red-nosed man barked at me.

'Yes, monsieur.'

'She has been apprehended in Moselle, the place of her birth. They are great patriots in Moselle and they knew her to be a conspirator.'

I regarded him with shock.

'They found upon her some documents and a book containing many pages of codes and ciphers. She had been in communication with émigrés, in Coblenz, Geneva, Turin and in London. Her case has been heard and she has been put to death.'

I could not mask the horror I felt at his pronouncement and began to shed tears for my unfortunate housemaid. I wondered why she had been willing to undertake the dangerous tasks requested of her by Mrs Elliot, or indeed if she had initially been deceived into performing this role, much as I had been. How I cursed that woman. Thérèse's blood would be upon her hands.

'You weep, citizeness?' He stared hard into my eyes. 'It is the guilty who weep. It only remains to be seen if your fate will be the same as your servant's.'

I now began to wait in earnest. Upon each occasion when a guard passed by our door or came abruptly into the common dining room, my heart began to race. I anticipated hearing my name, but those of others were cried out instead.

At the end of that month, I was shaken awake by a guard holding a great smoking torch above me. The dawn had not quite broken.

'Citizeness, you must come now. You are to be moved to the Conciergerie. Your trial is set for this morning.'

Madame Fourçon, who slept nearest to me, heard this and immediately sprang from her bed.

'Oh, dear God, child! You will be condemned to die!' she exclaimed. At the sound of this, the entire room of women, who now numbered fifteen, were roused from their slumber. They stared at me through the early blue light with sleepy, horrified eyes. Madame Fourçon reached tenderly for my hand.

'You must dress, mademoiselle.' Madame de Vollet spoke firmly. 'We shall prepare you.'

My turn had come.

I had participated in this ritual on at least a dozen occasions prior to this day. I had bid adieu to Madame Crozier and cried bitterly to observe Madame Desenfants wrenched from the arms of her daughter. I had threaded a fresh blue ribbon into her cap and smoothed her hair beneath it as she sobbed. I had tightened the stays of Mademoiselle Touret and tied Madame Le Donine's sash. Each woman took their leave of us attired in some part of their former existence, albeit creased, dampened and far looser fitted.

That which I had chosen to preserve was the gown made from the striped blue silk Allenham had once purchased for me.

In the corner of the dank room, six ladies crowded about me. One offered me a basin of cold water with which to wash my face and hands while Mademoiselle Desenfants removed me from my night shift. Another anxiously rifled through my box for a clean chemise, which she handed to me in silence. They assisted me in fastening my stocking garters, for my hands shook so. They tied me into my skirts. Madame de Vollet began to weep quietly to herself as she fixed the front of my bodice. There were hands upon my back, my hair, straightening my skirts. My feet were encased in a pair of blue shoes given to me by Orléans. My finest buckles had been seized and so these delicate slippers of Italian silk were adorned with no more than simple grosgrain ribbons.

When at last I was dressed, the lamentations and embracing began in earnest, until the guard returned and ordered me to come.

Madame de Vollet grabbed at my hand.

'My poor child, adieu! May God preserve you!'

I regarded her, my eyes dulled and tired of life.

'If I am to die, then I am not sorry for it.'

In truth, I wished for nothing more.

Chapter 28

The full light of morning had not yet penetrated the gloom. I took it to be perhaps six o'clock when they brought me and another prisoner, a man accused of forging documents for émigrés, by cart through the still, sombre streets. I was pleased there were few to assail me, to bellow out curses, to spit or throw filth. When I confess to you, reader, that I was not afraid, that I scarcely knew myself any more, that my mind and heart were as void and empty as dry amphorae, you must believe me. As we rattled slowly through the rue Saint-André-des-Arts to the pont Michel I considered the sky with the awareness of someone who believed they would never again witness dawn. Before me, the clouds turned the colour of roses against the indigo of morning. Where once I might have marvelled at this spectacle of nature, at the display of ever-altering hues, I now simply observed, feeling nothing stir in my breast. What life I had lived had now been spent and, after having glimpsed its horrors and delights, and all the most alluring and hideous faces of the human character, I was reconciled to death.

I did not expect to find what I did upon our arrival at the Conciergerie: despite the early hour, the room was entirely filled with clerks and those awaiting their trials. It was, as I recall, a forbidding, dark Gothic antechamber which vibrated with murmuring echoes; conversation, commands, coughs, sobs and clatter rose into the high, vaulted ceilings. The clink of keys jangled like a hundred little bells. Amidst this, small pools of light fell upon the stone floor from the grated windows above. At the end of this hall was a narrow stair and a gallery, which I was to learn led to the halls of Liberté and Égalité, the rooms where the trials were heard.

It was here, before a clerk, that my name was committed to a register. When I was asked it, I found myself so choked that I could scarcely speak the words. Indeed, I was forced to pause for a moment to think what name I would use.

'Henrietta Katherine Lightfoot.' That was the name which I had taken when I entered into my current life, and so it should be the one I bore when I quit it. With little more ceremony than that, I was then directed to take my seat upon the benches beside a collection of twenty or so of the most wretched souls I had ever glimpsed.

My friends, have you ever looked into the eye of a condemned man? Then you will understand the character of true desperation. There is to be found an ocean of remorse here, an endless depth of sorrow, a black fear as broad as the night sky. Women wept into their handkerchiefs; men too muttered and bawled into their hands. Others could not bear to sit in their final hours and paced mournfully or silently mouthed their prayers. In the corner, upon a filthy mattress, lay two men, too weak with illness to sit upright. Beneath the benches were scattered all manner of remnants: plates, bottles, crumbs of bread and the gristle of meat, provisions brought to them as they waited by suffering wives or children. All within that room bore faces etched with an understanding of their doom. Scarcely a word passed between us. Without uttering so much as a syllable to me, the thin, drawn lady who sat at my left reached for my hand. I permitted her to take it and hold it in hers as she shed tears.

An hour passed, and then perhaps two more. I observed as, one by one, those who occupied the room were summoned. With each name that was shouted through the hall, a soul rose humbly from their seat to meet with their fate. They were taken up the stair to the narrow gallery. The doors to the salon then swung wide, screeching ominously upon their hinges as they took in the accused and, on occasion, disgorged the innocent. Some would enter in tears and depart in elation, freed to return to their homes. Others would proceed with high heads, or take their leave in the depths of misery, wailing at the injustice of their circumstances. We sat below, as a silent, terrified audience.

I believe it was at some time in the afternoon when the name of Citizeness Saint-Clair was called and the unfortunate creature beside me stood to her feet.

'Mademoiselle, you have warmed my hand and my heart. I bid you well,' said she, before solemnly making her way to the stair.

'There is no hope for her,' whispered a man in a filthy gold-embroidered coat opposite me. His face had not been washed or shaven for several days and the white hairs upon his chin stood out among the black. 'She was an émigré and was foolish enough to return.'

No sooner had he spoken than my name was bellowed out.

A sharpness struck through me. It passed as swiftly as lightning from my head to my feet. I rose instantly as two guards approached and escorted me up the stair. We passed into the wooden gallery and then through the whining door and into a corridor glowing with daylight.

Two more doors were pushed wide, and then, reader, then I heard it, that noise of which I had been warned by my fellow prisoners: the braying and bleating of the gallery. Encircled by a wooden rail, they appeared like penned animals, like captured savages. They lit pipes, they drank and whistled, even the women jeered and hissed. What had become of civility? I wondered as I made my way upon the dais, to the spot designated for the accused. Certainly it did not follow that the acquisition of liberty should lead to the end of human compassion. This was never the intention of men like Monsieur Condorcet or Madame de Gouges, or even Madame de Buffon.

My eyes stared out at this congregation, through the blinding afternoon light. It flooded through the wide windows, bathing everything before me in a curious glow. I squinted and blinked.

'Citizeness, state your name, your age, your place of birth and your address before the tribunal,' a thundering voice implored me.

For a moment, I could not determine whence the question had come. My heart pounded as I searched about the room. So deadened to the world had my senses been that in the short time I had stood in that place I had failed to note who sat in judgement over me. I turned my head and then spied the judge, or president as they called him, and the jury to the other side of me, each of them a proud patriot, adorned in their rosettes and tricolour sashes.

'I am Henrietta Katherine Lightfoot. I am twenty years of age. I am an Englishwoman, living in Paris, until of late in the Hôtel Blanquefort, upon the rue Saint-Honoré, Section Saint-Honoré.'

At the announcement of my nationality there came a wild noise from the barn of beasts.

'Citizeness Lightfoot is charged with corresponding and conspiring with émigrés and assisting the counter-revolution. She is also charged with harbouring in her employment the conspirator and traitoress Thérèse-Marie Bertrand,' came a high-pitched cock's crow of a voice.

This last proclamation had been the cue for the prosecutor, Monsieur Fouquier-Tinville, to step forward. Such an odious, hateful scoundrel as he I have never had the misfortune of again encountering. He wore a scowl so unmoving, so deeply etched into his features that I was certain his very heart was hewn of marble. He wore his hair long, undressed and without a ribbon to tie it back, and two great hooped earrings, as if he were an African savage. I had come to notice that of late, many of the most zealous had taken to such an unkempt style. They preferred to attire themselves as would lawless bandits and ruffians so as to pretend that they had not been born as men of learning, nor practised as lawyers or schoolmasters. Striding across the courtroom in his jackboots, he looked more like a messenger just dismounted from his horse at an inn than an official of state.

Something in the sight of him stirred me. My otherwise muted heart, which until that instant felt nothing, sparked to life. Contempt began to burn within me. It rose into a sense of fury at those monsters who gathered in the gallery and who laughed at my misfortunes and howled for my death. It raged at Her. It was Her deceptions that had led me to this place, She, whom I had called mother. It was She who had sent Thérèse Bertrand to her death. Where was She now? I wondered. Where was She as I stood falsely accused for her crimes?

The hound Fouquier-Tinville then opened his jaws and launched his attack upon me. Standing at the centre of the court, he addressed those assembled, spreading wide his arms like a singer at the opera. He spoke as if reciting the words to some republican hymn. He offered thanksgiving to 'the great spirit of liberty who, in her wisdom, uncovers and spoils all plots and schemes against the fatherland. May the Republic ever triumph over such machinations and its despoilers,' cried he with a flourish of his hand.

The gallery whooped in appreciation.

'It is the plan of the Prince of Coburg, of the Duke of Brunswick and all their minions and émigré traitors to sow the seeds of division among us. It is their most ardent wish that we, citizens, are returned to our shackles, that our Republic is broken beneath the heels of their princely shoes. That, citizens, honourable patriots, will never be!'

Such a roar and a stomping of feet rose from the assembly that I believed it might shatter the windows. When the noise subsided, he turned his coal eyes to me.

'Citizeness Lightfoot's story is not an exceptional one. You have heard that she is an Englishwoman, one of those many votaries of decadence who came here to feed like jackals upon the scraps thrown to her by the depraved sons of aristocracy. So notorious were the excesses of our princes and counts, so renowned were they for their depravity and their inability to resist the lures of the flesh, that they issued forth a stink like that of a rotting corpse. This foul smell drew all the world's scavengers to our shores to feast. Since her arrival here, she has been known among the *filles de joie* of the highest order and, for some time, consorted with a Madame Elliot, a fellow countrywoman, until she found the politics of that lady repellent and was encouraged to break off the acquaintance by Citizen Égalité, whose particular friend she became. This, citizens, is to her credit, but does not explain why she chose to keep a memorandum of the days she passed in the company of Citizen Égalité and his household. Neither does there seem to be an answer as to why she chose to record her thoughts in a coded version of her native tongue. Nor does it forgive her for maintaining in her employment a traitoress, Thérèse-Marie Bertrand, who served as her housemaid and whose sole endeavour was to bring about the ruin of the Republic. Citizens, let it be known to you that Thérèse Bertrand was found guilty of the most heinous offences against the Republic; that of acting as an agent for the counter-revolution. She had been at the centre of correspondence with émigrés, including some of the most despised enemies of our Republic: the Comte d'Artois, the Duc and Duchesse de Polignac, the Duc de Noailles and the Prince de Condé, whose mistress she had once been while a maid in his household.' Fouquier-Tinville paused in his oration to pat his forehead with his handkerchief. The entire courtroom remained silent as he performed this task. He then cleared his throat.

'Prior to taking her place before the guillotine but a fortnight ago, Citizeness Bertrand offered her confession. In it, she described how she had received the communiqués of these émigrés. They were written in code. She was then charged with the task of deciphering them with the aid of a book of ciphers, before passing on the information through further coded letters to the parties concerned. The book containing her ciphers was retrieved upon her arrest by our brother patriots in Moselle.'

I stood aghast, my face blanched. This was the first I had heard of the subterfuge which had occurred beneath the roof of my own apartments. My correspondence with Mrs Elliot must have been but a small portion of the many letters to have passed through Thérèse's care. That she had employed a code and ciphers only served to aggravate my own situation.

'Let it be understood, citizens, that while the code committed to the pages of Citizeness Lightfoot's diaries does not correspond with those found within Thérèse Bertrand's book of ciphers, the suspicion which hangs about her, that she too was a participant in this treachery, cannot be dismissed – for certainly, my brothers, a mistress should have knowledge of the activities of her servants. Finally, it does not serve Citizeness Lightfoot well for it to be known that upon a search of her apartments, the place which she cites as her home, there was to be found no correspondence. There were no letters of any description, not a single line from a beloved parent or sibling, not a single *billet-doux* from one of her many lovers. When questioned as to this irregularity, Citizeness Lightfoot confessed that she had made a habit of disposing of her correspondence. I put to you, my brothers, is this not the action of one wishing to disguise her espionage?'

Fouquier-Tinville permitted this question to linger in the air. There came a beat of silence as he waited, head bowed with theatrical anticipation for the calls from the gallery.

'She is a traitoress! She is a whore! English bitch!' they came.

The president of the tribunal then cleared his throat and drew forth two sheets of writing paper.

'In defence of the accused, a letter of character has been submitted by Citizen Égalité.'

Upon hearing this, I took in a sharp breath of hope. Orléans. My letter written from the Abbaye had reached him. My eyes began to sting with tears. I waited for the president to read its comforting message to me, but instead his eyes rolled over the words.

'It is a substantial missive,' he pronounced with a half-grumble. 'It gives praise at length to Citizeness Lightfoot's love of liberty and her devotion to the Republic,' he summarized. He then took his eyes from the paper and folded it. My heart had begun to sink at the prospect of never hearing Orléans's final words to me, when he reached for a second letter.

'There is another statement from a Citizeness Buffon,' said he, opening another folded sheet. At this, my mouth fairly fell wide. I raised my hand to my breast. 'It is longer still than the first and filled with all manner of irrelevant female sentiment,' he sighed, before perusing its contents. 'It is claimed that the accused served as a *dame de compagnie* to this woman who declares herself a faithful champion of the Jacobin cause, one well known to Citizens Danton and Marat. This Citizeness Buffon proclaims the accused to be a passionate friend of the Revolution and greatly devoted to the writings of Rousseau, whose merits these women discussed upon many an occasion.'

There came sniggers from some quarter of the gallery.

'Furthermore, Citizeness Buffon attests that Citizeness Lightfoot attended sessions of the Legislative Assembly and the National Convention to observe debates. Upon the third of September she was gravely injured while championing the cause of liberty. Citizeness Buffon concludes by writing in favour of the accused that Citizeness Lightfoot is in every way a sister to her as well as to the Republic.'

Nothing I had heard until that moment struck me with as much force as those words from Agnès de Buffon. I was ashamed I had ever suspected that bitterness had led her to denounce me to the section house. The pain of my betrayal of her pierced through me. The ache was more terrible than any I had ever known. Tears of regret streamed uncontrollably forth, mingling with those of relief, for I felt myself to some degree absolved of my crimes against her. I knew she would not be among the assembly of spectators, but I could not prevent myself from searching for her familiar figure.

'The tribunal calls Pierre-Joseph Colbert,' the cockerel-like voice of the clerk sounded again through the court.

To the bench advanced a short, round-bellied man, upon whom, I confess, I had never before laid eyes.

'If you will, citizen, state your name, occupation, age and address for the tribunal.'

'I am Pierre-Joseph Colbert. I am thirty-one years of age, a member of the Jacobin Club and a surgeon. I live on the rue du Faubourg Saint-Honoré, in the Hôtel Blanquefort upon the second floor, above the accused.'

'Pray, citizen, tell us how you came to know Citizeness Lightfoot,' began Fouquier-Tinville.

'I am the patriot who raised the alarm,' said he proudly, not daring to spare me a glance. 'It was I who notified the section house upon several occasions when I noted the irregularities occurring below me.'

'Irregularities? Elaborate, Citizen Colbert.'

The impudent little man then began his tale, claiming that he and his family thought it most peculiar that Citizeness Lightfoot's housemaid came and went at such strange hours, even when her mistress was never at home. There seemed such a catalogue of errands to perform as to be improbable.

'My wife had commented on this to me,' said he, 'and also that there seemed too many people coming to call at a household where the mistress was absent. I thought I should put my enquiries to her one day when I met her in the courtyard. She was a haughty bitch. I might have known from her manner that she was a royalist.'

'What reply did she make to you upon your enquiries?'

He snorted.

'She said to me her mistress was an Englishwoman who made many demands upon her. I thought this curious indeed, for I had seen this lady once in the six months we had taken the lodgings.'

'And what was the occasion upon which you saw the accused, citizen?'

'It was in August past. On the day that followed the taking of the Tuileries Palace. Citizeness Lightfoot arrived and went up the stairs in a haste. I had never before beheld this woman and thought it curious she should arrive on such a day. As the guards had instructed all citizens to remain vigilant for irregularities, I lingered in the courtyard and observed her apartments. Shortly after Citizeness Lightfoot's arrival there came a cabriolet. A lady, modestly though well attired and with the air of an aristocrat, stepped from it and went above to the accused's apartments. She remained there for but a short time before emerging again. On this occasion she took her leave by the servants' stair where she stood part hidden with the traitoress Thérèse Bertrand for a moment. It was then that I spied Citizeness Bertrand hand the lady some letter or document which the recipient placed immediately into her pocket and departed.'

'And what of Citizeness Lightfoot? Pray tell us when you saw her next?'

'It was shortly after I witnessed this exchange. She then took her leave by a grand coach belonging, I believe, to some nobleman. I did not see or hear of her again until January.'

'What occurred upon that occasion, Citizen Colbert?'

'It was a day or so before the King was taken to the scaffold. When I returned for my dinner, there was a good deal of noise and commotion in the courtyard. A great cart of boxes and goods had arrived and was being portered to the apartments belonging to Citizeness Lightfoot. I enquired of the carters what this was about and learned of the gossip. They replied that Citizeness Lightfoot was returned from the Palais-Royal where Citizen Égalité had had enough of her for befriending royalists! It was then I knew I must make my denouncement to the section.' The fat barber Colbert puffed out his chest. His rosette seemed to grow larger with each wheeze of breath he took.

I did not disguise my disdain as this preposterous sham of a man removed his loathsome figure from the dais. After he had resumed his seat amongst the crowd, the president of the tribunal turned to me and enquired if I wished to refute these claims.

I opened my mouth to speak. My words sounded, to my ears, very weak.

'Monsieur,' said I, addressing him in the formal style. This caused him some embarrassment and he bristled visibly. 'I speak the truth when I declare that I knew nothing of Thérèse

Bertrand's associations, only that she came with good references from the household of the Prince de Condé.'

I might have spoken more, but stopped myself. I had to fairly bite my tongue to prevent my confession from flying free: that it was Mrs Elliot who had introduced Thérèse into my household. If she had not already suffered arrest, then those words would have incriminated her for certain. The guards would have pounced upon her and searched beneath every floorboard and cut open every mattress for her letters. Indeed, I could have informed them about the portrait of Grace Elliot's daughter, Georgiana Seymour. They need only pull upon the backing of it and there discover all they required to neatly remove Grace Elliot's head. But, reader, I resisted. You may wonder what compelled me, Henrietta Lightfoot, who has now become so corrupt of soul, to make such a display of her charitable nature. I am not the creature you take me for. I am not as my detractors would paint me. I am no worse, no more prone to the temptations of vengeance or the restraints of fear than you. You see, Mrs Elliot was profoundly clever. She understood that I would never decry her to the section house, to the Jacobin Club, to my prison keeper or to the Committee of Public Safety, for she held Allenham's fate in her hands. The letters that might have been discovered in any such search of her homes could well have borne his name. She knew I would go to my death bearing the weight of her secrets. And, as it had ever been, my consent to such a sacrifice had never been sought.

'I lived for a good while with the household at the Maison Égalité, at which time I had no dealings with my housemaid, nor was I aware of any of her unfortunate alliances,' I continued, my voice cracking. 'Furthermore, monsieur, I have never before in my life set eyes upon Citizen Colbert who accuses me, for I was but once at my home and upon that occasion it was to make certain that the lives of my household had not been imperilled by events. I was then resident at the Palais-Royal, where I lived in the Petits Appartements with the household of Citizen Égalité. Prior to that I had been in the country with Citizeness Buffon and absent from Paris. Had I been informed in any degree of Citizeness Bertrand's activities, I would have made a report to the section house post haste . . .' said I, now spewing forth falsehoods and beginning to tremble. 'I am, monsieur, not to blame for her disloyalty and machinations, for I was ignorant of them – entirely. Monsieur le président, I swear this upon my very life.'

And with that, it was as if I had opened my bodice to Fouquier-Tinville, to that devil who stalked the floor, and offered him a dagger. He turned, and came at me with an eager light in his eyes.

'Citizeness,' began he in a beguiling tone, 'you say you were resident in the Maison Égalité and not at your apartments at the Hôtel Blanquefort.'

'Yes, citizen.'

'Did you, at any time in your absence, not correspond with your housekeeper?'

My heart began to throb vigorously. I wondered if he knew, if indeed they had known all along, about the invisible ink or the letters Thérèse had passed between me and Mrs Elliot.

'Why . . . why . . . yes, I did.'

'Upon what matters, citizeness?'

'Why, the usual, monsieur . . . household accounts, purchases, etc.'

'Not upon any matters of politics?'

I forced a laugh, which echoed through the hall as if it were a shriek.

'I am not in the habit of discussing political matters with my household, monsieur.'

'No gossip from the Maison Égalité? None of those idle matters that pass between a lady and her maid?'

'No, monsieur. None. Never.'

'You will tell the tribunal then, Citizeness Lightfoot, for what purpose did you keep a memorandum of your conversations with Citizen Égalité, his family and household . . . if not to make gossip upon it?'

I stared at him. I could not think of an answer.

'It . . . was not . . . not for the purpose of gossip, monsieur . . . with my household . . .'

'Then for whom?'

'For . . . my own diversion, monsieur.'

'At no time did you send the contents of these diaries to Thérèse Bertrand?'

'No!' I snapped, perhaps too vehemently to be believed.

'But she has seen these diaries, has she not?'

'No. I swear it. No.'

'Upon their delivery to your apartments, Citizeness Bertrand was there to receive your effects, and the pocketbooks were among them. Is that not correct, Citizeness Lightfoot?'

He was, of course, correct. Though there had been nothing in the journals that Thérèse could have deciphered.

'Is that not correct, Citizeness Lightfoot? Your housemaid was privy to that which you had written upon that occasion.'

I swallowed. I slowly shook my head.

'I cannot imagine that she would have thought to look for such items among my effects . . .' My voice was now quite meek and thin.

'I propose to the tribunal that Citizeness Lightfoot conspired to share information to which she was privy from within the Maison Égalité, and at other times, with the traitoress Thérèse Bertrand!' Fouquier-Tinville announced with a rumbling roar.

The gallery erupted into shouts and heckles.

'She is guilty!' 'Traitoress!' 'Spy!' 'Enemy of the Republic!'

'No!' I cried. 'No, it is not true!' But my voice was drowned in a sea of shouts and expostulations.

The president nodded at my persecutor.

'The jury shall retire to contemplate the verdict.'

There was a great rush of commotion. The cries and howls did not abate, and through it, I felt my voice, my very life sucked from my throat, as all the sounds rose weightlessly into the dome above us, circling like buzzards overhead.

As a girl, I had once been swung by my brother Edwin Ingerton upon a swing, built by one of the servants at Melmouth. Instead of pushing me to and fro, we turned in the seat, twisting and knotting until we could draw the two ropes no tighter together. Then, with one hasty motion, we allowed the apparatus to spring free and spin us as rapidly as a toy top set loose from a whip.

I had never felt such a sensation again, until that moment in the tribunal. It was as if all the sounds and sights – the light, the smoking candles, the moving bodies, the squeal of door hinges, the shuffle of feet, the spitting, the jeering, the laughing, the distant conversation – churned about me, swirling into one confusion of noise and scene, so that I saw and felt nothing, and yet everything at once.

'Citizen Fouquier-Tinville! Citizen Fouquier-Tinville! Citizen President!'

I heard a voice cry repeatedly through the din.

'Citizen Fouquier-Tinville!'

It came from the gallery, from the crowd who were now rising to stretch their legs and make water in the stair behind.

'Citizen President!'

I looked, but could not steady my eyes. A man stood at the waist-high wooden partition which contained the spectators. He was wearing a black high-crowned hat, like most gentlemen, but the plain blue wool coat of a tradesman.

'Citizen Fouquier-Tinville, I am in possession of some information critical to this trial! This is an urgent matter, citizen!'

At that, the court halted. The president held up his hand. Fouquier-Tinville turned to face the gallery.

'Ah! Citizen Tyrone.' His voice lightened.

No sooner had the man's name been spoken than he removed his hat, slowly revealing his dark tresses, hanging loose to his shoulders.

At first I could not take him in, for in truth, reader, my heart and senses had suffered such wounds as to render me near insensible to any matter which passed before me. I stood entirely numb.

He did not venture to catch my eye. Truly, in my present circumstance I believe he could not bear to look upon me, while he himself appeared greatly shaken. His hands clenched in fists as he held the wooden dowels of the screen.

'Citizen,' he cried, 'this prisoner is innocent!'

All within the room fell silent. Fouquier-Tinville approached him slowly, an expression of bemusement on his face.

'I fear . . . I hope I have arrived in time to make a presentation to you, citizen . . . to the citizen president and to the tribunal . . .'

Fouquier-Tinville exchanged looks with the president, who nodded his assent.

'Citizen Tyrone, as an esteemed friend of the Revolution and as one known so well to your brothers here among the tribunal, this court will hear your submission,' said the prosecutor.

Allenham stood for a moment, his white stock tied high around his neck in the sans-culotte fashion, his ungloved hands resting upon the balustrade. He looked nothing like the image of the man I had kept locked safe within my breast. This new persona, Henry Tyrone, with his untied hair and fringe upon his forehead, this printer of angry bile-soaked cant – how far from this was the Allenham I had known at Orchard Cottage, with the gentle light from the fire falling on his face as he read to me in a soft, resonant voice. Was this truly him? Did my mind, now so disordered from my ordeal, not throw out hallucinations before me? I squinted, as if striving to see through the screen of my disbelief.

Indeed, at that moment, every eye was upon him; each pair of lungs had ceased to breathe.

'Citizen president . . .' he began. 'You and those who sit on this tribunal know me as Henry Tyrone. I am twenty-six years of age. I am a Jacobin, a printer and a secretary to Citizen Robespierre. I was born in Boston in the former British colony of Massachusetts, which is now recognized as the United States of America, but of late I have been made a proud national of France.' He inhaled and held his head aloft. 'Near to a fortnight ago, I was presented with the journals belonging to the prisoner and requested by the Committee of Public Safety to translate their contents. I was informed that they had been confiscated from the house of an enemy of the Republic. I knew no more than this when I opened their covers. As it has been asserted to the tribunal, they are written in code, though I can affirm this code bears no similarity to any found in the cipher book belonging to Thérèse Bertrand. Indeed, citizens,' said he, directing his gaze at the president and the prosecutor, 'it is merely a form of simple shorthand and obviously invented by the prisoner. It is elementary and easily deciphered by those familiar with the English tongue. The initials, are, as you correctly surmised, used to reference individuals, among them Citizen Égalité, as well as members of his family, household and guests. However, there is, citizens, nothing sinister in this, for as those in this tribunal can universally aver, shorthand is a convention most regularly employed in the keeping of memoranda and in correspondence. These were the facts I presented to the Committee of Public Safety, as was requested of me.'

Allenham drew breath, his hands tightening once more. His brow and hard jaw clenched in determination.

'There remains, of course, the question as to why the prisoner chose to maintain such a record as this, and for whose eyes it was intended . . .'

He paused. I observed him and, for a moment, my heart began to stir. I could not say what animated it, whether it moved from fear or from love, for I knew not what this pause in his narrative was to bring.

'Citizens, I lay before you my confession. This prisoner, Citizeness Lightfoot, is no stranger to me.' And with that, my beloved turned his gaze upon mine. His brilliant eyes, which had been so shy of meeting with my own, at last beheld me. His expression was just as I recalled it upon that dreaded day in the passage de Valois, consumed with trepidation. His finely shaped dark eyebrows arched backward. His eyes opened round and wide. The fear in his features was plain.

'In the course of performing the translation of the prisoner's diaries, I came to recognize that they belonged to her . . . to a woman to whom I had done a great injustice.'

At this, my mouth parted by the sheer force of surprise.

'My brothers, many of you know something of my story . . . for I have recounted it to some here, whom I number among my most intimate acquaintance. Before I came to reside in France, my father and I were engaged in the business of the import of paper to America. For some years we lived between London, Amsterdam and Brussels, and during this time I met the prisoner. She was then an actress upon the stage in London and consented to become my mistress.'

Hungrily, I awaited each word as it fell from Allenham's mouth, for I could see there was some scheme at work. He seemed to weave a tapestry from strands of truth and deceit.

'We passed for man and wife and, for all intents, lived in that capacity, but for the blessing of the Church, which we discounted as an irrelevance and a superstitious affectation of an old order. Citizeness Lightfoot accompanied me upon my travels to Brussels and to other parts . . . and bore me a child . . . who died shortly thereafter.'

Allenham lowered his head as he spoke those words. Although he believed them to be mere embellishment designed to heighten the emotion of his tale, they carried a certain truth unknown to him. To hear him speak of our son, the child about whom I had never told him, caused my eyes to grow instantly hot and sore with tears.

There was silence in the courtroom. I had scarcely noticed it until that moment. The howling from the gallery had ceased. Those who had, not moments before, been crying for my death were suddenly transported. They appeared tamed, enraptured. The men stood with folded arms, contemplatively smoking their pipes; the women sat transfixed, the babes in their arms uttering not so much as a mew. As I wiped the tears which now fell with abandon down my cheeks, I heard from across the room slight sniffles and sounds of weeping and looked to see three or four among these strangers partaking of my sorrows.

'It was in Brussels, not a month after this event that I, in an act of great callousness and cruelty, abandoned this fine woman, this sister and patriot, who was as dear to me as life itself.'

There was a jeer from the gallery, and then another.

'What shame I suffer now . . . It was the action of a fool,' said he, hanging his head. 'You see, my brothers, by then I could think of nothing but revolution. So fired up was I by the writings of Rousseau, of all I read, of Marat, of *Père Duchesne*, of all that was discussed in the rooms of the Jacobin Clubs . . .' Allenham's voice swelled with vigour. As I beheld him, I recognized that my beloved

336

was an actor! By Jove, to see him spouting and expostulating, standing at attention and delivering his lines to the tribunal, to the gallery – he was as accomplished as Kemble or Garrick himself! At that moment, in apprehending what he was doing, I felt the desire to smile. However, I knew better, and smothered that sensation immediately. It was now incumbent upon me to play my role too. Dear Allenham was transforming me from enemy to heroine and, in doing so, attempting with every breath in his lungs to preserve my life.

'. . . I could think of nothing else!' he continued. 'I wished to devote my entire person to the cause of the Revolution and I understood, in doing so, I could not afford the distractions of love – or the risks and consequences that flowed from such an engagement of the heart. And so my father and I set out for Paris. I bid Citizeness Lightfoot adieu in the belief that she would return to London. But she did not.' Allenham sighed and gazed at me longingly, so that my tears flowed steadily and genuinely.

'For some time, she endeavoured to locate me in this city and, after a spell, she was successful. Upon several occasions she came to the shop I keep with my father in the arcades of the Palais-Royal. It is with shame and sorrow that I confess to you that I turned her away out of coldness. Though she begged to be returned to my favour, I ignored the call of love. I eschewed all that I felt for this dear creature,' he cried, shaking his head in an anguished show of woe, his gaze locked on mine.

'She is the most beautiful woman I have ever beheld, and I have never loved another as I have loved her . . .' He turned again to the gallery behind him. 'Brothers, you cannot fault Citizen Égalité for falling prey to her charms!' There rose a great cheer. 'Indeed, I might not have wished for a more devoted and generous protector for her – one with whom she could share her passion for liberty. From Citizen Égalité's own hand you have heard the truth of this! Never was there one more dedicated to the ideals of the Revolution than she! She was born an Englishwoman: a hatred of tyranny courses through her very veins!' Again a cry of approval went up high into the dome of the ceiling. When it died away, Allenham, who now held an entire audience in his command, continued.

'You wish to know for what purpose she wrote – or scribbled, like any woman – these notes, this diary? There is not much of any meaningful intelligence in them. It is true she speaks in passing of Citizen Égalité's politics, of Citizeness Buffon's convictions, their polite conversation with Citizen Biron and with Citizen Beaujolais – with Citizen Égalité's English bankers. She records what he said to Marat, what he said to Danton . . . there is nothing in those pages but chatter and bons mots. There are no secrets, merely anecdotes: what wine was had, what dishes prepared, what gown Citizeness Buffon wore,' he fibbed. 'What you suspect is plainly untrue; not a word is spoken against the Revolution or the aims of the Convention. They sing in constant praise of it. Indeed, if ever aspersions are to be cast upon Citizen Égalité, upon his intentions and his love for the Republic, let these journals serve as testimony to his patriotism.' Allenham then softened his tone. 'But you wish to know, brothers, what was the cause of her keeping a memorandum of this nature? It was . . . for me.'

He smiled at me across the hall. His eyes luminescent with love, light and conviction.

'She hoped to entertain me. She wished to regain my affection by way of amusement. This she told me upon many occasions as she pleaded with me . . . pleaded for my love to be returned to her,' he fairly whispered, before raising his voice to a crescendo. 'Citizen Fouquier-Tinville wished to know why Citizeness Lightfoot possessed no correspondence among her effects. This is because, in a rage, she burned all of the letters that had ever passed between us – and I believe into that bonfire went other correspondence in an indiscriminate fit of passion.' He folded his arms against himself, in a gesture of defiance, and then pointed his chin towards the members of the tribunal.

'Citizen president, you would accuse this prisoner of wilfully conspiring with a traitoress, maintaining her within her household – a household, my fellow patriots, where she was scarcely in residence. This is so much the case that Citizeness Lightfoot failed to recognize the very neighbour who denounced her to the section house! She could have had no knowledge of her housemaid's activities for, as it has been evidenced in her pocketbooks, she was then residing at the Maison Égalité!'

'She is innocent!' came a cry from the gallery, and then another. A rumble of agreement rolled through the crowd.

Allenham paused. He permitted the calls of support and the murmurs to rise behind him. He wished them to gather volume before he continued, this time in a more measured, softer tone.

'I should like to address the prisoner . . . with your leave, citizen president?'

The hush returned once more. Neither the president nor Fouquier-Tinville made any motion to contradict him. He gazed at me, his face open and pleading, his expression a true one.

'I should like to beg the forgiveness of this innocent woman, whom I have so wronged . . . upon whom I have caused this misfortune to befall. I would beg her to believe that I have never ceased to love her, that I have not passed a single day without knowing remorse and regret for all I have perpetrated upon her. Should she be sent to her death on account of my follies, then I should rather die in her stead, for I could never lead a life upon this earth in the knowledge of my deeds, nor could I live without the reassurance of her love . . .'

All eyes were now upon me. I trembled. A stream of tears poured forth from me. Had the situation not demanded such a performance, it would have come entirely of its own accord.

'Dear Tyrone!' I cried. 'With the last breaths in my body I shall declare my eternal love for you!'

Such a howl burst from the gallery! Had you heard it, you would have believed yourself upon the benches at Drury Lane, rapt in the final acts of some great drama. The screams, the hollers!

'She is innocent!' 'Free the prisoner!' 'Preserve them! Save the lovers!'

The crowd then began to push in on Allenham, pulling at his coat, throwing their arms about him, kissing his face.

'He is an angel come to save her!' 'Have mercy upon them! Have mercy!'

My beloved wore something akin to a perplexed smile, his eyes not moving from mine.

The president and the clerk called for order. Once the room had fallen into a semblance of it, he looked anxiously at the jury.

'Citizen jurors, do you wish now to retire to consider a verdict?'

I shut my eyes tightly. All relief, what small sparks of joy had enlivened my breast, instantly dropped away.

There was a faint sound of whispering as they conferred, as they discussed the merits of ending my life. I would not open my eyes to see them make their pronouncement. I did not wish to witness the expression upon Allenham's face when they cried my death across the hall.

'No, citizen president. We have arrived at a verdict.'

'Then speak it plainly.'

'In the name of Liberté, Égalité and Fraternité, and in the defence of this Republic, the jury do not believe the prisoner Henrietta Lightfoot to be guilty of a conspiracy against the Revolution. Neither are we convinced of the evidence to suggest that she assisted the traitoress Thérèse Bertrand in her endeavours. Therefore we recommend to the president of the tribunal that she be acquitted and freed.'

When I opened my eyes, they were dazzled by light. The brilliance of late afternoon continued to illuminate the round window upon the opposite wall as the sounds of sobs and sighs soared through the room. I held my gaze there for a moment and drew in breath. When I lowered my eyes once more, he was gone.

Chapter 29

There was such a great deal of clamour and confusion. I turned this way and that, searching for him, but a guard came and brusquely pulled me from the dais. I was pushed through the crowd and beyond the doors and made to scrawl my name upon a ledger. The clerk nodded at me. 'You are at liberty, mademoiselle.'

I did not linger another moment, but passed into the public hall. Still awash with tears, I hunted for the figure I most hoped to find. There were many in this room, spectators and clerks and grieving friends, but he was not among them. It was then I heard a familiar cry.

Imagine my delight at beholding my devoted Lucy come to fling herself into my arms! How we wept together, maid and mistress, like two sisters. For among all the women in whom I had placed my trust, there had been not one who had proven themselves truer to me than her. I was incapable of speech, and she was so overcome with relief on my behalf that we clung to one another for a good while. When at last we gained command of our senses and our sobs dried into laughter, Lucy blurted her news to me.

'I am to be married, madam,' she exclaimed. 'Madame Vernet's brother has asked for my hand.' She then explained that he was a *traiteur* upon the rue de Richelieu and she had been given work at his establishment.

I congratulated her but lamented that she was not in possession of a dowry.

Lucy paid me a proud look and whispered that it was no matter, for she was already with child. 'I have learned enough of the male sex to understand how I might make what I want from this life,' she stated with a firm expression.

No sooner had she made this revelation to me than I became aware of a presence nearby. From the corner of my eye I spied a young man lingering, wishing to catch my notice. I turned and met his gaze, at which point he came forward, pressed a note into my hand and scampered away.

I examined the small packet and then exchanged a look with Lucy. It was in Allenham's hand.

'Make haste to Les Trois Pièces, a café in a passage that runs off the rue de la Harpe. I would urge you to take the greatest precautions and to proceed unaccompanied. Enquire there for Citizen Labroux.'

I did not for one instant hesitate but, after bidding dear Lucy farewell, set out for this place on foot.

I was in a state of near delirium. To sense the sun upon me and the breeze at my face, tickling my hair, seemed to me an inconceivable pleasure. I stepped out, entirely immune to the chill. Each sight and sound appeared as new to me, as if this were my first glimpse of Paris. I marvelled at the sun upon the river, glittering like a thousand silver scales upon a fish. I listened to the rhythmic knocking of wooden boats against the moorings, the cry of street-sellers. I breathed in the scent of the bakers, warm bread and burned sugar, the sharp onion of the cook shops, thick coal and wood smoke, the stink of the fish market, oil and hide, ink, earth, sour wine.

How briskly I strode through the narrow, filthy streets, as if I walked upon a ribbon of silk, untroubled by the beggars, the carts and cabriolets and carriages which halted my advance, the paving stones which gave way beneath my feet. All those inconveniences which had so troubled me in this city: I felt them not at all as I searched for the sign of the Trois Pièces.

I arrived at the place by way of a dank passage, which ran with all manner of grime. It was a squalid hostelry, patronized by the lowest sort. I cautiously picked my path into a courtyard and then entered through a low doorway. All was dark. The windows were shuttered fast, and no light could be seen but that provided by two candles and a rush light burning upon a table. A skittish girl peered at me from a corner.

'Citizen Labroux?' I spoke with apprehension. At the mention of that name she dashed quick as a sight hound through the door beside her. I stood for a moment, quite perplexed, believing she had gone to retrieve a gentleman, but instead she returned with a lantern and beckoned me to follow her.

The room into which she brought me was darker still. Without uttering a sound, she then opened the door to the cellar and proceeded down a set of narrow, wet stone steps which I could scarcely make out through the gloom. The walls within this place were ancient and narrow. I grew reluctant as she directed me into a dripping passage so small that it could not have been more than four feet in height, and scarcely that in width. I felt water beneath my feet and began to slow my pace.

'Where do you take me?' My voice reverberated.

She pressed her finger to her lips before pushing upon a door near rotted to its hinges. We emerged through this into a dwelling entirely different in appearance. She edged me forward, up a final pair of rickety stairs and into a room. It was a simple place with clay tiles upon the floor and poorly whitewashed panels. But for a table, a chair and the stub of a candle, long snuffed out, it was almost bare.

'He is there,' said she, gesturing to a door, before promptly disappearing below once more.

I looked about me uneasily and then approached the door.

'Citizen Labroux . . . ?' I called out softly.

I heard someone stir and waited for the door to open, but it did not. I called again and then rapped lightly upon it. Still uncertain, I stood for a moment before deciding I must try the handle. I pressed carefully against it. Sure enough, it creaked open to reveal a small room furnished with a simple bed and chairs, a table and a set of drawers. The shutters, however, were pulled. I spied not a soul. I took one step inside and then another, until all at once I felt a pair of hands about me.

Allenham kissed me fervently, and I him.

'I could not be certain you had arrived unaccompanied,' he said between breaths. 'Do forgive me, my angel, my beloved . . .' His words were smothered by the joining of our lips and then forgotten amid joyous laughter and tears of gratitude. He stroked my cheeks and hair, as if he could not believe I was real.

'That you live and are here is a miracle,' he said as he rubbed the wetness from his eyes.

'It is no miracle, my love, but your doing entirely,' I replied. 'I shall remain grateful until the last.'

'But it is I who am grateful to you, for your forgiveness.' He took my face into his hands. 'My dear Henrietta, now it is made plain to you that which I was unable to reveal in the past. Now you apprehend why it was impossible for you to have accompanied me to Paris. It was not because I did not love you or wish you to be at my side. In this matter I had no choice. Hetty, I have been a spy for His Majesty, in some capacity or other, since I was made to quit our life at Orchard Cottage. I was not at liberty to speak of it, to you or to any person. You cannot imagine what anguish this caused me. I could scarcely bear to consider the life into which you had been cast and then . . . in Paris, when I learned of your association with Mrs Elliot . . .' He shook his head. 'I glimpsed you with her, outside the printshop,' he whispered and shut his eyes. 'I could do nothing. I suspected that she had contrived a scheme. I begged her to relinquish you, to at the very least inform you of the truth of your situation, but she protested. She claimed that the plan was by then too far advanced to divulge. It was heedless of her, unjust, imprudent. I was unable to alert you to her design without placing myself, without placing all of us in the gravest peril.' He searched my expression with great sadness. 'And that dreadful day in September in the passage de Valois, you called my name – and were it not for the accident which befell you . . . Hetty, it was I who gathered you from where you had fallen. You were insensible. I prayed that you would live.' His tears glistened in his dark lashes. 'I could do nothing more.'

With that, I buried my head against his chest. I wished to feel him near to me and to banish the memory of how my heart had reproached him for his callousness. That I had ever judged him ill was unbearable to me. What shame I felt, and what sadness, too, that so many deceptions and secrets had lain between us. I understood then what I must say.

'George,' I said, my cheek against him. 'I beg *your* forgiveness.'

'There is nothing to forgive, sweet angel.'

'Pray, say you will forgive me, George,' I choked.

'Please . . .' He placed his hands upon my shoulders and stood somewhat apart from me so he might study my features. He appeared suddenly troubled.

'I . . . I have borne you a son.' I quaked as the words left my mouth. My nose and eyes streamed. 'I did not know myself to be with child until after you quit Orchard Cottage . . . I . . .

could not bring myself to tell you of it earlier . . . You claimed
. . . you claimed you had not the means to support . . .' I sniffed
and then collected myself. 'At the time of his birth, I lived as the
mistress of Mr John St John of Park Street. The child is George
Allen St John. I was several months gone when Mr St John took
me in. He believed the boy to be his and has acknowledged him
as his heir. Young Georgie is to be raised with his cousins, and
is currently with Lord Bolingbroke's children in Wiltshire. That
was the last I had heard as I have had no word of . . . our son
since I took my leave of England.' I swallowed and then ventured
to meet Allenham's gaze. I was most anxious about what I would
find there, but in his eyes there was only mildness, a gentle look
of surprise and then a smile. He drew me to him and crowned my
head with slow, pensive kisses, hushing me.

'It shall be made well. All shall be made well. Soon. One day,
soon,' were the only words he spoke, until silenced by the meeting
of our lips.

Caresses followed embraces followed more kisses until we
could no longer tolerate the space between our limbs, and retired to the thin, unsteady bed. There we lay in the lap of delight
for a good many hours, until the streaks of light which came
through the shutters had faded. Later, the girl from the Trois
Pièces returned and left for us a pitcher of cider, a cold roasted
chicken and a carp in sauce. It seemed to me the greatest feast
of which I had ever partaken. It was in the course of our supper
that Allenham revealed to me that the master of the Trois Pièces
was a fervent counter-revolutionary, who assisted in the smug-
gling of letters, gold and all manner of things to Coblenz and
abroad.

'He makes a business of procuring false passports.' Allenham
looked at me. 'Hetty, you know you cannot remain here; it is not
safe for you. As you have been accused once, so shall you ever re-

main suspect. The guards will not cease to trouble you and . . .' He paused, his expression turning quite grave. '. . . there is talk that Orléans is to be arrested.'

My heart dropped at hearing this.

'I fear it is but the beginning. There is not one among Orléans's associates who will not be considered suspect.'

'Madame de Buffon . . . what will become of her?' I whispered in horror.

My beloved returned my look.

'I cannot say . . . I do not know . . .'

'But certainly it is possible to—'

'My angel, you must hear me,' said he, reaching for my hand. 'It is not possible. Mrs Elliot attempted to persuade Orléans to make for England, even to seek refuge in America, but he refused. It is now too late.'

I stared at him. I did not wish to believe it so. My mind recalled Agnès de Buffon's cries of terror as she caught sight of Madame de Lamballe's head and entrails dragged through the Palais-Royal: *That will be my head there one day.* I closed my eyes against the thought. It was precisely as she had portended; she could have no more preserved me than I could her. The machine which whirled about us was too great a force to be slowed or altered in favour of a single life. Certainly, it was this which Orléans had implied to me. He had understood from the outset that it was destined to crush him in its wheels.

'And Mrs Elliot?' I enquired after a spell.

'She was arrested but last week.'

His answer startled me.

'But you are in jeopardy now!'

'Not upon this occasion, Hetty, no. She had no correspondence of mine in her possession, but the situation grows ever more perilous . . .'

I knew at that moment what he was about to say and I threw myself into his arms, as if to silence him.

'I shall do whatever you bid me. Anything you bid me to do . . . so long as you return to me . . .'

He tightened me in his embrace.

'I beg you not to reproach me, but I have made arrangements for this inevitability. You are to travel to Rome.'

'Rome!' I echoed with surprise, for I believed that he intended me to return to London.

'Yes. You must await me there, until circumstances permit me to join you.'

Allenham then made plain the details of this strategy. I was to journey to Italy with a consignment of paintings and objets d'art bound for the home of the British ambassador, a Mr Thomas Jenkins. It was explained to me that in addition to being a noted dealer in such treasures, Mr Jenkins was also a spy.

'There are messages contained within the pictures. The linings are made of dispatches: communiqués between émigrés, messages from spies here to others there, all variety of intelligence. You will be travelling with another, Monsieur Clement, who is an agent of the court at Coblenz. He is posing as a dealer of art and you will pass for his wife, an Englishwoman.' Allenham paused and gazed down at his hands. 'Dear Henrietta, I lament that too much of your life has been occupied in acting the part of a wife, whilst the advantages of that title have been denied to you.' He sighed before raising his bold blue eyes to meet mine. 'My angel, my dear sweet creature, you must understand, my existence has been a wretched one since our parting – upon both occasions. The existence I knew prior to my life here . . . I can never return to it. I can never undo that which I have witnessed and learned of men's hearts. Ambition, wealth, pride: a gentleman's life is predicated upon this . . . this flimsy tissue which is of no worth or meaning. If we exist for that alone, then we go to our graves without living. Here, I have watched men die for their passions, for that which they love; whether that be their convictions or those with whom they share their hearts. All that is true in this world is love. It is the stuff of our souls and it cannot be contained or directed like a channel of water to some place or person more or less appropriate. I love you, Henrietta, and I cannot think I should ever prefer the trappings of wealth and luxury, of false pride and surface pleasures to that.' He stopped. His eyes narrowed and began to move anxiously between mine, as if he searched for something. Then he took my hands firmly into his.

'My circumstances have not improved since we last parted. I fear that I shall one day lose Herberton and all that was bequeathed to me by my forebears. I shall not be able to maintain you in a manner befitting a gentlewoman. We shall have very little. It is likely we will be forced to live in retirement from society, or abroad for most of our days. But for the intercession of a relation – yours or mine – our children shall inherit very little, our daughters will not be provided for in marriage. However, if you will consent to accept my offer, though it is a paltry one and worthy of insult, I should like to make you my lawful wife in Rome.'

I know your thoughts, reader. Why, only a halfwit would assent to such a proposal, one which offered nothing but a future replete with want and anxiety. Likewise, only a fool would abandon all prospects of restoring his fortune and his family name by marrying his whore. Dear friends, if you have thumbed the many pages of my memoirs only to arrive at such a conclusion, then I fear you have failed to derive even the slightest scintilla of wisdom from my tale. I would implore you: return to your life of petty gossip, of sneering in your church pew or theatre box, of judgement and condemnation and outrage. Shepherd your daughter carefully through balls and gatherings. Read her letters, choose her books, dispose of her novels. Ensure your son never holds a hand of cards, nor tastes a glass of punch. Guard over your husband's or your father's business. Scrutinize each ledger, search his study, pick and pillage his locked drawers and cabinets. Accost his banker and solicitor regularly. After you have duly completed those tasks, rest assured, dear reader: my fate or Allenham's could never befall you or yours. Content yourself in the knowledge that wealth and title will preserve you from harm, just as it did the Duc d'Orléans and Louis XVI. We are all of us fools and halfwits. Our futures are never as certain as we would have them.

Upon that day, I chose the happiness laid before me. I chose hope. I chose love. And I have never had cause to regret it.

Afterword: An Incident in 1823

I was tormented for many years by the manner in which I made my departure from Paris. It had been in haste and in the midst of great turmoil. I fretted endlessly for those friends I had left behind. Of course, by the end of that year, 1793, I had learned of Orléans's tragic demise. I wept for him, boldly and without shame. I wept too for Madame de Buffon, for the grief visited upon her would have been insupportable. After a time, I mourned for her too. I could not have imagined that she would have been spared the guillotine when the Terror had harvested the lives of so many others less culpable.

Although I carried her memory in my heart, I had not spoken of her for many years. It was not until 1815, when I was in Brussels during the week of Waterloo and the Duchess of Richmond's ball that her name was mentioned in passing. Madame Le Grand, an intimate female acquaintance of Monsieur Talleyrand, there disclosed to me the most remarkable piece of intelligence: Madame de Buffon had survived.

'Why yes,' said she, 'I cannot say how, but by some miracle or accident she escaped arrest. She was divorced shortly before Monsieur d'Orléans's death, but then married another, a general by the name of Renouard de Bussière and bore him a child. For a time, she lived in Switzerland, I believe.'

'For a time?' I enquired.

'Yes, she died, seven years past. Consumption, I heard.'

This news brought such unexpected sorrow to me. For the briefest instant I believed that I might yet see her and make amends. Then, suddenly, that hope had vanished, as if the wind had whipped it away like a slip of paper. I vowed I should never again permit such an opportunity to escape me. You see, I am of the conviction that in life, all matters should be brought to a conclusion, and in no case does this hold truer than where erstwhile friends are concerned.

It was with this particular aim in mind that I returned to Paris in the spring of 1823. It had been many years since I had ventured there. I found the city a great deal altered. It had, like a recovered invalid, regained its colour and life.

One evening, whilst in the company of my friend Monsieur Stendhal, we attended the opera. It is remarkable with what varnish time paints former remembrances. The interior of the opera house had been altered from what it was, but I could still see in the boxes the faces I recalled from those final evenings when I sat with Agnès de Buffon. As my friend and I rode in a cabriolet to dine at Le Grand Véfour, which once I had known as the Café de Chartres, I could not help but speak a name I had withheld for some time.

'I have often wondered what became of Mrs Elliot, the Duc d'Orléans's former mistress. I do not know if she still lives. I am not of the belief that she returned to England – or else, if she has, she exists in some deep retirement, where she cannot be found,' I heard myself say.

Monsieur Stendhal turned to me; the shadow of his top hat was cast over his eyes.

'I have heard the name before, but I am afraid I do not know.'

He then suggested there were some associates of his to whom he could put the enquiry. Several days later, he returned to me and, in greeting me, took from his waistcoat a folded piece of paper.

'The lady you seek may be enquired for at this location.'

The address was not in Paris, but in the outlying part of Ville-d'Avray. It occurred to me to write a letter, but I soon abandoned that idea for I determined that a note alone would not serve my purposes. I knew I must see her, if not to lay to rest the matters which had plagued me since the day she swept me from her house at Meudon into the cold. The lesson she had imparted to me upon that day was perhaps the most formative instruction that I had ever received. I wished her to know this.

It was a clear day with a fresh wind in the middle of May; the sixteenth of the month, as I recall. The fields were newly verdant with the first scarlet poppies waving like flags among them. I travelled by chaise to the address I had been given: 'L'Hospice des soeurs de Dieu', upon the rue Fontaine.

It was a plain, whitewashed building set around a small, quiet courtyard. The house itself, a former monastery, was now inhabited by the mayor and his family.

I was shown to her rooms, or rather her room, where she sat with her back to me. There was little more to her lodgings than a trestle bed, some spindly chairs and a table, and a dark wooden chest of drawers. In the corner sat a small enamel stove, upon which was perched a copper kettle. A basin of white china and a pitcher were set out. The shelves were decorated with paper cuttings, which I supposed had been made by the sisters. Upon the wall were a few miniatures and silhouettes: no one whom I recognized. That image which I had painted of her in 1792 was not among them. Of all the furniture, jewels and attire she had owned, of her two houses, her carriages, and her sapphire (the true fate of which I could not begin to fathom) there remained only these scant remnants of her once opulent life. The annuities upon which she had staked her livelihood no longer sustained her. Indeed, half of the princes and dukes and marquises who might have paid them were dead, their estates long dispersed. *A house and furniture may be burned and jewels stolen . . .* I remembered her saying to me as we rode to the Comédie-Française.

Even from behind I knew her: the long back, though the neck was somewhat stooped and the shoulders curved. She had not the posture in her old age.

'Mrs Elliot,' I said. She did not turn. 'Mrs Elliot,' I said again, this time louder and more forcefully. She moved slightly.

With some hesitation, I approached her as she stared out of the window. Her features were as I recalled. Her nose was as beak-like, and her forehead as high, but her eyes seemed blank, clouded by near-blindness.

It was a curious thing to look upon that face once more. I felt a sudden jolt of coldness in my belly. The memory of the last day I saw her at Meudon came back like a sharp pain.

'Madame Elliot?'

She tilted her head up at me.

'*Oui?*'

'Mrs Elliot, do you remember me?' I tried a smile.

There was a long pause; her face quivered. Her lace cap tied beneath her chin held the sag of her flesh.

'I . . . do . . .' she said after a moment, and then held out her hand to me.

I let out a small sigh of relief.

'I have come to call upon you. I have brought you some loaves of bread, cheese, cream . . . and a box of tea, which you might enjoy.' My heart suddenly filled with sadness. Her hand was so frail in mine, like the bones of a bird. 'How do you do, Mrs Elliot?'

'I . . . I do well, child.' She smiled, but too broadly, for near to half her teeth were gone. 'Tell me . . . do you come from London, my dear?'

'Yes. Yes, I do.'

'And what is the gossip in London?'

I told her of the King upon the throne, George IV, and of the building works. I talked of Mr Kean's last season at Covent Garden.

'Yes, I know of that . . . but tell me of you . . . tell me of Cholmondeley.'

'I . . . am afraid I know nothing of Lord Cholmondeley.' I peered closely at her face. 'Mrs Elliot, do you . . . remember me? Do you know my name?'

There was a pause.

'I do, child . . . Why, you are my daughter . . .'

It was a curious thing, but my heart, which had not felt that tug for so many years, jumped.

'You are my Georgiana Seymour.'

'No, madam. I fear I am not her.' I smiled sadly and then turned from her. 'Would you care for some tea, Mrs Elliot?' I enquired after a moment.

The kettle upon the stove was still warm. There was no elaborate tea service like those she had once owned, but a plain white pot and a single white chipped cup and saucer. I opened the small box of leaves and dropped into the water two spoonfuls. I then allowed it to steep, to turn amber. She possessed no sugar to disguise its bitter flavour, but I supposed she would not complain. I handed her the cup and saucer and watched her press it to her lips.

'Would you care for me to read to you?' I asked. 'I have brought a book from London. You have probably not been read to in

English for some time. It is Sir Walter Scott – he is most popular. *Ivanhoe.*

I then read to her for the better part of an hour. She listened and in that time scarcely moved so much as a finger. Then, quite unexpectedly, she drew breath.

'Miss Lightfoot.' Her mouth trembled. 'That is your name.'

I leaned in and looked directly into her foggy eyes.

'It is. You remember me.' I smiled, faintly.

She nodded, her expression quite solemn.

'You recall our last meeting, so many years ago? How well you instructed me, madam. Why, I have come to live by the advice you imparted to me. *It is trust that weakens us,*' I reminded her of her words.

I waited for a further response, but there came none.

'I shall brew you another pot of tea, for I believe you are in need of it,' said I, rising to my feet.

On this occasion, when I handed her the dish, I studied her long sips. I observed her throat move with each swallow, drawing the tea downward.

'There now,' said I, removing the empty cup from her and guiding her back against the chair. This at last succeeded in lulling her.

I resumed reading, pausing to examine her at every turn of the page. I listened to her breath move gradually from deep to shallow. Her expression slackened as she seemed to slip comfortably into the grip of a sleep. I waited, and after a spell, rose and bid her a silent farewell. I could not bring myself to kiss her, as might a dutiful daughter, or even a dear old friend, but reached for her cool hand and touched her shoulder, in the manner of a pupil bidding her tutoress adieu.

Author's Note

One of the joys of writing historical fiction is the freedom to embellish and amend the truth. All of the gaps in our knowledge can be filled with speculation and imaginative invention. However, while this is a fun exercise for a historian, it can sometimes leave the reader confused as to where fact ends and fiction begins.

Many of the names mentioned in *The French Lesson* will be familiar to those with a working knowledge of the events of the French Revolution – Marie Antoinette, Louis XVI, Robespierre, Danton, Marat – but the principal characters in the book – the Duc d'Orléans (Philippe Égalité), Agnès de Buffon and Grace Dalrymple Elliot – are less likely to be recognized. These figures are real, as are all of the members of Orléans's household: his sons, their tutor, his physician, his secretary and his servants. So too are Mrs Elliot's friends: the notorious Madame de Flaghac, Mrs Meyler, Madame Laurent, and Orléans's closest companion, the Duke de Biron. In fact, only Henrietta, Lord Allenham, Andrew Savill and a number of peripheral characters are invented.

Where I drew upon real people I made certain to undertake a significant amount of research in order to animate them in an accurate, yet colourful way. Of course, I employed some artistic licence. This is, after all, fiction.

Louis Philippe Joseph d'Orléans, 'Philippe Égalité' (1747–93)

For centuries, Orléans has been maligned as one of the villains of the French Revolution, a member of the ruling Bourbon family who sent his own cousin, Louis XVI, to the guillotine. But Orléans's relationship with his family had been a complex one long before the first stirrings of revolution. He had never seen eye to eye with the court and his relationship with Marie Antoinette was notoriously bitter. This, and his vast wealth (which was in part due to his wife's enormous dowry), made him an obvious person around whom those opposed to the King could rally. For a time, Orléans was celebrated as 'the Godfather of the Revolution', the man who funded Danton and Marat and who opened his palace to the people of Paris, but politics was never his passion. Ultimately, the Revolution forced him to make a terrible choice: whether he would sacrifice his own life and, inevitably, the lives of his family and friends, or that of the King. He came to regret what he did for the rest of his foreshortened days.

When Henrietta meets Orléans he has parted with both his wife and the most famous of all of his mistresses, Madame de Genlis, a talented writer and educator. His power is on the wane. As he was required to pay back his Duchess's dowry, Orléans was indeed strapped for cash in the final years of his life, and after his death in November 1793 the Palais-Royal was stripped bare of its remaining treasures by the Revolutionary government.

Orléans's sons, the Dukes of Chartres and Montpensier and the Count of Beaujolais, escaped the guillotine by going into an exile worthy of the pages of an Alexandre Dumas novel. They wandered

Europe and the Americas and lived for a time outside Richmond, Surrey. Eventually, Louis Philippe (Orléans's eldest) returned to France to be made 'King of the French' in 1830. Henrietta would have lived to see this and, after witnessing Orléans's torments, I have no doubt that it would have made her smile.

Marguerite Françoise 'Agnès' de Buffon, née Bouvier de la Mothe Cepoy (1767–1808)

Agnès de Buffon is an author's gift. We know tantalizingly little about the woman who played such a significant role in the life of the Duc d'Orléans. She is mentioned only fleetingly in memoirs and letters. Louis Philippe refers to her as his father's 'only friend in Paris' (aside from Biron) and remarks that their 'liaison was unfortunately very public'. He defends her by saying that 'she never gave him anything but good advice' and that 'her affection for him never failed'. Others were not so kind. The Duke de Lauzan commented that her 'stupidity' was convenient, as one didn't have to worry that she was filling Orléans's head with inflated notions. However, it's more likely that Agnès was playing a careful game. Grace Elliot asserts that she was a firm supporter of the Revolution and very close to Orléans's political advisors. She was also known to attend the sessions at the Assembly, with or without the Duke at her side. Perhaps it was this that gave rise to concerns that she was manipulating Orléans into believing he could rule as a constitutional monarch.

Whatever the case, Agnès did not trust Grace Elliot. 'Madame de Buffon and the Duke's friends did everything they could to prevent his coming to me,' Grace writes. 'They used to tell him that as I saw none but royalists and his enemies, I should get him assassinated.'

That which is written about Agnès's relationship with Orléans suggests that theirs was truly a union of hearts and certainly contained a lot of sexual passion. 'She's like a little animal in bed,' Orléans writes to Lauzan at the outset of their affair. She accompanied him on his visit to London, and when he joined the Army of the North she took a house to be near him at Valenciennes. During the troubled second half of 1792, she seemed to take up permanent residence at the Palais-Royal. As I have written in *The French Lesson*, Agnès was pregnant during that summer of bloodshed and gave birth as the September Massacres raged. Perhaps the most widely repeated anecdote about her is the story of her breakfast with Orléans and his bankers, when the crowd outside their window raised the decapitated head of the Princess de Lamballe. Agnès is said to have become hysterical and cried, 'My God! That will be my head there one day!' before collapsing. Shortly thereafter, Victor Leclerc de Buffon, Orléans's illegitimate son, was born. He became the Chevalier de Saint Paul and for part of his short life was looked after by his exiled half-brothers. He died in 1812.

Grace Dalrymple Elliot (or Elliott) (1754–1823)

Grace Dalrymple Elliot's autobiography, *Journal of My Life During the French Revolution*, is one of the best-known English-language accounts of the conflict. It was this book more than any other that inspired me to write *The French Lesson*, as a sort of answer to Grace Elliot's record of events.

Orléans had numerous dalliances with women, but Grace was among his favourite mistresses. Like so many British women who took up residence in Paris during the eighteenth century, her past was a chequered one. She had been disgraced after an affair with Lord Valentia, whom her much older husband sued for criminal conversation, or adultery, before divorcing her. Following the scandal, Grace embarked upon a life as a 'professional mistress' or courtesan, or, as the French termed it, a *dame entretenue*. She did well in her profession and before her association with Orléans enjoyed the favour of both the notorious Marquess of Cholmondeley and the even more notorious Prince of Wales. However, it was in Paris, through her affairs with a number of French noblemen, that she truly prospered and was able to make a home.

The events of Grace Elliot's life have often been called into question. Like Henrietta, she can be an unreliable narrator when it comes to recounting details. Many of the assertions that appear in her *Journal* have yet to be substantiated and in some cases seem improbable. Dates and names are confused and it has still to be proven where, and for how long, she was incarcerated during the Revolution. However, recent research has begun to throw further light on her somewhat mysterious life. Jo Manning, in her biography *My Lady Scandalous*, has put together a convincing case that Grace acted as a spy for the British and seemed to have been trafficking correspondence. She and her friend 'Mrs Meyler' (a woman whom I suggest in my non-fiction book *Lady Worsley's Whim* is actually Seymour, Lady Worsley) also famously helped the Marquis de Chansenets to escape from Paris after the assault on the Tuileries. Sarah Murden and Joanne Major, in *An Infamous Mistress: The Life, Loves and Family of the Celebrated Grace Dalrymple Elliott*, have unearthed more about her cloak-and-dagger activities and her life in Paris. To these three authors, I am especially grateful.

The French Revolution is a fascinating episode in history – it was a modern political conflict where the state reigned by means of widespread propaganda, indoctrination, fear, and a campaign of systematized murder. Fortunately for us, those who lived through it have left an array of gripping first-hand accounts, of which Grace Elliot's is just one. In writing *The French Lesson* I made use of a number of these, including those of Gouverneur Morris, Élizabeth Vigée-Lebrun, Thomas Blaikie, Marie Louise Victoire Marquise de la Rochejaquelein, Restif de la Bretonne, Louis Philippe and Granville Leveson-Gower.

I'm equally indebted to a number of living writers and their scholarly books on late-eighteenth-century France and the French Revolution. Professor David Andress's work *The Terror* and his general counsel on the Revolution between 1792 and 1793 was enormously useful, as was Nina Kushner's *Erotic Exchanges: The World of Elite Prostitution in Eighteenth-century Paris*. Evelyn Farr and her book *Before the Deluge* were both very helpful to me in painting a picture of Paris on the edge of revolution. The knowledgeable David Downie and Alison Harris must be thanked for taking me on one of their tours through what remains of eighteenth-century Paris (not a great deal, sadly), and Agnès Montenay for generously offering me a peek into a set of Palais-Royal apartments.

For those interested in learning more about the French Revolution, life in Paris and the real characters in my book, I can recommend:

Godfather of the Revolution: The Life of Philippe Égalité, Duc d'Orléans, by Tom Ambrose (Peter Owen Publishers, 2008)

Liberty: The Lives and Times of Six Women in Revolutionary France, by Lucy Moore (Harper Collins, 2006)

Panorama of Paris: Selections from Le Tableau de Paris *by Louis Sébastien Mercier*, edited by Jeremy D. Popkin (Pennsylvania State University Press, 1999)

Citizens: A Chronicle of the French Revolution, by Simon Schama (Penguin, 2004)

Acknowledgements

I would like to thank my wonderful editor, Jane Lawson, for her never-faltering belief in me. She and the team at Transworld have been supportive from start to finish. Gratitude is also due to my agent, Hellie Ogden, for cracking the whip over my back and holding my hand in equal measure. Finally, I would never have crossed the finish line were it not for the unwavering support of my husband, family and devoted friends.

Hallie Rubenhold is a historian and broadcaster and an authority on women's lives in the eighteenth century. She has worked as a curator for the National Portrait Gallery and as a university lecturer. Her first novel, *Mistress of My Fate*, was received with great acclaim and her biography *Lady Worsley's Whim* was made into the BBC drama *The Scandalous Lady W*. She lives in London with her husband. Chat with her on Twitter @HallieRubenhold.